Twenty

ALSO BY JAMES GRIPPANDO

The Big Lie★

The Girl in the Glass Box★

A Death in Live Oak★

Most Dangerous Place★

Gone Again★

Cash Landing

Cane and Abe

Black Horizon★

Blood Money★

Need You Now

Afraid of the Dark★

Money to Burn

Intent to Kill

Born to Run★

Last Call★

Lying with Strangers

When Darkness Falls★

Got the Look★

Hear No Evil★

Last to Die★

Beyond Suspicion★

A King's Ransom

Under Cover of Darkness

Found Money

The Abduction

The Informant

The Pardon★

Other Fiction

The Penny Jumper

Leapholes

★ A Jack Swyteck novel

Twenty

A Jack Swyteck Novel

James Grippando

HARPER LARGE PRINT

An Imprint of HarperCollinsPublishers

TWENTY. Copyright © 2021 by James Grippando, Inc. All rights reserved. Printed in the United States of America. No part of this book may be used or reproduced in any manner whatsoever without written permission except in the case of brief quotations embodied in critical articles and reviews. For information, address HarperCollins Publishers, 195 Broadway, New York, NY 10007.

HarperCollins books may be purchased for educational, business, or sales promotional use. For information, please e-mail the Special Markets Department at SPsales@harpercollins.com.

FIRST HARPER LARGE PRINT EDITION

ISBN: 978-0-06-306302-0

Library of Congress Cataloging-in-Publication Data is available upon request.

21 22 23 24 25   LSC   10 9 8 7 6 5 4 3 2 1

For Tiffany.
Remember that trip to Australia?

Twenty

Chapter 1

"Everything I learned, I've forgotten since kindergarten," said Jack. He was behind the wheel of the family SUV with his wife, Andie, beside him. Their daughter was behind Andie, strapped into her car seat, her curious expression lighting up Jack's rearview mirror.

"What does that mean, Daddy?"

"Oh, there was this book some time ago. It was called—"

"Actually," said Andie, "it was called *Everything I Need to Know, I Learned in Kindergarten.* So I think what your daddy is saying is that he needs to *go back* to kindergarten."

"You mean he wants a do-over?" asked Righley.

Jack smiled. "Yes, honey. Daddy wants a do-over."

"No do-overs! That's our rule."

Jack was the assistant coach of Righley's peewee soccer team. "You're right, honey. That is the rule."

Had a do-over been possible, Jack would have chosen Riverside Day School for his own education. Seated on ten picturesque acres of green space in one of the oldest neighborhoods along the Miami River, Riverside was South Florida's premier K-through-12 private academy. Ninety percent of the faculty had a postgraduate degree, no teacher had more than eighteen students, and every classroom had the latest SMART Board technology. The parent directory read like a Who's Who of Florida business leaders, which left Jack and Andie in the proverbial no-man's-land on the financial spectrum, too rich for financial aid and not nearly rich enough to afford the tuition. So they stretched, remaining conspicuously silent when other parents waxed on about their ski trips over winter break or summers in the South of France.

"Park right there," said Andie, pointing to an open space on the street.

They were still more than two blocks from the campus entrance, just outside the blinking amber lights of the designated school zone. The school had a parking lot, but Jack understood the issue. Andie was an FBI agent, and although she was dressed for a day of field work, she was not yet on duty, and Florida law prohibited law enforcement officers from carrying weapons into school zones if they were off duty. Jack parked the car and unloaded Righley from the back seat while Andie discreetly locked her sidearm and holster in the glove compartment.

It was mid-September, a Wednesday morning, the final week during which kindergarten parents were allowed to walk their children to the classroom. Hand in hand, they entered the campus and went to the flagpole on the quad, where the elementary-level students assembled every morning in a circle, placed their hands over their hearts, and recited the pledge of allegiance. Or some reasonable facsimile thereof.

And to the Republic, for Richard Stanz.

One day Jack wanted to meet this Richard Stanz.

Jack's law office was within walking distance, a historic coral-stone house that, like most residences in this gentrified circa-1920s neighborhood, had been refurbished and converted to commercial use. He gave Andie the car keys and a kiss, hugged Righley, and headed off beneath the sprawling limbs of century-old live oaks. It was a perfect morning, still hours away from the heat and humidity that would return every afternoon until about Halloween, a wet blanket of a reminder that there really was no such thing as autumn in the subtropics. It made Jack think of the walks he would have liked to have taken with his father when he was in kindergarten, when a young Representative Harry Swyteck was away in Tallahassee for legislative sessions and Jack's stepmother was too hung over to get out of bed.

Jack enjoyed his walk along the river, thanking his lucky stars for the life he and Andie had made for themselves and their only child.

The mother-daughter good-bye at the classroom door was without tears, at least not from Righley. Andie's commute to the FBI's field office in North Miami was by way of the dreaded Palmetto Expressway, a miles-long, bumper-to-bumper nightmare of blinking red taillights, the thought of which made her downright envious of Jack's lovely walk from the school to his office. Deciding to let rush-hour traffic subside before getting on the road, Andie joined the other parents in the recreation center for the regular second-Wednesday-of-the-month coffee with the head of school. It was Andie's first, but it wasn't limited to new parents, so it was mostly "the usual suspects." Working mothers dressed for the office in one cluster. Stay-at-home mothers in workout spandex or tennis skirts in another. Off to the side, alone, stood a tech-world multimillionaire who had sold his company and retired way too young, not really sure how he fit into this overwhelmingly female group. Andie felt almost as out of place, dressed in law-enforcement khaki pants and black tactical boots, which made her look more like the head janitor than a Riverside parent. She was relieved to find her friend Molly near the basket of bagels.

"Glad to see you here," said Andie.

Molly had two boys and a girl at Riverside, a senior, a sophomore, and her "happy accident," a daughter in the second grade. After the third, she'd stopped teaching Lamaze, but it was in Molly's course that Andie had first met her. They'd lost touch after Righley's birth, but she was once again Andie's rock, her only familiar face at Riverside.

"There's a fresh patch of vomit on the gym floor," said Molly. "Could you please fetch a bag of sawdust?"

"Right away, ma'am."

The "janitor look" was a running joke between them. The first few weeks of school were filled with countless orientations and meetings for Riverside parents: meet the math department, meet the coaches, meet the science teachers, meet the alumni parents who are so glad they spent a fortune on private school because their kids are rockin' it at Harvard. At the first gathering of the year, a tenth-grade mother had asked Andie to look into the condensation dripping from the AC vent. Andie had since made a habit of latching on to Molly.

"Have you decided what committee you're going to volunteer for?" asked Molly.

"Committee? I wasn't planning on volunteering."

"Oh, no, no, no, dear. You can attend all the welcome meetings you want. But if you're going to come to the monthly morning coffees with the head of school, you can either volunteer or write a check big enough to have a classroom named after you."

"Jack volunteers. He helps with the soccer team. Doesn't that count?"

"Technically, yes. But that doesn't give you much to talk about with this group of women."

"What committee are you on?"

"Me? Volunteer? I don't think so."

"So you write a check?"

She stepped closer, as if letting Andie in on a secret. "Of course I write a check. But I still come to the coffees."

"Why?"

"Because I like coffee."

Andie laughed, though not everyone at Riverside was as quiet about the checks they wrote, as if they weren't already saying enough with their Cartier bracelets stacked seven or eight high à la Kylie Jenner, engagement rings of at least three karats (extra points for a marquis-cut canary diamond), and sparkling stud earrings that resembled something out of the Milky Way. Andie's entire net worth paled in comparison to the "everyday" bauble collection of the average mother at Riverside.

"Come on," said Molly, still playing the poor-mouth game. "It's time for us commoners to pay our respects to the head of school."

They started across the room, but the sudden blare of a fire alarm stopped them in their tracks. All conversation ceased. The head of school moved to the center of the room and addressed the parents in a calm and even tone. "Everyone, please stay where you are." She quickly made a call on her cell. Despite the pulsing alarm, Andie heard her say into her phone, "Judy, is this a drill?"

The response was heard only by the head of school, but in a moment, every woman in the room had an answer. An unmistakable noise—*pop, pop, pop!*—sounded in the hallway.

"That's gunfire!" shouted Andie.

The screams inside the room weren't nearly loud enough to drown out the blaring alarm or the continued *pop, pop, pop* of semiautomatic gunfire outside the rec center. As an FBI agent, Andie knew that activating a fire alarm to create chaos was a tried-and-true modus operandi in school shootings. The screams of children in the hallway confirmed they were caught in the middle of one. Andie hurried to the door, but before she could open it, the next three pops resulted in three bullet-sized dimples in the bullet-resistant steel.

"This way!" the head shouted. "Follow me!"

She led them to the door on the opposite side of the room, pushed it open, and stepped aside to let parents exit first. It was anything but orderly, elbows flying and parents pushing other parents to the floor in a mad scramble to safety.

"Let's go!" shouted Molly.

Andie switched off the lights. "You go! I got the rear."

The gunfire in the hallway was nonstop.

"Are you crazy?

"Just go, Molly! Run!"

Molly did. Andie was alone in the rec center. As an agent, she was familiar with the active-shooter response protocol. Option one: run. Option two: hide. Last resort: fight. As a mother, the protocol went right out the window. The sound of the semiautomatic gunfire—loud, very loud, then more distant—told her that the shooter was headed south. The kindergarten classrooms were at the south end of campus. Righley was in danger. Andie had no choice.

And no weapon.

Andie spotted a fire extinguisher on the wall. With a tap of the metal hammer, the glass case shattered, and she grabbed the extinguisher. Fire-retardant foam was no match for a semiautomatic firearm, but a sudden burst in an ambush might confuse or blind the shooter long enough for her to overtake him. There was no time to lose. Andie pushed open the door, stepped out of the rec center, and came face-to-face with a stampede of screaming children running for their lives. They were running from a masked shooter at the end of the hallway, a man walking with purpose as he squeezed off round after round from a semiautomatic pistol with an extended magazine. A *long* extended magazine.

To Andie, it looked as long as a child's arm.

"Righley!" she shouted instinctively, and she started down the hallway, braving the noise and the chaos, armed with only a fire extinguisher.

Chapter 2

J ack was at his desk preparing for a deposition when an emergency text from Riverside popped up on his cell phone: ACTIVE SHOOTER ON CAMPUS.

"Clear my morning calendar!" he said to his assistant as he rushed out the door, cell phone in hand.

The race back to Riverside was like a high-speed rewind of Jack's lovely walk on a perfect morning, a panic-driven sprint through a parent's worst nightmare. He speed-dialed Andie, never breaking stride, but the call didn't go through. Cell-phone service was already overloaded around the school. Traffic was backed up for blocks, horns blaring. Frightened and frustrated parents abandoned their vehicles in the street and joined Jack on foot. Inside of a block from campus the crowd was so large that people could barely move. Obviously, Jack had not been the first to receive the "Active Shooter" alert by text message. Helicopters whirred overhead, some from law enforcement, others bearing the colorful logos of local television news stations. Jack pushed forward, wending his way toward the police perimeter outside the campus gate.

"You can't go any farther," said an officer in uniform.

"But my daughter's in there!" he said, and it sounded as if a dozen other parents behind him had said the same thing in unison.

"No one goes in," the officer said firmly. "We've locked down the premises."

Locked down the premises. Police jargon seemed only to underscore the insanity of the fact that Righley had skipped through these gates holding hands with her parents, and two hours later Jack was at the gates to hell—parents searching for their children, teachers trying to account for their students, children crying and clinging to one another, ambulances and police cars with beacons flashing.

"Out of the way!" a paramedic shouted.

Jack turned to see first responders whisking a victim from school grounds on a gurney. They nearly had to run over a camera crew to get past the scores of television journalists who had descended on the scene. A sickening feeling came over Jack as the paramedics loaded the unconscious student into the back of an ambulance. The boy wasn't even old enough to shave.

Jack tried dialing Andie again, but the call failed. Righley's teacher had given all parents her cell number on the first day of classes, and Jack kicked himself for not having entered it into his contacts. Not that her cell-phone service would have performed any better. He needed information, and he needed to gather it the old-fashioned way. Down the sidewalk, Jack spotted a field reporter speaking into the camera with a live *Action News* update. He moved closer to hear her report in real time.

"The active shooting from inside the building seems to have stopped," she said in an urgent voice. "A scattering of students have fled to safety, but most are still in their classrooms. The entire campus is on lockdown. Information is spotty. Rumors abound. Some say the shooter is dead. Others say he got away. As best we can piece it together, most of the shooting occurred at or near the rec center."

Jack froze. *The rec center.*

The reporter wrapped up her live update, her crewman lowered his camera, and Jack pushed his way forward to get the reporter's attention.

"Excuse me, but did you say there was shooting at the rec center?"

"You can get instant updates if you follow me on Twitter," she said, but Jack wasn't listening as she shared her handle. His gaze drifted toward the chaos on the campus grounds. More gurneys, flanked by first responders, were speeding toward the waiting ambulances. He was certain that he'd heard the reporter right the first time, and Jack's words came like a reflex.

"My wife was in the rec center."

On a dead run, Andie put herself into a base-stealing slide across the tile floor and hunkered down outside Righley's classroom, still armed with the fire extinguisher. Her shoulder was against the steel door, and the entranceway was a recessed alcove, so she couldn't see left or right down the hallway. It was like peering out from inside a tunnel. She knocked on the door so hard it hurt her hand. The teacher didn't open it, and Andie didn't blame her. No matter: if the shooter was going to get to her daughter, he'd have to get past the mother bear.

Ninety. Ninety-one. Ninety-two.

Andie's estimate of rounds fired was certainly low. She hadn't even started counting until she'd bolted from the rec center, and she'd surely missed a few in the noisy sprint down the hallway. Her singular objective had been to reach the kindergarten classroom before the shooter did. Adrenaline had propelled her. Instinct and training had probably kept her alive. Or luck. The blaring alarm, punctuated by screams and gunshots, made it impossible to think straight, let alone hear. It was the classic fog of war. In a school.

Thirty feet. Andie had switched to counting the 12x12 floor tiles. She was trying to gauge the width of the hallway, trying to guess how far the foam might spray—the range of her makeshift weapon. The sight of a spent ammunition round on the floor made her heart skip a beat.

She checked her cell phone. She'd texted her location to every law enforcement officer on her list of contacts, but reception was spotty, and not one had gone through immediately. She was checking the SEND status when her cop instincts kicked in, and she detected a change in the air—something afoot. She put her phone on silent mode and listened more intently. The fire alarm continued to whine, but the shooting seemed to have stopped. It had been at least a minute since anyone had passed in the hallway from either direction.

Then she heard it—even over the piercing alarm. Footfalls in the hallway. Heavy footfalls, like marching boots on the move.

Is he coming back this way?

Andie gripped the fire extinguisher, not sure if the

best defense was to spray the shooter with foam or to throw the entire metal canister like a mortar shell.

"Are you hurt?" a man shouted.

Andie recognized the black uniform of Miami-Dade SWAT in the nick of time, sparing him a face full of fire retardant.

"I'm FBI!" she shouted, as she flashed her credentials.

"Come with me!"

"My daughter's in this classroom!"

"My job is to clear this hallway!"

"I'm not leaving my daughter!"

He seemed to comprehend that the children would be safer with a law enforcement officer there, but it was obvious that standing guard with a fire extinguisher wasn't a viable plan. He reached for the electronic passkey that was linked to his belt and stepped closer, to be heard over the blaring alarm.

"Announce yourself before you enter," he said. "Lock the door and barricade it once you're inside. Don't let anyone leave until I come back with the 'all clear.'"

He inserted the passkey. The electronic lock clicked. Andie called out to the teacher at the top of her lungs.

"Ms. Hernandez! It's Righley's mother! I'm coming in!"

"Mommy!" the reply came, and the little voice from inside nearly crushed her.

Andie turned to thank the SWAT officer, but he was already gone. She opened the door and hurried inside a kindergarten classroom under siege.

Chapter 3

Jack watched from outside the campus grounds, having positioned himself as close to the entrance gates as possible without crossing the yellow police tape. The hysteria around him was palpable, the desperate pleas of parents blending into a cacophony of English and Spanish. Jack's español wasn't bad—his *abuela* gave him about a C minus—but in all his years in Miami, he'd never heard it spoken with such urgency. He was pretty sure he'd heard the group of Latina moms behind him correctly, but he needed to clarify.

"Excuse me," he said slowly in Spanish, overenunciating in hopes that the woman behind him would take his cue and answer in the same cadence. "Did you say they are evacuating students?"

The woman's emotions were running too high for

her to speak slowly, and Jack's loose handle on Cuban American Spanglish was no match for a native Colombian speaker. But he got the gist: police had begun to evacuate students through the riverside access to campus. The implicit good news was not lost on him.

The police must have been confident that the shooting was over.

The crowd outside the gate was growing larger by the minute, and getting from one side of campus to the other wouldn't be easy. But Jack had still heard nothing from Andie, and he needed to find his wife and daughter. He squeezed his way around one person after another, zigzagging his way past uniformed police, scrambling journalists, and tearful parents. It took ten minutes just to get to the end of the block, where he made a left turn toward the river. With each passing square of sidewalk underfoot, he sensed that more and more frantic people were moving with him in the same direction. News of the evacuation appeared to be spreading. Jack hoped it wasn't just another worthless rumor. He'd heard plenty of misinformation already, everything from "It was just a bunch of firecrackers" to "Dozens of children and teachers dead."

Jack was getting close to the campus's rear exit. The attractive coral-rock wall that protected three sides of the ten-acre campus gave way to a purely functional chain-link fence. On the other side of the fence was an open athletic field, and through the gaps in the eight-foot privacy hedge, Jack spotted lines of students, each line led by an adult, leaving the building. They were moving quickly but in orderly fashion, each student with one hand in the air and the other resting on the shoulder of the boy or girl they followed. Jack found an opening in the crowd and sprinted the last hundred yards to the field exit. A police officer was at the gate.

"Have they evacuated kindergarten yet?" Jack asked.

"I really don't know, sir." A line of older students passed, and her attention shifted fully toward crowd control. "Don't crowd the gate, please!"

"Where would they be, if they came out already?"

The officer's focus was entirely on the students. "Keep moving! Don't stop until you get to the high school parking lot."

It wasn't a direct response to Jack, but it answered his question. He ran ahead of the last line of students, passing a second and third line on his way to the parking lot. The children he saw were too old for elementary school but not yet teenagers. Probably middle schoolers—not a one of them too cool to be caught crying under these circumstances. Jack approached a teacher at the head of the line.

"Has kindergarten come out yet?" he asked, alarmed

by the level of desperation he detected in his own voice.

"That's Building G," she said. "We're F. They'd be somewhere behind us."

Jack did a quick pivot and ran back in the direction of the school. The lines were coming nonstop. The school was in full-throttle evacuation mode. Kindergarten had to be part of it. Unless the worst thing imaginable had happened.

The thought propelled him to an all-out sprint back to the rear gate.

The officer stopped him. "Nobody goes in, sir."

"I need to find my family."

"Jack!"

He turned at the sound of Andie's voice. He'd run right past her in the crowd. Righley was in her arms. He ran to them and wrapped his arms around them so tightly that he could barely breathe.

"Are you okay?" he asked.

"Yes. We're okay. Her whole class is okay."

Jack couldn't let go.

"Let's walk to your office," said Andie. "I want Righley out of here."

Righley's teacher was fending off questions from every angle. Jack was able to get her attention long enough to let her know that they were leaving with their daughter. Andie was already on her way and carrying Righley with her. Jack caught up and offered to give Andie's arms a rest, but Andie refused to give up her daughter.

"Have you heard anything?" asked Jack.

Andie threw him a look that said, *Not in front of Righley.*

Jack placed his set of earbuds in Righley's ears, opened the Spotify app on his smartphone, and tuned to the playlist labeled Righley's Stuff.

"How about some music, Pumpkin?"

Righley nodded, and the playful sound of her favorite music took some of the fear out of her eyes. Jack and Andie kept walking toward his office. Andie seemed satisfied that they were free to talk.

"You probably know more than I do," said Andie. "I've been locked in a classroom with zero information. My cell didn't even work."

"I've picked up a few things from reporters here and there."

"Have they identified the shooter?"

"If they have, they're not saying. But all the networks are saying that they recovered a semiautomatic pistol. It's registered to a forty-one-year-old man who has kids in the school."

"Are you kidding me? A school parent?"

"Amir something is his name. Begins with a 'K.'"

Andie brought them to a dead halt. "Amir Khoury?"

"Yes, that's it. Do you know him?"

Andie's expression ran cold. "My friend Molly—that's her husband."

Not another word was said until they reached Jack's office.

The Law Office of Jack Swyteck P.A. was on the first floor of a ninety-year-old house near the Miami River, and, more important, blocks away from the Criminal Justice Center. The first time Jack had set foot on the old Dade County pine floors, this old house was home to the Freedom Institute, a ragtag group of talented lawyers who specialized in death penalty work. It was Jack's first job fresh out of law school. Four years of defending the guilty proved to be enough for Jack, so he struck out as a sole practitioner. A decade later, when his mentor passed away and the Institute was on the brink of financial collapse, Jack bought the building. He set up shop downstairs. His old friends from the Institute leased space upstairs. Jack couldn't remember the last time they had actually made a rent payment.

Jack's assistant met them at the door. Bonnie had been with Jack for years. Andie called her "the Roadrunner," so named because she knew only one speed—full throttle—when zipping around the office.

"Is she—" Bonnie started to ask, but Jack gave her a quick shush signal. Righley was sound asleep in her mother's arms.

"Poor angel," said Bonnie.

Andie took her into what had once been the dining room of the old house—now Jack's private office. Jack cleared away the trial notebooks, and Andie laid Righley on the couch.

"She's wiped out," said Jack.

"Better off in her dreams," said Andie.

They stepped out of Jack's office and into the reception area. Bonnie had the television tuned to the local news coverage. Amir Khoury's name and photograph were on every broadcast in America, confirming Jack's info. But Jack was confused on many levels.

"Your friend Molly strikes me as WASPy enough to be a member of the Daughters of the American Revolution," said Jack.

"She is. She fell in love and married a Muslim."

"Where's he from?"

"What do you mean 'where's he from'? Camp al-Qaeda—is that what you're implying?"

"I'm not implying anything," said Jack. "His gun was found on the scene of a school shooting. I'm just asking the question."

"He's from Fort Lauderdale. Whenever anyone raised

an eyebrow, as if lily-white Molly and her Muslim husband were the odd couple, she'd say it was destiny: they were born in the same hospital, Broward General. I cannot believe this is happening."

Andie's cell rang, and she checked the incoming number. "It's Schwartz."

Guy Schwartz was the assistant special agent in charge of the FBI's Miami field office. Jack knew him better as that guy who always called right before Andie had to leave in the middle of dinner, cancel her daughter's birthday party, or disappear on assignment for days or even weeks at a time.

Andie stepped to the other side of the reception area to take the call. It lasted only a minute, and she didn't look happy when it ended. Jack had seen Andie's work face before, and he knew that there would no explanation coming. Just an announcement. It was all part of being married to an FBI agent.

"I have to go," she said.

Andie's partner picked her up at Jack's office. He brought a replacement sidearm, since Andie's was still locked in the glove compartment of Jack's SUV, and the SUV was parked on a street so crowded that it was impassable.

Andie knew Molly's address. Their friendship was

precisely the reason for the call from the assistant special agent in charge of the FBI's Miami field office.

"Miami-Dade Police have a no-knock warrant for the Khoury residence," ASAC Schwartz had told her. "No knock" meant that law enforcement would literally break down the door.

"Have they executed?"

"About to. And they want you there when they do."

"Why?"

"No one knows how this might go down. You know the Khoury family. You might be useful in de-escalating the situation, if need be."

Andie could have resisted and said she wanted to be with her daughter the moment Righley woke, but Schwartz's directions had left her no option: "Andie, the bureau could have jurisdiction here, if this turns out to be terrorist related."

Andie's partner turned at Santa Maria Street, one of the most prestigious addresses in Coral Gables that was not on the waterfront. Lined with majestic live oaks and some of the best preserved colonial-style and other historic mansions in South Florida, the quiet old side street bisected the golf course of the famous Riviera Country Club, offering residents drop-dead views of beautiful fairways, not to mention a lifetime supply of golf balls, compliments of innumerable club members with a nasty slice. Molly had joked about not being able to cut a donation check to Riverside on top of three tuitions, but it was indeed a joke.

They parked on the street. Andie and her partner simultaneously climbed out of the vehicle. The front door to Molly's house was wide open. Two police officers were standing guard on the porch. A line of yellow police tape demarked the entire front yard as a crime scene.

"Looks like they executed without us," said Andie's partner.

"Wasn't the whole point that they wanted me here?"

A Miami-Dade police officer approached and explained. "We couldn't wait any longer. The suspect's name has gone viral. The media is hyper-focused on the school, but any minute now this entire street is going to be a mob scene. More packed than Halloween night."

Andie took his point. For Andie, Jack, Righley, and about fifty thousand other annual visitors, Santa Maria was the South Florida trick-or-treating destination of choice. Many a law enforcement officer had done Halloween crowd-control duty on Santa Maria.

As if on cue, the first media van pulled up and stopped across the street from the Khoury residence. Seconds later, Molly's midnight-blue Mercedes arrived and stopped in the driveway. Molly and her three children were inside. The front doors swung open, and as Molly stepped out from behind the wheel, Miami-Dade police officers surrounded the vehicle, weapons drawn.

"Freeze!" an officer shouted.

"Don't shoot!" Molly screamed.

Molly's younger children were in the back seat, the older of the two stunned into silence and Molly's eight-year-old daughter crying hysterically. Molly's oldest son was standing beside the open passenger's-side door with his hands in the air. Xavier was a high school senior at Riverside. Last Andie had heard, he was heading to MIT after graduation.

"Mom, it's okay," said Xavier. "I did it."

Chapter 4

Not until late afternoon was the neighborhood around the school clear enough for Jack to walk over and retrieve the SUV. On a normal workday he would never leave his office between four and six p.m., but Righley desperately wanted her mother, so he pushed through rush-hour traffic out of downtown Miami.

Their house was on Key Biscayne, a tropical island community that connected by causeway to the entirely different world of high-rise condominiums along Miami's Brickell-area waterfront. Many thought of "the Key" as paradise. Jack felt lucky to live there. Real estate was priced way beyond his means, but years earlier, before he'd even met Andie, he'd cut a steal of a deal on one of the last remaining Mackle homes, basically a 1,200-square-foot shoe box built right after

World War II as affordable housing for returning GIs. Those had to be some of the happiest veterans in the history of warfare. On a day like this one, the fact was not lost on Jack that the Key still had one of the lowest crime rates in America.

Jack pulled into their driveway, a crunchy swatch of crushed seashells that was big enough for just one car. Righley unbuckled herself from her car seat and ran to the front door. Andie met her there.

"Mommy!"

It wasn't the usual "Mommy" of pure joy and excitement. Righley's voice had a more distressed quality. Back at the office, Jack had been under the impression that he and Bonnie were doing a pretty good job with Righley in the wake of trauma. The way she was clinging to her mother, however, made Jack realize that this was going to be a long road.

Andie led Righley back to her bedroom to change out of her school uniform. Jack went to the kitchen, opened a beer, and turned on the five o'clock news. All day long, the "breaking news" alerts had been about the shooting at Riverside. The young reporter on the screen was standing about a block away from the school, not far from where Jack had parked the SUV that morning. This time, the breaking news was actually something he didn't already know.

"Nationwide, this is the two-hundred-and-ninety-fifth mass shooting so far this year," said the reporter, "and it is one of the most deadly. Thirteen are confirmed dead. The identity of the victims has been withheld pending notification of next of kin. Now our sources are also telling us that the terrorist organization al-Qaeda has claimed responsibility for the shooting. Law enforcement has yet to confirm that information."

Andie entered the kitchen. Righley was showered and in her room. The nightly routine of trying on every nightgown she owned, deciding which princess to be, had begun.

"A link to terrorism would change the complexion of this investigation," said Jack. "Is the FBI going to take jurisdiction?"

"I can't talk about that, Jack."

The separation of work and family was standard operating procedure for any FBI agent, and that was especially true when the agent was married to a criminal defense lawyer. Still, Jack thought she might make an exception for a criminal matter that directly affected their family.

"What can you tell me?" asked Jack.

"The standard-issue magazine on the semiautomatic pistol used in the shooting is thirteen rounds. The shooter went through four extended magazines, thirty-three rounds each. Over a hundred and thirty rounds fired in less than five minutes."

"That sounds like a lot. Is it, as far as school shootings go?"

"Not as many as Sandy Hook; a few more than Parkland. But keep in mind this shooter was using a handgun, not an assault rifle."

Jack found it interesting that she didn't refer to the shooter by name. "What's happening with Xavier?"

"He's in custody."

"Are they questioning anyone else in the family?"

"Molly's husband isn't even in the country, if that's what you're asking. He's in London on a business trip."

It wasn't like Andie to sling passive-aggressive reminders of "innocent until proven guilty" in Jack's direction. But nothing was normal about this day. Andie seemed in denial, clinging to the irrational hope that by some miracle things had not forever changed between Molly and her. Jack left her alone for a while and went back to Righley's room. Her wet towel was on the floor, as were Mulan, Ariel, and Jasmine. She'd selected her Rapunzel nightgown and was standing in front of the full-length mirror, trying to run a comb through her tangled, wet hair.

"Let me help you, honey."

"No!"

That took him aback. When it came to girl stuff, untangling wet hair was one of the few things Jack did better than Mommy. He even did it *on* Mommy.

"I just want to—"

"Daddy, don't touch me!"

Jack froze. The day had left even Andie, a trained FBI agent, out of sorts. Righley's outburst was so out of character as to be downright worrisome.

Like a godsend, Jack's grandmother appeared in the doorway. *"Hola, mi vida!"* Literally, "my life." To Abuela, Righley was as precious as life itself.

Righley rushed across the room and hugged her. Abuela was too old to pick her up, but as she liked to say, the way she was shrinking and Righley was growing, they'd be eye to eye soon enough. Jack was glad she'd agreed to spend the night. Abuela had a way of shrinking any life trauma down to size. It wasn't exactly a gift. Not only had she lost a daughter—preeclampsia claimed Jack's mother way too young—but it had taken Abuela forty years to escape Castro's Cuba to visit the grave.

"You sure you two will be all right while we're gone?" asked Jack.

Riverside had a satellite campus in South Miami for students with special needs. An emergency parents meeting was scheduled there for seven p.m. If not for Abuela, Jack and Andie probably would have skipped.

"Go," said Abuela.

The drive to the Riverside satellite was thirty minutes. Jack and Andie arrived to a packed gymnasium. This meeting was only for families with children who were neither victims nor eyewitnesses to the carnage; individual counseling sessions were underway at a separate facility for those more directly affected. Still, it was a solemn crowd, easily more than three hundred parents. Jack found two of the last open seats in the third row of bleachers. He and Andie were squeezing into place, bumping shoulders with each other and the parents beside them, when the head of school stepped up to the microphone.

"Good evening. I'm Cynthia Mickelson, and I want to thank all of you for coming tonight."

The first order of business was an ecumenical prayer. The bleachers rumbled as the crowd rose. Leading the convocation were a minister, a priest, and a rabbi. No imam, it occurred to Jack as the prayer ended.

"Amen," the crowd said in unison.

Mickelson waited for all to be seated and then started with a series of announcements. School would be closed for at least a week. Counselors were available to students and parents upon request. Support animals would be allowed in classrooms when classes resumed.

"Also," she continued, "I received a call from the

Florida attorney general this afternoon. I have his word that the state will pay all expenses for the funerals of the victims."

"How many are there?" a man shouted. He was a few rows behind Jack.

"Excuse me?" asked Mickelson.

The man rose. "How many teachers and students have we lost? No one will give us a straight answer."

The head measured her words. "The official count has not yet been released. As soon as we have that information, we will post it on the school website."

Another man rose. "It's at least one more than it had to be."

Mickelson hesitated, confused. "I don't understand."

"My middle son, David, was caught in the hallway when this lunatic opened fire. He and his friend Lucas Horne tried to hide in the bathroom. But the bathroom door was locked. My son was lucky. Lucas is dead. So I want know: Why was that bathroom door locked?"

"The bathrooms in our middle school and high school buildings are locked. Students must ask their teacher for permission to use the bathroom, and if permission is granted, they are given a key."

"Why is that?"

"That was a decision we implemented at the beginning of this school year. As a preventive measure."

"Preventative of *what*?"

"Last semester we had to expel two eighth-grade students for vaping in the bathroom."

"So you *locked* the bathrooms? The only place my son and his friend had to hide was the bathroom, and you locked it?"

The pain in his voice drew a rumbling from the crowd. The head of school went into damage-control mode.

"I am so truly sorry, for your son, and for the Horne family. I should point out, however, that if your son was an eyewitness to this unfortunate turn of events, your entire family should be at the other meeting."

"No," he said firmly. "These families here, whose kids will be going back to school in a week with their puppies and kittens for support, need to know the truth. They need to know some of us will be paying the price forever because of *your* stupidity."

"I completely understand your anger."

"No!" he said, his voice booming loud enough to fill the gymnasium. "You *don't* understand. But if you *think* you do, then, by God, you had best not get anywhere near Lucas Horne's father."

He lowered himself into his seat, emotionally spent. His wife slid her arm around his shoulder, as if to say he'd done the right thing.

Another man rose in the next bleacher section. "While we're on the subject of stupidity: Don't we have background checks for families before they are accepted to this academy?"

Mickelson paused, thinking through her response. "As everyone in this gymnasium knows well, the application process at Riverside is highly selective and very comprehensive. And of course we interview all students and their parents."

"What if people lie?" the man asked.

"Lie about what?"

"About who they are?"

"I don't think that's the issue here," said Mickelson.

"I do. Let's say only the mother comes in for the interview and not the father. How much do you really know about that family?"

Jack and Andie exchanged anxious glances. The man might as well have asked, *How'd you let Molly's Muslim husband slip through?*

"I see where you're going with this," said Mickelson. "And I want to address this as fully and as directly as I can. We all want answers."

"You bet we do."

"Hold on," said Mickelson. "Just because someone called the media to claim responsibility on behalf of al-Qaeda doesn't mean that al-Qaeda was necessarily behind this. And just because the shooter—alleged shooter—has a Muslim father doesn't mean that this shooting had anything to do with radical Islam."

"That's all very nice and politically correct, Mrs. Mickelson. But do you expect us to believe it?"

"I expect everyone in this room to let law enforcement do its job without feeding the rumor mill."

"It's not a rumor. My brother is a cop at Miami-Dade. He says the FBI's Joint Terrorism Task Force is already involved. Why would the FBI's terrorism task force be involved if al-Qaeda's claim of responsibility was not credible?"

"I don't know how to answer that question," said Mickelson.

His gaze swept the bleachers. "Isn't one of our parents an FBI agent? Maybe she can answer it."

Heads turned, and dozens of parents were suddenly looking in Jack and Andie's direction.

Mickelson seemed to sense Andie's discomfort even from thirty feet away. "I don't think it's fair to put Agent Henning on the spot like that. That's not the point of this meeting."

"Maybe we should let her speak for herself," the man said. "It's a simple question. Would the Joint Terrorism Task Force get involved if al-Qaeda had nothing to do with this?"

The crowd fell silent, which sent a clear message. Andie was suddenly the official spokesperson for the FBI. She rose slowly.

Jack heard whispering all around them, which made him wish all the more that they had never come.

Who's she?

Absentee mom. Hardly ever at the school.

I think she's friends with that Muslim boy's mother.

"I can't comment on that," said Andie. She sat down and looked at Jack, but he didn't have to tell her what she already knew.

This crowd had all the confirmation it needed.

Chapter 5

Jack and Andie were the last to leave the school parking lot. Not that they weren't eager to get home. After being singled out as the "FBI mom," Andie needed to find a private place and call her ASAC.

"How'd it go?" Jack asked as she climbed into the passenger seat.

"You don't want to know, and I can't tell you."

The drive from the mainland to Key Biscayne was mostly in silence. Crossing the causeway, Andie's profile was a pensive silhouette against the backdrop of city lights in the distance. They were home a little after nine o'clock. Righley was sound asleep in her room. Abuela was nearby in her favorite rocking chair, literally snoring. Andie wanted their little girl in their bed, so she gently picked her up and carried her down the hallway.

Jack heard a car pull up outside the house and then a timid knock on the front door. He went to the living room and opened it.

"May I come in, please?" asked the woman.

Although Jack had met Molly before, it took him a moment to recognize her as the woman standing on his front porch. She was normally a stylish dresser, but the cashmere wrap she wore was better suited for January, and there was nothing stylish about the broad-brimmed hat that left her face in the shadows and the sunglasses so dark that not even eighties heartthrob Corey Hart would have worn them at night.

"It's me, Molly," she said as she removed her sunglasses.

Without them, she looked broken, desperate. Jack couldn't help but feel for her.

"Who is it, Jack?" asked Andie, entering the living room.

Molly went straight to Andie, but it seemed that Molly's need for a hug was not exactly reciprocal. Just a few hours earlier, Andie had been quick to show her support for her girlfriend, at least in conversation with Jack. Maybe it was the phone call with her ASAC, or maybe a gymnasium full of angry parents had unlocked the voices of child victims in her head, but something had changed since the school meeting. Psychologically speaking, it seemed that Andie had already moved from denial to anger.

"Molly, I know you must have a lot to talk about," said Andie. "But right now I just want to lie down with my daughter and thank God she's still here."

"I won't be long."

"I'll let you two talk in private," said Jack.

"No," said Molly. "I'd like you to be part of this, if you would, Jack."

Jack took a seat with Andie on the couch. Molly sat in the club chair, facing them.

"I heard about the meeting at the school," said Molly. "I didn't go, of course. I've been at the jail all night, trying to speak to Xavier."

"Trying?" asked Jack. "Are the police not allowing it?"

"It's a different problem," said Molly. "Xavier refuses any visitors."

"You're his mother," said Andie. "If you want to see him, you have the right."

"I'm told that's not the case. He's eighteen. Since he's no longer a minor, the police are telling me that his parents have no right to visit him and no ability to force him to see us."

"When did he turn eighteen?" asked Jack.

Molly hesitated, then answered in a weak voice. "Today."

The gravity of a high school student embarking on a shooting spree on his eighteenth birthday sent chills through the room.

Molly continued. "I suppose Xavier waited until he was eighteen so that his parents would have no say over what happens to him after the . . ." She seemed unable to even say the word.

"After his arrest," Jack offered.

"Yes," said Molly. "After his arrest."

"Has anyone told you what was said at tonight's meeting?" asked Andie.

"Not directly. But I see the chatter on social media. Not everyone at the school has deleted me from their list of friends yet. They might be surprised to know that I agree with much of what is being said."

"Like what?" asked Andie.

"Al-Qaeda, for one. I'm sure our head of school means well by telling parents not to jump to conclusions about a connection to Islamic terrorism. But al-Qaeda claimed responsibility."

"And you believe that the claim is real?" asked Jack.

"Yes. Someone must have radicalized Xavier to do something as horrible as this. Contrary to what people might say on social media, my son was not 'born to kill.'"

"Molly, if I could give you any advice, it would be this," said Jack. "Don't go on social media. Stay off the Internet."

"I know. It's horrible what people will say. The whole world wants my son executed so he can start burning in hell as soon as possible."

"No one said that at tonight's meeting," said Jack.

"They're definitely saying it online. I can't explain or excuse what Xavier did, but a high school boy who is the victim of brainwashing should not be executed."

"It will be up to the state attorney to decide if she'll seek the death penalty," said Jack.

"Can he be executed?" asked Molly. "Legally, I mean. Can a boy who's still in high school get the death penalty?"

Jack took no joy in being the one to tell her, but soon enough Molly would learn what a difference a day makes. "The Supreme Court has held that the death penalty is unconstitutional under the Eighth Amendment as 'cruel and unusual punishment' for anyone under the age of eighteen. Xavier made the cutoff by one day."

Molly closed her eyes and opened them slowly, absorbing the blow. "So that's the answer? If the state attorney chooses to seek the death penalty, there is no mercy?"

Jack understood the arguments on both sides: What mercy had Xavier shown his victims? "If he's found guilty, there will be a second trial on the issue of sentencing. So it's up to the jury to decide if he gets death or life in prison. Xavier's youth and impressionability would be relevant mitigating circumstances that jurors can consider."

"Thank you for that," she said. "I put a lot of stock in what you say. I understand you've done a lot of death penalty work."

"I have," said Jack.

"Some would say too much," added Andie.

"I googled you," said Molly. "You're a very courageous man. You've taken some very tough cases. For some pretty notorious clients."

"Most of those were a long time ago," said Jack.

"Before we were married," said Andie.

Molly paused, and Jack sensed she was building up the nerve to ask him something. Finally, she spoke.

"Could you be Xavier's lawyer?"

Andie answered for him. "No."

"We would pay you, of course."

"Molly, he can't," Andie said firmly.

"I'm sorry," said Molly. "I shouldn't have asked."

"There's nothing wrong with asking," said Jack.

"I wish you would at least think about it. I don't know how I'm going to find a good lawyer."

"You don't have to worry about that," said Jack. "Your son is an adult, even if it is just by one day, and he has no job. It makes no difference that his parents have enough money to afford a private attorney. Your son is indigent for purposes of court-appointed counsel and will be represented by the Public Defender's Office."

"But I don't want him to have a public defender," said Molly.

"The public defender is well qualified to make all of the arguments that need to be made at Xavier's sentencing hearing to avoid the death penalty."

"No, he's not. I spoke to him. He called me earlier today because Xavier wouldn't talk to him and he thought I might have some insight on how to break through. Frankly, I don't trust him."

"Don't trust him in what way?" asked Jack.

"It goes back to what I said before. Xavier wasn't born a murderer. I do believe he was radicalized. But this is key: he was *not* radicalized *at home.*"

"Is someone saying that he was?" asked Jack.

"Not yet. But the public defender is already heading in that direction."

"How do you know?"

"It was clear from the questions he asked me. He's going to tell the same old story that lawyers always tell. His client was the victim of his upbringing. The parents are horrible people. How could a boy who was raised in this household grow up to be *anything but* a mass murderer?"

Jack had made similar arguments—the dysfunctional family, physically and emotionally abusive parents— many times on behalf of death row inmates. "The public defender can't make those arguments if they're not true."

"Baloney. My husband is a Muslim. He's a sitting duck for the bogus argument that he radicalized Xavier. It's not fair to Amir, who loves this country as much as any other American. And it's not fair to Xavier's brother and sister, who will have to live with this stigma for the rest of their lives."

"Everything you're saying is valid," said Jack. "But there isn't much you or I can do. It's up to Xavier to choose his own lawyer. He's eighteen."

"What if he called you? Maybe I can get through to him and give him your number. Would you talk to him?"

Jack cut another glance at Andie, who even in her silence was making her position clear.

"I don't know," said Jack.

"I don't expect anyone to prove my son's innocence. That's impossible. All I'm asking is to keep him off death row. And do it without labeling my entire family as Islamic-extremist sympathizers. Is that asking too much?"

Jack considered it. Molly was beyond desperate. "I'm not saying I'll take his case. But if he calls me, I might take the call."

"Thank you," she said. "Thank you so very much."

Molly rose. She and Andie shared a hug more awkward than the first one. Jack showed her to the door. Molly thanked him again, and Jack closed the door. Andie had more to say.

"I don't want you getting involved in this case, Jack."

"I'm not getting involved."

"Xavier is going to call you. How is that not getting involved?"

"I told her I *might* take the call."

"Before you do, I suggest you call Nate Abrams."

Nate was a respected lawyer in town and one of the dads at Riverside Jack had become friendly with. "Why?" asked Jack.

"It was bad enough to get chewed out by my ASAC after the parent meeting," said Andie. "But the reason that call took so long is that he gave me some information that isn't public yet. The names of the victims."

Andie paused, and Jack gave her a moment.

"Lindsey Abrams was shot in the back running from her classroom," said Andie. "She's fighting for her life at Jackson Memorial."

"That's horrible. I'm sorry to hear that."

"Tell it to Nate. Then ask him how he'd feel about your defending the monster who shot her."

It was like a slap to the face. Jack watched as Andie turned and headed toward the bedroom to sleep with Righley.

Chapter 6

Jack was in the Richard E. Gerstein Justice Building early the next morning. His client was a nineteen-year-old first-time offender who "forgot" that the recreational marijuana she'd bought legally in Illinois wasn't legal in Florida. It took Jack less than five minutes to get the assistant state attorney to agree to dismissal of the charges upon completion of a pretrial intervention program. Jack had plenty of other work to do back at the office, but he made a stop on the first floor, where it wasn't just the usual courthouse buzz.

"Standing room only," the deputy at the door told him.

Felony arraignments started every weekday at nine a.m. in Courtroom 1-5. The morning docket included everyone in Miami-Dade County who'd been arrested in the previous twenty-four hours on a felony charge. The routine played out in a spacious old room with high ceilings and a long mahogany rail that separated the public seating from the business end of the justice system. A junior assistant state attorney was seated at the government's table in front of the empty jury box, working his way through the stack of files, one at a time, as each case was called. Jack watched from the back of the courtroom, standing, not a seat to be had. The draw was not the usual parade of accused armed robbers, drunk drivers, and others proclaiming their innocence. The crowd had come to see Xavier Khoury. Jack was one of many Riverside parents and supporters in attendance.

"Next case," said Judge Feinstein. He was moving quickly. They were at number nine. Feinstein was the oldest judge on the criminal circuit. Some said he no longer had the stamina for lengthy trials, but he still seemed to enjoy the frenetic pace of arraignments.

"Case number seventeen oh-three oh-one," announced the bailiff. "State of Florida versus Xavier Khoury."

The side door opened, and a pair of deputies brought Xavier into the courtroom. The atmosphere was suddenly charged, as a packed gallery and the rest of the world, via television, got its first look at the shooter in his orange prison jumpsuit and shackles, flanked by muscle-bound guards. Reporters in the designated media section took notes, furiously recording their front-row impressions, as the accused shuffled across the courtroom with head down. The guards seated him alone in the empty jury box, almost separate from the proceeding, as if to keep the prisoner from continuing his rampage and lashing out at the public. Jack had seen that done before, on occasion, with particularly dangerous defendants.

"Mitchell Karr for the defendant," said Xavier's court-appointed lawyer, announcing his appearance.

The junior prosecutor who had handled the first ten arraignments stepped aside and was replaced by the chief prosecutor of the homicide division. "Abe Beckham for the state of Florida."

Jack had squared off against Beckham in several capital cases. The state attorney was bringing in the big gun for *State v. Khoury.*

"Good morning, everyone," said Judge Feinstein. "Mr. Beckham, may I have the date and time of Mr. Khoury's arrest?"

"Yesterday at approximately two twenty p.m."

The judge swiveled his high-back chair toward the jury box to address the defendant more directly. "Mr. Khoury, the purpose of this proceeding is, first of all, to advise you of certain rights that you have and to inform you of the charges made against you under Florida law. Do you understand?"

Xavier was staring at the floor, motionless.

"Your Honor, the defendant stands mute," his lawyer said.

Judge Feinstein recited the Miranda warnings, though it hardly seemed necessary to remind Xavier of his "right to remain silent."

"Mr. Khoury, you have been charged with thirteen counts of murder in the first degree," the judge continued. "As of this initial hearing, those charges are supported by affidavit of the Miami-Dade Police Department. A grand jury will be convened in accordance with Florida law. If the grand jury returns a true bill, your conviction on these charges may be punishable by death. Do you understand?"

No response from the accused. "The defendant stands mute," his lawyer answered.

"Count one charges that without justification Xavier Khoury did cause the death of Kaleb Greene, a first degree felony. Count Two charges that—"

"Your Honor, my client is aware of the charges," said Karr. "We will waive formal reading."

A smart move from the defense standpoint. Tensions

were high enough in the courtroom without reading aloud thirteen counts of homicide in the first degree.

"Mr. Khoury, how do you plead?"

His lawyer interjected. "Judge, I have a matter to take up with the court in regard to the defendant's plea."

"Go ahead, Counsel."

"On my client's behalf, we reached out to the state attorney. Mr. Khoury offered to plead guilty to thirteen counts of homicide and seven additional counts of attempted murder—*twenty* life sentences to be served consecutively without possibility of parole—if the government will waive the death penalty. The state attorney has refused that offer. He insists on taking this case to the grand jury, proceeding to trial, and seeking the death penalty."

"Which is the state attorney's job," said the judge.

As a defense lawyer, Jack could only cringe. If the public defender had been hoping that a public announcement might make Judge Feinstein browbeat the prosecution into accepting the proposed plea deal, Karr had badly misread the tea leaves.

"Mr. Khoury, how do you plead?" asked the judge.

The accused didn't look up, didn't move, and didn't say a word.

"The court will enter a plea of not guilty," said the judge, and then his gaze swung to the other side of the courtroom. "Since this is a first-degree murder case, there is no bail. Does the defense have any argument to the contrary?"

"Not at this time," said Karr.

"The defendant shall be remanded to custody. Anything else?"

The state attorney brought up a few "housekeeping matters," as judges called them, but Jack had seen enough. He slipped out the rear exit, continued through the courthouse lobby, and left the building through the main entrance doors. At the bottom of the concrete steps, he stopped, turned, and noticed that another lawyer from the PD's Office, Sheila Kinkaid, had followed him out.

"Buy you a coffee, Swyteck?"

Jack held Sheila in high regard—much higher than his regard for Xavier's lawyer. He was happy to share a coffee with her. There was an old man who sold Cuban café out of the back of his truck right outside the courthouse. Sheila ordered two espressos.

"What did you think of round one, Jack?"

"You mean announcing to the world that your client is guilty before he even gets the chance to plead not guilty?"

"The Broward PD did the same thing in the Nikolas Cruz case after the Parkland shooting," said Sheila.

"I didn't agree with it then, either. For one, it all but takes an insanity defense off the table. Anyone who is rational enough to offer a guilty plea in order to save his own life is rational enough to know the difference between right and wrong."

"Good point," she said.

"I can rattle off about ninety-nine other ones, if you have the time."

"No need," said Sheila. "I agree with you. But it wasn't my decision."

"You should be handling this case, Sheila. Not Mitchell Karr."

"Makes no difference in the long run. The PD's Office will be withdrawing as counsel tomorrow."

"On what grounds?"

"Xavier is far from indigent. Independently wealthy, you might say."

The vendor poured two steaming espressos into little poly-paper cups and placed them on the counter at the back of the truck. Jack paid before Sheila could.

"I spoke to his mother last night," said Jack. "She didn't mention anything about Xavier having money."

"She didn't know. We didn't know, either, until we spoke to Xavier's father. Amir Khoury established trusts for each of his three children at birth. The two boys get two hundred grand a year starting on their eighteenth birthday. Their daughter gets hers in one lump sum when she marries."

Jack couldn't even imagine Andie's reaction to a plan like that for Righley. "I'm guessing that's why Amir never told his wife."

"Probably. The bottom line is that taxpayers will not be paying for Xavier's lawyer. He will. Which means he has to find a private attorney."

Jack was on to her, smiling and wagging a finger. "No, no, Sheila. I see where this is headed. Molly Khoury asked me the same thing last night."

"Jack, this is a capital case. Judge Feinstein won't be happy if the PD's Office withdraws without lining up substitute counsel. We want a seamless transition: we're out; you're in."

"I can't."

"Actually, you're one of the few private attorneys in this town who *can*."

"There are others."

"Yes," said Sheila. "But the last thing your school community needs is a grandstanding criminal defense lawyer who parlays this case into his ticket to TV talking-head stardom."

He took her point. Jack had defended one innocent

client while working for the Freedom Institute. Out of respect for the families of victims, he never went on television proclaiming the innocence of any other client. "Some lawyers seem to forget that the Constitution guarantees a right to counsel, not to a publicity agent."

"Amen to that."

"But here's the problem," said Jack. "Both Righley and Andie were at the school when the shooting happened."

"So, if they had not been there, you *would* take the case. Is that what you're saying?"

Jack added a little sugar to his espresso. "I don't know."

"Will Righley be a witness for the prosecution?"

"No."

"Will Andie?"

"No."

"Then it's not that you *can't* take the case. You choose not to."

"What are you getting at, Sheila?"

"Look, if I dodged every capital case that made my husband squirm, I might as well hang it up and become an accountant. I know you, Swyteck. You'd make a lousy accountant." She tossed back her espresso and then leveled her most serious gaze at him. "Tell me you'll think about it."

Jack glanced back at the courthouse. Camera crews were at the top of the steps outside the main entrance, and local television reporters were grabbing any available lawyer to comment on the case. There was no shortage of "experts" willing to talk, talk, talk about something that was way outside their sphere of knowledge.

Jack downed his espresso and then noticed the man and woman getting into their car across the street. The sticker on the bumper read MY CHILD IS AN HONOR STUDENT AT RIVERSIDE DAY SCHOOL.

Was, thought Jack. *Was an honor student.*

"I'm sorry, Sheila," he said, as he crushed the little paper cup into a ball, "I really can't see myself making any other choice than the one Andie and I have already made."

He pitched the ball into the trash basket, nothing but net.

Chapter 7

Jack drove straight from the courthouse to UM Jackson Memorial Hospital.

Jackson was Miami's premier public hospital, which meant that in addition to its stellar reputation for groundbreaking research in everything from cancer to spinal injury, its world-class emergency room was the city's go-to trauma center for gunshot wounds. Located just across the river from the Criminal Justice Center, it wasn't at all unusual for the victims of violent crime to land within walking distance of the initial court appearance for the man who'd put them in the hospital. If they could still walk.

"I'm here to see Lindsey Abrams," Jack told the receptionist.

Jack's public-defender friend Sheila had said nothing that made him want to take Xavier's case. Andie's angry reaction—*Ask Nate Abrams how he would feel if you defended this monster*—wasn't the reason Jack went to the hospital. He just felt the need to see his friend Nate.

"She's a minor in the intensive care unit. Are you on the visitation list?"

"I just spoke to her father on the telephone. They're expecting me."

The receptionist called upstairs, checked out the story, and printed out a "visitor" badge that Jack stuck to his lapel. A painfully slow elevator ride took him to the fifth floor. Polished tile floors glistened beneath bright fluorescent lighting. The hallway led to a set of locked doors marked INTENSIVE CARE UNIT. Jack identified himself over the intercom, and a nurse's response crackled over the speaker.

"Room Six," she said, "but only one more visitor can come in now. Maximum of three at a time."

Jack took that to mean that both parents were at their daughter's bedside, which only added to the heartbreak. "I'm alone," said Jack.

The door opened automatically, and Jack entered to the steady sound of beeping patient monitors. In the center of the ICU was the nurses' station, an open island of charts and records surrounded on all sides by a wide corridor. Lining the outer perimeter were the glass-walled rooms for patients, most of whom were in open view. The unit appeared to be full, but in some rooms the privacy curtains were drawn, so it was hard to know. A busy nurse passed with a tray of medications. As Jack approached Room 6, he noticed several visitors outside adjacent rooms wearing hats or T-shirts emblazoned with the Falcon logo—the school mascot for Riverside. The Abramses were not the only Riverside family with a child in the Jackson Memorial ICU.

"Thanks for coming," said Nate.

Jack and Nate were about the same age, but the stress of the past twenty-four hours had already aged him. The privacy curtain prevented Jack from seeing inside Room 6. It made his chest tighten to think of Nate's wife in there with a critically wounded daughter.

"Let's take a walk over to the lounge," said Nate.

Jack followed him around to the other side of the unit, where there was a small room for visitors to catch a moment alone when needed. Nate bought two bottled waters from the vending machine, and they sat across from each other at a small table.

Nate glanced at the calendar on the wall. "Exactly two weeks from today is Lindsey's fourteenth birthday."

It was a painful place to start. Jack wasn't sure what to say, so he simply allowed Nate to continue.

"They tell me Lindsey was running toward the stairwell when she was shot. She had no pulse by the time paramedics finally got to her. They were able to restart the heart with a defibrillator. But . . . uhm . . ."

"You don't have to tell me, unless you want to," said Jack.

Nate looked past Jack, numbness and disbelief leading his line of sight off to somewhere in the middle distance. "I spoke with three different neurologists this morning. Cardiologist came in after that. A pulmonologist is keeping an eye on her to see if she needs any assistance in breathing. Just before you got here, we met a gastro specialist about inserting a feeding tube, if it comes to that. A physical therapist is scheduled to come by twice a day to move her limbs."

Jack said, "They have excellent doctors here."

"Yes, they do," said Nate, and then he took a deep breath. "But not a single one of them can tell us if Lindsey will ever regain consciousness."

"I'm very sorry to hear that," said Jack.

"They say if she lives, she'll be paralyzed from the chest down."

Silence hung between them. Jack suddenly was aware of the hum of fluorescent lights above them. He had no idea how to help. Nate did him the favor of changing the subject. Slightly.

"How did it go in court this morning?" Nate asked.

Jack could have run with it, but he didn't. "A lot of Riverside families showed up."

"Is the state attorney seeking the death penalty?"

"No formal announcement yet. But it's clear enough that he will."

"Such a mistake," said Nate.

Jack wasn't sure he'd heard right. "A mistake?"

"It is in my mind," said Nate.

"Why do you say that?"

Nate breathed in and out. "I remember reading an op-ed that one of the parents wrote in the *Sun-Sentinel* after the Parkland shooting. Of course I never dreamed I'd be in this situation. Anyway, I remember feeling sorry for the man. He'd lost his son. But I didn't agree with what he wrote. Until now."

"What did he write?"

"He started with the fact that in Florida, the average time from arrest to trial in a death penalty case is . . . I forget how many years he said."

"Four years," said Jack, something he knew.

"Right. So this dad pointed out that there would be countless hearings along the way. Worse, the families of all seventeen victims, and every child in that school who witnessed the shooting, would have to relive the experience as witnesses in videotaped depositions and then again at the trial. In the Parkland shooting, the lawyers had to postpone depositions of some of the students because parents were seriously concerned that their child would commit suicide if forced to relive that experience in deposition or at trial."

"So his point was—"

"His point was that the state attorney should accept the shooter's guilty plea and let the court sentence him to seventeen consecutive life sentences with no chance of parole."

"Is that what you think should happen here?"

"I do. And that's why you should take the case."

Jack was dumbstruck. "How did you know I'd even been asked?"

"All of us parents are glued to social media. I saw the update ten minutes before you called. Isn't that what you came here to talk about?"

Jack didn't know who had twisted his words and put it out there. Sheila? Molly? All that mattered was that it was *out there.*

"Please, get involved, Jack," said Nate. "I trust you to convince the state attorney to accept a guilty plea and a sentence of twenty consecutive life sentences without parole. Don't force my daughter and dozens of other traumatized kids to relive this nightmare for the next four years, just so that the state attorney can someday run for governor as the 'pro-death-penalty, tough-on-crime' candidate."

Jack wasn't sure if the allusion had been intentional, but Jack's father had run on that platform twice—and won. "I take your point and can see this in a different light."

"You'll do it?"

Jack paused. "I need to talk to Andie."

Jack met Andie for lunch. He ordered a Cuban sandwich *sin mostaza,* as most of the so-called Cuban joints in Miami didn't seem to know that a *real* Cuban didn't have mustard on it. Andie ordered only an iced tea, having lost her appetite.

Andie was unlike any woman Jack had ever known, and not just because she worked undercover for the FBI. Jack loved that she wasn't afraid to cave dive in Florida's aquifer, that in her training at the FBI Academy she'd nailed a perfect score on one of the toughest shooting ranges in the world, that as a teenager she'd been a Junior Olympic mogul skier from her home state of Washington—something Jack hadn't even known about her until she'd rolled him out of bed one hot August morning and said, "Let's go skiing in Argentina." He loved the green eyes she got from her Anglo father and the raven-black hair from her Native American mother, a mix that made for such exotic beauty.

He hated when she tried to manage his career. But the case of Xavier Khoury was different.

"This one's outside the agreement," said Andie.

The "agreement" was for the sake of their relationship: Jack didn't question her FBI assignments; Andie didn't judge his clients.

"I get it," said Jack. "It affects Righley."

Andie drank from her iced tea. "I'm not going to tell you what to do, Jack. No, let me restate that: if anyone but Nate Abrams had asked, I *would* tell you what to do. But . . ."

He knew Andie would never approve. The question was whether he could live with her mere acquiescence.

"But there's one condition," she said.

"Okay. What?"

"I want to know why that boy wanted to kill my daughter. I want to know what he thought it would accomplish. I want you to ask him. And I don't want to hear any bullshit from you about the attorney-client privilege. You're going to tell me what he says."

Jack didn't say yes. He didn't say no. He wasn't sure what he was going to say—to Andie or to Nate Abrams.

Chapter 8

Jack needed some therapy. He drove to Cy's Place in Coconut Grove and took a seat on a stool at the U-shaped bar.

"You look like you could use a Cy Bender," said Theo, offering up his version of a shot-and-beer: craft-brewed IPA paired with 150-proof whiskey.

"Just a draft," said Jack. "No disrespect to Uncle Cy."

The "Cy" in Cy's Place was Theo's great-uncle Cyrus Knight, a saxophonist who'd in younger days—nights, actually—played in Miami's Overtown Village, once known as Little Harlem. It seemed fitting to put his name on the club, the second bar Theo had purchased with the settlement money from the state of Florida—Theo's "compensation" for spending four years on death row for a murder he didn't commit. Cy's vibe and occasional riff inspired the place, drawing weekend crowds from all over South Florida. Creaky wood floors, redbrick walls, and high ceilings were the perfect bones for a jazz club. Art nouveau chandeliers cast just the right mood lighting after dark. It had been Theo's goal to "do something right." He'd nailed it.

Theo placed the draft in front of him. "Funny thing about you, Jack. Whenever there's something on your mind, it's all over your face. Talk to me."

Theo was Jack's best friend, bartender, therapist, confidant, and sometime investigator. He was also a former client, a one-time gangbanger who easily could have ended up dead on the streets of Overtown or Liberty City. Instead, he landed on death row for a murder he didn't commit. Theo was the one innocent client Jack had represented during his stint at the Freedom Institute.

And he was one damn good listener.

Jack unloaded—the plea from Molly, the "ask" from the public defender—and then Nate Abrams, speaking on behalf of his daughter and every other child who might have to relive the nightmare by testifying as a witness in deposition, at trial, and again at the sentencing hearing.

"Nate's the only one who has me thinking," said Jack.

Theo leaned onto the bar top, as if to level with his friend. "Maybe I can get you off the fence. No extra charge."

"*Extra?*" said Jack. "You've never let me pay for anything here."

It was Theo's way of paying back the young lawyer who'd never stopped believing in him and never stopped fighting to get him off death row—for no pay.

"Figure of speech," said Theo. "Let me tell you this story."

"Only if I haven't heard it before."

"Guaranteed," said Theo. "I used to think my land-lord was the most generous man in Miami. When my bar shut down because of the coronavirus, I couldn't pay my staff *and* pay the rent. He said no problem. We'll waive the rent. You don't even have to pay it back."

"That sounds too nice to be true."

"No shit. Here's where it gets interesting. Later on, his partner comes by to check on the place. I thanked him personally. 'God bless you, man,' was all I could say. 'You kept me in business.' He looked at me like I had three heads. That's when I found out the truth."

"Which was?"

"Molly Khoury paid my rent. She told the landlord not to tell me."

"Why would Molly pay your rent?"

"That's what I asked myself. Then I remembered: I coached her son. Xavier was on my eighth-grade-boys basketball team when I ran the program over at the Boys and Girls Club. He wasn't very good. Terrible, actually. But he tried hard, and got nothing in the way of sports from his old man, so I used to run extra drills with him and a couple other kids after practice. I guess that meant a lot to Molly. So when every bar and restaurant around me was boarding up from the virus, I wasn't the one lucky tenant who had a saint for a landlord. Molly paid my rent. It was her way of saying 'Thanks, Coach. Thanks for being the only man who ever cared enough to get my son off the couch.'"

"Wow," said Jack. "She must know we're friends, right?"

"Yeah, we ran into each other at Righley's birthday party. She says, 'Theo, what're you doin' here?' I say, 'I'm Righley's godfather. What're *you* doin' here?'"

"But she didn't mention anything about paying your rent when she asked me to be Xavier's lawyer."

"That's because she didn't help me so that she could call in a favor someday."

"Rare," said Jack.

"Very," said Theo. "So, let me put in my two cents.

No one's asking you to put a school shooter back on the street. Nate sure isn't. It doesn't sound like Molly is, either. She's just a mom trying to figure out how to pull her life back together. She needs this to end. We both know that a death sentence is far from 'finality' or 'closure' or whatever you want to call it. It means another fifteen years of appeals and stays of execution. Life in prison without parole: *that's* finality. If you can get that, Molly can put this behind her for herself and for her other two kids. It's step one to getting her life back."

Jack considered Theo's words, and his thoughts kept tumbling back to the way Molly had comported herself in his living room. "She could have easily played that card—paying your rent—when she came to see Andie and me and asked me to defend her son. She didn't."

"I respect that," said Theo.

Jack watched the little bubbles rise up from the bottom of his beer glass and explode at the surface. "So do I."

"Maybe you should go talk to her."

Jack nodded. "Maybe *we* should."

Jack braced his hands against the dashboard as Theo maneuvered around a slow-moving camper with Quebec license plates. "Dude, this is Miami, not Daytona, so there's no need to drive five hundred miles an hour."

"I don't think the Daytona Five Hundred means they actually go five—"

"Just slow down, will you?"

Theo grumbled something to the effect of "old fart" as they joined the normal traffic flow.

The meeting was at the Khoury residence on Santa Maria Street. Law enforcement had finished the execution of the search warrant and allowed the family to move back in that morning. Lamps were aglow inside, situation normal, just like any other house on the street. But the porchlight was out. In the darkness, Jack stepped on a stray strip of yellow police tape that the police had left behind. Walking up the driveway, he felt like the hapless teacher who lights up the laughter by entering a classroom with a trail of toilet paper stuck to his shoe. He finally shook the tape loose, continued to the front door, and rang the bell. Molly answered and invited them into the living room, where her husband was on the couch, waiting. Jack had never met Amir, but he'd gathered as much publicly available background information about him as he could, so it came as no surprise that Molly's Muslim husband spoke with no Middle Eastern accent. According to his online bio, he had a BS from Duke and an MBA from Wharton. He was fluent in Arabic, French, and English, which was true of many people of Lebanese heritage, especially businesspeople. For the last decade he'd worked at an elite private equity firm on Brickell Avenue, the heart of downtown Miami's Financial District.

"Thank you for taking our case," said Amir.

"I actually haven't decided yet," said Jack. "But I should point out that even if I do defend Xavier, it's not quite accurate to call it 'our' case."

"Excuse me?"

"First thing you need to understand is that I'm meeting with you and Molly as witnesses, not prospective clients. Xavier would be the only client. Everything I discuss with his parents would be useable in court, just like my conversations with any other school parents."

"That seems odd," said Amir. "But if that's the way it is, we'll deal with it."

"Let's start with the search warrant," said Jack. "I've seen a copy of it, but I'm not sure what it turned up."

"The house looked like a bomb went off," said Amir.

"It wasn't that bad," said Molly.

"You didn't see the worst of it, Molly," said Amir.

"The police aren't supposed to break anything, unless it's necessary to execute the warrant," said Jack. "But it happens."

"Happened every fucking day where I grew up," said Theo. "Cops called it tossing the place."

"We got tossed," said Amir. "And please don't use that word in front of my wife."

"Tossing?"

Jack shot Theo a look that said, *Let me do the talking*, and then he turned his attention back to the Khourys. "Have you been able to determine what's missing since the police left?"

"They definitely took Xavier's cell phone and laptop," said Molly. "And the family computer in the den."

"Anything else?"

"Like what?" she asked.

"Weapons? Ammunition?"

"There's none of that in the house," said Amir.

"I don't allow it," said Molly. "Not with children."

"That rule is a little hard to square with the fact that the gun used in the shooting was registered in Amir's name."

"I kept that gun in my car," said Amir. "Locked in the glove compartment."

"Do you have a concealed-carry permit?"

"Yes."

"Do you mind if I ask why you got one?"

"Because I was hoping that my son would someday grow up to be a school shooter."

"Amir, please," said Molly.

"That was clearly the point of his question," said Amir.

"I'm just asking why you had a concealed-carry permit," said Jack.

"Fine. It goes back almost twenty years. Two weeks after the nine-eleven attacks I got into a fender bender. My luck, I hit a monster red pickup truck with a stars-and-bars decal stretched across the entire rear window. When the driver saw the name on my driver's license was Amir Khoury, I honestly thought he might grab the shotgun from his rack and kill me. Anti-Muslim sentiment in this country was out of control. It's gotten almost that bad again. Molly doesn't want a gun in the house. I keep it in my car."

"Did Xavier know you kept it there?"

"Yes. I told him. I took him to the shooting range and taught him how to use it, too."

"For—"

"For self-defense," Amir said sharply. "Not for murdering innocent children."

Molly reached over and took his hand. "Amir, honey. Take a deep breath, okay?"

"I'm sorry I have to ask these questions," said Jack.

"But I do have to ask them. When was the last time you saw the gun in your glove compartment?"

"I don't remember. How often do you look in your glove compartment?"

"Fair point," said Jack. He wanted to ask about the extended magazines, but Amir seemed to have reached his limit on guns and ammo questions. "Let's talk about the laptop and family computer taken in the search. Is there anything on those devices I should know about?"

"Can you be a little more specific?" asked Molly.

"Sure. Here's what the police will be looking for. First they're going to check every email, text, and social media post to see if there were any threats or red flags about a school shooting."

"Xavier isn't on social media," said Amir.

Jack looked at Molly, as if the moms always had the real story. "Seriously?"

"We didn't allow it," said Amir. "Social media is a complete waste of time, and Xavier has no time to waste. How do you think he was accepted to MIT?"

"Ordinarily, I'd be skeptical of any parent's blanket claim that their high school student was not on social media. But it's been forty-eight hours, and the media hasn't turned up a single social media post by Xavier. So you may be right."

"I am right," said Amir.

"What about his Internet searches?" asked Jack. "How closely did you monitor Xavier's online activity?"

"As closely as any parent."

"The police will be all over his search history. And so will I, if I take the case," said Jack. "It could be a key part of his defense."

"Part of his defense?" said Amir. "How?"

Jack paused, not sure how his answer might be received. "Let me take a step back and explain the process. A death penalty case has two phases. Guilt or innocence is decided at phase one. If the defendant is found guilty, the trial moves to phase two: sentencing. Both phases are decided by a jury of twelve. Sometimes the strategy in phase one is completely different from phase two. Here, not necessarily."

"What do you mean?" asked Amir.

"Our legal strategy may be to convince the jury in both phases of the trial that Xavier was radicalized. In phase one, proving that Xavier was radicalized by Islamic extremists—perhaps even by members of al-Qaeda itself—is the best shot at proving that he's not guilty by reason of temporary insanity, however slight the chance of success may be. More realistically, radicalization will be a persuasive mitigating circumstance at the sentencing phase of trial and could convince at least one juror that Xavier should not receive the death penalty. One vote is all he needs. The jury must be unanimous for the death penalty in Florida."

"So that's where the Internet comes in?" asked Molly. "Finding evidence to support a radicalization theory?"

"Yes. More to the point, that's where your help comes in. As Xavier's lawyer, I would need to know every possible source of radicalization that Xavier could have been exposed to. Internet. Friends. Relatives."

Amir's eyes were like black, smoldering embers. *"Family?"*

"Is there someone you have in mind?" asked Jack.

"Is there someone *you* have in mind, Mr. Swyteck?"

Molly squeezed his hand. "Honey, you're taking this too personally."

"How else am I supposed to take it? I've seen the posts on social media. They might not come right out and say it, but every parent at Riverside thinks the same thing."

"Thinks what?" asks Jack.

"That—"

"Amir, please," said Molly.

Amir took a breath. "Let me set something straight. Molly and I disagree completely about this being an act of international terrorism."

"You don't think it was?" asked Jack.

"I believe the claim of responsibility by al-Qaeda is a hoax. Al-Qaeda hasn't claimed credit for an attack in the US since 2001. As a terrorist organization, they are yesterday's news."

"Who do you think made the phony claim of responsibility?" asked Jack.

"Some ignoramus racist who hates Islam, that's who."

Jack collected his thoughts, trying not to push Amir into a corner. "First, let me say I disagree with you that al-Qaeda is yesterday's news. They're on a comeback."

"So you're not only a crackerjack criminal defense lawyer, but also an expert on international terrorism, is that it?"

Jack did know more than most people, but he didn't want to bring his wife into this discussion. "You and I just disagree on that point."

"Yes, and we also disagree on the best strategy for my son. I forbid you or whoever defends him to make the argument that Xavier was radicalized."

"I'm sorry, but—"

"No, *I'm* sorry, Mr. Swyteck. Molly and I did not raise a *terrorist.* We raised a *Muslim.* Your strategy plays right into the hands of racists who think every child who is raised in a Muslim household is a terrorist threat. If a white supremacist shoots up a synagogue, not all white people are white supremacists. But as soon as a Muslim opens fire, all Muslims are terrorists."

"That's not the argument."

"That *is* the argument. And it's the same argument the public defender wanted to make. Thankfully, that lawyer is off the case. I hope we don't have to fire *you*."

"You can't fire Xavier's lawyer."

"I can fire anybody I want."

"No. Your son is eighteen. Only he can hire me. And only he can fire me."

"Xavier will do as I say."

"No, he won't!" Molly shouted.

The room went silent. If Molly wasn't about to snap, she was darn close.

"Listen to me, Amir," she said, her voice tight but racing. "This family is never going to be the same. Our lives are never going to be what they used to be. But we have to do what we can do to make things a little better. Talitha is eight years old. I don't want her to be a senior in high school having to deal with the fact that her brother is front-page news again because after ten years of legal gymnastics he's finally being executed. If there is a lawyer on this planet who can convince the state attorney that the death penalty is the wrong decision and that this needs to end *now*, life without parole, you are looking at him. I will *not* let you interfere with that because you have a chip on your shoulder as big as the entire fucking Middle East!"

The f-bomb was lost on no one, but not a man in the room said a word.

"Do you understand me, Amir?"

Her husband didn't answer.

"Amir. Do you—"

"You sort it out," he said, getting up and storming out of the room. Jack and Theo sat in stunned silence, not sure what to say. Molly was about to cry.

"Are you okay?" asked Jack.

She dabbed away a tear from the corner of her eye. "No, I'm really not. I'm sorry. Amir has a bit of a temper. More than a bit, since this happened."

Jack heard little footsteps in a hallway. A young girl dressed in her nightgown took a timid step into the room and stopped. "Mommy?"

Molly smiled. "Come here, honey."

The girl hurried across the room, and Jack was struck by her beauty. She was blond, like her mother, with olive skin and a natural waviness to her hair that hinted at her father's Lebanese ancestry.

Molly wrapped her daughter in her arms. "Why are you awake?"

"Why were you and Daddy yelling?"

"Oh, don't worry about that, honey. We were just

talking loudly. Say hello to Mr. Swyteck and his friend Theo Knight."

Jack leaned forward, speaking eye to eye. "Hi, Talitha. I'm Righley's daddy. She's in kindergarten."

Talitha smiled. "I know Righley. I was her reading buddy in library studies last week. I like her. She's funny."

"Yeah, she is funny."

"Are you going to help my mommy?"

"Help her?" asked Jack.

"Uh-huh. I heard Mommy say things are never going to be like they used to. But you could help make it better."

Molly smiled awkwardly. "Kids are all ears, I guess."

"Are you going to help?" asked Talitha.

"Well, I have to think about it."

"Why?"

The question made Jack squirm. "Why do I have to think about it?"

"Yeah. When somebody needs help, why do you have to think about helping them?"

Why? Because I'm a big-shot lawyer, son of Florida's former governor, and I'm worried what people might think if I take this case. Because you're eight years old, toxic, and don't deserve a chance in life because of something your brother did. Because your mother didn't think twice when Theo needed help. Because I'm a piece of shit.

"You know what, Talitha? I've made up my mind. I am going to help you. And your mommy."

Chapter 9

At nine p.m. the criminal courthouse was dark, but the lights were burning across the street—Lucky Thirteenth Street, as it was known—at the pretrial detention center. The multistory facility housed roughly 170 inmates awaiting trial on charges that ran the legal gamut, from traffic offenses to capital murder. Among them, in Protective Custody Level One, was Xavier Khoury.

Jack parked in the jury lot, which was empty for the night. With him was Theo Knight.

"Ah, memories," said Theo. He may have been the only innocent man Jack had ever defended on death row, but Theo had grown up no choir boy. He wasn't kidding about his "memories" of the stockade.

"Seems like a lifetime ago," said Jack.

"Yeah, to *you*," said Theo.

They went in through the visitors' entrance on the ground floor. Normal visitation hours had ended, but visits by attorneys—who were apparently something other than "normal"—were allowed anytime. Jack gave his name and his Florida Bar card to the corrections officer seated behind the glass window at registration.

"I'm here to see Xavier Khoury," said Jack.

The corrections officer answered from inside the booth, speaking into a gooseneck microphone. "You his attorney?"

Technically, not yet. The Public Defender's Office had filed the motion to substitute counsel recommending Jack. But Jack had not accepted, and Xavier had yet to say anything to anyone since his arrest, let alone designate replacement counsel.

"Prospective counsel," said Jack.

"Who's he?" he asked, meaning Theo.

"My investigator," said Jack.

The officer shook his head. "I'll let you go, Mr. Swyteck. But until you're officially retained as counsel, no nonlawyers can go with you."

It was a rule that he seemed to be making up on the spot. Jack wanted Theo with him because, in Jack's experience with past clients facing the possibility of the death penalty, there was no better icebreaker than a former death row inmate who swore that he owed his life to Jack Swyteck. But this corrections officer from his throne inside the glass booth had the power to keep Jack waiting for hours, if he chose, so Jack didn't fight the no-Theo edict, however arbitrary. He and Theo took a seat in the waiting room. After about fifteen minutes, a guard escorted Jack to the attorney-client conference room, where Xavier was waiting for him. Jack entered. The guard closed the door and locked it from the outside, leaving Jack alone with someone who didn't look at all like a mass murderer.

Jack introduced himself and offered a handshake. Xavier didn't move or speak. They were surrounded by windowless walls of glossy white-painted cinder block, bathed in the bluish-white hue of LED bulbs that lent the room all the warmth of a workshop. Jack sat opposite him at the table.

Xavier looked nothing like his little sister. Never in her life would Talitha and her golden locks have a problem with airport security. Xavier was the guy who came to mind during media reports of dark-skinned young men who claimed they were being profiled by the TSA. As the father of an only child, Jack was forever amazed how children from the same womb could be so different.

"How are you holding up, Xavier?"

No reply. It was a fundamental problem—the client who would talk to no one, not even his lawyer—but Jack had encountered it before. The only way to handle it was to let the monologue begin.

"You're in deep shit," said Jack. "You need a lawyer. The public defender is withdrawing. I may be willing to step in. But that's hard for me to do if you won't talk to me."

Xavier remained mute.

"The first thing I'd like to do, if I were your attorney, is to have a criminal psychiatrist evaluate you for a possible plea of not guilty by reason of insanity."

No answer.

"It's nothing to get your hopes up about. It's a very low-percentage strategy. Nationwide, about one out of every one-point-two million felony cases that go to trial end with the defendant not guilty by reason of insanity. Florida's legal test for insanity is stricter than most states, so the odds are even worse here. Last time I even attempted an insanity defense was for a client whom the cops dubbed the Fiddler on the Roof. You ever heard of that case, Xavier?"

No answer.

"Maybe you're too young. It got a lot of press. My client was arrested at the murder scene. Above it, actually. He was found sitting on the roof of the house. Masturbating."

Xavier still refused to speak, but Jack had actually drawn a reaction from him. The Fiddler on the Roof was eighteen-year-old boy humor, an icebreaker.

"I'm not going to lie to you, Xavier. Evidence of guilt is strong here. Maybe overwhelming. Other than a long-shot insanity defense, my brain isn't bursting with ideas of how to convince a jury that you're not guilty. But if I become your lawyer, it's also my job to keep you alive. Now, you might be sitting there thinking 'Screw you, Jack, I don't want to live.' I've had clients like that before. But guess what?"

Jack leaned closer, trying to get Xavier to look at him more directly. "When they finally get shipped up to Florida State Prison, and they get assigned to a solitary cell on death row, and they start moving down the line one cell at a time, until there's no more cells between them and the gurney and a needle in their arm . . . that's when a lot of them change their mind."

Jack poured himself a glass of water from the pitcher. He poured one for Xavier, too. Jack drank. Xavier didn't.

"I'm going to ask you a few questions, Xavier. If the answer is yes, just sit there and say nothing. If the answer is no, speak up and tell me no. Got it?"

Silence.

"Good. Here we go," said Jack. "Do you understand that the state attorney is seeking the death penalty in this case?"

More silence.

"Are the Marlins going to win the World Series this year?"

Even *de minimis* baseball knowledge was enough to recognize that as a joke. It drew a hint of a smile from Xavier, like Fiddler on the Roof. Jack seized on it.

"Your mother doesn't want you to die. Does that matter to you?"

All traces of a smile faded.

Jack pushed a little harder. "Xavier, I'm asking: Does that matter to you?"

Xavier sat quietly for almost a full minute. Jack waited. Finally, his client shrugged. Jack smiled on the inside.

It was a start.

Chapter 10

J ust south of the day school campus, two blocks from the river, was a public playground. Andie had stopped there many times with Righley to push her on the swing. "Higher, higher, Mommy!" she'd shout, hair flying in the wind, toes pointing to the sky. Just when Andie was ready to put her foot down and tell her "That's high enough," Righley would shriek in delight and say, "I see it, I see it, Mommy!" At the high point of her path, at the tip of the invisible arc that stretched like a giant smile from one side of the swing set to the other, Righley could peer over the treetops all the way to her classroom windows. The classroom she loved. A place where, Andie had told her, she would always be safe.

That evening, fifty-some hours after the shooting,

Andie went to the park without her daughter. But she was not alone. More than a thousand people had gathered for a candlelight vigil.

"Where's Jack?"

It was Rolanda Suarez, one of the mothers from Righley's class. Dozens of high school students had turned out for the vigil, but for the lower grades it was just parents. Andie, Rolanda, and several others were standing near a chain-link fence that had been transformed into a makeshift memorial laden with so many flowers, crosses, and teddy bears that it might have collapsed of its own weight if not for the support of countless helium balloons of orange and white, the school colors. A sea of glowing candles flickered in the warm night air between Andie and the amphitheater. On stage at the podium was a grief-stricken father with a microphone. His son, Scott, was in the ninth grade, the shooter's first victim. The man said he wasn't sure if he'd told Scotty he loved him that morning. "My job is to protect my children," he said, his voice quaking. "I screwed up. I sent my kid to school."

His words hit Andie hard. It could have been any father up there. It could have been Jack.

"Jack couldn't come," Andie whispered.

"I heard a rumor," said Rolanda.

School gossip was the extracurricular activity of

choice for certain mothers at Riverside. Andie had no use for it, and it bugged her that Rolanda seemed to think it was okay even at a vigil.

"I heard he might be the lawyer for the shooter," said Rolanda.

"He's—" Andie stopped herself. It didn't seem like the right time to tell Rolanda or anyone else that Jack was at the shooter's house. But she wasn't going to lie. "He's thinking about it."

Scotty's father put down the microphone, walked slowly off the stage, and nearly fell into the arms of his grieving wife. Silence came over the crowd, except for the sobbing.

Rolanda looked at Andie in disbelief, but it was the mother right behind them who verbalized it.

"Why on earth would you let Jack do something like that?"

Eavesdropping was second only to gossip in the school-mommy skill set. The chain of whispers hopped from one mother's ear to the next, as Andie's confirmation of Jack's new client spread out of control. Andie felt the urgent need to get away. She excused herself and walked toward the baseball diamond on the other side of the amphitheater, weaving through a mostly silent crowd of parents and teenagers, past a church group embracing in quiet prayer, stopping as she came upon a group of teenage girls dressed in softball uniforms. Riverside had been regional champions two years running. They'd lost their star pitcher in the shooting. The only way her teammates could turn tears to smiles was to tell people about her, tell anyone who would listen.

"She was our MVP," said one.

"She had a ponytail all the way to her butt," laughed another.

"She's not a bragger," added another girl, clinging to the present tense. "She makes us all better players."

Andie moved along, then stopped as a woman stepped in front of her and said, "Agent Henning, I'd like to ask you a question."

Andie didn't recognize her.

"We were in the recreation center with you," the woman explained, and only then in the glow of burning candles did Andie understand the "we" reference. It was a group of women from the rec center, and Andie's read of the body language was that this was not a friendly visit.

"What's on your mind?" asked Andie.

The woman folded her arms, making the body language even clearer. "We've been talking among ourselves a lot since that morning. All of us wondering if there's something we could have done."

"That's a natural reaction to any tragedy," said

Andie. "But trust me, there's nothing anyone could have done."

"Well, that's mostly true. But what about you?"

"Me?"

"We all heard the shots right outside the door. You're right. There's nothing *we* could have done. We're not FBI agents. You are. No offense, but why didn't you act like one?"

The *No offense but* qualifier, three words that somehow made it okay to say the most offensive things imaginable. "What is that supposed to mean?" asked Andie.

"I'm just saying. If I'd had a gun and was trained to use it—"

"I was unarmed," said Andie. "I was off duty."

"You were *off duty*?" said another woman, offended. "That's why you did nothing? Because you were *off duty*?"

"Oh, my God," groaned another mother.

"You're not listening to me," said Andie. "I said *I didn't have a gun* because I was off duty."

It was too late. The gossip chain was growing link by link.

Did you hear what she just said?

I can't believe it.

No wonder she's best friends with Molly Khoury.

Did you hear about her husband?

Others quickly piled on, and although Andie couldn't overhear all of it, she somehow knew that she was being compared to that notorious armed security guard at the Parkland shooting in 2018, who'd cowered outside Building 12 and done nothing to protect the children being massacred inside. The distinction Andie was trying to draw—that she was prohibited by law from carrying her weapon onto school grounds—was valid. But no one seemed the least bit interested in hearing it.

Andie hurried to the parking lot, found her car, and headed home, her tires squealing and the glow of burning candles fading in the rearview mirror as she exited the park. She was speeding down the expressway toward Key Biscayne but didn't care. She couldn't get away from that place fast enough. Andie told herself that those women weren't being malicious—that people were so broken and devastated that they just needed to direct their anger at someone. But it still hurt.

Andie was almost home, and Key Biscayne stretched out before her as she reached the very apex of the bridge that arched across the bay from the mainland. She rolled down the window, welcoming the fresh sea air. Questions clouded her mind, and not just the question that had chased her from the vigil. She, too, had been second-guessing her actions that morning. Instinct and adrenaline had propelled her down the hallway to Righley's classroom. But why didn't she rush the attacker? She had a pretty clear memory of at least one momentary pause in the semiautomatic gunfire that must have been a magazine change. In hindsight, that would have been the time to rush him. Maybe she could have saved someone else's child.

Andie parked in the driveway and walked quickly into the house. She dropped her purse on the couch, went straight to Righley's room, and sat on the edge of the bed. It wasn't her intention to wake her, but Righley's eyes blinked open. Andie had been completely unaware of how distraught she must have looked until Righley asked the question.

"What's wrong, Mommy?"

"Oh, it's just been one of those days, honey."

"Do you want a do-over? You can have one. I won't tell Daddy."

Andie smiled sadly. "It's not up to Daddy."

"You can ask God. Maybe if you ask, He'll say I can have one, too."

Andie recalled the conversation Jack and Righley were having on the way to school, and it broke it her heart. "Honey, it's good to pray. But we don't pray for do-overs. Daddy's right. There are none."

"Why?"

Tough question. "Why? Well, I think the reason there are no do-overs, is because . . ."

"Because why?"

"Because we have each other," said Andie. "As long as we have each other we don't need any do-overs."

"Promise?"

Andie brought her closer and held on tightly. "Yeah. I promise."

On Saturday morning Jack took a long bike ride, up and over the Key Biscayne bridge—the only real "hill" in Miami—and onto the mainland. He rode right past Cy's Place in the Coconut Grove business district and didn't stop pedaling until he was in South Grove.

George Washington Carver Middle School is a top-ranked magnet school in an area that was once known as the Grove Ghetto. The Grand Avenue neighborhood isn't the war zone it had been when Janet Reno was state attorney in the 1980s. Back then, butting right up against Miami's most expensive real estate was a ghetto that could service just about anyone's bad habit, from gangs with their random hits, to doctors and lawyers who ventured out into the night to service their addictions. That had been Theo's neighborhood. For some of his friends, Carver Middle had been the first punch in their ticket out. Theo and his brother weren't as lucky, having wandered the streets too late at night for too many years. At least Theo had made it out alive.

The neighborhood wasn't quite so bad anymore, but it was fair enough to call it hardscrabble, especially after dark. One thing surely had not changed: basketball ruled. Jack found "Coach Theo" with his eighth-grade-boys team in the Carver gym.

"Be with you in a minute, Jack," Theo shouted from across the court.

His players were running "suicides" up and down the court, the sprint-until-you-puke ritual that the toughest coaches imposed on the best teams. Jack took a seat in the bleachers, ready to dial 911 or administer artificial resuscitation, as necessary.

"This ain't a walk!" he shouted to his team. "Everyone under thirty seconds!"

Jack's first meeting with the prosecution had not gone well. Abe Beckham was senior trial counsel at the Office of the State Attorney for Miami-Dade County, the go-to prosecutor in capital cases. He'd recently earned the moniker Honest Abe, a courthouse joke that marked an impressive milestone of four-score-and-seven murder convictions without a loss. Two of those victories had been against Jack, and if their first

conversation about Xavier Khoury had been any indi-
cation, Beckham was highly confident of a third. Jack
had paid the prosecutor a visit on Friday, seeking only
to break the ice and suggest that, perhaps, Beckham
should at least consider backing away from the death
penalty. It had been a short conversation.

"Sorry, Jack. This is a capital case if ever there was
one."

"You have to get a conviction before you can get the
death penalty."

"Right. See that barrel of fish over there? Shoot one
on your way out, would you, please?"

Getting Beckham to budge was going to be even
harder than Jack had thought.

"Family on three!" Theo shouted, and his players
did their practice-ending ritual, gathering in a tight
circle, a mix of black, brown, and white hands at the
center.

"Family!" they shouted in unison, and then it was a
mad dash to the drinking fountains. Theo walked over
to Jack.

"Coming back to be my assistant?"

Jack stepped down from the bleachers and smiled.
"I wish."

Theo's team was in the locker room, and it was just
the two of them courtside.

"Give me a hand with the equipment?" he asked.

"You got it." Jack draped a dozen jump ropes around his neck, gathered up as many basketballs as he could carry, and followed Theo into the storage room.

"I met with the prosecutor yesterday," said Jack.

"How'd that go?"

Jack summed it up in two words. "Not well."

"You come here to tap my brilliant legal mind?"

"Sort of."

Theo shoved a stack of orange training cones onto the top shelf. "Talk to me."

"The prosecution is way too confident. Legally, guilt or innocence is supposed be a separate question from life or death. But sometimes strong evidence of guilt bleeds over in the prosecutor's mind. The death penalty becomes a foregone conclusion. End of story."

"Why is he so confident?"

"Why?" Jack asked, scoffing. "Well, for one thing, Xavier said 'I did it' in front of three police officers."

"That's bullshit."

"Maybe it is to you. To Abe Beckham, it's a confession."

"Confession, my ass, Jack."

"How do you see it?"

"I see a brown kid looking at three white cops pointing their guns at him. You, his mom, and every other white person in America hears him say, 'I did it, I'm the shooter, I'm a mass murderer.' I hear, 'Don't shoot me, I did whatever you say I did, just please don't shoot me.'"

"I don't know, Theo. You really think I should turn this into Black Lives Matter?"

Theo locked the storage door—three megalocks, Jack noted, a reminder that crime in the Grove Ghetto was not just a distant memory from Theo's youth.

"I'm not telling you to turn it into anything, Jack. Just tell it like it is."

Chapter 11

On Monday morning Jack was inside the criminal courtroom of Circuit Court Judge Humberto Martinez, seated at the table for the defense, alone only in the sense that his client was not with him. Xavier had refused to attend, which was his choice, but the gallery was packed with parents, teachers, members of the media, and dozens more. Riverside would not reopen for at least another week, and Jack noticed a few high school students in the crowd.

At 8:59 a.m., precisely one minute before the scheduled hearing, the prosecutor entered through the swinging gate at the rail behind Jack and started toward the other table.

"Good morning, Abe," said Jack.

"Jack," he said, opting for a one-word response that barely passed as a greeting.

"All rise!"

The call to order brought the crowd to its feet, and the packed courtroom fell silent as Judge Martinez ascended to the bench.

With experience as both a prosecutor and defense lawyer, Martinez was a good fit for a high-profile case that demanded an evenhanded jurist. His reputation wasn't one of pandering to the media, but he definitely wasn't camera shy. As a younger man, his good looks and decisiveness had put him on the short list to star in the Latin version of *The People's Court* on Spanish-language TV. It hadn't worked out. "Too polite," the producers had told him.

"Take your seats," he said, and when everyone was settled, he looked straight at the prosecutor.

"Mr. Beckham, I've read your motion. As I understand it, the state of Florida seeks a court order directing Mr. Swyteck to file a formal notice of appearance in this case as counsel for the defendant, Xavier Khoury."

"That's correct, Your Honor. This is a capital case. The public defender has withdrawn as counsel. We are at a critical stage where important decisions are being made. If Mr. Khoury has no lawyer of record, all the work we do to secure his conviction over the coming months will be for naught. His appellate lawyer will argue that the conviction is invalid because he was deprived of his constitutional right to counsel."

"I understand your concern," the judge said. "But what is the basis for ordering Mr. Swyteck, specifically, to be his counsel?"

"On Friday, Mr. Swyteck visited my office and said he's representing Mr. Khoury for purposes of negotiating a plea, but he has not agreed to be trial counsel."

The judge looked at Jack. "Is that true, Mr. Swyteck? Has Mr. Khoury engaged you as his attorney?"

Jack rose. "Judge, I met once with Mr. Khoury. He has yet to say a word to me. I explained that I would be willing to meet with the prosecution on his behalf to try to negotiate a plea. I'm not comfortable saying anything more than that in open court, as what I said is protected by the attorney-client privilege. But I asked Mr. Khoury to nod his head if he would like me to do that for him. He nodded."

The judge leaned back in his oversized chair, looking up at the ceiling, thinking. "So it's your position that you're his lawyer for the limited purpose of negotiating a plea."

"Correct," said Jack. "I have not made an appearance in this case."

"Which is the point of my motion," said Beckham. "He needs to get off the fence."

The judge shifted his attention from the ceiling to Jack. "Seems to me you're splitting hairs, Mr. Swyteck."

"Judge, I have not agreed to defend Mr. Khoury at trial."

"Well, you're here now, and as an officer of the court, you'd be doing this community and the justice system as a whole a great public service by acting as Mr. Khoury's counsel."

"Judge, I—"

"As far as I'm concerned, you're in," said the judge. "File your notice of appearance in the record at the conclusion of this hearing. You are counsel of record for Mr. Khoury until you can demonstrate good cause why I should relieve you of that obligation. Anything further?"

"No, Your Honor," said Beckham.

Jack felt as though he'd been run over by a bus, but he knew the rules. Once a lawyer was counsel of record in a criminal case, it was virtually impossible to get out, even if the client stopped paying. It was the reason defense lawyers asked for the entire fee up front.

All Jack could do was take solace in the fact that this would come as good news to his friend Nate Abrams.

"Judge, there actually is one thing more," he said, casting his gaze toward the prosecutor. "If I'm in, I'm all in. I have a motion for the court's consideration."

"Judge, I object," said Beckham.

"Overruled. As they say, Mr. Beckham, be careful what you wish for. What's your motion, Mr. Swyteck?"

The only way to make death by lethal injection a negotiable item was to take Beckham's confidence down a peg. And that was the point of Jack's first motion before the court—with a little help from Theo Knight.

"Your Honor, both the Miami-Dade Police and the state attorney have stated publicly that Mr. Khoury confessed to the shooting at Riverside. It's our position that this statement is not a confession. Alternatively, if it was a confession, it was obtained in violation of Mr. Khoury's constitutional rights and should be suppressed."

Beckham groaned. "Judge, this is a completely frivolous motion."

"Mr. Beckham, someone who has been in my courtroom as many times as you should know by now that I generally make my decisions *after* I've heard the evidence. Mr. Swyteck, have you any evidence to support your motion?"

Jack's gaze landed on the police officer standing by the door in the back of the courtroom, whom Jack had noticed on the way in. "The defense calls Miami-Dade police officer Glenn Donner."

Beckham rose. "Judge, this is highly irregular."

"Officer Donner was one of the MDPD officers on the scene when my client was arrested," said Jack. "His testimony goes to the heart of the defense's motion."

"Officer Donner, come forward and be sworn," the judge said.

All heads turned as a middle-aged man dressed in the distinctive taupe MDPD uniform walked down the center aisle, his steady footfalls on the tile floor the only sound in the room. He stopped, raised his right hand, and swore to tell the truth.

"I most certainly do," he said.

His embellishment on a simple "I do" was a little thing, but like any good trial lawyer, Jack picked up on the little things. Right out of the gate, this witness had violated rule number one of "Courtroom Testimony for Dummies": never say more than you have to, not a single word more.

"Good morning, Officer," Jack said as he approached.

"Good morning."

The witness was wringing his hands, even before the first question. His anxiety was understandable. It was easy for the prosecutor to dismiss Jack's motion as frivolous, but Donner was the man in the hot seat, and no one wanted to be known as the MDPD officer whose testimony got a confession to a school shooting kicked from the case.

Jack went straight to work.

"Officer Donner, you were one of the MDPD officers on the scene at the Khoury residence on the morning Xavier Khoury was arrested, correct?"

"I was one of four. It was our job to secure the perimeter while the search team entered the residence to execute the warrant."

"You were not part of the search team?"

"No."

"But you and the other officers on perimeter security went there knowing that a handgun had been found on school grounds, and that this handgun was registered in the name of Amir Khoury. Right?"

"We knew the basis for the issuance of the warrant, yes."

"The search team was inside the house when Mrs. Khoury drove up in her sedan?"

"Yes. Her *Mercedes*," Officer Donner added, as if it were a crime to be rich.

"Molly Khoury was driving. Was she armed?"

"We didn't know."

"Her two younger children were in the back seat.

Talitha, age eight, and Jamal, age fifteen," said Jack. "Were they armed?"

"There was no way to know."

"Her son Xavier was in the passenger seat. Was he armed?"

"We thought he might be."

"Did he make a sudden move when he exited the vehicle?"

"No."

"Did he have something in his hand that looked like a gun?"

"Not that I saw."

"Did you see anything inside the car that looked like a gun?"

"I don't believe so."

"Did he say he had a gun?"

"No."

"Did he threaten you in any way?"

"Not really."

"But as soon as Xavier and his mother stepped out of the car, you drew your weapon, correct?"

"Yes, of course. There had just been a school shooting."

"You weren't there to arrest Xavier, were you?"

"No."

"No arrest warrant had been issued, correct?"

"That's correct."

"No one had accused Xavier of being the school shooter, right?"

"Not to my knowledge."

"You didn't ask him if he was the shooter, did you?"

"No."

"None of the other officers asked him. Right?"

"They did not."

Jack checked his notes, though they were mostly chicken scratch, since this was a motion on the fly. "So let me see if I have this straight. An eighteen-year-old boy rides up in the family car with his mother."

"Objection," said Beckham, rising. "According to *Roper v. Simmons*, the defendant is an eighteen-year-old *man*."

He was referring to the US Supreme Court decision that prohibited the execution of juveniles as cruel and unusual punishment.

"Let me rephrase," said Jack. "An eighteen-year-old high school student rides up in the family car with his mother. The instant they step out and set foot on the ground, four armed police officers surround the vehicle and draw their weapons."

"As I said, there had just been a deadly school shooting."

For effect, Jack assumed the stance, arms extended, as if he had a gun. "You yelled 'Freeze!'"

"Yes."

"Mrs. Khoury shouted back, 'Don't shoot!'"

"Yes."

"Her two younger children were crying in the back seat, terrified."

"I don't know if—"

"Really, Officer Donner?" said Jack, dropping the marksman's stance and resuming his posture as lawyer. "You don't know?"

"I suppose they were frightened."

"And it was at that moment—with four police officers aiming their loaded weapons at his mother, his sister, his brother, and him—that Xavier Khoury said, 'Mom, it's okay. I did it.'"

"That is what he said."

"And you took that to mean he did *what*?"

The witness hesitated, as if sensing that the lawyer was setting a trap. "I have no idea what he meant."

"Precisely," said Jack, pouncing on the answer he wanted. "You never asked him if he was the school shooter, did you?"

"No."

"You didn't tell him that his father's gun was found at the scene, did you?"

"No."

"So when he said 'I did it,' you had no way of knowing if he meant the shooting at Riverside."

"I—" Officer Donner started to say, then stopped, seeming to sense that Jack liked the way this was going. He was suddenly backpedaling. "I can't read his mind, if that's what you're asking."

"When Xavier saw the police and said 'I did it,' he could have meant that he was guilty of downloading music illegally from the Internet, like millions of other high school kids. Right?"

"I don't think that's what he meant."

"He could have meant he was watching porn the night before, right?"

"Or he could also have meant he did the school shooting."

"Yes, he could have," said Jack. "And he could have thought that a confession was the only way to stop you and three other officers from shooting him and his mother."

"Objection!" shouted Beckham.

"Sustained," said the judge.

Beckham stepped forward. "Your Honor, this charade has gone far enough. Mr. Swyteck knows the law as well as I do. To suppress Mr. Khoury's statement, this court is required to find that the police said something that was likely to elicit an incriminating response before advising him of his Miranda rights. Here, all they said was 'Freeze!'"

Jack had to concede the point—but only half of it. "Judge, I'm not accusing the police of having done anything wrong. This is not a situation where the police said something they shouldn't have said, or did something they shouldn't have done. It's simply a statement that has zero probative value of anything. Xavier said 'I did it,' having no idea what crime he was confessing to."

"I agree with Mr. Beckham," the judge said. "This does not meet the legal standard for suppression."

"Thank you, Your Honor," said the prosecutor.

"Not so fast," said the judge. "I also take Mr. Swyteck's point. This is a high-profile case, and I intend to give this defendant, like every defendant in my courtroom, a fair trial. From day one, we've been hearing from the state attorney and from other sources in law enforcement about a so-called confession. If this is the 'confession' you're talking about . . ." The judge shook his head, measuring his words. "Well, I'm not making an evidentiary ruling today, but let me say this. You need to tone down the rhetoric, Mr. Beckham."

"Understood," said the prosecutor.

"Anything else, Counsel?"

A public admonition from the court was more than Jack could have hoped for. "Nothing from the defense, Your Honor."

"Then we're adjourned," the judge said, with the crack of his gavel.

"All rise!"

Behind Jack, in the packed galley, the bumps and thuds of a rising crowd thumped like a ragtag army on the march. The judge disappeared behind the paneled door to his chambers, and members of the media rushed to the rail, peppering the lawyers with questions.

"Are you saying he didn't do it, Swyteck?"

"Mr. Beckham, is there another confession?"

Jack didn't answer. It was his job to argue his client's position before the judge. It was not his job to vouch for his client's innocence before the media.

"Swyteck, you got a minute?" asked Beckham.

Jack followed him to the far end of the jury box, where they were out of earshot from the media.

"I don't care how many holes you try to poke in my case. I'm not going to lose, and I'll never back away from the death penalty."

"Killing Xavier won't deter other eighteen-year-old boys," said Jack.

"I'm a big believer in specific deterrence. Your client will never shoot up a school again."

"He won't do it again if he's in jail the rest of his life. This is a case in which life means life."

Beckham glanced toward the gallery, toward the sullen expressions of parents and teachers still in shock from the shooting. "When I hear you defense lawyers say that—life means life—it really bugs me."

"Bugs you? Why?"

"You ever read Vladimir Nabokov?"

Jack had read *Lolita* in high school. The story of pedophilia and serial rape was not his cup of tea. "Not a fan."

"Neither am I," said Beckham. "But there's one thing he may have gotten right. Nabokov said, 'Life is the brief crack of light between two eternities of darkness.'"

"That's pretty grim, Abe. I'm not following your point."

"What your client took away from those thirteen children is unforgivable. Why should his brief crack of light be any longer than theirs?"

"I don't have an answer to that."

"I think you know the answer," said Beckham. "And I'm absolutely certain you know how this is going to end. With or without a confession."

Beckham slung his computer bag over his shoulder and walked away. All Jack could do was watch as the prosecutor stood at the rail, confidence unshaken, and reassured some very concerned parents about the strength of his case.

Chapter 12

It was a short walk from the justice center to his office, and Abe Beckham made it in record time. Anger propelled him.

The official name for the main facility of the Office of the State Attorney for Miami-Dade County was the Graham Building, but Abe called it the Boomerang. The building had two wings, and the footprint was angled like a boomerang, but the appellation had more to do with the fact that it seemed he could never leave without coming right back. Ten-to-twelve-hour days were normal. Longer when the lawyer on the other side was as good as Jack Swyteck.

"Mary, I want the whole team in the twelfth-floor conference room," he told his assistant as he hurried by her in the hallway.

"When, Mr. Beckham?"

"Now."

Abe went back to his office to make a phone call. The State Attorney's Office had a victims' relations unit, but Abe had always considered it part of his job to keep families informed. That was especially true in the case of Elena Hernandez, a woman he'd met minutes after rushing over to Riverside on the morning of the shooting. The victims had yet to be identified, but Elena couldn't find her son, and she was convinced that she'd lost him. He was a senior, brave, strong, and with dreams of joining the US Marine Corps, the type of young man who would do everything in his power to save his friends before himself. Sadly, her instincts had been spot-on. The tributes posted on the fence outside the school included dozens of thank-you notes from students who'd survived only because her son, Carlos, had held the classroom door shut.

"Call me anytime," Abe said into the phone. "Be well."

He hung up, took a breath, and walked down the hall to the conference room. The team was waiting for him: Liz Kaplan, who would sit beside him at trial, and two junior prosecutors who were relatively new to the adult felony division. Abe grabbed an erasable marker from the table and wrote on the whiteboard in big red letters: NO CONFESSION.

"That's how we have to try this case," said Abe.

One of the junior lawyers spoke up. "Didn't Judge Martinez reserve ruling?"

Abe underlined the word *No* on the whiteboard. "I'm not talking about the rules of evidence. And your instincts are right. The judge won't exclude this statement. But we have to be prepared to deal with Swyteck's spin to the jury. Our best strategy is to move forward as if there's no confession. There's a hole in our case. How do we fill it?"

Silence.

"Jessica, let's start with the search of the Khoury residence. What can we pull from that?"

The junior prosecutor checked her notes. "Well . . ."

"Go item by item," said Abe, as he wrote the word *Evidence* on the whiteboard. "Start with the digital evidence."

Jessica flipped the pages ahead to the forensic report. "The parental control filters on the family computer were set very high—keep in mind their youngest daughter is in elementary school—so that hard drive was squeaky clean, PG-13 at worst."

"How about Xavier's cell phone?"

"Just as clean. No texts or emails of concern. No suspicious content in any of the files he created."

"No manifesto? No diary?"

"Nope. And his Internet search history shows no visits to the dark web, terrorist websites, or so-called radicalizing elements."

"What kind of music did he listen to?"

"Apparently he was a big fan of Bangtan Sonyeondan."

"Sounds promising. Is that connected to al-Qaeda?"

"No, it's a South Korean boy band. Very popular in the United States. Totally mainstream."

Abe would have laughed if the situation weren't so serious. "What about social media?"

"As best we can tell, he wasn't on social media."

"Huh. So Swyteck wasn't blowing smoke about that, after all. Fine. Let's talk physical evidence."

Jessica flipped to the next page of her notes. "Nothing in the way of weapons. No handguns. No rifles. No ammunition. No magazines. No knives."

"No cache," he said, writing it on the whiteboard. "What about clothing or accessories? Any Kevlar vests?"

"No."

"Anything like the shooter was wearing in the video? Camouflage jacket? Shoe covers? Balaclava? Tactical gloves?"

"Nothing. Well, there was an Elsa ski mask."

"Elsa?"

"The princess from *Frozen*. You know: 'Let it go.' They found it in his sister's bedroom."

"Not helpful," said Abe, popping the cap back onto the marker for emphasis. "I presume the search warrant you drafted specifically asked for each of these items."

"Yes."

"Teaching moment," said Abe, trying not to come down too hard on a newbie. "Never ask for something in a search warrant unless you know it's there. This search warrant is an outline for Swyteck's cross-examination of our lead detective. He'll go point by point: no handgun, no rifle, no ammunition, and on and on. The only answer we have for the jury is that we tore the house apart looking for each and every one of these things and found nothing."

"I'm sorry," said Jessica. "But if you look at the history of mass shootings, the items I listed in the warrant always turn up."

"I understand," said Abe. "It's puzzling. And one more reason this case is not the cakewalk that everyone seems to think it is. Nothing in the hands of a jury is easy."

There was a polite knock at the door. It opened,

and Abe's assistant stuck her head into the conference room. "Lieutenant Vega is on the line. It's important. Good news, she says."

Vega was the lead homicide detective on the case. "Patch her through on the speaker," said Abe, which sent his assistant racing back to her desk.

Abe had been just a "pit assistant," a C-level prosecutor in his first year of adult felonies, when he'd met Claudia Vega—"Cloud," as he called her, since she was always correcting gringos on the Hispanic pronunciation of her name: "*Clow*-dia," not "*Claw*-dia." They'd worked at least a dozen homicide cases together. Abe still considered her a friend, though much had changed since the days of double dates to the movies or the Miami City Ballet, the cop, the prosecutor, and their spouses. Samantha loved the ballet almost as much as Claudia's husband did. Abe could take it or leave it. But he would have feather-stepped across hot coals for the chance to sit through another one, holding hands with the love of his life. Abe had always worked long hours, but only after Samantha's death did he come up with the name Boomerang for the building he never left, except to go home and sleep. Alone.

The phone beeped to announce the transferred call. Abe hit the SPEAKER button. "What you got, Cloud?"

The detective's voice filled the room. "The lab finally lifted a print from the murder weapon that doesn't belong to Xavier's father. It wasn't easy. That gun is more than twenty years old, and I don't think Amir ever wiped it clean. Forensics had to deal with fingerprints on top of smeared fingerprints. But finally we got a clean one."

"And?"

"A match," she said. "Right index. One hundred percent certain it belongs to Xavier Khoury."

"Good work," he said with a little smile. "I can't wait to tell Swyteck."

"Wish I could be there," said Claudia.

"Here's what I wish," said Abe. "I wish someone would find the clothes Xavier was wearing when he shot up his school."

"It's not for lack of trying."

"We know exactly what he had on. It's right there on the school security video. Somehow he got rid of everything between the time he left the school grounds and the time he showed up at his house in his mother's Mercedes."

"I printed hundreds of pictures from that video. Teams of officers have checked every culvert, every Dumpster, every alley, every place you could imagine within a mile of the school. Nothing turned up."

"Listen to me more carefully, Cloud. I said somehow all of it disappeared by the time he pulled up at his house *in his mother's Mercedes.*"

There was a pause on the line, and Abe could almost hear the wheels turning in the detective's head.

"You think the mother dumped all the gear?" she asked.

"I don't think a Kevlar vest, camouflage, and all that other shit that makes a punk feel powerful vanished into thin air. But I need evidence."

"I'm on it."

"I'm waiting," said Abe, and with the push of the orange button he ended the call.

Chapter 13

Icy glares followed Jack down the granite steps as he left the justice center. The pursuit of justice, whatever that meant, sometimes required a quick exit from the courthouse. Jack needed to clear his head. And fill his stomach. He drove to Coconut Grove for lunch at Cy's Place, pulled up a barstool, and glanced over the menu.

"Try the conch chowder," said Theo. "It's Uncle Cy's recipe. Extra sherry."

"Sounds good," said Jack, laying the menu aside.

Theo put the order in to the kitchen and set up Jack with a cold draft.

"I didn't order a beer," said Jack.

"You look like you could use one," Theo said, in the

knowing voice of a bartender. "How did your hearing go this morning?"

"Better than expected," he said without heart. "And worse than expected."

Jack's gaze drifted toward the café tables that fronted the stage, where musicians played till two a.m. on weekends. It was at one of those tiny tables, barely room enough for two pairs of elbows, that Jack had put a ring on Andie's finger, surprising her on what she'd dubbed "the second anniversary of Jack's thirty-ninth birthday." Seemed so long ago. It was sometimes hard to remember life BC, before child. Harder still to imagine life after losing a child, the way thirteen families from Righley's school would live the rest of their lives.

"It's so crazy," said Jack.

"What?"

"If Xavier Khoury had done this one day earlier, I wouldn't be his lawyer. On Tuesday, death by lethal injection was cruel and unusual punishment. On Wednesday, no punishment but death fit the crime. Thirteen life sentences with no chance of parole isn't enough."

"I was sixteen when I was on death row. What do you think the Department of Corrections would have said after I was dead and gone, and the Supreme Court said no executing kids convicted of murder."

"Probably the same thing they said in their press

release after trying to execute you three times before DNA proved you innocent."

"Yeah," said Theo, summarizing: "'Oops.'"

Jack turned serious. "To be honest, I do see why a parent would want the shooter dead. My wife and daughter were at the school. How would I feel if Andie and Righley were on the list of victims?"

"You'd want the death penalty?"

"I'm saying that I can understand why someone would."

"Well, excuse me for having strong views on the subject, but I got a problem with it."

"Everybody has a problem with executing innocent people. I'm not telling you my client is guilty, but—well, you get my point." The server brought Jack's chowder. Jack tasted it. "Wow, that *is* good."

Theo didn't want to talk food. "Are you getting out of the case?"

"It's almost impossible to withdraw in a death case. Once you're in, you're in. Unless the client fires you."

"*Would* you get out? If you could?"

Jack put down his spoon. "I'll say this much. Right out of law school, when I went to work at the Freedom Institute, all fired up to seek truth and justice in the world, there was no doubt in my mind that the death penalty was cruel and unusual punishment. I don't know if I'm getting old, or if the world is just becoming a darker place. Maybe the way Andie thinks is rubbing off on me. Part of me almost wants to say that, for certain crimes and certain people, maybe there's room for capital punishment."

"Seriously?"

"Yes," said Jack. "Seriously."

"To me, it's a simple equation. We're human. Anytime you put humans in charge, there will be mistakes."

"I get that argument."

"Maybe you need a little refresher. How many innocent people are on death row?"

"Depends on whom you ask. According to the inmates, probably in the neighborhood of ninety-nine-point-nine percent."

"Let's stick to reliable sources."

"National Academy of Science says four percent."

"There you go," said Theo, doing the math in his head. "Are you okay strapping one innocent man onto the gurney so that you can execute twenty-five guilty ones? Or, to put a more personal spin on it: Is it okay to execute one Theo Knight so you can execute twenty-five Xavier Khourys? If your answer is yes, then get the hell out of the case, Jack. If the answer is no . . . then you're doing the right thing."

Jack actually felt a little better. A little. "You're a pretty smart guy, Theo Knight."

"Hanging around dumb fucks makes anyone look smart."

"Thanks, man. Really appreciate it."

Abe ate lunch in his office. Detective Vega joined him.

"Really, Abe?" she said, watching him unload his paper sack. "Cheesesteak sub, barbecue potato chips, two chocolate chip cookies, and a can of *diet* soda?"

"Gotta cut back somewhere."

It was a working lunch. Abe had watched the video from the security cameras at Riverside at least a dozen times, but he needed to sit down and go through it with someone who could tell him what he was missing. That was Detective Vega.

"What a monster," she said, her gaze locked onto the flat screen on the wall. They were watching the first images picked up on school surveillance cameras, seconds before the shooting started. He did look like a monster, dressed in a camouflage flak jacket and black pants, his face hidden behind a black ski mask and dark goggles, his cloth shoe covers lending a creepy slide to his gait. He had tactical gloves on his hands. In one hand was the pistol with extended magazine. In the other were the extra magazines that had pushed the number of rounds fired to well over a hundred.

"Does that look like Khoury to you?" asked Abe.

"Can't really tell."

The video quality suddenly changed, and there was audio with the next frames. Riverside had no surveillance cameras in the hallways outside the recreation room, so police had patched together clips of video from a handful of students, some on a dead run, who managed to record snippets of the shooting on their cell phones.

"How does a kid get caught in a school shooting and think to record video?"

"It's in this generation's DNA," said Abe.

The image bounced on the screen, but it was taken from behind the shooter. It was utter hysteria, screaming punctuated by the crack of semiautomatic gunfire. A teenage girl came out of her classroom, saw the shooter, ran for her life—and then dropped to the floor. The shooter turned around and faced the student holding the camera.

Abe froze the image on the screen. "There it is. The best look of the shooter we have on video."

The detective studied the image, then looked at Abe. "That's the best we got? A face covered by a hooded ski mask and dark ski goggles?"

"I'm afraid so," said Abe. "What do you think?"

The detective rose, walked closer to the screen, and looked harder, as if trying to see behind the mask and goggles. "One thing's for sure," she said.

"What?"

She turned and looked at Abe. "There's no way anyone could say that's Xavier Khoury."

"More to the point: If someone *did* say it, there's no way a juror would believe it beyond a reasonable doubt."

Abe switched off the screen with the remote.

Vega threw him a puzzled look. "There's more, isn't there?"

"Yeah. Almost two gigs of video from SWAT body-armor cameras when they rushed in and found the victims." Abe tossed the remote control onto his desk. "I don't have the stomach for it right now."

"When are you taking the case to the grand jury?"

It was a good question, as the detective knew that a grand jury indictment was needed in a death penalty case. "Soon."

"Are you going to show them the video?"

"You think I should?"

"You'll probably have them in tears if you do."

Abe walked to the window and peered out toward the detention center where Xavier Khoury was housed. "Might shed a few myself."

Jack was back in his office by two o'clock and spent the rest of the afternoon working only on things that had nothing to do with a school shooting. Not that there wasn't plenty to be done in the Khoury case. The real work would come after Beckham presented the case to the grand jury—it was only a matter of time—but already there were boxes and boxes of materials to comb through. Hannah Goldsmith had offered to take a first cut, and Jack was more than grateful.

"Got a minute, Jack?" asked Hannah, appearing in the open doorway.

"Yeah, come on in."

Hannah's father, Neil, had founded the Freedom Institute in the 1960s. It was Neil who'd found the run-down, historic house made of coral stone and Dade County pine just a few blocks from the courthouse and converted it into office space for the Institute. And it was Neil who'd hired Jack out of law school to handle capital cases at a time when Jack's father, Governor Harry Swyteck, was signing more death warrants than any governor in Florida history. When Neil died, Hannah took over. When Hannah ran out of money, Jack bought the old house, set up his own practice downstairs, and let Hannah run the

Institute out of the old master suite and bedrooms up-stairs, rent free.

Hannah took a seat in the armchair facing Jack's desk. "I may be on to something."

"Tell me."

"I went through all the witness statements. I count eleven witnesses who say they recognized the shooter as Xavier Khoury. Nine students and two teachers."

"More than I thought there would be," said Jack.

"But here's the interesting thing. I checked the date and time of each eyewitness identification. There's not a single witness who said Xavier Khoury was the shooter until *after* al-Qaeda claimed responsibility for the shooting."

"So your argument is that it's the radical Islam con-nection that made these witnesses say the man behind the mask and goggles was the eldest son of the only Muslim family in the school. Is that it?"

"Yes, Jack. Have you seen the surveillance camera images that have been released to the media? The shooter is unrecognizable."

"Hannah, that's all very interesting. But I'm not going to cross-examine nine traumatized children and discredit them until they break down in tears and admit they can't possibly be certain that the man behind a ski mask and goggles was my client. I just won't do it. We have to figure out a way to get Beckham to bite on life in prison instead of death. Taking this case to trial is in nobody's best interest."

"We don't have to go after the children," said Hannah. "We need the notes and recordings of the interviews. Let's say the police told the witnesses that al-Qaeda claimed responsibility or that the shooting was an act of radical Islamic terrorism, and only then did they ask the question: Who does this look like to you? The whole preface to the question could have suggested the answer and caused these witnesses to finger Xavier."

"All right. That's an angle that may be worth looking into."

"But not tonight," said Hannah, smiling. "Evan and I are celebrating our one-year anniversary."

"Wow. Has it been a year already?"

"Yeah. One down. Forever to go."

"You make marriage sound so magical," said Jack, teasing.

"What can I say? Mom was a child of the sixties, and Dad was the prodigal son. The apple doesn't fall far from the tree."

"Enjoy your celebration," said Jack.

Hannah assured Jack that she would and nearly collided with Jack's assistant on her way out. Bonnie, it seemed, was always running into or over someone.

"There's a visitor here to see you," said Bonnie. "Nate Abrams."

Jack had not spoken to Nate since visiting him at the ICU. He was happy to talk to the one and only school parent who approved of his defense of the alleged shooter. Jack followed Bonnie out of his office to the lobby. Nate rose from the couch. It was readily apparent that he'd come directly from the hospital, as he was still wearing the VISITOR badge from Jackson Memorial on his shirt.

"How's Lindsey?" Jack asked, but by the time the words crossed his lips, the answer was written all over Nate's face.

"She's gone," he said.

"I'm so sorry, Nate." He lowered himself slowly into the armchair, his heart aching. "I can't begin to say how sorry."

"Her mom and I were with her," he said in a distant voice. "That was good. I suppose."

Jack just listened.

"Her mom is still there," said Nate. "I had to walk. Had to get out of that place. You know what I mean?"

"I think I do," said Jack.

"I just kept walking. Thinking. Walking. Crying,"

Nate said, adding a little laugh at himself. "And walking some more. I was going to walk over to the school. It's not that far from the hospital, actually. Just on the other side of the river."

Silence hung in the air.

"Did you go?" asked Jack. "To the school?"

"Almost," said Nate. "I got about two blocks away, and I just stopped. I don't why. Honestly, I don't know why I started walking over there in the first place. I don't know why anything happens anymore, Jack."

There was only sadness in Nate's eyes, and Jack could only wish that he had an answer.

"So I ended up here," said Nate. "Lucky you. You're three blocks from the school."

"I used to think of it as a blessing," said Jack.

"Yeah, all us dads married to our hour-long commutes were jealous."

Jack smiled a little, then turned serious. "Something tells me you didn't just happen over here."

Nate shook his head. "No. I came because I'm angry."

"At me?"

"Yes."

"Because of the argument I made in court this morning?"

"No. As a lawyer, I totally get why you're trying to suppress the confession. It's what all trial lawyers do when they have an unwinnable case. Give the other side a little something to think about and make them come to the bargaining table. My anger isn't that focused. I'm mad at you, at the world, at the universe. And mad at myself."

"Why at yourself?"

"I hope I can explain this. And not everyone will agree with what I'm going to tell you now. But this is from the heart."

"Okay. What is it?"

He leaned forward a bit, as if to plead his case. "I want your client dead."

"Are you saying that you take back everything you told me in the hospital? You don't want me to defend Xavier?"

"I'm saying I want to kill him myself. I want to take a hammer and bash his skull in."

It wasn't the first time Jack had heard such words from a grieving father. The popularity of Hollywood revenge stories notwithstanding, real people in real life almost always reached the same conclusion.

"It's not worth it," said Jack.

"That's why I came here. I don't need this, Jack."

"This what?"

"A crusade to put a needle in Xavier's arm sucking the energy out of me for the next ten years. When I asked you to take Xavier's case, I never thought I'd get caught up in it, even if I lost Lindsey. I was wrong. I can tell already. It's going to consume me. That's why I'm angry at myself. I want to focus on something positive. Maybe create a dance scholarship in Lindsey's memory. God, she loved to dance. I'm just thinking off the top of my head. I don't know what my purpose will be. But anything is better than giving my time, my energy, *myself* over to this monster."

Nate took a deep breath, then rose. "I need to get back to the hospital. Left my car there. But that's what I came to say. I want you to stay on the case. Get the prosecutor to agree to thirteen"—he paused, choking back the correction—"*fourteen* life sentences, and let's get this over with. Save me from myself."

Jack walked him to the door. "You're a good man, Nate."

"You're a good lawyer. Put it to good use."

Jack shook his hand, the firmest promise without words he'd ever made to another man. "Can I give you a lift?"

"No, thanks. I need the walk."

Nate walked down the stairs, his footfalls crunching in the pea gravel as he continued down the driveway to the street. Jack went back inside. Bonnie stopped him on his way to his office.

"Oh, Jack, I forgot to tell you. The check came today."

"What check?"

"From the Trustee of the Xavier Khoury Irrevocable Trust."

"How much?"

"Your full retainer. A hundred thousand dollars. Do you want me to split it with the Freedom Institute for Hannah's work?"

Jack thought about it, but only for a second. "No. I want you to take it to the bank and cash it. Then get a money order for one hundred thousand dollars."

"Payable to whom?"

"The Lindsey Abrams Dance Scholarship Fund."

"Oh, how nice. Is there such a thing?"

"There will be now," said Jack.

"Do you want to do a letter with it?"

"No. Just put the check in the envelope. No return address. It's anonymous."

Jack went to the window and looked out toward the street. Nate was long gone, well into his lonely walk back to the hospital, but Jack spoke to him anyway.

"You take care of yourself, Nate," he said softly.

Chapter 14

Alone, Molly walked into her living room and stopped.

As in most homes, the Khoury living room was the most underutilized square footage under the roof. The only room Molly had spent less time in—recently, at least—was Xavier's bedroom. He'd told her to keep out, which to her seemed normal for a teenage boy. Everything about Xavier had seemed normal. She no longer knew what "normal" was.

She stepped toward the fireplace. Talk about under-utilized. Every expensive home in Coral Gables had one, and Molly couldn't understand why. Amir lit a fire about once every three years, and every time he did, Molly got new draperies because he turned the entire room into a smoker. Worse than useless, as far as she was concerned.

It had fallen to Molly to explain to their children why Santa Claus didn't come down the Khoury fireplace.

Slowly, Molly allowed her gaze to drift upward, above the mantel, settling on the enormous family portrait in a beautiful gold-leaf frame. Amir had commissioned an artist to paint the portrait from a photograph taken on the first family trip to Lebanon that included their youngest daughter. Talitha was three. Jamal was nine. Xavier was thirteen. Molly's gaze locked onto the smiling face of her eldest son.

Why?

Before the shooting, removing that portrait from its place of honor above the mantel would have been unthinkable to Molly. But what was she to do now? Take it down immediately? Wait to see if he was convicted? And if a jury said "guilty," would that mean going through every family album and Photoshopping her son out of their memories? Do sons convicted of murder cease to exist? Or would her son continue to exist as captured in the perfect photograph that an artist's brushstrokes had transformed into the perfect portrait. Everything about it was perfect. Her family was perfect. Until it was destroyed from within.

For what?

The front door opened, startling Molly. Amir was home.

"What are you doing?" he asked from the foyer, as if to confirm that she was in the room no one ever entered.

Molly went to her husband and held him. Amir put down his briefcase and returned the embrace. Molly broke away, glanced at the family portrait over the mantel, and then looked into Amir's eyes, unable to speak.

"You're grieving," he said.

"Yes," she said in a voice that cracked.

"You need to stop."

Molly swallowed hard, confused. "Stop? Why?"

"We are still a family without"—he paused, alluding to the portrait—"*him*."

The pronoun hurt. "You won't even say his name?"

"Do you have any idea what it was like for me going back to the office today? The looks on people's faces? I've spent my entire adult life beating back the notion that Muslims are anti-American. And now this happens."

"That's what really bothers you, isn't it, Amir? Not that our son is in jail. Not that fourteen children are dead. You can't get over the fact that your reputation has taken a hit."

"Reputation? You think hate and prejudice are about

reputation? I don't want to have this conversation." He started down the hallway toward the kitchen.

Molly followed. "I'm not going to let this go. You need to stop making this about you."

He turned and faced her. "It *is* about me. I'm the father in this family. I'm *the Muslim*!"

They locked eyes for a moment. Then Amir went to the refrigerator and grabbed a beer.

"Do you think Xavier did it?" asked Molly.

The question seemed to annoy him. "I don't know."

"I didn't ask if you *know*. I asked what you think."

"All I can tell you is that if Xavier went into his school with a gun and killed fourteen children, he was not acting in the name of Islam."

"How do you know that?"

"Because I pray, Molly. Try it sometime. It might surprise you to learn the things you can know through prayer."

"Just because I don't kneel down and face east five times a day doesn't mean I don't pray. And my prayers tell me to keep my heart and mind open to possibilities."

"Xavier told you he did it. He said it right in front of four police officers."

"Jack Swyteck explained all of that to the judge. I thought his argument was quite convincing."

"He's doing what lawyers do—the courtroom tap dance. What you don't hear is Swyteck trumpeting his client's innocence, do you? You don't even hear your own son saying he didn't do it."

"We should hire our own private investigator," said Molly.

Amir twisted off the bottle cap and pitched it into the trash. "To do what?"

"The police aren't even considering that someone broke into the glove compartment of your car and stole the gun that was used in the shooting."

Amir took a seat on the barstool at the granite-topped island. "Is that where your head is now? Someone broke into my car, stole my gun, and shot up the school?"

"It's possible, isn't it?"

"It doesn't make any sense."

"As if *any* of this makes sense."

"Molly, think about it. Why steal my gun? It would have been much easier to walk into any gun shop in Florida and buy a shiny new assault rifle—which, by the way, would have done even more damage than my gun."

"Maybe the shooter wasn't interested in 'easy.' Maybe the goal was to make everyone *think* it was the Muslim kid who did it."

Amir drank his beer, thinking. "A setup?"

"It could have been."

Amir narrowed his eyes, the anger returning. "Don't do this to me, Molly."

"Do what?"

"Last week you embarrassed me in my own house in front of Swyteck, accusing me of having a Muslim chip on my shoulder as big as the Middle East. Now you're telling me that our son was set up by an anti-Muslim conspiracy. I can't take your mood swings."

"It's not a *mood* swing! I've had more time to think about it."

"Maybe you should stop spending so much time cooking up conspiracy theories and start worrying about yourself."

"What does that mean?"

"I got a phone call from Detective Claudia Vega at Miami-Dade homicide today."

"What did she want?"

"They subpoenaed my cell-phone records."

"*Your* cell phone?"

"The family plan. Everybody's calls are on it, including Xavier's. The detective is focused on the incoming and outgoing calls on the morning of the shooting."

"And?"

"There was a flurry of calls from you right after the shooting."

"Of course there was. Like every other mother in that school, I was frantically trying to find my children."

"That's what I told her. But here's where I think the detective was going. The police still can't find the clothes and the vest the shooter was wearing. They think he ditched the clothes, but they can't find anything."

"What do cell-phone records have to do with that?"

"Obviously, the police think he coordinated with someone."

"'Someone' meaning you?"

"No. I was out of town," said Amir. "They suspect you."

"That's insane. They think I helped my son shoot schoolchildren?"

"No. They think you're an accomplice *after* the fact."

"That's preposterous."

"Is it?"

"Yes! Amir, I swear. I did not help Xavier in any way. Until the police pointed their guns at us and Xavier said 'I did it,' I didn't even consider the possibility that it was him."

Amir finished his beer and tossed the bottle into the recycling bin. "I'm going to send the phone records to Swyteck. He should have what the police have. Maybe we can stop the bleeding."

"Bleeding?"

"Financial bleeding. If you're a suspect, maybe we can work this out so we only have to pay one lawyer."

"Wonderful, Amir. Our son may be headed to death row, your wife could be charged as an accessory to murder, and all you care about is the two-for-one plan. Do you ever think of anyone but yourself?"

"I'm not making it about me, damn it! I'm trying to salvage what this family has left! I'm just—"

"Just go to hell," said Molly. She turned to leave, but Amir's booming voice—*"Molly!"*—brought her to a dead stop. It was that burst of anger she'd experienced only a handful of times in their marriage, the one that sent a chill down her spine. Molly turned slowly to face him.

"Xavier is *your* son," he said, no longer shouting, but deadly serious. "To me, he no longer exists."

Molly hurried from her kitchen, avoiding even a glimpse of the family portrait as she passed the living room on her way to the master suite.

Chapter 15

Jack flipped to the next page of his print magazine, a two-year-old edition of *Sports Illustrated* that he'd picked up in the detention center's waiting room.

Jack did most of his reading online these days, but cell phones were considered "contraband" in the jail visitation lexicon, even for attorneys. Xavier was seated across from him, on the other side of the table. His lower lip was swollen. The left side of his face was bruised. Clearly, he'd been in some kind of tussle, which was why the corrections officer had left him shackled for this meeting—unusual for a prisoner's meeting with his attorney. The guard had given Jack no explanation for Xavier's bruises, and, as per usual, Xavier refused to speak a word about anything. So Jack sat there, reading. Finally, he laid the magazine aside.

"I blocked out an hour for this meeting," said Jack. "You can sit there in silence and watch me read, or you can talk and let me help you."

No response.

"Letting your whiskers grow, I see," said Jack.

It wasn't idle chitchat. Appearances mattered. Jack had cleaned up many a client before letting him set foot in a courtroom, including a former Gitmo detainee.

"Brilliant move on your part," said Jack. "You're accused of carrying out a terrorist plot. Might as well look the part. You going for the al-Qaeda suicide-bomber look, or the Isis foot-solider look?"

The remark was intended to draw a reaction of some sort, but Xavier gave him nothing.

"Some of your fellow students have been telling the media that they saw you on the campus after the shooting. Not that it helps you in any way. Nikolas Cruz did the same thing at the Parkland shooting. Ditched his gun and his 'work' clothes and then tried to blend in with the students as the police led them to safety."

Jack tightened his gaze, trying to force Xavier to make eye contact. He wouldn't.

"So what'd you do with your 'work' clothes, Xavier?"

Jack didn't expect a response. He rose, walked to the other side of the room, and then glanced back to see if Xavier's gaze had followed him. Jack caught him looking, but Xavier quickly averted his eyes.

"The cops think your mother helped you lose the clothes you wore during the shooting," said Jack.

Xavier offered no verbal response, but the body language told Jack that he finally had his client's attention. Jack returned to his chair and laid the Khoury cell-phone records on the table for Xavier to see. It was several pages in length with each call identified by the ten-digit number of the caller or recipient.

"The police have focused on these calls," said Jack, pointing to Molly's phone number. "The ones from your mother to you right after the shooting. I guess their theory is that you were coordinating a rendezvous. Pretty far-fetched, if you ask me. What mother wouldn't be calling her son's cell phone after a school shooting? But this wouldn't be the first time the cops put the pressure on the mother to get the son to confess."

Xavier was staring down at the page.

Jack continued. "I don't know how hard the prosecutor intends to push the idea that your mother helped you. He may just be rattling your cage, hoping you'll sign a nice and clear confession to keep the police from charging your mother with a crime. Or maybe he really does intend to charge your mother as an accessory after the fact to murder. Either way, your parents want me to be her lawyer."

Xavier continued his stare at the printed page. Jack laid his hand flat on the paper, palm down, to break Xavier's concentration.

"Under the professional rules of ethics, I need your consent to represent both you and your mother. It's called joint representation. Honestly, I don't think it's a good idea. It's not in your mother's interest to be linked to you in any way, and joint representation only reinforces the link. My advice to your mother was to get separate counsel. But your father is determined to pay only one lawyer. So I'm asking you, as my existing client: Do you object to joint representation?"

Jack waited. Silence.

"I'm not going to take silence as acceptance," said Jack.

More silence.

"Okay, I have my answer. I'll let your parents know that you do not consent to joint representation. All for the better, as far as I'm concerned."

Jack shuffled through the next few pages of cell-phone records until he found what he was looking for. He laid a new page on the table.

"Here's what interests me," said Jack, pointing. "This number, right here. It's not your mom's number or your dad's number. In fact, when I asked your parents, they had no idea whose number this is. Which is interesting because you called it every day. Multiple times a day. Until five days before the shooting. Then the calls stopped."

Jack gave him a moment to review the record, to see it in black and white.

"Whose number is that?" asked Jack.

Xavier was staring down at the page.

"You obviously know," said Jack. "You talked every day. Why did the calls stop? Why did you stop talking just five days before the shooting?"

The silent stare continued.

"Fine," said Jack. He folded the papers and tucked them away in his coat pocket. "I'll pick up my cell phone on my way out of the building and dial the number. Let's see who answers."

Xavier's eyes widened, and for a second Jack thought he might say something, but he didn't. Jack rose, went to the door, and called for the guard.

"I'm not bluffing," Jack said to his client. "I'm giving you this one chance to tell me. If you don't, I'm going to dial that number the minute I leave this building."

He gave Xavier a moment to reconsider. Not a word.

The door opened. "I'm finished," Jack told the guard.

Jack took the elevator down to the lobby and retrieved his smartphone from the custodian. He walked straight out of the building, crossed the street to his car, and got inside. He turned on the air-conditioning but left the car in PARK. Then he made good on his threat. He dialed the number, and the call linked to his Bluetooth on speaker.

"Hello?"

It was the voice of a young woman, which took Jack by surprise. "This is Xavier Khoury's lawyer, Jack Swyteck."

He wanted her name, but fishing for it would only increase the chances of a hang-up. Better to act like he already knew who she was. "Your number is in Xavier's cell-phone records. Are you a friend of his?"

No response.

"Are you still there?" Jack asked.

"What do you want?"

"I'd like to talk to you."

"What about?"

"Xavier."

"I'm sorry. I don't want to talk."

"If you're worried about talking on a cell phone, I understand. I'd be happy to meet somewhere in private."

"I just don't want to talk."

"We could meet wherever is convenient."

"I don't want to meet."

"I'm not asking you to tell me anything that makes you uncomfortable."

"That leaves us nothing to talk about," she said, and the line went silent.

"Hello?"

Jack waited, but she was gone.

"Damn it!" he said, pounding the steering wheel, angry only at himself.

Andie was at her desk, working on a witness statement, when the assistant special agent in charge of the Miami field office stepped into the doorway and invited her to lunch.

"We need to catch up," he said, but Andie sensed there was something more to it. Schwartz was a well-known brown-bagger who ate almost every day at his desk, working. Just before noon, they left the building together and went to Andie's car. She drove in the direction of a local sandwich shop that had the best tuna salad on pita around.

"Tell me something, Henning," said Schwartz.

Andie kept her eyes on the road but braced herself. Her instincts had been right: clearly more to it.

"Do you think the al-Qaeda claim of responsibility is real?" he asked.

She knew exactly what he meant, but she asked anyway. "You mean about the school shooting?"

"Yes. The school shooting."

"Terrorism is not my turf, as you know. So I really can't say any more than anyone else who watches the nightly news."

"What does Jack think?" he asked.

"I don't know what Jack thinks."

"Two possibilities, right? A terrorist cell radicalized the shooter and made him an instrument of al-Qaeda. Or someone wants law enforcement to think it was an act of Islamic terrorism."

"I agree," said Andie. "Which way Jack is leaning I can't say. We never talk about his cases. At least not until the trial is over."

"I find that hard to believe in this situation. A shooting at your daughter's school. You and Righley could have been killed. And you don't talk about it?"

Andie steered into a parking space outside the sandwich shop and stopped the car. "Maybe it is hard to believe. But it's true."

They climbed out of the car, shut the doors, and started toward the restaurant. Andie heard the click of heels on the sidewalk behind them. She walked a little faster, and the footfalls quickened. She turned and stopped. The man kept coming and then stopped.

"Andrea Henning?" he asked.

"Yes."

"This is for you," he said, handing her a large manila envelope.

Andie took it, and the moment she did, the man hurried away.

"What the hell was that?" the ASAC asked.

Andie opened the envelope and looked inside. "*That* was a process server," she said, leafing through the pages. "And this is a civil summons and a complaint."

"Huh?"

Andie looked up in time to see the process server drive away.

"I'm being sued," she said in disbelief.

Chapter 16

Jack met MDPD Homicide detective Vega outside the front gate to Riverside.

The defendant's motion to allow his counsel to tour the campus grounds had drawn no opposition from the state attorney. Jack had visited the campus before, of course, but only casually, as a parent. Before the students returned to classes—the target date was the following Monday—he needed to view the grounds as counsel for an accused killer. It was an entirely different way of looking at a familiar place filled with mostly fond memories.

"Here's how we're going to proceed," said Vega.

The detective was in control, and she laid out the rules. The motion Jack had filed with the court also asked to see any hand-drawn diagrams or electronic graphics the homicide team had created to document the shooter's movements. Jack was given an iPad to use during the tour. A room-by-room simulation would unfold on the handheld LCD screen in real time, as Vega led Jack in the shooter's footsteps.

"We'll start in Building E," she said, as she unlocked the gate and pushed it open.

Jack followed her across the grounds. "Ghost town" was a cliché, but the term nonetheless came to Jack's mind. It was just after the lunch hour on a school day. In the courtyard, picnic tables that should have been filled with schoolchildren and their cafeteria trays were empty. Silence replaced the usual school-day sounds—no bells, no commotion, no laughter, no snickering boys and girls who couldn't heed their teacher's command to stand silent. Even the flagpole was barren.

They stopped at the entrance door to Building E. It was the logical starting point, as Jack knew that Building E was where surveillance cameras had picked up the earliest images of the shooter.

"On my signal, hit the START button on your screen," said Vega. "Just follow me, and walk exactly at the pace I set. Don't stop unless I stop. This tour proceeds at the exact speed of the shooter's movement across campus."

"Got it," said Jack. He checked the screen on the tablet. It was a blueprint-style diagram of twelve classrooms, six on each side of the hallway that ran the length of the building. Inside each classroom were a dozen or more green dots and one blue dot.

"The green dots are students," said Vega. "Blue is a teacher. As soon as we enter the building, you'll see a black dot. That's the shooter. Ready?"

"Yes."

She opened the door. On her signal, Jack followed her inside, and the on-screen demonstration began. A black dot appeared at the building entrance, exactly where they were standing. The detective walked calmly toward the fire alarm, as did the on-screen black dot.

"First thing the shooter did was pull the fire alarm," she said, but she didn't actually pull it. On screen, green dots inside the classrooms formed lines, exactly the way students would in response to an emergency drill. The blue dots went to the front of the lines.

"The teachers opened the doors," said Vega.

They were just dots on a screen, but Jack felt his heart pounding as lines of unsuspecting students filed out of the classrooms and into the hallway.

Vega stepped into the stairwell. Jack followed.

"The shooter waited for the classrooms to empty," she said.

Ten seconds passed, and then she stepped back into the hallway.

"And then he opened fire," she said.

The green dots scattered across the screen in every direction, some running away from the shooter, others running toward him in obvious confusion, still others racing back in the classrooms and clustering in the corners.

Before Jack's eyes, green dots in the hallway changed color.

"The purple dots are hits," said the detective.

Jack counted four. The detective continued down the hallway. Jack followed, putting one foot in front of the other, hardly able to imagine what it must have been like for those scattering and screaming "green dots" on that morning. The detective stopped briefly outside the door to Classroom E-101, and then kept walking.

"We don't know why the shooter didn't go inside," she said. "Maybe he was looking for a particular teacher or student. Maybe you can tell us."

Jack didn't acknowledge the remark, but he didn't hold it against her either, given the horror of the virtual reenactment.

Vega stopped at the next classroom. "Seven-oh-three had the most victims."

Vega opened the door, and Jack followed her inside. A blue dot moved precipitously across the LCD screen toward the black one. Blue turned to purple.

"That was Mr. Davis," said Vega. "Science teacher. Thirty-two years old. Wife and three kids."

Over the next fifteen seconds, the dots that had clustered in the corner changed from green to purple, one innocent child at a time, leaving Jack breathless.

"There's more," said Vega.

Jack was all too aware. He followed her out. The virtual hallway on screen was empty, save for the random purple dots that marked the shooter's first victims. Vega continued down the hallway.

"He changed magazines while walking to the south exit. A fully spent extended magazine—almost forty rounds—was found right there," she said, pointing to a piece of ballistics marking tape that was still on the floor.

Jack followed her out of the building, the movement of the black dot on the screen synced perfectly with their walk through the courtyard.

"The shooter's next stop was the rec center," said Vega. "I'm guessing you knew that."

"Yes," said Jack.

Vega opened the door, and they entered a wide hallway. To the left were classrooms. To the right was the recreation center.

"Your wife was in there," said Vega. "Those yellow dots on your screen are the parents who attended the coffee with the head of school."

Vega walked. Three green dots were in a vestibule outside the second classroom on the left.

"By now, word was starting to spread that there was a shooter on campus," said Vega. "Unfortunately, three students didn't make it out of the building with their classmates. They hid right over there."

They stopped outside the vestibule. Two of the green dots turned purple. The third dot moved quickly down the hallway, then stopped. Green turned to purple. Jack could not contain his reaction.

"Lindsey," he said softly.

"What?"

Jack cleared his throat. "That was Nate Abrams' daughter. Lindsey."

"Yes. I was so sorry to hear we lost her. Victim number fourteen."

The screen went dark. The detective took Jack's iPad. "That's as far as our tech team has gotten with the virtual reenactment."

Jack was in some way relieved. He wasn't quite ready to see how close to the black dot the yellow "parent" dot had come after leaving the rec center, racing down the hallway, and standing guard outside Righley's classroom.

"The graphic designers are incorporating new information into the model every few days," said Vega.

"You should coordinate directly with Abe Beckham for the latest updates."

"I will," said Jack. "Thank you."

Together they left the building, but instead of retracing their steps, Jack followed the detective on a shortcut directly to the front gate. He thanked her again and walked alone toward his office, just a few blocks away. The front porch outside the old house-turned-law-office was in sight when his cell phone rang. He checked the number. It was the number he'd dialed earlier that morning, the one from the Khoury family cell-phone records. Jack answered eagerly, and her words were music to his ears.

"I've been thinking," she said.

Jack stopped on the sidewalk. Detective Vega's tour had all but convinced him that someone had radicalized his client. The young woman on the line might know something about that.

"Maybe we should talk about it," said Jack.

"Maybe."

"I can come to you," said Jack.

"I don't know."

Jack didn't want to push too hard—but he needed to close the deal before she changed her mind again. "Where are you now?"

"I'm at work."

"Where do you work?"

"Uhm. Little Havana. Do you know San Lazaro's Café?"

"Yes. That's ten minutes from my office. When's your next break?"

"Three."

Jack checked the time. He had twenty minutes. "That would work perfectly for me. How about you?"

"I guess. But . . ."

Jack was afraid to ask. "But what?"

"If you get here before three, take the booth in the back. The one with the old map of Cuba on the wall. Wait there."

He breathed a sigh of relief. That was a but he could deal with. "Got it. Oh, one other thing. What's your name?"

"Maritza."

"Thank you, Maritza. I'm on my way."

Chapter 17

Jack made it to San Lazaro's Café with time to spare, ordered a *café con leche* at the counter, and found the booth in the back. Maritza hadn't been kidding about the *old* map of Cuba on the wall. This one was from pre-Castro Cuba, more than sixty years old.

Just after three p.m., a young woman brought him his coffee and took the seat across from him. She was a little older than Xavier, Jack guessed, a dark-eyed Latina with long brown hair and a face like a younger Selena Gomez. Younger and tired. "I'm Maritza," she said.

Jack thanked her and kept the preliminaries short. He had a thousand questions but only a few minutes. "How do you know Xavier? From school?"

"No," she said, scoffing. "I didn't go to Fancy-Pants Day School, if that's what you're asking. I graduated from Miami Senior High two years ago."

"Is that your term or Xavier's—'Fancy-Pants Day School'?"

"Mine. He called it 'fuck-wad penitentiary.'"

She was already more helpful than Jack had anticipated. "How did you meet?"

"Xavier stopped here for coffee almost every day on his way to school. Large American coffee, two sugars. He drives a BMW convertible, so one day I was like, 'Hey, nice car.' We started talking every day after that. Chitchat. It grew from there."

"Grew in what way?"

"We became friends."

"Just friends?"

She smiled. "More than friends."

"Were you his girlfriend?"

"Not officially."

Jack stirred a packet of sugar into his coffee. "What does that mean?"

"Xavier's parents have a problem with Latina chicks. Especially his father. Apparently we're all sluts. His parents are such assholes."

"So you kept your relationship a secret?"

"Yeah. If we went out, it was to somewhere no one

would know us. Anyplace north of Miami Gardens was safe."

"His phone had no text messages from you. Did you ever text each other?"

"Never. No Snapchat, no social media. Just phone calls. We had to do it that way. Xavier said he had like a ton of money coming to him in trust on his eighteenth birthday. He didn't want his parents finding a text message and cutting him off over a girlfriend."

"Did anyone ever find out that you two were an item?"

"An item?"

Jack was dating himself with the terminology. "Did anyone know that you and Xavier were, you know—"

"We weren't just fuck buddies, if that's what you're asking."

"That wasn't exactly my question, but thank you for that."

"In fact, that morning was supposed to be 'the day,'" she said, using air quotes.

"Are you talking about the morning of the shooting?"

Maritza was noticeably less cheerful. "Yeah. That morning."

"What did you mean when you say it was supposed to be 'the day.'"

"It was his birthday. The big one."

"I know. Eighteen."

She looked away, then back. "I was his present."

Jack suddenly hoped Righley would never grow up, then shook it off. "I get your drift. So what was the plan? Meet after school?"

"No. Instead of school."

"What?"

"I took the day off. Xavier skipped school that day and came to my apartment. My roommates were at work, so we had the place to ourselves. That's where he got his present."

"I'm less interested in *what* the present was than *when*," said Jack. "You're saying that Xavier was at your apartment the morning of the shooting?"

"Yes."

Jack took a moment to process that answer. "Until what time?"

"Until his phone started ringing. And ringing. And ringing. His mother was psycho-calling him, and he freaked out. He thought his mom was on to him and somehow knew he was with me."

Her story jibed with the cell-phone records, the flurry of calls from a panic-stricken mother to her son. "What did you do?"

"Xavier said he needed to go back to school."

"Go back? I thought you said he skipped school and went to your apartment."

"He parked his car in the school lot, like usual. His father had one of those electronic gizmos on his BMW—the ones the insurance companies have, so you can see where someone drives, how fast they go, and stuff. So he couldn't drive to my apartment."

"How did he get from the school?"

"The parking lot is right next to the athletic field. I picked him up at the back gate."

Jack drank his coffee. "Did you drive him back to school after his mother called?"

"Yeah. Left him off where I picked him up. The back gate."

"What time?"

"I'd say around ten thirty. Maybe eleven."

The shooting had ended before ten a.m. "What did you see when you got there? It must have been pandemonium."

"To me, it looked like there was some kind of fire drill going on. Which I thought was pretty lucky for us. Xavier could just jump the fence and fall in line somewhere. Not until later did I find out this was no drill. People were getting shot."

The café manager approached their table. "Break's over, Maritza. Need you at the drive-through."

"Coming," she told him. She waited for him to leave before saying more to Jack. "Sorry, I have to go. I hope this is useful."

"It's useful," said Jack. "If it's true."

"Why would I lie?"

"Don't take this personally, but girlfriends are the number one phony alibi in the history of homicide. Mothers a close second."

"I'm not a phony."

"I understand. But I'd like to ask you one favor: Would you be willing to sit for a polygraph examination?"

"A what?"

"A lie detector test."

She looked at him harshly, clearly offended. "You don't believe me, do you?"

"I'm just being careful."

"No one will believe me. Even if I pass a stupid lie detector test."

"Passing a polygraph will help."

"No way. You just said yourself that girlfriends are the number one phony alibi. That's who I'll be the rest of my life: the slutty Latina who slept with the Islamic terrorist and then lied to help him get away with shooting up his school."

"I'm sorry. I wasn't trying to offend you."

"My first reaction was right," she said, rising. "I should never have talked to you."

"All I was suggesting is that a lot of people have made up their mind about Xavier. They'll question your story."

"They can't question it if I don't tell it," she said, sliding out of the booth.

"Please don't leave like this."

"Just forget it. This meeting never happened. Don't call me again."

"Maritza, please—"

"I said *forget it*. I won't testify. I won't say anything to anyone. *Ever.*"

Jack could only watch as she made an angry pivot and marched back to work.

Chapter 18

Jack and Andie were side by side in the moonlight, holding hands, seated in matching Adirondack chairs. A gentle breeze blew in from the bay, adding warmth to the glow of downtown Miami's magnificent skyline on the mainland. Their little vintage-fifties house was tiny by Key Biscayne standards, one of the few remaining Mackle homes that hadn't been bulldozed to make room for elevated three-story McMansions built on concrete pilings. Jack and Andie were among the holdouts. It worked just fine for their family of three, might get crowded if they became four, or might be under three feet of water by the time Jack and Andie were grandparents. The trade-off was life on the Key Biscayne waterfront.

Andie had a glass of sauvignon blanc in her free hand. Jack held the complaint in his, reading.

"Exactly what is a declaratory judgment anyway?" asked Andie.

"The Board of Trustees is asking the court to issue a declaration that the school has good cause to terminate our contract."

"So they can kick Righley out of the school?"

"Yes," said Jack. "And still make us pay the full year's tuition we owe."

"Can they do that?"

"It's frivolous. If the board wanted me to stop representing Xavier Khoury, they should have talked to me about it. Not file a bullshit lawsuit against my wife."

"The lawsuit doesn't have anything to do with your representation of Xavier Khoury."

"It has everything to do with it," said Jack. "They could have just sent us a letter and terminated the contract. Instead, they filed a lawsuit and made this a public statement."

"You're talking about the motive. I'm talking about the substance of the lawsuit. This is serious." Andie took the complaint from him and read aloud.

"'Agent Henning disregarded the explicit instructions of the head of school, putting the lives of students in danger. As a law enforcement officer, Agent Henning was familiar with the well-established "Run, Hide, Fight" response protocol to an active shooter in public places. By her own admission, Agent Henning violated that protocol.'"

Jack stopped her. "There's bogus allegation number one. When did you admit to violating the 'Run, Hide, Fight' protocol?"

Andie considered it. "I guess at the candlelight vigil in the park. A few of the kindergarten moms confronted me and made some pretty harsh accusations. I didn't deny anything. I guess by not denying it, I admitted it."

"Yeah, you and Jesus."

"But that's not the main point. What this lawsuit is alleging is that it would have been fine for me to run for an exit. Instead—well, it says it right here. 'Agent Henning proceeded directly to a classroom filled with kindergarten students, potentially leading the shooter to the youngest and most vulnerable students in the school. Agent Henning's negligent and unprofessional actions caused unknown additional casualties.'"

"That's just outrageous," said Jack. "No one in Righley's classroom was hurt. In fact, the argument could be made that you *prevented* the shooter from going in that classroom by standing guard outside the door."

Andie drew a deep breath. "I just don't believe this is about you, Jack. These are smart people on the Board of Trustees. Would they file a lawsuit like this just because you're defending Xavier?"

"It's also a proactive move," said Jack. "Yes, the trustees are smart. But the school also has smart lawyers. It's not a pleasant topic while families are still grieving, but wrongful death lawsuits are already in the pipeline. This claim against you is step one in taking control of the narrative: the school did everything it could, and to the extent that any safety measures failed, it was the fault of people like you who broke the rules."

"Maybe it *was* the fault of people like me."

"Stop," Jack said.

Andie turned her gaze toward the distant city lights on the mainland. "The crazy thing is, I had to leave my gun behind in the glove compartment. Not only am I an FBI agent. I was the only one in my class at Quantico who made the Possible Club. You know what that means, Jack? It means I shot a perfect score on one of the most difficult training courses in the country. It means that if you put me at the other end of the hallway with that shooter, I could have shot the teenage stubble off of his chin. I could've put a bullet between his eyes and ended it. Instead, all I could do was hide in a vestibule outside my daughter's classroom, armed only with a stupid fire extinguisher, while he just kept shooting and shooting and—"

"Hey, hey, stop," said Jack. He went to her quickly and held her tight.

"I'm sorry," said Andie, sobbing.

"It's okay."

"It's not okay."

Jack kissed her on the forehead. "You're right. It's not. I was moved when Nate Abrams walked me down the hall from his daughter's room in the ICU and asked me to take this case. Even more moved when he walked all the way from the hospital to tell me to keep on doing what I was doing. But you're my wife. This is our family. I'm not going to do this at your expense. I'll file a motion to withdraw as counsel in the morning."

"That's not what I want," said Andie.

"You don't have to say that. No need to put on the happy mask and play 'the good wife.'"

"It's not that," said Andie, and her expression turned from sadness to resignation. "We never really fit in there anyway, Jack."

"What do you mean?"

"You know exactly what I mean. I'm pretty confident we're the only family at Riverside that uses coupons at the grocery store."

"What's wrong with coupons?"

"Nothing. All I'm saying is that changing schools is not the end of the world. How is Righley going to feel when she's sixteen years old and still riding the bus while her friends are driving to school in a new Audi or Range Rover? We have an amazing daughter who will do amazing things at her new school. And in the long run, she'll learn a lot more from a father who does what he believes in than she would ever learn from attending 'the right school.'"

Jack smiled a little. "Thank you for that."

"I meant it."

Jack held her closer. "One way or another, I have to wrap this up as soon as possible. And it starts tomorrow."

Chapter 19

Abe Beckham and a junior prosecutor entered the grand jury room at eight a.m. Inside were twenty-three grand jurors who had sworn an oath to keep secret all matters that occurred before them, and to consider all evidence presented against Xavier Khoury. There was no judge. The prosecutor was the virtual writer, director, and producer of this nonpublic proceeding.

It was day three of the presentation. It was Abe's decision, with the state attorney's approval, not to call any children as witnesses before the grand jury. Instead, the prosecution team read witness statements into the record, which had taken most of the first day. Day two had been forensic evidence and testimony from law enforcement officers. On Wednesday morning, exactly one week after the deadly shooting, the prosecution was ready to call its final witness.

"Let's get started," said Beckham.

The junior prosecutor opened the door, and a Florida state trooper escorted the witness into the room.

By law, everything presented to a grand jury is eventually disclosed to the defense, and it was usually Beckham's strategy to present just enough evidence to secure an indictment—in other words, only the truly essential witnesses. In some cases, however, it made sense to call a nonessential witness just to see how he performed on the witness stand. Better that he fall on his face in front of a grand jury than before the real jury at trial. That was the case with Simon Radler, owner of Tactical Guns & Ammo in Jupiter, Florida.

"Mr. Radler, how long have you owned your gun shop?" asked Beckham.

"Forty-eight years," Radler said in a strong voice. His weathered skin and his beard the color of driftwood made it no surprise to hear how old he was, yet his solid physique and crusty demeanor would have made much younger men afraid to mess with him. Beckham had seen other men shrink in the witness stand. Radler sat tall on the hardwood chair, like the captain of a ship, his tattoos swelling as he folded his forearms across his chest.

"What kind of weapons do you sell?"

"All kinds."

"Do you sell semiautomatic firearms?"

"Of course."

"Pistols?"

"Yes."

"Rifles?"

"Yup."

"Are you familiar with a semiautomatic rifle known as the AR-15?"

"I am. I own one myself. I take it to the Everglades for target shooting. It's a lot of fun. Arguably the most fun sporting rifle in America."

"Tell the grand jurors a little more about the AR-15."

Radler turned in the chair to face the grand jurors more directly. "First thing you need to know is that 'AR' does not stand for 'assault rifle.' It stands for Armalite Rifle. The first ones were made by Colt, and Colt still owns the AR-15 trademark. So, technically speaking, if the rifle is made by a manufacturer other than Colt, it's an AR-15–*style* rifle. Not an AR-15."

"Understood. Are all AR-15–style rifles alike?"

"Nope. You got your standard full-size rifles with 20-inch barrels, short carbine-length models with 16-inch barrels, long-range target models with 24-inch barrels, and so on. Even more different calibers. Depends on the manufacturer."

"Tell me how the AR-15–style rifle performs."

"It's semiautomatic, not fully automatic. That means to fire a round, you have to pull the trigger. It's not a machine gun or tommy gun like the old Chicago gangsters used in the St. Valentine's Day Massacre."

"But they have been used in mass shootings, correct?"

"I knew you'd bring that up. Yeah, some very sick people have *mis*used the AR-15 and AR-15–style rifles."

"The AR-15 was used in the Aurora movie theater shooting that killed twelve people in Colorado, right?"

"I believe so."

"In the Sandy Hook school shooting that killed twenty first-grade students and six teachers and staff in Connecticut?"

"Yes."

"The AR-15 was the weapon of choice for the husband-and-wife terrorist attack that killed fourteen people in San Bernardino, California. The murder of twenty-six victims at the First Baptist Church in Sutherland Springs, Texas. The massacre of fifty-eight concertgoers in Las Vegas. Am I right?"

"Like I said: It has been *mis*used by very sick people."

"Closer to home, the AR-15 was used in the Parkland shooting that left seventeen students and teachers dead at Marjorie Stoneman Douglas High School. Right?"

"Same answer."

Beckham flashed a photograph on the screen for the witness and jurors. "Let me state for the record that I am displaying the defendant's headshot from his Florida driver's license. Mr. Radler, have you ever seen this man before?"

"Yeah. I have."

"When?"

"About a month ago. He came into my store."

"Let me tell you, sir, that Mr. Khoury's house was in Coral Gables. How far is that from your store in Jupiter?"

"About a two-hour drive."

"So Mr. Khoury drove for two hours to your shop for what? Was he looking to buy something?"

"He said he was interested in a rifle."

"What kind of rifle?"

"An AR-15."

"What did you tell him?"

"He looked kind of young. So I asked if he was twenty-one years old. That's the minimum age now in Florida to buy an AR-15–style rifle. He said he was still a teenager."

"Did you sell him the rifle?"

"No," Radler said, annoyed by the question. "All our sales comply with the law."

"Thank you, Mr. Radler. Those are all the questions I have."

Radler rose, but the prosecutor halted him.

"Just a second, Mr. Radler. A grand jury proceeding is different than a trial. The grand jurors can ask questions. So let me turn it over to these fine ladies and gentlemen to see if there's anything they would like to ask."

A juror in the back row raised her hand, and Beckham acknowledged her.

"I'd like to know if Mr. Radler asked Mr. Khoury why he wanted the AR-15."

"I didn't ask him," said Radler.

A woman in the front row spoke up. "Did you call the police?"

"Excuse me?"

"A high school student who looks like an Arab drove all the way from Miami-Dade County to buy an assault rifle. Did you call the police?"

Beckham interrupted. "First of all, let's be clear that Mr. Khoury is an American citizen born in this country."

"No, *first of all*, let me reiterate that this is not an

assault rifle," said the witness. "Second of all, I bought my first AR-15 when I was eighteen years old. I've never even aimed it in the general direction of another human being, let alone used it in a mass shooting."

The grand juror didn't seem satisfied. "So the answer is no, you didn't call the police?"

"If I had, I probably would've been sued by the ACLU and put out of business for discriminating against Muslims."

The room fell silent. Another juror spoke up, a man. "When he was in your store, did he tell you his name?"

"No. Or maybe it was on his driver's license. I don't remember. I didn't remember hardly nothing about this until Mr. Beckham showed me his picture and said it was Xavier Khoury."

Beckham interjected. "Just to clarify: I didn't tell you that Xavier Khoury went to your store."

"Well, maybe not in so many words. You showed me a copy of his driver's license with his picture and his name on it, told me he was charged in the school shooting, and asked 'Could this be the guy who came into your store?' I said it could be."

The same grand juror followed up. "How sure are you that it was Xavier Khoury who visited your store? Ninety percent sure? Seventy-five percent?"

"I can't put a percentage on it. I run one of the biggest operations in South Florida. On a typical weekend, over a thousand people come into my store. This was over a month ago, at least. In hindsight, it makes sense that it *would be* him, now that we know he shot up his school. It could be him. That's what I'm telling you."

"Thank you very much, Mr. Radler," said the prosecutor, shutting it down. Beckham was glad he'd taken this witness for a little test-drive before trial. Mr. Radler wouldn't be back.

Radler showed himself to the exit, the door closed behind him, and the junior prosecutor locked it. With a push of a button on the remote control, Beckham darkened the on-screen image of the defendant and queued up the next item. It was the powerful simulation of the shooting that the tech team had prepared—the same one Detective Vega had shown to Swyteck on the school tour.

"Ladies and gentlemen," the prosecutor said in a solemn voice. "Before you retire for your deliberations, there is one more thing I would like you to see."

Jack walked into the clerk's office on the ground floor of the criminal courthouse, affixed his signature to his motion to withdraw as defense counsel for Xavier

Khoury, and slid it across the counter to the intake clerk. She thumbed through the pages, cocked her head, and raised an eyebrow at Jack.

"This one'll be in the news," she said.

"I suppose," said Jack.

He could have filed it online, but there was something therapeutic about handing the paper motion to a human being, watching her log it into the docket, and walking out with a file-stamped copy in hand. It felt final. But it wasn't. He was still Xavier's lawyer until the judge granted the motion to withdraw, which was not a given in a capital case. Until then, it was still Jack's mission to persuade the prosecutor to back away from the death penalty—to convince Abe Beckham that the best result was a guilty plea, life without parole, and no trial.

To that end, Jack took a seat on a wood bench outside the grand jury room and waited.

The prosecutor was the only lawyer allowed inside the grand jury room, but the hallway was fair game for other members of the bar. Defense lawyers and even members of the media sometimes parked themselves near the entrance door just to see which witnesses the prosecutor was summoning. This time, Jack had come only to talk to Beckham, and he sprang from his slumber on the bench the instant the door opened.

"Abe, you got a minute?" asked Jack.

Beckham sent his assistant along to the elevator without him and walked toward Jack. They were alone in the long corridor, standing in the shadow of a curiously situated support pillar that blocked the window and the midmorning sunshine.

"What's on your mind, Jack?"

"I don't know how close you are to an indictment, but I wanted to give you a heads-up that I may ask you to present exculpatory evidence to the grand jury."

"You can ask, but you know I'm under no obligation to present it."

That was the law, and Jack was all too aware of it. A defense lawyer could show up with a truckload of evidence that his client was innocent, and the prosecutor could simply refuse delivery. "I hope you'll at least consider it," said Jack.

"Is this what I've seen in the media the last couple of days—students who saw Xavier mixed in with other students during the evacuation? I don't consider that exculpatory at all. That's exactly what the Parkland shooter did to slip through the police perimeter and head over to McDonald's for a burger and fries after a hard day's work."

"That's not what I'm talking about. We may have an alibi witness."

Beckham showed surprise, probably more than he would have liked. "An alibi? Really? Who?"

"I'm not prepared to say just yet. I'm here to ask you to slow down the train for a day or two. I'd like to gather my facts and offer this evidence to you in a reliable way. Then you can decide whether to present it to the grand jury."

"Delay, delay, delay," said Beckham, groaning. "That's the game you defense lawyers always play—until your client is convicted. Then you file an appeal arguing that I violated your client's constitutional right to a speedy trial. I'm not slowing down. I'm getting my indictment on fourteen counts of first-degree murder today, we're going to trial as soon as possible, and I'm seeking the death penalty."

"That's what I thought you'd say. I understand. Go ahead and announce the indictment. But throw me this bone, will you? Do not make a public announcement that you are seeking the death penalty."

"It's already out there. I've been talking about the death penalty since the arrest."

"Talking, yes," said Jack. "Up until this point, I think it's fair to say that the State Attorney's Office has rejected any request by the defense to take the death penalty off the table. Once you have the indictment in hand and make a formal announcement that you are seeking death, that's a game changer. Politically, it's almost impossible for the state attorney to back away from it in a case like this. So wait a week. Wait a *day*. Just *wait*."

Abe didn't answer right away. "I'll consider it," he said finally.

"Thank you," said Jack.

They walked toward the elevator together, but before Jack could push the CALL button, the bell rang and the chrome doors parted. A gaggle of reporters spilled out of the crowded elevator, and from the looks on their faces, they smelled a breaking development in the case. Jack suspected that Beckham's assistant had put the word out that an indictment was imminent.

"Mr. Beckham!" they shouted. "Mr. Beckham!"

Within seconds the prosecutor was surrounded, the blinding media lamps were up, and the cameras were rolling. Jack watched and listened as the prosecutor spoke into the bouquet of microphones thrust toward his face.

"Let me say this," said Beckham. "The state's presentation of evidence is complete. It is now up to the grand jury."

A reporter pushed forward. "Mr. Beckham, if the grand jury returns an indictment for first-degree murder, will you be seeking the death penalty?"

"Without question," said Beckham, looking straight into the nearest camera. "As I've said all along, this is a capital case if ever there was one. Thank you all very much."

He broke away from the crowd and headed for the stairwell instead of the elevator, walking right past Jack on the way.

"Thanks for considering my request," said Jack, and he let the prosecutor go up the stairwell alone.

Chapter 20

The package from Abe Beckham landed in Jack's office the next morning.

Federal law referred to it as "Jencks material," so named for the 1957 Supreme Court case that defined the government's initial disclosure requirements in a criminal case. Florida has similar rules, and it was the defense team's first look at the evidence presented to the grand jury. The government was also required to turn over evidence that wasn't presented to the grand jury and that could help the defense. Potentially, it was like Christmas morning; more realistically, like Christmas morning for the kid whose parents didn't get to the store in time to buy the hot new toy. Nonetheless, you open the package, hoping.

"How can I help?" asked Hannah.

They were in the kitchen, the one room in the old house that Jack had left exactly the way it was after Hannah's father passed away. When Jack was a newbie at the Freedom Institute, the vintage-sixties kitchen was not only where lawyers and staff ate their bagged lunches, but it also served as the main (and only) conference room. Hanging on the wall over the old Joe DiMaggio Mr. Coffee machine was the same framed photograph of Bobby Kennedy that had once hung in Neil's dorm room at Harvard. Jack loved that Hannah was filling his shoes.

Jack gave a quick once-over to the stack of banker boxes on the Formica countertop. There would be hours of work ahead of him—if he stayed on the case.

"Let's give it a day or two. See how this plays out."

"See how what plays out?"

Jack had told her about his motion, but Hannah obviously had not given up hope that Jack would change his mind. She was already tearing off box tops, looking for something that piqued her interest and expertise. "What's the name of their fingerprint expert?" she asked, flipping through the printed transcript. "I'll start there."

"Granger, I think," said Jack.

"I'm curious to read his testimony about the extended magazines."

"There were five of them," said Jack. "Thirty rounds apiece."

"What I'm asking is whether Xavier's fingerprints were found on the extended magazines. It's no big deal if his prints are on the gun. His father owned it for twenty years, and he told you he taught his son how to use it, right?"

"Right."

"So we can explain the gun. But if Xavier's fingerprints were found on the extended magazines, that's not so easy to explain. Unless he's the shooter."

"Good point," said Jack. "I don't know if they're on the magazines."

"That's why I'm looking."

Jack's assistant knocked on the doorframe. "You have a call from Judge Martinez's chambers," said Bonnie.

Jack excused himself, went to his office, and picked up the phone on his desk. The judge's assistant was on the line.

"Judge Martinez has scheduled a hearing at four p.m. on your motion to withdraw. Can you please confirm your availability?"

"Yes, I'm available."

"The hearing will be in chambers, not in the courtroom. The judge has granted the request that the hearing be closed to the public."

"I'm sorry, I didn't make that request."

"Ms. Gonzalez did," said the assistant.

"Who?"

"Sylvia Gonzalez. She's an attorney with the National Security Division of the United States Department of Justice. They are opposing your motion to withdraw as counsel."

"Excuse me?"

"That's all I know, sir. Can I tell Judge Martinez you will be here at four o'clock?"

"Yes," said Jack, puzzled. "I'll definitely be there."

Andie was in the field office, working through lunch at her desk, when security called from the main lobby. "Agent Henning, there's a Molly Khoury here to see you."

Her empty stomach filled with pangs of guilt. Andie had always thought of herself as a compassionate person. But Molly was complicated territory. "I'll come down," she said into the phone.

Andie rode the elevator down alone, fairly certain that she knew what this was about. She'd told Jack that he didn't have to withdraw as counsel, but she was happy with his decision. Molly, no doubt, was not.

The elevator doors opened to the lobby, and Andie found Molly seated on the vinyl couch near the window.

Molly rose and greeted her with a pained expression. "I'm so sorry, Andie."

They took a seat on the couch. "Sorry about what?"

"The lawsuit. I heard you got sued."

"No need to apologize," said Andie. "I don't see that as your fault."

"As soon as I heard, I had to come and see you. I want to do the right thing."

"I don't really know what that means, but you don't have to do anything, Molly."

"I know how much you and Jack sacrifice to afford the tuition at Riverside."

"Everybody sacrifices."

"No," said Molly. "They don't."

"Jack and I will figure it out. He's trying to set up a meeting with the school's attorney."

"You've been a good friend, Andie. I don't want you to spend another minute worrying about this." Molly opened her purse, dug out a check, and offered it to Andie, who didn't take it.

"What are you doing?" asked Andie.

"Amir and I want to reimburse you and Jack. For the tuition you have to pay to Riverside."

"No," said Andie. "I can't take your money."

"Please," Molly said, pushing it toward her. "We want you to have it."

"Molly, please," Andie said, rising and taking a step back.

Molly rose, too, but she spilled her purse all over the floor. Andie bent over to help gather the mess, but Molly leaned in the same direction, and they bumped heads. Andie laughed, thinking it comical, but Molly shrieked so loudly that it was anything but funny.

"Molly, are you okay?" Andie asked with concern.

Molly was in obvious pain, and she settled back into the couch holding the side of her head.

"I didn't think we'd bumped that hard," said Andie.

"We didn't," said Molly, wincing. "I have this . . . this thing."

Andie took a seat beside her and looked more closely. The knot on the side of her head, right behind the ear, was as big as a golf ball. It couldn't possibly have been caused by their head-to-head collision. It was purple and already yellowing—not fresh—at least a day old.

"Molly, my God. What happened here?"

"Nothing."

"It's *not* nothing. The last time I saw something like this it turned out to be a fractured skull. Did you get in a car accident?"

"No."

"Fall?"

"Uh-uh."

Andie hesitated, but she had to ask. "Did . . . did someone hit you?"

Molly blinked hard. "It's nothing."

"Molly?"

She zipped up her purse and rose to her feet, leaving the check on the couch. "Please keep it, Andie. It would be the first time money made me happy."

It was the saddest smile Andie had ever seen. She just watched as Molly hurried to the exit.

Chapter 21

A judicial assistant directed the lawyers into Judge Martinez's chambers for the four p.m. hearing.

"Please have a seat," the judge said cordially. He was behind a massive antique desk, directly in front of which stretched a rectangular table in a T-shape configuration. Jack and Hannah Goldsmith were on one side of the table. Beckham and the Justice Department lawyer sat opposite them. A court reporter was the only other person in the chambers, tucked away in the corner between the American flag and a life-sized plastic replica of Sebastian the Ibis, the sports mascot for the University of Miami—"The U"—Judge Martinez's alma mater.

"It isn't every day that I have a lawyer from the

DOJ's National Security Division in my chambers," the judge said.

"It's an unusual and important matter," she said.

"Emphasis on 'unusual,'" said Jack. "Your Honor, I don't see how the federal government has any say as to whether you, a state court judge, should allow me to withdraw as defense counsel in a criminal case prosecuted under state law by our local state attorney."

"Nor do I," said Beckham.

The judge smiled. "Well, Mr. Beckham, not to be cynical, but I can certainly see why you'd want a lawyer of Mr. Swyteck's experience and ability out of the case. But let's hear what the department has to say. Ms. Gonzalez, if you please."

"Your Honor, the federal government is not the outsider to this action that Mr. Swyteck would have this court believe. One of the first things he did as counsel was submit a written request to our office under the Freedom of Information Act."

"Is that true, Mr. Swyteck?"

"Yes," said Jack. "As I'm sure everyone here recalls, within hours of the shooting, the media reported that al-Qaeda claimed responsibility. If that claim is legitimate, my client was obviously radicalized as a juvenile. It's the defense's position that radicalization by a terrorist organization at such a young age is a mitigating factor that should weigh against the death penalty."

"If he's guilty," added Hannah. "It may also be that radicalization will support a plea of not guilty by reason of insanity."

"Got it," the judge said. "So I presume the defense seeks information from the federal government as to the bona fides of al-Qaeda's claim of responsibility."

"Correct," said Jack. "But this issue will be central to the case whether I'm counsel or someone else is counsel. Ms. Goldsmith is prepared to step in as my replacement, and she fully intends to pursue the issue of radicalization."

"Which is exactly why the Department of Justice is here," said Gonzalez.

The judge peered out over the top of his reading glasses. "You're going to have to elaborate, Ms. Gonzalez."

"Happy to," she said. "Ten years after the terrorist attacks of nine-eleven, Mr. Swyteck was appointed to serve as counsel in the case of *Khaled Al-Jawar v. The President of the United States of America*, a habeas corpus proceeding filed in the District of Columbia. Mr. Al-Jawar was a Somali enemy combatant detained at the US Naval Air base in Guantánamo, Cuba."

"No kidding?" said the judge, half smiling. "You're just a veritable box of surprises, aren't you, Mr. Swyteck?"

Gonzalez continued. "The point here is that there is an ongoing investigation into the possible al-Qaeda connection to this school shooting. We recognize that the defendant has a legitimate right to pursue his radicalization defense. To the extent that the federal government is called upon to provide any information relating to 'radicalization,' it is of paramount concern that this information be handled in a way that does not compromise matters of national security."

"So you want Mr. Swyteck to stay on the case?"

"In a word, yes. Mr. Swyteck was thoroughly vetted before he was allowed to travel to Gitmo. He was even more thoroughly vetted before he was allowed to interview witnesses and review classified evidence relating to the accusations that his client sheltered al-Qaeda operatives in East Africa and posed a serious threat to this nation's safety. Simply put, he is no stranger to the NSD, and he has a known track record in litigating a case that raises issues of national security."

"I'm sure Ms. Goldsmith is willing to stipulate to any reasonable protections," said Jack.

"It's not that simple," said Gonzalez. "Mr. Swyteck was even issued 'secret' security clearance under the

Rules of Procedure for the Foreign Intelligence Service Court of Review. That's a small universe."

"I take your point, Ms. Gonzalez," the judge said. "Mr. Swyteck, let me ask you this question. Has your client refused to pay you?"

It wasn't the time to mention his donation to the Lindsey Abrams dance scholarship fund. "It's not an issue of payment, Your Honor."

"Has your client asked you to do something unethical?"

"No. Actually, he won't even talk to me."

"So you're seeking to withdraw because . . ."

Jack didn't want to drag Andie into this. "Personal reasons," said Jack. "Withdrawal is in the best interest of my family."

"Well *boo-hoo*," said the judge. "I'm not going to force Ms. Gonzalez to beg you to stay in this case. You know the rules. Courts frown on the withdrawal of counsel in a criminal case. The stakes are even higher in a capital case. I'm denying the motion to withdraw."

"Thank you, Judge," said Gonzalez.

"Sorry, Mr. Swyteck," the judge said. "You're in for the long haul."

Jack felt a congratulatory kick under the table from Hannah, the footsie version of a high five.

"Understood," said Jack.

Chapter 22

J ack's court-ordered stint as "counsel for life" to Xavier Khoury began the following morning.

It was not Jack's first visit to a mosque. Some years earlier, after back-to-back mass shootings at two New Zealand mosques claimed fifty-one lives, he and Andie had attended an interfaith memorial service for the victims. But this was his first visit to the mosque in Hialeah, Florida—the one attended by Amir Khoury and his sons. Jack's top priority was to find out whether Xavier had fallen in with the wrong people and been radicalized. Talks with Xavier's father had gone nowhere, so the imam seemed like the next logical interview.

"I've never met an imam," said Theo. Theo was with him, wearing his figurative investigator's hat.

"Treat him the way you would any other leader in a place of worship," said Jack. "And keep in mind this is a Sunni mosque. Not Shiite."

"I know there's a difference, but I can't honestly say I know what it is."

Jack probably could have left it at that, but there was no telling what might come out of Theo's mouth. "Just don't mention the Ayatollah."

Theo parked the car on the south side of the mosque, near the minaret, the tower from which the Muslim crier traditionally called worshipers to prayer five times a day. They walked past the restrooms, past the separate women's entrance to the prayer hall, and then entered the administrative offices. Imam Abbas Hassan greeted them and walked them back to his office, making small talk.

"I know Jack is not Muslim. Are you, Mr. Knight?"

"No," said Theo. "But I did get asked to join a Muslim gang when I was in prison."

Jack could have clubbed him.

"That's not really very funny, Mr. Knight."

"No joke," said Theo. "I did time in Florida State Prison, and they asked me to join. So did the Jamaican gang, the Cubans, the Bloods, the Crips, and about a dozen others who wanted the added status of a six-foot-six brother on death row."

"Theo was innocent," said Jack, quickly in damage-control mode. "It's a long story."

"Gangs are not real Muslims," said Hassan. Then he directed them to the armchairs and took a seat behind his desk. His tone was cordial enough, but he was obviously less than pleased about the purpose of Jack's visit.

"Let me say up front that news of the school shooting made my skin crawl," said Hassan. "What in the world would trigger a young man to do something like that? It makes you sick. We reject it."

"That is the question," said Jack. "If Xavier did it, what made him do it?"

"Is there any doubt in your mind as to his guilt, Mr. Swyteck?"

"I'm not at liberty to discuss what's in my mind," said Jack. "I'd like to limit our discussion to facts. Who were Xavier's friends? Who were his contacts?"

The imam listed several boys, and Jack jotted down the names. For the next few minutes, Jack stuck to that format—just the facts, and strictly about Xavier. Then he shifted gears.

"Is Molly Khoury part of your religious community?" asked Jack.

"No. Amir came only with his sons."

"Was she ever?"

"A very short time. She refused to use the women's entrance. Amir and I had a discussion with her, and that frankly is the last time I have ever spoken with her. As far as I know, she is without religion. I'm sure this was not helpful to Xavier's development, spiritual or otherwise."

"Did you talk with Xavier about that?"

"Those conversations are confidential."

"I'm his lawyer."

"I understand. And as soon as Xavier tells me that I can reveal our confidential conversations to his lawyer, we can talk."

"Got it," said Jack.

"Don't misunderstand," said Hassan. "Nothing I know or even heard about Xavier would have made this shooting foreseeable. Our community director already had Xavier's name on the list of singles for our 'Muslim Matches' under-twenty-one icebreakers. I liked Xavier. We all liked him. This is tragic on so many levels."

The imam appeared truly heartbroken. Jack gave him a minute, then continued.

"What do you make of the claim of responsibility by al-Qaeda?" asked Jack.

"My opinion is the same as Amir's. It's fake. Xavier

is from a good family and is part of a solid religious community."

"Do you have any idea why Xavier would have done something like this?"

"None. Why did those boys open fire on their classmates at Columbine? Why did Nikolas Cruz kill all those children at Parkland? Those school shootings had nothing to do with Islamic terrorism. Neither does this. This was a Muslim boy who lost his way in a world that sometimes loses its mind. Not a Muslim boy who was radicalized by his religious community to kill in the name of Islam."

Hassan checked his watch. "I'm sorry, but I have an appointment, and I cannot be late."

"One quick thing," said Jack. "Did Xavier ever mention to you a young woman named Maritza?"

Hassan's expression soured. "I met this Maritza. Xavier brought her to services once or twice. He was quite taken with her."

"You don't seem to approve."

"Not for the reason Xavier thought. She told him that I was opposed to their dating because Maritza was Hispanic. That's not true. In fact, Hispanics are one of the fastest-growing demographics in conversions to Islam."

"I did not know that."

"People forget that Spain has had a large Muslim population for over a thousand years." He checked his watch again, then rose. "I really must be going."

"Sorry," said Jack, "but I have to ask: What was it about Maritza that made her so wrong for Xavier?"

The imam drew a breath, as if reluctant to say. "She's a prostitute."

Jack bristled. "Let's not get into name-calling."

"I'm not calling anyone names. She has sex with men for money. She's a prostitute. A lady of the night. Whatever you wish to call it."

It took Jack a second to comprehend. "How do you know that?"

"Ask her. She'll tell you."

"All right," said Jack. "I will."

Chapter 23

Jack was eager to speak with Maritza at the coffee shop, but it would have to wait. He had a two p.m. meeting with Duncan Fitz, the attorney for Riverside Day School in the lawsuit against Andie. Theo drove to Fitz's office on prestigious Brickell Avenue, while Jack rode in the passenger seat, preparing for the meeting.

Theo glanced over from the driver's seat. "What's that famous saying from Abraham Lincoln about a lawyer and his client?"

"'A lawyer who represents himself has a fool for a client.'"

"No, I mean the other one. 'A lawyer who represents his wife is just a fucking lunatic.'"

"I don't think Lincoln actually said that."

"He would have, if Mary Todd had asked him to defend her."

"Hannah will be representing Andie if this case goes forward. This is my one and only shot to see if I can make this go away."

Fitz was the senior litigation counsel at the Miami office of one of the world's largest law firms, Coolidge, Harding & Cash—"Cool Cash," as it was known in the power circles, since every one of its equity partners in seventeen different offices across the globe drew a seven-figure bonus year in and year out. Fitz's typical client was a Fortune 500 company, not a private day school, but his three children had attended Riverside Day School, so Jack assumed he was personally invested in the case against Andie.

"You nervous?" asked Theo, as they rode up alone in the elevator.

"Why should I be nervous?"

"He's a son of a bitch. One of his lawyers stopped in my bar to drown his sorrows. Fitz fired him for missing a conference call to be in the delivery room for the birth of his son."

Jack had heard worse. Fitz actually bragged about his creative approach to settling a "bad drug" case brought by a retired police officer, Gilbert Jones, who was permanently disabled by a weight-loss medication that the pharmaceutical company knew was dangerous. "Mr. Jones, it will take you five years to get this case to trial and through all appeals. You can wait that long for your money or we can end this today. Before you, on this table, are three briefcases. One contains a check for three million dollars, your lawyer's latest settlement demand. One contains fifty thousand dollars in cash, my client's latest settlement offer. The third contains nothing. Think of me as Howie Mandel, and I'm giving you one chance to bring this lawsuit—and the wait for your money—to an immediate end. Deal? Or no deal?"

Gilbert walked out with nothing. The lawyers spent the next two years litigating whether the "settlement" was an illegal form of gambling.

"Mr. Fitz will see you now," the receptionist said. Theo waited in the lobby as Jack followed Fitz's assistant to her boss's corner office on the forty-second floor. Fitz had a drop-dead view of downtown Miami to the north and the blue-green waters of the bay to the east. Jack could almost see his house on Key Biscayne in the distance.

"I've heard a lot about you, Jack."

With lawyers of Fitz's generation there was the usual chitchat about Jack's father, former governor Harry Swyteck, with the added twist of how much money

Cool Cash and Duncan Fitz personally had contributed to Harry's gubernatorial elections back in the day. Then the conversation turned even closer to home.

"Andie doesn't deserve this," said Jack.

"We'll see what the judge says."

"I was hoping to stop this case from getting that far."

Fitz chuckled. "What do you want me to do? Take a voluntary dismissal?"

"Yes," Jack said in a serious voice. "If the Board of Trustees is unhappy about my decision to represent Xavier Khoury, this lawsuit is not going to change anything. I filed a motion to withdraw as counsel. The court denied it."

"Is that what you think? That we filed this lawsuit to bully you into withdrawing?"

"The thought crossed my mind."

"Erase the thought," said Fitz. "This is a simple breach-of-contract action. All families execute a binding agreement to abide by the Riverside's rules and procedures. Your wife breached that agreement."

"Then let's address this on a business level. We will agree to leave the school quietly. The school waives its right to tuition for the rest of the school year."

"That hardly leaves my client whole," said Fitz. "Riverside Day School is a not-for-profit institution. The Board of Trustees approves its annual budget based on the number of tuitions coming from enrolled students. Even if one of those students leaves, the school still depends on that tuition to meet its operations."

"You'll find another family to step in. The waiting list to get in to Riverside Day School is as long as my arm."

Fitz shook his head. "That waiting list has evaporated into thin air."

Jack had heard the rumors. "So what people are saying online is true?"

"I wouldn't know what is being said online," said Fitz.

"The buzz is that Riverside is in panic mode. They think families are going to pull out in droves and demand a tuition refund."

"That's a legitimate fear," said Fitz. "Any reasonable parent might ask himself or herself, 'Do I want to pay top dollar to send my child to a school that will forever be linked to a massacre like this one?'"

The lightbulb switched on for Jack. "Now I get it. The Board of Trustees is making an example out of us. The message to the school community is this: every family—even the ones we *kick out* of this school—will be held to their contract for the full amount of annual tuition."

"Plus payment of my attorneys' fees. Which I believe are in the neighborhood of twenty-eight thousand dollars. *Twenty-nine*, once I bill for this meeting."

Fitz rose from his desk chair and offered a handshake, which Jack ignored.

"I can't dismiss the case, Jack. I'm sure you understand."

"I'm trying to," said Jack, leaving the office with the firm impression that everything he'd heard about Duncan Fitz was true—and then some.

"Let's get out of here," he said, as he blew past Theo in the lobby. In five minutes they were down the elevator and in the car. It took another five just to get out of the parking garage and into the stop-and-go traffic of Brickell Avenue, the heart of Miami's Financial District. Jack had no desire to move his office downtown, but it was a beautiful afternoon, and the reflection of palm trees and sunshine against Brickell's glass towers made him long for the old convertible he'd swapped out for life with Andie, Righley, and a golden retriever named Max, who had no idea he was a dog.

"You want me to drop you at your office?" asked Theo.

"Stop by San Lazaro's Café first," said Jack. "I have a few pointed questions for Maritza."

The drive to the coffee shop was just long enough for Jack to call Andie and give her the highs and low, mostly lows, of his meeting at Cool Cash. She took it as well as could be expected, and Jack assured her that Hannah was a pit bull, every bit the match for Duncan Fitz.

Theo found a parking spot next to the one for the Employee of the Month. Jack led the way inside to the booth in the back where he'd met Maritza. Theo's head covered half the map of Cuba. A server approached.

"Is Maritza here today?" asked Jack.

The server suddenly seemed flustered. "Uhm. Maritza? Uh . . . one second."

Jack and Theo exchanged puzzled looks as she walked away.

"Did you see that face she made?" asked Jack.

"That was weird, dude."

The manager appeared a moment later, the same one Jack had met the day before. "You were asking about Maritza?"

"Yeah, I was here yesterday. We talked over her break."

"I remember."

"Is she here?" asked Jack.

"No."

"When will she be back?"

"That's impossible to say. Probably never."

"Do you know where she is now?"

"I'm guessing she's on an airplane to Mexico City. ICE was here yesterday. I'm told she has been deported."

"She was illegal?" asked Jack, though it was more of a reflex than an inquiry.

"Look, I don't know all the details, and I have a café to run. Do you fellas want to buy some coffee? If not, I'd like to turn this table."

"I'd like an espresso," said Theo.

"I'll send your server," said the manager, and he stepped away.

"What do you make of that?" asked Jack.

"It's like the old joke," said Theo. "What's worse than a prostitute for an alibi? A deported prostitute."

"Never heard that one," said Jack.

"A moldy oldie, I call it."

Jack considered how quickly he'd lost his potential alibi witness after mere mention of her to the prosecution. "I call it a little too convenient for coincidence."

Chapter 24

"Is it safe?" asked Righley.

The question cut to Jack's core. He was leaning over her shoulder at the kitchen table, cutting her toasted waffle—"No black stuff on the edges, Daddy"—into bite-sized pieces on her breakfast plate. Righley was dressed in a blue skirt and white polo shirt, the mandatory uniform of her new school. It was the family's morning routine. Andie got her up and dressed. Jack took Max outside to do his morning business and made Righley breakfast. They'd followed the same routine when Righley was at Riverside Day School, but there was a twist of late, with Righley asking the same question she'd asked every morning since day one at Key Biscayne K through 8.

Is it safe?

"Yes, sweetie. It's safe, it's fun, and you're going to learn so much there." Jack was sure of it. Then again, hadn't every parent at Riverside Day School made the same promise to their children just by virtue of sending them off to school each morning?

Max jumped up on his hind legs, front paws on the tabletop, and licked the syrup from Righley's chin. She laughed the way every child should laugh. There was nothing like an eighty-pound golden retriever licking your face to make you feel safe.

Righley finished her waffle in what seemed like record time, though Jack suspected that Max had claimed more than his fair share. Andie entered the kitchen.

"Ready, Righley?"

Righley looked at Max. "Ready?"

The real winner in the new routine was Max. The best thing about Righley's new school was that it was close enough to walk. The downside was that, with fourteen hundred students, Key Biscayne's K through 8 enrollment was almost triple Riverside's K through 12, which was precisely the reason Jack and Andie had stretched their wallet to send Righley to Riverside in the first place. Andie affixed Max's leash and took Righley's hand. Jack kissed them all good-bye, and the threesome was out the door. He topped off his go-cup with hot coffee and glanced at the newspaper on the kitchen counter. The remaining memorial services for victims of the Riverside shooting were scheduled for the coming week. Jack wondered if his name would come up. He grabbed his computer bag, jumped in the car, and headed across the bridge to Doral.

Most people who'd heard of Doral thought of the legendary Blue Monster golf course, home to PGA events for over fifty years and host to virtually every great player in the sport. Doral was also home to the Forensic Services Bureau of the Miami-Dade Police Department. Jack was pushing Xavier's case forward as fast as possible, and at the top of his priority list was the deposition of the state's fingerprint expert. At nine a.m. Jack was in a windowless conference room, and the stage was set. Jack was on one side of the rectangular table. Abe Beckham was on the other. The witness was seated at the head of the table next to the court reporter. It was Jack's deposition, so he was asking the questions.

"Good morning, Dr. Granger," said Jack, beginning much in the same way he would at trial, eliciting the witness's background and qualifications. Granger was a skinny fellow, mostly bald, save for an exceedingly long wisp of hair that attached at what was formerly his hairline, reached back over his shiny scalp, and disappeared somewhere behind his right ear. It was the gray and self-grown version of the hair extensions that Riverside mothers paid ridiculous sums of money to have taped to their heads, only to lose them in a tennis match or a windy convertible. Granger had a nervous habit of pushing his wisp into place once every minute or so, though it wasn't readily apparent to Jack what was "in place" as opposed to "out of place." That aside, there was no challenging Granger's expertise in his field. He held a PhD and had served as chief of the MDPD Forensic Bureau's Latent Unit for almost fifteen years.

"What is the primary function of the Latent Unit?" asked Jack.

"We evaluate physical evidence from crime scenes for the presence of latent prints through friction ridge analysis."

"What is a friction ridge?"

He used his own hand as a prop. "On the palm side of our hands and on the soles of our feet are prominent skin features that single us out from everyone else in the world. These so-called friction ridges leave impressions when they come into contact with an object. The impressions from the last finger joints are known as fingerprints."

"What is a latent fingerprint?"

"Let me back up a second," said Granger, pushing

the wisp of hair back into place. "There are two different types of friction ridge impressions. The first are of known individuals recorded for a specific purpose, like the prints that you gave to the Florida Bar when you became a member, or that your client gave to the police when he was arrested. The second type involves impressions of unknown persons on a piece of evidence from a crime scene or related location. These are generally referred to as latent prints."

"Did you analyze latent fingerprints recovered from the crime scene at Riverside Day School?"

"I did."

"On what piece of evidence were those fingerprints found?"

"From the weapon that was recovered on the scene."

Jack put the next question with some trepidation, as it was a key issue that he and Hannah had focused on. "Were any latent prints found on the extended magazines recovered from the crime scene?"

"No."

"None?" asked Jack.

"No. My assumption is that the shooter wiped those magazines clean after purchasing them, probably with alcohol, and thereafter handled them only with gloves, like the gloves the shooter was wearing in the surveillance video I watched."

It was the kind of long-winded and speculative answer that Jack would have shut down at trial, but he was interested in hearing the expert's assumptions in a discovery deposition.

Jack handed the witness a photograph of the pistol. "Dr. Granger, this photograph is marked as Grand Jury Exhibit Ninety-Two and was produced to us by the state of Florida. Is it your testimony that the only latent fingerprints you examined are those found on this weapon?"

"That is my testimony."

"Were you able to identify any of the fingerprints found on this pistol?"

"Yes. We identified several prints from the gun's registered owner, Mr. Amir Khoury. And one print from the defendant, Xavier Khoury."

"Using the photograph, could you please point to the exact location of these fingerprints?"

"I'd rather use the diagram I prepared," said Granger. "It's in my report."

Jack located it, and reasked the question. Granger first identified the location of Amir's fingerprints, which were not important. "Where did you find Xavier Khoury's fingerprint?" asked Jack.

"There was only one print. It was the right index finger. Found here," said Granger, pointing to the diagram, "on the top of the barrel near the fixed sight."

"Your examination of Mr. Khoury's fingerprint was done in accordance with best practices, correct, Doctor?"

"Of course."

"Consistent with the exercise of best practices, what conclusion did you reach as to the age of Xavier Khoury's fingerprint that was found on the pistol?"

Granger looked puzzled—so puzzled that he pushed the wisp of gray hair back into place when, as far as Jack could tell, it wasn't even out of place. "The age?" he asked.

"Yeah," said Jack. "How long had Xavier's fingerprint been on the gun?"

"I didn't reach any conclusion in that regard," said Granger.

"Why not?"

"There's no reliable scientific test to determine the age of a fingerprint. We can only deduce it from circumstantial or anecdotal evidence."

"How would you deduce the age of a fingerprint?"

"For example, if a latent print is lifted from a newspaper dated June first, twenty-nineteen, you know the fingerprint isn't older than that."

"Let's keep our focus on the weapon at issue in this case. Is there such a way to 'deduce' the age of Xavier Khoury's fingerprint?"

"Not in our lab. The Netherlands Forensic Institute

has made progress on a technique that can be used on fresh fingerprints—prints less than fifteen days old. They claim that their technique can pin it down to within a day or two."

"The fingerprints from the weapon found in this case were not examined by the Netherlands Forensic Institute, were they, Doctor?"

"No."

"As far as you know, Dr. Granger, my client's fingerprint could have been a day old?"

"Yes."

"A week?"

"Yes."

"A month?"

"Sure."

"A year?"

"When you start talking years, then it becomes a question of whether the print really could have lasted that long. That all depends on the surface, the firmness of the imprint, and other factors, including the salinity of a person's skin. On porous surfaces, like paper, fingerprints can last forty years."

"What about a gun like the one used in the Riverside shooting? How long?"

"I'm going to object," said Beckham. "That's pure speculation."

There was no judge at a deposition, but the prosecutor had the right to make his objections for the record. Clearly, Beckham didn't like the point Jack was making—that the only time Xavier had ever handled this gun was *years* before anyone had planned the school shooting.

"Let me rephrase," said Jack. "Are you aware of any studies regarding the recovery of latent prints some number of years after those prints were impressed on a firearm?"

"I've read a number of excellent studies. For one, Sheffield Hallam University developed a technique to recover latent marks from spent casings using an electrolysis process. They've examined spent casings and weapons up to twenty years old, in various states of decay, and recovered latent prints that are legally admissible in a court of law."

"In our case, Mr. Khoury's gun is more than twenty years old," said Jack. "In theory, the fingerprints you recovered from Amir and Xavier Khoury could be that old, correct?"

"Not Xavier's. He's only eighteen. And in my opinion the size of the impression indicates that his hands were fully grown."

"So the most your report can say is that Xavier laid a finger on his father's gun sometime after he went through puberty. Say, sometime in the last three or four years."

"Objection," said Beckham. "Dr. Granger has already testified that there is no test to confirm the age of a fingerprint."

"You can answer," Jack told the witness. "Xavier touched his father's gun sometime in the last three or four years. That's all you can say, right?"

"It could have been that long ago."

"And for the same reasons, Mr. Khoury's print could be twenty or more years old, correct?"

"Yes," said Granger. "And the same goes for the unidentified print."

Jack did a double take. It never ceased to amaze him the way smart people couldn't resist showing off how much they knew, even if it helped the other side. It took all of Jack's professional discipline to contain his excitement.

"Dr. Granger, I've read your report. I didn't see any mention of an *unidentified* latent fingerprint on the murder weapon."

"It's not in my report."

"Why not?"

"Additional tests are being run to identify it."

"Where was this unidentified fingerprint found?"

"On the inside of the pistol's slide. I'm not a ballistics expert, but a pistol doesn't have an exposed barrel the way a revolver does. The barrel is inside the slide. So, for a print to be found inside the slide, the firearm must have been disassembled for cleaning, maintenance, gun-safety training—whatever the reason."

"Let me make sure I understand," said Jack. "You've been unable to link this latent fingerprint to any known individual, correct?"

"Correct."

"But you have concluded that this fingerprint *does not* belong to either Amir Khoury or Xavier Khoury."

"Objection," said Beckham. "That was not Dr. Granger's testimony. Your question fails to account for the fact that the impression could have been blurred or smudged, which prevented Dr. Granger from concluding that it belonged to either Xavier or Amir Khoury."

"Is that the case, Dr. Granger?" asked Jack. "Or is the prosecutor putting words in your mouth?"

"I object to that remark," said Beckham.

Jack tightened his gaze, as well as his figurative grip, on the witness. "Dr. Granger, there was nothing wrong with the quality of the fingerprint you were unable to identify, was there?"

"No," Granger said, too much of a professional to mince words. "Actually, it's of even higher quality than the latent print of Xavier Khoury. It oxidized into the metal, which can happen with certain types of firearms or casings."

"In other words, if this fingerprint did, in fact, belong to Xavier or his father, the print was of sufficient quality for you to make that determination. And you ruled them out. Correct?"

He paused, not because he didn't know the answer, but because he seemed to appreciate the gravity of his admission. "That is true. The unidentified print does not belong to either Xavier or his father. As a forensic scientist, I'm certain of that much."

"Thank you, Doctor," said Jack, and he was happy to end it right there.

Chapter 25

On Thursday Jack paid another visit to the Miami-Dade Pretrial Detention Center. It was a standing appointment with his client. Sort of.

Jack was fed up with the silent treatment from Xavier. He wanted to talk about Maritza, but the emphasis was on *talk*. So Jack had written his client a letter about his meeting with Maritza and said, "Let's have a real conversation." He'd made it abundantly clear that it would not be another session of Jack talking and Xavier listening. "I will come to the lobby every day at 10 a.m. and wait five minutes. If you're ready to *talk to me*, have the guard send me up." A week had passed, and with each visit Jack had come and gone in five minutes with no word from Xavier or the guard.

On a Thursday, fifteen days after the shooting, Jack's conditions were met.

"Your client will see you, Swyteck," the guard told him.

Jack felt optimistic as he rode up the elevator with the guard. Progress, it seemed, was being made. Xavier was waiting for him in the attorney-client meeting room, seated in a chair at the table with his arms folded across his chest. No shackles this time, and no bruises about the face, which Jack took as a sign of Xavier's adjustment to life behind bars, the most important aspect of which was learning how to stay out of trouble. Jack waited for the guard to close the door on his way out. He then pulled up a chair, turned it around backwards, and sat rodeo-style, facing his client.

"Ready to have a conversation?" asked Jack.

Xavier said nothing.

"I know you can speak," said Jack. "The guard told me he heard you praying in your cell this morning."

Jack waited, but it was back to the old routine. Nothing from Xavier.

"You did read my letter, right?" said Jack.

Xavier lowered his gaze, breaking eye contact.

"We had a deal," said Jack. "I offered to come up here if you agreed to talk. You accepted that offer. Now it's time to honor your end of the bargain."

Xavier drew a deep breath and let it out. But no words followed.

It was frustrating, but Jack had dealt with worse. A client who wouldn't talk was probably better than a client who lied constantly or threatened to kill you. Jack had to change strategies.

"Here's my dilemma," said Jack. "The defense has a legal obligation to tell the prosecution if there will be an alibi witness. I also have a legal obligation not to put a witness on the stand who I know is lying. I'm not going to spin my wheels trying to track down Maritza if my own client tells me she's lying." Jack leaned a little closer. "Is she lying, Xavier?"

Again, no reply.

"I think she is," said Jack. "And I think you're the shooter. What do you have to say about that?"

Xavier lifted his gaze and looked at Jack, but that was the extent of his reaction.

"Let's put my opinions aside," said Jack. "This may sound a little far afield to you, but I want to tell you this story. It's about an ol' friend of mine from college. Ray married his college sweetheart and started a family long before I did. He has a grown daughter now who's fantastic. Ray had a son, too. Jason was his name. He died when he was seventeen. Suicide."

Xavier shifted in his chair, clearly listening.

"Jason was a lot like you. Good-looking boy. Excellent student. You were accepted to MIT; I think Jason was headed for Cal Poly or some other top engineering school. Jason never had a girlfriend, though, until his senior year of high school. He was nuts about her, his dad told me. Then she dumped him. Jason was devastated. As much as his dad tried to help him through it, Jason just couldn't get over it. So one Saturday night when his parents went out on their weekly date night, Jason grabbed the keys to his car, closed the garage door, rolled down the car windows, and started the engine. Two hours later his father found him slumped over in the front seat. Jason was gone.

"Terrible story, I know. What his dad can't get over is that Jason didn't want to die. He knows that because Jason recorded a video on his cell phone while he was fading away inside the car. Jason was professing his love to this girl who had dumped him. His dad says that every psychiatrist and health-care professional who watched that video and heard Jason's last words reached the same conclusion. Not only did Jason not *want* to die. He didn't even believe that he was *going to die.* Jason had cooked up this fantasy in his head that his parents would come home from dinner, find him, and rush him to the hospital. And when the doctors revived him and he came to, this girl who had dumped him would be standing at his bedside, and she'd throw her arms around him, kiss him, and say, *Oh, Jason, you really do love me!*"

Jack gave his client a minute to absorb the story, and then continued.

"Like I said, Xavier. I think you did it. But for one moment, let's step into that alternative world of possibilities, the one percent chance you're innocent. Is all of this some kind of romantic fantasy for you? You sit in this room in silence, not helping yourself, not letting me help you. Do you have a tortured vision in your head of this case going all the way to trial, all the way to the *last day* of trial, and it looks like you're going to be convicted and sentenced to death? Then let me guess. Suddenly the doors in the back of the courtroom swing open, and in walks Maritza. She tells the jury that she loves you and that the two of you were making passionate love all morning while the real shooter was murdering innocent students across town at Riverside Day School. You and Maritza lock eyes from across the courtroom, the two of you unable to comprehend another minute apart from each other. Maritza saves you from the needle, and the two of you live happily ever after.

"Is that the game you're playing, Xavier?"

All expression drained from Xavier's face. He was a complete blank.

"I hope not," said Jack, "because that is not going to happen. If you don't open up and talk to me, this is not going to end well for you. I speak from experience. I'm not bragging, but I'm highly regarded in this unpleasant line of work in capital cases. Even so, I have more dead former clients than living ones."

Jack waited, hoping that the weight of his story hanging in silence between them would impel a response. But the ticking seconds turned to minutes, and Xavier said nothing. Jack had one last card to play.

"I spoke with Imam Hassan from your mosque," said Jack. "He told me that he met Maritza."

Xavier didn't deny it, but given the track record, it was impossible to infer an admission from silence. So Jack dropped the bomb.

"He said Maritza was a prostitute."

Jack waited. A slow but steady transformation was underway, right before Jack's eyes. Something at a very primal level was churning inside Xavier, not just in his mind but throughout his entire body, as if those little bubbles that form in a pot of water on the stove were rising ever faster. Xavier didn't speak, but Jack thought he saw him mouth the word *prostitute*—and the pot boiled over. Xavier sprang from his chair, roiling mad, as fifteen days of self-imposed silence erupted from his molten core. He grabbed the chair and threw it across the room, smashing it against the wall.

"Xavier!" Jack shouted.

The door burst open, and two guards rushed in. Xavier was about to slam the table against the wall when the guards tackled him, pinned him facedown on the floor, and cuffed his wrists behind his back.

"Don't resist!" the guard shouted, and Xavier's body went limp.

The other guard checked on Jack. "Are you all right?"

"I'm fine," said Jack.

The guards lifted Xavier from the floor and took him toward the door.

"Wait," said Jack.

They stopped, but only the guards glanced back at Jack. Xavier kept his head down, facing the exit. His anger seemed to be under control.

"We'll talk again, Xavier," said Jack.

"Maybe when he gets out of disciplinary confinement," said the guard.

Xavier was silent, but fully compliant, as the corrections officers took him away.

Chapter 26

On Friday Jack was again before Judge Martinez—without Xavier, who was in day two of ten days of disciplinary confinement for his violent outburst. Hannah was at the defense table with Jack. Abe Beckham, on behalf of the state of Florida, and Sylvia Gonzalez, for the Justice Department, shared the prosecutor's table to Jack's right. The proceeding was open to the public, and several rows of seating behind the lawyers were filled with friends and family of the victims. They were almost outnumbered by the media.

"Good morning," said Judge Martinez. "We are here on Mr. Swyteck's motion, is that correct?"

Jack rose. "That's correct, Your Honor."

The judge flipped through the file before him, reading. "The defendant seeks an order of the court compelling the production of all evidence, including forensic reports, concerning an unidentified fingerprint found on the firearm allegedly used in the shooting at Riverside Day School."

"The defense also subpoenaed the federal government to produce any similar records," said Jack.

"Which the National Security Division of the Department of Justice opposes," said Gonzalez, rising.

Beckham rose. "I can simplify matters, Judge. The state of Florida has no objection to turning over whatever records it has in its possession. But the National Security Division has asked us not to."

"On what basis?" the judge asked.

"I'll defer to Ms. Gonzalez on that point," said Beckham.

"National security, Your Honor," said Gonzalez.

The judge threw up his hands, looking at Jack. "Mr. Swyteck, you need to enforce your subpoena against the federal government in federal court in Washington, DC. Not here."

"And I will," said Jack. He stepped to the podium, taking charge. "Your Honor, I'm before you today because the existence of an unidentified fingerprint on the murder weapon clearly raises questions as to the guilt or innocence of my client. The prosecution has an obligation to turn over to the defense all exculpatory evidence. If Mr. Beckham has that information, this court has the power to, and should, order the state of Florida to give it to me. Whether the federal government must give me that information is an argument for another day in another courthouse. But my client has a right to have whatever Mr. Beckham has in his possession."

"I think I understand the issue Mr. Swyteck is raising," the judge said, "and it's an interesting one."

Gonzalez spoke up. "Yes, Judge, it's an interesting issue for a law professor to research for two years before publishing some bleeding-heart article in a highbrow academic journal."

"It goes to the heart of my client's constitutional right to a fair trial," Jack fired back. "Can the prosecutor withhold vital evidence simply because the NSD tells him that handing it over to the defense would be contrary to the interests of national security? The answer has to be no."

"I agree with Mr. Swyteck to a point," the judge said. "Evidence of an unidentified print on the murder weapon is vital evidence. But there has to be a balance of interests. Ms. Gonzalez, exactly what is the national security interest here?"

Gonzalez glanced over her shoulder at the crowded gallery. Members of the media were literally on the edge of their seats. "Judge, I would ask the courtroom be closed for my response to that question."

A chorus of groans coursed through the gallery.

"Everyone keep your seats," the judge said. "Counsel, let's do this in my chambers."

The judge stepped down, and the lawyers followed. There were no assigned seats, but everyone took exactly the same seats as the last hearing in chambers. Ivan the life-sized Ibis hadn't moved.

"Ms. Gonzalez, let's hear it," said the judge.

"The short answer is that al-Qaeda claimed responsibility for this shooting," said Gonzalez. "That claim is being taken very seriously, and there is an active investigation underway involving multiple agencies. The information sought by Mr. Swyteck goes to the heart of that investigation."

"That's it?" asked the judge. "That's your explanation?"

"That's all I'm at liberty to reveal."

"Ms. Gonzalez, I closed this hearing to the public at your request so that you would be free to convince me that a vital national security interest is at stake. This is your opportunity."

"Your Honor, I'm limited as to what I can say by NSD policies, as well as specific orders entered in this investigation by the FISA Court."

"FISA" was her shorthand reference to the Foreign Intelligence Surveillance Court, which entertains government requests for approval of electronic surveillance, physical search, and other investigative actions for foreign intelligence purposes.

Jack needed to jump in—with both feet. "Your Honor, the government is talking out of both sides of its mouth. Two weeks ago, Ms. Gonzalez opposed my request to withdraw as counsel because I could be trusted to handle sensitive information. Now it's her position that she can't even tell *you* what national security interest is at stake."

"I do recall your saying that, Ms. Gonzalez," the judge said.

Gonzalez hesitated, then replied. "I can tell the court this much. There is a vital national security interest. It is to prevent more terrorist attacks, possibly more school shootings. On behalf of the United States Department of Justice, I'm asking you *not* to be the state court judge who derailed a federal investigation that could have stopped another school shooting."

Gonzalez had the judge thinking, and Jack had to hand it to her: Gonzalez didn't practice regularly in Miami, but she knew exactly the right argument to make in a state where trial judges are elected and can't survive bad press.

"Well, the safety of our schoolchildren is certainly a vital interest," Judge Martinez said.

Jack repackaged his argument on the fly, knowing that he would never get this judge to side with the defense on the issue as reframed by the government. "Judge, I don't want to be the *lawyer* who derailed this investigation, either. But I'm also fighting for my client's life, and apart from the fact that he has not yet been adjudicated guilty, there's something important that's being overlooked."

"Tell me," the judge said.

"The very existence of the unidentified print only came to my attention because I elicited the information while deposing the government's fingerprint expert. That's not the way the process is supposed to work. The existence of that print should have been disclosed to the defense immediately. I'm not sure Mr. Beckham would have *ever* told me about it if his own witness had not let the cat out of the bag. That's a clear violation of the government's disclosure obligations."

Beckham was in the hot seat, and Jack's read of the situation was that he could pull one of two pages from the time-honored, unwritten prosecutor's manual: the Aw-shucks-Judge-I'm-sorry page, or the When-dead-wrong-become-indignant page.

Beckham chose the latter. "For a second there, Judge,

I thought Mr. Swyteck was serious when he said he was interested in saving innocent lives. I certainly am. The NSD told me to treat the unidentified print as a matter of national security, so I did."

Jack caught Gonzalez's eye from across the table, and apparently it was enough to get her to do the right thing. "Your Honor, if I may clarify the communication?"

"Please do."

"I asked Mr. Beckham to treat as confidential all matters relating to the identity or possible identity of the person whose fingerprint was found on the gun. The mere *existence* of an unidentified print is, by itself, not a matter of national security and will not compromise the investigation."

Beckham shrank in his chair, and Jack could almost see him shift gears and reach for the "aw shucks" page in the unwritten prosecutor's manual. "Oh, well, my mistake, Your Honor. I'm terribly sorry. It won't happen again. Just an honest miscommunication."

Judge Martinez, too, had apparently "read" the manual and was completely on to him. "It had better not happen again, Mr. Beckham. Because if this had happened closer to trial, I could very well be entering an order dismissing the indictment. Understood?"

"Yes, Your Honor."

"Has this court addressed everything?" the judge asked.

"For now," said Jack.

"Then we're adjourned. Thank you, Counsel."

The lawyers rose, and Beckham was the first one out the door. Jack caught up with Gonzalez in the hallway outside the judge's chambers.

"Thank you for that, Sylvia."

"You're welcome," she said.

"I hope you won't take this as ingratitude, but I do plan to file a motion in federal court. I need to know whose fingerprint is on that gun."

"I would expect no less from you, Jack."

"See you soon," he said.

She just smiled and was on her way.

Chapter 27

Xavier waited on the bench for the corrections officer to come.

The incident on Friday had cost him two nights in solitary confinement. Unlike the guy in the cell next to him, who'd kept howling like a wounded wolf, Xavier had behaved himself. So he was being moved from solitary to a shared cell, though still in disciplinary confinement. Apparently, it was taking longer than planned to find an open bunk. No shortage of badasses at the Miami-Dade Pretrial Detention Center.

Xavier was on week three as a Level One detainee, and things weren't getting any better. He'd felt untethered from reality the minute he'd set foot in the building. No wristwatch. No cell phone. No talking allowed. Those first few hours had been a blur, but in slow motion. Up and down several flights of stairs. In and out of different holding pens. He'd been shackled, unshackled, and shackled again. The body search had been especially memorable, not so much for what actually had happened, but for fear of what might. Fingerprinting took another hour. Not even the prisoner's obligatory "one phone call" had gone smoothly. Xavier had waited in line for an hour and was reaching for the phone when another inmate came up from behind him and whispered a threat into his ear. "Tanks for holdin' my spot in line, mon—now get the fuck away from me." It had been just as well. Even local calls were collect only, and probably no one would have accepted Xavier's charges anyway.

"Got a bunk for you," said the guard. "Let's go."

Xavier rode up the elevator flanked by a pair of corrections officers. The doors opened to the disciplinary cellblock, where a third officer completed the disciplinary check-in procedures. It had taken so long for a bed to free up that it was already "lights out." The cells were dark, but the long corridor remained lighted. The guards escorted Xavier past one locked door after another until they stopped at cell number 511.

"You're bunking with Roosevelt," the guard said. "It's your lucky day."

Xavier had no idea who Roosevelt was, but the way

the other guard snickered at the "lucky day" comment, it was a safe bet he was no relation to the former presidents.

Maybe I should've stayed in solitary.

The cell door buzzed open. The guards removed the shackles. Xavier entered quietly, trying not to disturb Roosevelt on the top bunk as he climbed onto the mattress below. The metal frame squeaked as he settled in. The cell door closed, and then it hit him. This was no ordinary inmate. He was locked in a cell with a man who was being punished for breaking the rules. Maybe it was his imagination running wild, but Xavier quickly convinced himself that Roosevelt had done something far worse than throw a chair against the wall.

"Hey, you that shooter, ain't you, pretty boy?"

Apparently, Roosevelt had only pretended to be asleep. Xavier kept quiet, hoping his cellmate would let it drop. No such luck.

"Yeah, you is. I saw you walk in. Shooter is a fuckin' pretty boy."

Xavier lay still, praying for silence. It was dark. It was scary. His pillow stank so bad that he wanted to throw it on the floor. Maybe Roosevelt had sprinkled it with toilet juice: the joke's on the pretty boy.

A minute later, Roosevelt's voice again pierced the darkness. "Wanna know somethin', pretty boy? You is better off with the death penalty. You get yo' own private cell on death row. Takes years to move on down the line to the gurney. And when you finally get there, you lay down, take a needle in the arm, and go to sleep. That don't sound so bad, does it?"

Xavier didn't answer.

"But a life sentence?" he said, chuckling. "Shit. You in the general population, pretty boy. You understand what I'm sayin'? If you take the needle, you get stuck once. But if you in the general population—shit, a pretty boy like you? You get stuck every night."

Xavier had already gone down that line of thinking, many times, since his arrest.

"You don't talk, huh?" asked Roosevelt. "I get it. You afraid to open your mouth. You don't have to worry, pretty boy. You can open your mouth. I ain't gonna stick my dick down your throat.

"Not tonight."

Xavier froze. This was the first of ten disciplinary nights with Roosevelt. Xavier could ask for a transfer to another cell, but he could end up with worse. Or his request could easily be denied. Either way, he'd need to state the reason for the request, and he'd have to tell the guard that Roosevelt threatened him. Then Xavier wouldn't just be the "pretty boy." He'd also be a snitch who needed to be taught a lesson. "Snitch bitch" was what the other inmates had called that guy in the shower who was down on his knees.

Roosevelt was right. The needle was preferable.

"Hey, pretty boy," said Roosevelt. "I'm gonna do you a favor."

Xavier felt a chill down his spine. Did he mean *sexual* favor?

"Listen good," said Roosevelt. "I don't do this for everyone. And you don't even have to thank me. Just listen real careful to what I'm saying. Then take the time you need to think it over. And while you thinkin', be sure to pay attention to the schedule the guards follow to check on us at night. Okay? You listening?"

Xavier remained still.

"I'm gonna tell you how to make a good, strong fucking rope out of a bedsheet."

Chapter 28

Around four a.m. Jack phoned Molly Khoury from his bedroom. She answered on the second ring and sounded wide awake. A good night's sleep was obviously not part of this mother's current existence.

"I just heard from Jackson Memorial Hospital," said Jack. "Xavier is in the intensive care unit. He tried to hang himself."

Molly's shriek on the line was so loud that it made Andie stir on the other side of their bed. Jack went into their master bathroom and closed the door. It took a minute to calm Molly down and tell her what he knew, which wasn't very much.

"They wouldn't give me details over the phone. I pushed so hard to speak to him that I must have ticked off the nurse. She got a little testy and said Xavier couldn't talk to me even if phones were allowed in the ICU. He's unconscious and breathing on a ventilator."

"Oh, my God," said Molly. "Why did no one call me?"

"You're the first person I called," said Jack.

"I mean the hospital or the jail!"

The harsh reality was that Xavier had listed neither of his parents as "contacts," but there was no need to make her feel worse than she already did. "I'm leaving in five minutes. I can meet you at the hospital and we can get a handle on what's going on."

She agreed, and as quickly as Jack could get dressed, he was out the door and on the causeway to the mainland. Molly had a shorter drive to Jackson and was already in the waiting room by the time Jack made it over from Key Biscayne.

"They won't let me go up to see him," she said. "How can they not let his own mother see him?"

Molly seemed to have mentally blocked out the fact that her son was not only an accused mass murderer, but also a Protective Custody Level One detainee who was in disciplinary detention for bad behavior. Jack went to the admissions window. The clerk took the necessary information from him and called for a security guard to escort him to the ICU. Molly was much like any concerned mother, filling Jack's head with her son's complete medical history.

"Xavier had his wisdom teeth removed six months ago. Probably should have had his tonsils out in the fifth grade, but we decided not to. He tolerates acetaminophen well but has trouble swallowing the tablets, so be sure to tell the nurse to break them in half or give him gel caps."

Molly was so scattered that she seemed to have forgotten that, at last report, Xavier wasn't even breathing on his own. "Got it," said Jack.

She handed him the file she'd grabbed from home. "Everything is right here. Please give it to the nurses in the ICU."

"Will do."

The security guard took him up the elevator. They rode in silence, which gave Jack another opportunity to wrestle with the guilt he was feeling. Xavier's attempted suicide had come on the heels of Jack's story about the teenage boy who'd taken his own life—his old friend Ray's son. It was enough to make Jack wonder.

The elevator door opened, and as he stepped into the bright hallway, Jack felt a strange sense of déjà vu. Two weeks earlier, he'd walked down this same hallway to visit Nate Abrams, whose daughter was barely clinging to life. It was almost too bizarre for words. All he could hope was that Lindsey's killer—*alleged* killer—wasn't lying in the very same bed. Jack reached the pneumatic doors and pressed the CALL button, but this time there was no crackling response from the nurse over the intercom. The door opened, and a physician dressed in scrubs walked out.

"Please don't come in," he said.

"Who are you?" asked Jack.

"I'm Dr. Henderson. Infectious disease. I've been with Emily Ramirez almost all night. The infection from the gunshot wound to her abdomen is back with a vengeance. She could easily become your client's fifteenth victim by the end of today."

"I'm so sorry to hear that."

"Her parents are with her now. They don't need to see your face. Please, don't come in."

Jack didn't make an issue of it. "I presume my client is under armed guard?"

"Yes. Two of them. They're posted right outside his bay, which is distressing enough for Emily's parents, not to mention our other patients who have never committed mass murder."

"I don't want to add to anyone's stress," said Jack. "But can someone give me an update? I was told Xavier is on a ventilator."

"Then you got bad information. He's breathing on his own. Vitals are good. Pupils respond to light, so no sign of depressed brain-stem reflexes. Reflexes are normal, and he responds to pinprick and other painful stimuli."

"So, he's going to recover?"

"Let's put it this way: people who want your client to be fully aware and conscious when the executioner sticks a needle in his arm will not be disappointed."

"So he's going to be fine?"

"Yes," said the doctor, and then he glanced back at the ICU entrance. "How the good Lord squares that with the innocent children who didn't come out of here alive is beyond me."

"I understand."

"No you don't," said the doctor. "No lawyer who does what you do understands anything but money and some kind of perverse high that comes from defending despicable people."

"My wife says the same thing," said Jack. "Except the money part. She's on a government salary and makes more than I do."

The doctor didn't so much as acknowledge Jack's attempt to defuse the situation. "I need to get back to my patients."

"One second," said Jack. "Can you give me some idea of what happened?"

"What I know is all after the fact. You'll have to talk to the detention center. I gotta go." As the doctor stepped away, he seemed to reconsider his attitude. He stopped. "Hey, sorry for what I said about what you do and why you do it. It's been a long night."

Jack had been on the receiving end of much worse. "No problem," he said.

Jack was in court before his client was fully awake. Judge Martinez was starting a jury trial in another case that morning, so he squeezed in Abe Beckham's request for an emergency hearing at eight thirty a.m.

The judicial assistant brought a big mug of coffee up to the bench. "Mr. Beckham, I presume this emergency relates to the attempted suicide and hospitalization of the defendant?"

"That's partially correct," said the prosecutor. "The state of Florida disputes that this was an attempted suicide."

The judge reviewed the file in front of him. "The incident report states that the detainee tore off three long strips from his bedsheet, braided the strips together like a rope, tied the rope to the bed frame in the bunk above him, and hanged himself by the neck until he was unconscious. Does that not sound like attempted suicide to you, Mr. Beckham?"

"Things are not always what they appear to be."

"Especially in this town," the judge added. "But

why has the prosecution brought this matter before the court? If anything, I would have expected a motion from the defense arguing that Mr. Khoury is mentally incompetent to stand trial."

"I'm being proactive," said the prosecutor. "I, too, fully expect the defense to latch on to this incident and postpone the trial until Mr. Khoury dies of old age. My goal is to nip this stunt in the bud."

Jack rose. "Your Honor, I have to object to the characterization of a medical emergency as a 'stunt.'"

"Yes, Mr. Beckham. Let's tone down the rhetoric, please. Especially in the absence of any factual record to support your allegation."

"My apologies," said Beckham. "With the court's permission, I would like to establish that factual record."

"When?" the judge asked.

"I have Dr. Andrew Phillips waiting in the hallway. He is with the Office of Health Services, Florida Department of Corrections, and oversees the administration of health care at Miami-Dade Pretrial Detention Center."

Jack was on his feet again. "Your Honor, I've had no time to prepare."

"*Prepare*," said Beckham, almost snarling. "Judge, that's exactly why we need to move quickly. We all know exactly what Mr. Swyteck means by 'prepare.' He needs time to prepare his client to say exactly the right words in a psychiatric evaluation. He needs time to find the right psychiatrist who will listen to this beautifully prepared presentation so that he, in turn, can prepare an ironclad report. And Mr. Swyteck then needs time to prepare his disingenuous argument to the court that the trial must be postponed indefinitely because his client thinks the judge is a kangaroo, thinks the prosecutor is from planet Mars, and thinks the FBI is spying on him through a camera implanted in his penis."

"Judge, this is beyond the pale," said Jack.

"Really, Mr. Beckham. What is it that you want?"

"I want the *immediate* opportunity to demonstrate to this court that the defendant is mentally competent to stand trial."

"Judge, I have not yet asserted that my client is mentally incompetent," said Jack.

"But it's coming!" said Beckham. "We all know it. Hollywood makes it seem that claims of not guilty by reason of insanity are an everyday occurrence in a criminal courtroom. They're not. But I can tell you what is: a claim by a guilty-as-sin defendant that he is mentally incompetent to stand trial, followed by a flurry of motions from death row arguing that he lacks the mental capacity to understand why he is being executed.

"Well, what about the mental state of the good people who are grieving for the children who were shot down in their own school, Your Honor? What about *their* mental anguish? I'm here for them this morning. I will not be caught flat-footed and watch the defense use this so-called attempted suicide to delay this trial for months, if not years, which will only deprive the victims and their families of the justice they deserve."

Jack kept his seat. Even at such an early hour, and even for a last-minute hearing, more than a dozen friends and relatives of the victims had gathered in the gallery. They were the core group who had vowed to "be there, no matter what" for a lost loved one—wounded souls who would have shown up in their pajamas at three a.m. if someone in Victims Services at the State Attorney's Office had called to tell them that a hearing was scheduled at the last minute. Finally, the prosecutor had pushed the right button with Judge Martinez: justice for the victims.

"All right," the judge said. "We have time for one witness."

Beckham thanked him, and, as if on cue, Dr. Phillips entered through the rear doors of the courtroom. The witness was sworn and settled into the chair. The prosecutor quickly established his credentials as chief physician at the detention center with more than two decades of experience at the Florida Department of Corrections. The questioning quickly transitioned to Jack's client.

"Dr. Phillips, when did you find out that Mr. Khoury had been taken to Jackson Memorial Hospital?"

"I received a phone call from the warden around one a.m. He informed me that the ambulance was already on the way."

"What did you do?"

"I have staff privileges at Jackson, so I went straight to the emergency room."

"Did you provide any information to the emergency room physicians about Mr. Khoury or the events that led to his visit to the emergency room?"

"Officer Jenkins was the corrections officer who found Mr. Khoury in his bunk. He rode in the ambulance to the ER. He provided that information to the doctors."

"Were you there for Officer Jenkins' report?"

"I was."

"Could you summarize, please?"

"Jenkins was on his regular rounds when he checked Mr. Khoury's cell. Mr. Khoury appeared to be sitting up in the lower bunk. Jenkins called to him, but Mr.

Khoury did not respond. Jenkins switched on the light and then saw the rope around Mr. Khoury's neck. He immediately radioed for assistance and entered the cell. He removed the rope and administered CPR. Mr. Khoury was breathing when paramedics arrived."

"Dr. Phillips, have there been suicides at the Pretrial Detention Center in the past?"

"Sadly, yes."

"And I suppose there have been attempted suicides, where the inmate survived?"

"Yes."

"Did any of those suicides or attempted suicides involve hanging?"

"Yes."

"Now, Doctor. Can you tell me if in any of those previous cases, the detainee tried to hang himself while lying down?"

"Lying down," he said, searching his memory.

Jack rose before the witness could answer. "Your Honor, I see where this line of questioning is going, and I object. Any qualified expert on this subject would testify that death by hanging doesn't require a drop from the highest gallows. Hanging is deadly in any number of positions: sitting, kneeling, toes touching the ground—and yes, even in a prone position with nothing but the weight of the head and chest as the constricting force."

"That's not my point," said Beckham. "Judge, may I continue without interruption, please?"

"You may continue," the judge said, "but please make your point soon."

"Dr. Phillips, when you heard that Mr. Khoury hanged himself, what was your first thought?"

"Tragic. We do everything reasonably possible to ensure the safety of our inmates."

"When you heard that Mr. Khoury tried to hang himself while lying down, what was your first thought?"

"Well," the doctor said, almost smiling, "I don't mean to sound insensitive. But we actually have a term for that."

"What is the term?"

"Sympathy hanging."

Jack thought again of the story he'd told Xavier about Ray's son—the teenage boy who didn't really want to kill himself.

Beckham asked, "What does that mean, Doctor? A sympathy hanging?"

Jack sprang from his chair to object, but the judge overruled him. "There's no jury here," the judge said. "The witness may answer."

"It's like the person who takes one too many sleeping pills and then dials nine-one-one before dozing off. They don't really want to die. They do it for sympathy."

Jack objected again. "Your Honor, we are way beyond this witness's sphere of personal knowledge, and ever futher beyond his area of medical expertise."

The judge peered out over the top of his reading glasses, toward the scattering of victim supporters in the gallery, as if to assure them that he'd allowed the prosecutor to go as far as legally permissible. "I have to say I agree with the defense," he said with some reluctance. "Mr. Beckham, if your goal is to convince me that this was all a stunt to set up a claim that Mr. Khoury is mentally incompetent to stand trial, this witness isn't going to do it for you. No offense to you, Dr. Phillips. Counsel, let's schedule this matter for a proper hearing."

"Very well," said Beckham. "To that end, the state requests that the court appoint a psychiatrist to conduct a full competence evaluation of the defendant."

"I'll say it again," said Jack. "The defense has made no claim that Mr. Khoury is mentally incompetent."

"The rules also allow for evaluation at the request of the prosecution," said Beckham. "Why wait for Mr. Swyteck to make his request two hours before the start of trial, which will only delay justice? Let's do it now."

"The state's request is granted," the judge said.

"Thank you," said Beckham. "We ask that the court appoint Dr. Howard Meed."

Jack and every other defense lawyer in Miami knew of Meed. In Meed's judgment, Beckham's hypothetical defendant—the one who thought the judge was a kangaroo and the prosecutor was from Mars—was not only competent to stand trial but also quite qualified to operate his own think tank. "Judge, I suggest that the court direct the prosecutor and defense to confer and select a mutually agreeable psychiatrist."

"More delay," said Beckham. "Dr. Meed is eminently qualified."

"He is, indeed," the judge said. "Dr. Meed's evaluation shall take place as soon as Mr. Khoury's treating physician clears him. Anything further from counsel this morning?"

There was nothing.

"Then we're adjourned," the judge said, with a crack of his gavel.

Lawyers and spectators rose on the bailiff's command, and the judge exited to his chambers. Jack approached his opposing counsel while Beckham was at the table and packing up his trial bag.

"There's still a way to avoid all this," said Jack. "Offer me a plea that doesn't include the death penalty, and I will do everything in my power to make sure my client gives it serious consideration."

"I have no reason to change my mind," said Beckham. "If hanging himself was a stunt pulled purely for sympathy, your client is evil and manipulative. If it was a genuine attempt to kill himself, it shows consciousness of guilt. Either way, he deserves death."

Jack glanced toward the friends and family in the gallery. Some were making their way toward the exit in silence. Others just sat there, staring, as if still coming to terms with the fact that someone they loved was gone, that nothing that transpired in this courtroom was ever going to bring them back.

"I wish I could convince you that this isn't about sparing my client," said Jack. "It's about sparing them."

"You keep on telling yourself that, Swyteck, if it helps you live with yourself."

Beckham turned and exited through the swinging gate at the rail. Jack started back toward the defense table to gather his belongings, glancing once more toward the friends and family who'd come to support the victims, feeling the weight of one woman's stare from the back of the courtroom. Jack averted his eyes—then he stopped and did a double take, his gaze shifting back toward the double-door exit.

The young woman was gone, but Jack suddenly realized that it hadn't been a glare from a total stranger. It had taken a moment for his mind to sift through the confusion and recognize the face beneath the broad-brimmed hat she'd been wearing, but he was certain that he knew her, that he'd met her before.

That it was Maritza from the coffee shop.

Jack grabbed his computer bag from the table, hurried to the exit, and pushed through the double doors to the lobby. He was caught in the nine a.m. rush with hundreds of lawyers and jurors trying to be on time for the start of another day in the justice mill. Jack saw no sign of Maritza in the crowd, and he wasn't sure which way she might have gone. He took two quick steps in one direction, then changed his mind and started in the other, running head-on into a Miami-Dade cop who had apparently missed his calling as a Miami Dolphin running back. He hit Jack so hard that the collision sent his laptop flying right out of his computer bag. It landed with a distressing *crack* on the floor.

"Oh, man, I'm so sorry," the cop said. He helped Jack gather up the pens, Post-Its, and other tools of the trade that had scattered across the floor. "You got it all, pal? Hope you didn't lose nothin'."

Jack glanced toward the escalators at the end of the long hallway. No sign of Maritza.

"No telling what I lost," said Jack.

Chapter 29

Andie didn't want her husband in the room with her. It was Tuesday morning, and Andie's deposition in the school's lawsuit against her was scheduled for nine a.m. at the law offices of Cool Cash. Jack had assured her that he was fully on board with President Lincoln's view, as amended by Theo Knight, as cleaned up by Jack Swyteck, that "the lawyer who represents his wife is an effing lunatic." But on the morning of the deposition, before they left the house, he seemed to be wavering.

"Hannah will appear as the attorney of record," said Jack. "I'll attend strictly as an interested observer."

"You won't just observe," said Andie.

"Only Hannah will speak on your behalf. I promise."

"You lie, Jack."

"Come on, Andie. What can it hurt if I'm there?"

"You said it yourself when we agreed you were not going. All I need to do is tell the truth. The only way for me to get into trouble is if I start worrying how you might react to my answers to Fitz's questions."

Andie had him there. His own words. Jack went to his office like any other workday. It was Andie and Hannah at the deposition—unlike any day Andie had ever experienced.

"Agent Henning, have you ever been deposed before?" asked Fitz.

Duncan Fitz, lead lawyer for the plaintiff, was seated across the conference table from Andie and Hannah, his back to the floor-to-ceiling windows and the view of Biscayne Bay. With him on his side of the needlessly long table were a Cool Cash junior partner, a Cool Cash senior associate, a Cool Cash junior associate, and two Cool Cash paralegals. Andie wondered if the deposition of President Clinton had been this overstaffed.

"I have not," said Andie.

Fitz launched into a five-minute explanation of the rules of a deposition, which included everything she'd already heard from Hannah in their prep session the day before. Hannah had also told her that background questions would come next—education, employment history, current employment, and the like. But Fitz surprised her—as Jack had warned her he might—by going straight to the heart of the matter.

"Agent Henning, you are familiar with the 'Run, Hide, Fight' protocol in response to an active shooter in schools, correct?"

"Yes, I am."

"Let's focus on step one, 'run,'" said Fitz. "I'm reading from the Riverside safety pamphlet that is part of the school information package given to all parents. 'If there is considerable distance between you and the gunfire/armed person, quickly move away from the sound of the gunfire/armed person. If the gunfire/armed person is in your building and it is safe to do so, run out of the building and move far away until you are in a secure place to hide.'"

Fitz handed the pamphlet to Andie and her counsel. "Does that comport with your understanding of 'run,' in the 'Run, Hide, Fight' protocol?"

Andie read it to herself, then answered. "It does."

"The protocol dictates that you *run away* from the sound of gunfire, correct?"

"That is what it says here."

"And that if the shooter is inside the building you run *out of the building*, correct?"

"Yes."

"In fact," said Fitz, "on the morning of the Riverside shooting, that's exactly what the head of school directed every parent in the rec center to do: follow her away from the shooter and out of the building."

"That is my recollection," said Andie.

"Let me ask you this," said Fitz. "If one of the other mothers in that room had decided to run anywhere but out of the building and away from the shooter, you, as an experienced FBI agent, would consider that a violation of the 'Run, Hide, Fight' protocol. Would you not?"

"Objection," said Hannah, though it wasn't at all clear to Andie what the objection was. "You can answer," said Hannah.

"No other mother in the rec center was a trained law enforcement officer," said Andie. "I thought I could help."

"You were off duty and unarmed that morning, correct?" said Fitz.

"Yes."

"So, let's be honest. Did you really think you could help? Or did you think you were special and that the rules didn't apply to you?"

Hannah objected again, but it all seemed pointless to Andie. "You can answer," said Hannah.

"I didn't think I was special," said Andie.

"Well, did you think it was okay to disobey the explicit directions of the head of school to exit the building and follow her to safety?"

"Like I said, I thought I could help."

"All right," said Fitz. "Let's talk about how much help you actually were. After you exited the rec center, did you confront the shooter?"

"No."

"Did you throw anything at him to distract him?"

"No."

"Did you call out to him to confuse him?"

"No."

"The fact is, you did nothing more than run to your daughter's classroom and sit outside the door, correct?"

Andie paused, not liking the way Fitz had phrased it. "I waited outside the door and prepared myself as best I could to confront the shooter if he tried to enter the kindergarten classroom."

"I see. In your view, you committed an act of bravery."

"I think it was pure instinct."

Fitz smiled insincerely. "Well, don't sell yourself short, Agent Henning. We've all seen the diagrams of the shooter's path prepared by the Miami-Dade Police Department. You agree that you ran toward the shooter, not away from him. Correct?"

"That appears to be the case."

"You were putting yourself in danger, right?"

"I suppose so. I wasn't thinking about that."

"Did anyone follow you down the hallway as you moved toward the shooter?"

"No."

"How do you know that?"

Andie understood the question, but she still puzzled over it. "I didn't see anyone follow me."

"So your answer is you *don't know* if anyone followed you because you didn't see anyone."

"Right. I didn't see anyone."

"Someone *might* have followed you, right?"

Hannah interjected. "Please don't ask the witness to guess."

Fitz didn't give up. "Agent Henning, are you going to tell me that it is *impossible* that someone followed you?"

"I would say it's possible."

"More than possible, wouldn't you say? A child is caught in a hallway during an active shooting. Gunfire is popping like an exploding brick of firecrackers. Bodies are on the floor. Students are screaming and scattering in every direction. A lost and confused child doesn't know what to do. The child sees an adult running down the hallway with purpose. The child follows the adult. Wouldn't that be a natural thing for any child to do?"

"Objection, calls for speculation."

"I don't know," said Andie.

"You *don't know?*" asked Fitz, his tone more aggressive. "As an FBI agent and *a mother*, you have no view as to whether or not a terrified child who doesn't know where to run would follow an adult? *That's* your testimony under oath?"

"Objection, asked and answered," said Hannah.

Andie was struggling. She did have an opinion. But clearly her lawyer was sending her a signal not to answer Fitz's question. "I really can't say," she said.

Fitz leaned forward, forearms resting on the table, forcing Andie to look into the eyes of an experienced litigator who knew exactly how to control a witness. He didn't shout. He didn't get nasty. He simply gave the witness no option but to say what he knew, in her heart, she believed to be true.

"Agent Henning," he said in a firm voice. "Let's see if we can agree on this much: if *any* child followed you down that hallway instead of running for the exit, you put that child at greater risk. Didn't you?"

"Objection," said Hannah. "Counsel, now you are simply harassing the witness. Agent Henning, as your lawyer I'm directing you not to answer that question."

"That's completely improper," said Fitz. "If you stick to that position, I will take it to the judge and seek sanctions against you and your client."

The Cool Cash associates at the end of the table were feverishly tapping the keys on their laptops, probably at work on the motion already.

"Do as you think you must," said Hannah. "But move on."

Fitz turned his attention back to Andie. "Agent Henning, are you going to follow the instruction of your counsel? Or are you going to give me an honest answer to a question that you know is fair and proper: If any child followed you down that hallway toward the gunfire instead of running for the exit, that child was at greater risk. Agreed?"

"I object," said Hannah, "and I repeat my instruction to my client."

Andie was thinking—but not about her lawyer's instruction.

"How about it, Agent Henning?" asked Fitz. "Your answer, please?"

Hannah jumped to her feet and said, "That's it. We're leaving. Come on, Andie, let's—"

"Yes," said Andie.

The room was silent.

Then Fitz followed up. "Yes, what?"

He may have been out of line, but Andie felt the need to answer. "If any child followed me, that child would have been at greater risk."

"Thank you," said Fitz. "Now, Ms. Goldsmith, if you will retake your seat, I'd like to ask your client about her educational background and employment history."

"I think my client would like a break," said Hannah.

Andie swallowed the lump in her throat. In the first ten minutes of the deposition, Fitz had drilled to the very core of her own second-guessing of her response to the gunshots that morning.

"Yes, thanks," said Andie. "A break would be good."

Chapter 30

Jack worked through dinner and wasn't home until nine. The house was quiet. He assumed Righley was asleep, so he chose not to tap into his half-Cuban roots, play Ricky Ricardo, and announce *Looo-cy, I'm home!* with all the volume of "Babalú." He went quietly to the kitchen, heated up leftover spaghetti Bolognese in the microwave, and took a seat at the counter.

It had been a wasted day at the office. One of Theo's many buddies happened to be a top tattoo artist who'd created one-of-a-kind images for NBA players. Sports video companies paid the players big bucks to use their likeness in their games, and the graphic artists copied the tattoos with impressive precision. Theo's friend thought the video company should pay him for copying the tattoos he created. Jack was no copyright expert, but like most sole practitioners, he thought of himself as a "Jack of all trades," no pun intended. This claim, however, was dead by sundown. Jack found lawsuits over tattoos on LeBron James and other NBA stars, all decided against the artist.

He switched on the TV but kept the volume low. The Miami Heat were battling the Los Angeles Lakers. LeBron was at the free-throw line.

"Nice tats," said Jack.

He ate about half his bowl of spaghetti and cleared the rest into the trash can. It was then that he noticed the empty bottle of wine on the counter. Andie's voice got lower when she was drunk, and Jack heard that voice coming from the dark living room.

"Jack? Is that you?"

She was lying on the couch. Jack went to her and gave her a kiss. She could barely lift her head to meet his lips, and she was still wearing the silk blouse and pants that she'd worn to the deposition. At least she'd removed her shoes. Jack sat at the end of the couch, put her feet in his lap, and massaged the ball of the foot the way she liked.

"Ahhh," she said, almost purring.

"You're drunk."

"Ya *think*?"

"Did you finish that whole bottle of wine yourself?"

"Yup."

"When we talked on the phone, you said the deposition went well."

"It did. I was the perfect witness. I'm celebrating!"

Jack's eyes were adjusting to the darkness, and he could see pain in her expression, feel it in her toes as the phony exuberance faded. "Tell me what happened," he said.

"I don't want to talk about it, Jack."

"Getting drunk isn't going to help."

"Sure didn't hurt."

"Do you want me to call Duncan Fitz?"

"No!" she said, almost jackknifing on the couch, suddenly finding the energy to sit up. "You can't fix this, Jack. Nobody can fix this."

"Fix what?"

"Fix *what*?" she said, overenunciating, her mouth forming the words in such exaggerated fashion that Jack could have understood without a sense of hearing. "You don't think something is *broken*?" she asked.

Jack dropped her left foot into his lap and started on the right, trying to relax her. "Why don't you tell me what you think is broken?"

"Us, Jack. *Us.*"

Jack stopped the foot massage. "What are you talking about?"

"I was talking to Molly."

"Today?"

"No, no. Like two months ago. We were talking about religion. She's not a Muslim, so I was curious to know how that worked for her and Amir."

"The imam told me she has no religion," said Jack.

"That's not true. She's not without religion. She was raised Episcopalian. She just doesn't practice, and she chose not to convert to Islam."

"What does this have to do with us?"

"Just listen to me, Jack. When Molly decided not to convert, she and Amir reached an understanding. Since Molly doesn't practice, their children would go to the mosque with Amir."

"That's the way it is in a lot of interfaith families. You go with the parent who considers religion to be a more important part of their life. But I still don't see how this pertains to us."

"It's . . ." She paused, but it appeared to be just a head rush. "It's like us because they had an under-standing, and it doesn't work."

"Andie, we're both Christians. We don't have that issue."

"I'm not saying it's the same issue. But we have the same problem."

"You're drunk, and I'm not following you at all."

"No, don't dismiss what I'm saying. We really do have the same problem. It's like Molly told me. The understanding worked for a while. But as you get older, and you have kids, and things get more complicated, you realize that the old understanding isn't working. You're only pretending it works."

"So religion became more important to Amir as they got older. Is that what you're saying."

"Yes!"

"Fine. That's them. That has nothing to do with us."

"Yes, it does! We have an understanding. It's not exactly like theirs, but it's just as important to our marriage."

Jack finally had a sense of where this conversation was headed. "You're talking about our agreement: I don't ask you about active investigations you're working on; you don't ask me about criminal cases I'm handling."

"Yes! Our agreement," said Andie. "The one that we fool ourselves into thinking can make a marriage work between an FBI agent and a criminal defense lawyer."

Jack was starting to worry. "I don't see the comparison between our agreement and the one that Molly and Amir have."

"Before you agreed to defend Xavier, I wouldn't

have seen it either. But now it's so clear to me. After the deposition today, it's crystal clear."

"You're going to have to explain it to me, honey."

"Jack, before I met you, you did nothing but defend guilty murderers on death row."

"Theo wasn't guilty."

"One," said Andie. "*One* innocent client."

"What's your point?"

"It's like a religion for you, Jack. Defending guilty people. Amir went back to his religion stronger, more devoted, as their marriage went on. I'm afraid. I'm so afraid you're going back to *your* religion. Because I can't handle it, Jack. I can't. It's not who I am."

Jack took a deep breath. He'd known this was hard on Andie, but he'd clearly underestimated how hard. "I'm sorry."

"Sorry for what?"

"For all this pain. I can't make it go away now. I'm in this case, and the judge isn't going to let me out. But if it's any consolation, defending Xavier has taught me something."

"What?"

"It's not who I am, either," he said, shooting a quick glance down the hallway to Righley's bedroom. "Not anymore."

Chapter 31

Jack drove to work in the morning with one of the biggest songs of the nineties in his head. The one about the guy in the corner. In the spotlight. *Losing my religion.*

Jack considered it a rock trivia nugget to know that the old R.E.M. hit had nothing to do with religion. Not until he went to college in North Florida did he hear anyone say "losing my religion," an Old South expression for losing your temper or feeling frustrated and desperate. "Frustrated" seemed to fit well enough on the heels of Jack's conversation with Andie. Maybe even "desperate." Jack didn't hold out much hope that his meeting with the Justice Department would improve things.

The James Lawrence King Federal Justice Building is a twelve-story government office building in downtown Miami. Glass-and-concrete construction made it a relatively modern addition to a jigsaw complex that included the old and new federal courthouses, all connected by courtyards. Surrounding streets were cordoned off by concrete car-bomb barriers, a part of life across the country after domestic terrorist Timothy McVeigh detonated a truckload of explosives outside the Alfred P. Murrah Federal Building in Oklahoma City, murdering 149 adults and 19 children. Had Xavier been indicted under federal law as a terrorist, he would have been housed in the federal detention center right next door to the US Attorney's Office.

It was Sylvia Gonzalez who'd requested the meeting, and she'd traveled down from Washington to attend on behalf of the National Security Division. Jack assumed it was about federal charges. They met with Jack in the US attorney's spacious corner office, so technically he was the host. The US attorney's post was a political appointment, changing like clockwork with each presidential election, which meant that the best lawyers didn't necessarily rise to the top. Grady Olson was more of a CEO than a lawyer, and apparently he had more important things to manage than this meeting.

He was glued to his smartphone, not even trying to hide the fact that he was reading and answering emails, thumbs in high gear.

Gonzalez was in control.

"Let's start with this unpleasant reality," she said. "Because the shooting has been designated an act of terrorism, the DOJ has the power to prosecute your client and seek the death penalty under federal law."

"You also have the power to prosecute my client and seek life in prison without parole," said Jack. "Which is what I hope you'll do. And because I'm feeling particularly lucky this morning, I hope you'll convince Abe Beckham and the state attorney to do the same under Florida law."

"This indeed may be your lucky day, Jack."

Her words took Jack by surprise. He'd come prepared to talk about the dents he'd put in the prosecutor's case, maybe even spring the alibi that Xavier was in bed with Maritza, though he was saving Maritza until he knew whether she was his ace in the hole or a bald-faced liar.

"Come again?" said Jack.

"There's one way to get death off the table," said Gonzalez. "Tell us who Xavier's accomplice was."

"I don't represent Molly Khoury," said Jack, "but I can tell you this much, based on what I know about her. Molly would gladly tell you that she went to Riverside Day School after the shooting; that she gathered up the shooter's hat, goggles, clothes, and vest and then dumped all of it deep in the Everglades where it could never be found. She would happily plead guilty as an accessory after the fact and even do jail time. And she would do that even if it wasn't true—if it would save her son from the death penalty."

Gonzalez poured a glass of water from the pitcher on the coffee table. Jack declined her offer, and Grady was too focused on his phone to notice, so she kept it for herself.

"We're not talking about Molly Khoury," she said. "And we are definitely not talking about an accessory after the fact."

"I'm listening," said Jack.

"You've seen the evidence Abe Beckham presented to the grand jury. Your client's confession may or may not meet the standard of guilty beyond a reasonable doubt. The gun belonged to his father, so you'll tell the jury that it was stolen from his glove compartment by the real shooter, who is not your client."

"It's more than a colorable argument," said Jack. "The government's own fingerprint expert has confirmed the existence of a print that doesn't belong to Xavier or his father. And the gun-shop owner's testimony that Xavier tried to buy an automatic rifle from him is unusable."

"Shaky," said Gonzalez. "I'll give you that."

"There's also no evidence to connect my client to the purchase of extended magazines," Jack continued. "No surveillance video to confirm his identity. No credible eyewitness identification of him as the shooter. No one could have identified the man behind the ski mask and goggles in the fog of war."

Gonzalez chomped on an ice cube from her water glass. "I didn't invite you here to debate the evidence," she said. "Every prosecutor's case has weaknesses."

"These are holes, not weaknesses," said Jack. "More holes than the state attorney wants to admit."

"Not one of these holes, as you call them, will stop a jury from convicting him of murder in the first degree. Nor will they save him from the death penalty. Which leads me back to where I started."

"The accomplice," said Jack.

"Yes," said Gonzalez, placing her water glass on the coffee table.

Grady quickly moved it to the tray, grabbed a napkin, and wiped the condensation from his gorgeous mahogany tabletop. Then he went back to his phone.

Gonzalez continued. "Your client didn't do this alone. Someone planned it, recruited him, educated him, supplied the extended magazines, told him what to wear, and helped him escape. It wasn't Molly Khoury. Tell us who it was, and the United States will not seek the death penalty when we indict him under federal law."

"If you could prove an al-Qaeda connection, you would have already charged him under federal terrorism laws. Without a terrorist connection, you might as well throw double jeopardy out the window and charge him twice for the same crime. Frankly, I'm more concerned about the good, ol' fashioned homicide charges. Beckham doesn't have to prove it was terrorism under state law."

"I believe we can persuade the state attorney to fall in line."

"Let me make sure I understand the deal. If my client names his accomplice, he gets life without parole."

"Put another way, if he doesn't give up his accomplice, he's looking at the death penalty under Florida law and under federal law."

"I don't think he's all that concerned about being executed twice."

"You know what I mean, Jack. At least one of us is going to make it stick."

"I understand," said Jack. "But isn't your offer overlooking one thing?"

"My offer is tailored to what your client is lucky to get."

Jack hadn't pressed the "wrong man" argument so far, but the existence of an accomplice and recitation of "holes" in the government's case had him thinking: *What if Maritza wasn't a liar?*

"Have you considered the possibility that Xavier wasn't the shooter?" asked Jack.

The US attorney chuckled, his second contribution to the meeting, this time without a napkin. "Don't get cocky, Swyteck," he said.

"There's no doubt in anyone's mind who did it," said Gonzalez. "We want to know who helped him."

Jack paused, but only to increase the effect of his next suggestion. "What if Xavier has an alibi?"

"Beckham spoke to me about that," said Gonzalez. "He told me you raised the possibility of presenting an alibi to the grand jury. You came forward with nothing."

"I'm in the process of verifying it. I don't want to put it out there only to have it picked apart. Under the rules, I don't have to disclose an alibi until ten days before trial."

"I'm not going to tell you all of the evidence I'm sitting on, Jack. But know this much: any alibi would be taken not with a grain, but a boulder, of salt."

"We'll see."

Grady rose, as if to signal it was time for his next meeting. "Seriously, Swyteck, do you really believe your client is not the shooter?"

Jack didn't have to answer, and he wasn't sure if the US attorney expected him to. But he gave him an honest one.

"I don't know what to believe anymore," said Jack.

Chapter 32

Jack left the US Attorney's Office certain of one thing: if Xavier was the shooter, and if he had an accomplice, Jack wasn't going to get a name from a client who was giving him the silent treatment. The long and impressive run of the Miami-Dade Detention Center Monologues, starring Jack Swyteck, had to end.

The court order directing the defendant to submit to a psychiatric "competence" evaluation was still in effect. Jack had managed to stave off the prosecutor's repeated demands for a firm date, taking the position that he needed to speak to his client—or, more precisely, his client needed to speak to him—before any session with a psychiatrist chosen by the prosecution. Jack's meeting with Sylvia Gonzalez had attached some urgency to the process, so he modified his position: if he wouldn't talk to Jack, Xavier at least had to talk to a psychiatrist chosen by Jack.

"Hypnosis?" asked Dr. Moore. "Really, Jack?"

Elaine Moore, M.D., used hypnosis in her practice, but she used it cautiously. So cautiously that, in one of his capital cases at the Freedom Institute, Jack had called her as an expert witness to *attack* the use of hypnotically induced memory recall in a police homicide investigation. It was Dr. Moore's testimony—"Uncorroborated, hypnotically elicited memories can lead to the wrongful imprisonment of innocent people"—that had won a last-minute stay of execution for Jack's client.

"Can you help?" said Jack. "I'm desperate." *Losing my religion.*

"For you, I'll give it a shot."

Jack arranged for the session to take place the next day in the detention center's police interrogation room. It was a tiny space, the perfect cramped rectangle for one good cop, one bad cop, and any suspect who was pliable enough to trade away the rest of his life for a cheeseburger, fries, and a milkshake. Dr. Moore and Xavier were inside alone. Jack and Hannah were standing in the adjacent room. Hidden behind a one-way mirror and connected by a hidden microphone, they could see and hear the doctor and her patient.

"So this is what it's like to be on the other side,"

said Hannah. "I wonder where they keep the rubber hose."

"That's not funny," said Jack. Hannah sometimes forgot that Jack was married to a law enforcement officer.

Jack stepped closer to the glass, his gaze focused on his client. Dr. Moore had requested a comfortable cot for her patient, which the warden had denied, so she'd brought a beanbag chair from her office. Xavier was half submerged in a big ball of blue velour, seemingly relaxed, with knees bent, feet flat on the floor, and hands on his thighs. The lights were dimmed to create the right mood. The doctor spoke in a calm, soothing tone.

"Just begin to allow yourself to relax . . . Letting all your cares and worries go . . . And at this moment in time . . . Nothing matters . . . As you switch off your thoughts . . . And let your eyelids close."

Xavier's eyes remained open. The doctor continued in the same even tone, as if her voice were on a recorded audio loop. "Just allow this time for yourself . . . So that you can unwind completely . . . And as you begin to feel more and more relaxed . . . Letting go of any worries or problems . . . That may have been on your mind lately . . . And there is no need to fight any unwanted negative thoughts . . ."

Xavier closed his eyes.

"You think he's faking?" asked Hannah.

"Damned if I know," said Jack.

"Usually you can tell," said Hannah. "My college roommate used to pretend to faint every time her boyfriend broke up with her. We knew she was faking because her eyelids quivered. Xavier's aren't quivering."

They weren't, but Jack was skeptical. "I'm not sure quivering eyelids is a medically sound litmus test."

The doctor's voice continued. "I want you to take me back now, Xavier. Back to that day."

Jack and the doctor had agreed on "that day" as a handle for the shooting. A more explicit reference would have been contrary to the instructions to relax and release all negative energy.

Dr. Moore continued. "You're with your mom . . . In the family car . . . She's driving . . . Your sister and brother are in the back seat."

The clinical approach, as Jack understood it, was to take Xavier back to the last time he'd spoken in the presence of another human being. The hypnosis would elicit the next words out of his mouth. At least that was the plan.

"The car is moving down the street . . . Where you walked the dog . . . Rode your bike . . . You see the house . . . Where you grew up . . . Where your family lives . . ."

Xavier appeared to be very relaxed.

"I don't think he's faking," Hannah whispered.

"We'll see," said Jack, allowing for the possibility that perhaps Dr. Moore had made a breakthrough.

"The car stops . . . You open the door . . . You get out . . ."

She was reaching the critical point, and Dr. Moore had forewarned Jack that even if things were going well, the moment of confrontation with the police could be jarring and might bring the session to a screeching halt.

"Men in uniform approach the car . . . They want something . . . You put your hands in the air . . . You say something to your mother . . ."

Xavier didn't flinch. His eyes remained closed. The doctor gave him a moment and then modulated her tone, as if trying to explore a deeper place in Xavier's psyche.

"You say, 'It's okay, Mom. I did it.'"

More silence. No reaction from Xavier. Best of all, Jack saw no sign of distress.

Dr. Moore leaned closer, further adjusting her tone, probing even deeper. "Tell me why you said 'I.' . . . Did you leave someone out? Was there someone else?"

Jack watched, hoping to see Xavier's lips move. But he was perfectly still.

"Why?" the doctor asked. "Why did you say '*I did it*'?"

It was almost imperceptible, but Xavier's breathing seemed to change. Something about him seemed different, as if he could truly be in a state of hypnosis.

Slowly, he sat up in the beanbag chair, eyes closed, as if rising from the dead. His head turned slowly toward the glass. His eyes blinked open, and he uttered his first words since being taken into custody by police, apparently speaking directly to Jack, as if he were completely on to the fact that he was being watched.

"Because I fucking did it," he said. "That's why."

Jack stared back at his client. Although they weren't technically locking eyes through the one-way mirror, it felt like it.

"Whaddaya know," said Jack. "He speaks."

Chapter 33

On Friday morning Jack drove to Miami's Financial District on Brickell Avenue. He had Theo on speaker. Maritza was the topic of conversation.

"Let me get this straight," said Theo. "On Monday, you see a woman in the back of the courtroom who looks like Maritza, even though her boss said ICE hauled her away from the coffee shop and deported her. Five days later you call me and say it's urgent to find Maritza's last name. What's up with that?"

"I was going to do this myself, but I've just been too busy. I didn't want to hire you if I can't pay you. I'm watching my pennies here."

"Bullshit."

"Seriously. I just got the bill from Dr. Moore for her hypnosis session. Blew my budget for the whole month."

"Money's not the reason you're moving so slow on Maritza, Jack. When did you first meet her?"

Jack stopped at the traffic light. He had to think. "A good two weeks ago. More."

"A witness hands you a possible alibi, and you sit on it for over two weeks. That tells me one thing. You don't believe her."

Jack hadn't realized how transparent he was. "You're right. I don't."

"Shit, Jack. When you gonna catch up with the rest of the legal profession and have no problem putting a liar on the witness stand?"

"Very funny, Theo."

"Dude, I wasn't kidding."

The light changed to green, but Jack was a nano-second slow on the acceleration—a capital offense in Miami. The guy behind him laid on his horn. Jack ignored him.

"The goal isn't to prove an alibi," said Jack. "We're looking for an accomplice."

"You think it's her?"

"No, but it wouldn't surprise me if she knows who it is. If somehow she's back in Miami, I need to talk to her. A last name would help."

"I'm on it."

Jack ended the call and steered his car into the multistory garage. It was a relief to see that parking was only twelve dollars, until he read the fine print: FOR THE FIRST FIFTEEN MINUTES.

There goes the rest of the case budget.

Amir Khoury worked on the east side of Brickell Avenue, in the waterfront office tower directly across the street from the law firm of Coolidge, Harding & Cash. The South Florida branch of GC Capital was a lavishly appointed penthouse on the fiftieth floor, which meant that Amir was one of the lucky few who could literally look down on Duncan Fitz and the two hundred other lawyers at Cool Cash.

"Elevator number one," the security guard told Jack. It was an express ride to the penthouse, and in sixty seconds the doors opened to a cavernous lobby that resembled a glass atrium in the sky. Views stretched all the way to the Turkey-Point Nuclear Generating Station, some thirty miles south, the one potential target that put all of Miami on edge when the terrorist threat level on the Homeland Security advisory scale inched toward red.

"I'm here to see Amir Khoury," Jack told the receptionist, and he gave her his name.

"Do you have an appointment?"

He'd left a voice mail to say he was coming, albeit a bit vague. You didn't just come out and say, "I need to find out if your son was dating a prostitute," even if the son was a mass murderer. Alleged mass murderer.

"He's expecting me," said Jack, and he waited as she dialed Amir's assistant.

GC Capital was a private equity and credit investment firm that targeted "distressed" companies—high risk, but potentially high reward. Some said GC was a loan-to-own specialist, making its real money not from long-term business strategy but from betting on the borrower's quick default, picking up the pieces in foreclosure, and then selling off the assets at a huge profit. No laws were broken, but it wasn't exactly the "win-win" approach to business.

"Mr. Khoury will see you now," the receptionist said.

With parking at forty-eight bucks an hour, Jack was happy for no wait. An assistant entered the lobby and led him down the hall to a corner office. Amir was behind his desk, pacing as he spoke into his headset on a phone call, and he waved his visitor in. The assistant directed Jack to the armchair and then exited in church-mouse fashion, closing the door on the way out.

"We need to hit the links again soon," Amir said into his headset, about to wrap up his call.

Jack allowed his gaze to wander across the cherry-paneled walls, a quick survey of the trappings of Wall Street success, South Florida–style. Some people found success and favored expensive art. Others built a self-congratulatory shrine. Amir was in the latter camp, the wall behind his desk covered with plaques, awards, and more than a dozen framed photographs. His MBA diploma from the Wharton School. His elbow rubbing with the right politicians. A signed picture of Amir and Molly with Jeff Bezos, himself a product of South Florida, land of the Everglades, before moving to the Pacific Northwest to build his Amazon. And, of course, there was the obligatory display of Lucite cubes across the credenza. Deal toys, they were called. Little desktop mementos that, depending on the nature and size of the transaction, might encase anything from the iconic facade of the New York Stock Exchange to a pair of knights in shining armor jousting over an engraved sum of eight, possibly nine, figures.

Amir ended his phone call and laid his headset atop his desk. It had been a pleasant call, judging from his expression, but the pleasantries faded as he came around to the front of his desk, leaned against the edge, and faced Jack.

"Got your message," said Amir. "I understand you want to know about this Maritza."

This Maritza. Not Jack's words. Obviously, Amir was no fan. "No one told me that Xavier had a girlfriend," said Jack.

"She was *not* his girlfriend. What she is," added Amir, "is a pathological liar."

"What she is and who she is: that's what I came to talk about. I spoke to Imam Hassan."

"Yes, we spoke. He told you what she is. A prostitute."

"I'm curious to know how the imam knows that. Did you tell him?"

"No, *she* told him. Xavier brought her to the mosque as a guest. Imam Hassan has known Xavier since he was born, so naturally he's protective. He asked to speak privately with Maritza, and she agreed."

"She just came right out and told the imam: 'Oh, by the way, I'm a prostitute'?"

"I don't know *how* it came out. I wasn't there. All I cared about was getting Xavier away from her. He was my—he was part of our family."

Jack noted not only his inability to say the word *son*, but also his use of the past tense. "What did you do?"

"Xavier told me where she worked. Apparently, that coffee shop has a reputation for hiring illegals. I didn't know for sure that she was illegal, but I had a hunch. I called ICE to report an illegal, a prostitute, preying on my seventeen-year-old son."

"The manager told me she was deported," said Jack. "Just last week, in fact."

"Okay, I was right. About time, then."

Jack debated whether to mention the "sighting" at the courthouse on Monday. He decided against it. "Do you know Maritza's last name?"

Amir sighed, thinking. "I honestly don't remember. Something Hispanic. Perez, Mendendez, Martinez, Jimenez, Gonzalez, Hernandez, Fernandez, Rodriguez—one of those 'ezzes.'"

"I'm afraid that's not much help," said Jack. It was the Miami equivalent of looking for "stein" in the Long Island phone book.

"You could ask around the coffee shop," said Amir.

"I tried that. No one at the coffee shop will talk to me, now that word is out that Maritza was deported."

"No one wants to be next," said Amir. He checked his watch and reached for his headset, making it clear that Jack's time was up. "I'm sorry, but I have a conference call with a group of Zurich bankers who will be out the door to happy hour if I dial in a minute late."

"Understood," said Jack, rising. "I'm sorry."

"No need to apologize."

Jack wanted to circle back, discreetly, to Amir's use of the past tense—*was* a member of our family. "No, I really am sorry. I can't reveal privileged information, but I should have asked if there is anything you would like to know about Xavier or his case."

Amir's expression ran cold. "No. There's nothing. Absolutely nothing I want to know."

They shook hands, and the strength of Amir's grip only seemed to reaffirm the point: *absolutely nothing.*

"Donna will show you to the elevator," he said, opening the door for Jack.

"I'll find my way."

Jack retraced his steps down the hallway to the lobby. He said good-bye as he breezed past the receptionist and then stopped and did a double take. Theo was seated on the white leather couch taking in the view of Miami Beach.

"What are you doing here?" asked Jack.

Theo smiled as he approached. He was holding a sheet of paper. "Maritza's job application," he said, offering it.

Jack didn't take it. "How'd you get that? And so fast?"

"Me and the manager—we did a little *bizniz.*"

"Doesn't sound like my kind of *business.* Maybe you should get a job working at this place."

Theo dangled it before Jack's eyes, pinching the corner. "Got her name. And her address."

"Let me see that," said Jack, snatching it. He read quickly: Maritza Cruz. Amir's recollection was a little off. At least he'd gotten the *z* right.

"She lives in Uncle Cy's old neighborhood," said Theo. "Ten minutes from here."

Jack double-checked the address. "Let's take a ride," he said.

Andie spent the morning at the field office firing range. She had her Sig Sauer P250, the same 9 mm pistol that she'd used to earn a perfect score on the qualifications course at Quantico—the same pistol that had been locked away in the glove compartment of the family car on the morning of the Riverside school shooting.

The FBI had changed its qualifications course at least twice since Andie's graduation from the National Academy. It wasn't any easier. Agents fired on the target from distances of three, five, seven, fifteen, and twenty-five yards. Each distance posed a different challenge of speed, skill, and accuracy. Draw. Switch hands. From the ready. Standing. Drop to kneeling. Empty-gun reload. Three rounds in two seconds. Six rounds in four seconds. Fifty rounds total, two points for each hit. The target was the QIT silhouette, which looked more like a box-headed robot than a human being. Agents were advised not to distract themselves by personalizing it; no imagining the face of an old boyfriend in the box. From twenty-five yards, Andie jettisoned the warning.

In her mind's eye, the target was wearing a camouflage jacket, ski mask, and goggles. He was at one end
of the hallway outside the Riverside recreation center.
Andie was at the other end. She had twenty seconds.

Go.

Draw and fire four rounds from standing. Drop to
kneeling and fire more rounds.

She did it in eleven seconds. Eight out of eight hits.
Forty-eight out of fifty overall.

If only she'd had her Sig Sauer with her outside the
rec center.

Andie recorded her score in the ledger, cleaned up
her station, and put the ear-protection muffs back in
her locker.

"Henning, can I speak with you a minute?"

It was the ASAC. She did one more safety check and
holstered her sidearm. "Sure."

"In my office," said Schwartz.

The "in my office" part wasn't necessarily a concern. The seriousness of his tone, however, left Andie a
little worried. She followed him out of the locker room
and down the hall to his office. Schwartz closed the
door and went straight to the leather chair behind his
desk. "Have a seat, Henning."

It sounded more like an order than an offer. "This is
not the part of my job I enjoy," he said.

Andie lowered herself into a chair that was definitely starting to feel like the hot seat. "What's this about?"

He pushed a manila envelope across the desktop toward her. "This letter arrived today."

Andie opened it. The name of the law firm on the letterhead made her stomach churn. "Coolidge, Harding and Cash represents Riverside Day School," she said.

"I know all about the lawsuit," said Schwartz. "I was there when the process server handed you the summons."

"Then what's the problem? The case is ongoing. Nothing has been decided yet."

"It's not just a lawsuit anymore. Duncan Fitz—on behalf of the school—has lodged a formal complaint against you with the Office of Professional Responsibility."

Andie swallowed. "For what?"

"Your conduct during the school shooting."

"I was off duty."

"Agents are responsible for their off-duty conduct."

"Yes. But I did nothing wrong."

He took the letter back from her. "According to Mr. Fitz, you admitted under oath at your deposition that you needlessly put the lives of Riverside students in danger by violating written school policies on active shooter protocols, and by disregarding direct verbal instructions from the head of school in an emergency situation."

"This makes me sick," said Andie. "This is all because the school insists that Jack and I have to pay a full year's tuition to a school that Righley no longer attends."

"It's not about tuition," said Schwartz. "The first wrongful-death action was filed yesterday. One of the science teachers lost his life. His wife wants a million dollars from the school for loss of consortium."

"What does that have to do with me?"

"I'm sure the school knows there will be more lawsuits to come, probably well in excess of their insurance coverage. It seems clear to me that the legal strategy is to prove that the school did everything right by pointing the finger at someone who did something wrong."

It was exactly what Jack, from the get-go, had told her the lawsuit against her was really about: "The school did everything it could, and to the extent that any safety measures failed, it was the fault of people like you who broke the rules."

"I'm the scapegoat."

"I'm afraid so."

Andie sat in silence, absorbing the blow. "Am I suspended?"

"Not by me," said Schwartz. "But the review board has the power to suspend you pending the investigation."

"Do you think they will?"

"I'll recommend against it."

"Thank you."

"But let me be up front about this, Andie. A lot depends on how Duncan Fitz works this in the media. A story about an FBI agent taking matters into her own hands and putting schoolchildren in danger could be very bad for you. And bad for the bureau. Between you, me, and the lamppost, the bureau can be very image conscious. The review board will not want to appear soft on school safety."

Andie didn't need to be reminded of the FBI image. Fidelity. Bravery. Integrity. She'd worked to uphold it her entire career.

"Anything else?" she asked, rising.

"No. But I do hope this all works out. I'll do what I can."

"Thanks," she said, and she left his office.

Jack was in the passenger seat, nonstop busy on his computer, as Theo drove.

They were north of downtown Miami, on Second Avenue between Sixth and Tenth Streets, once a lively stretch that, back in the day, was known variously as Little Broadway, the Strip, and the Great Black Way. Once Miami's jazz mecca, the historic village of Overtown bore little resemblance to its former self. The nightclubs had closed decades earlier, many before Jack was even born. But he and Theo had heard the stories of Uncle Cy's glory days blowing an old Buescher 400 saxophone at places like the Cotton Club, the Clover Club, and the Rockland Palace Hotel. Theo seemed to enjoy repeating them, playing tour guide.

"Right over there used to be the Knight Beat," said Theo, "the 'swingingest place in the South.' I'll bet that sly dog Cyrus Knight impressed a lady or two saying he owned the joint."

Jack was only half listening. He was on the Internet running searches for "Maritza Cruz." It wasn't exactly an unusual name in Miami, but it wasn't as common as Maria Cruz. As best Jack could tell from the photographs associated with the name, the Maritza Cruz he wanted had no Instagram, no Twitter, and no Facebook presence. It was the search for deportations, however, that he found most remarkable.

"Immigration Court docket shows no deportations of anyone named Maritza Cruz in the last two weeks," said Jack.

"It's that up to date?"

"Good question. She could also be locked up somewhere until they put her on a plane."

Theo stopped the car. "We're here."

Jack looked up from his computer. "Where?"

"Maritza's address," said Theo, pointing across the street with a nod of his head. "From her job application."

Jack saw a vacant lot surrounded by a chain-link fence. A faded billboard promised condominiums "Opening Summer 2015"—a deadline that could now be met only with the aid of time travel. There were a few mounds of gravel and deep ruts from truck tires, but the weeds had taken over.

"I think this used to be a joint called the Harlem Square Club," said Theo. "Long gone."

"Yeah," said Jack. "Like Maritza."

Chapter 34

Jack didn't like what he heard in Andie's voice. She wasn't suspended, but she'd cashed in a sick day and was calling from home. Andie was not a crier, and the verge-of-tears moment they'd shared that night on their patio, right after she was hit with the lawsuit, was a rarity. But there was something in her voice that Jack had never heard before, something more worrisome: defeat.

"What's happening to me just sucks beyond belief."

"Andie, I don't think you should have left the office."

"You have no idea what a rumor mill that place is, Jack. I had to get out."

He listened in private, through earbuds, as Theo drove them out of Overtown. Andie recounted the whole conversation with the ASAC. Schwartz was a decent guy and, Jack had always thought, a genuine fan of Agent Henning. But they didn't call it the Federal *Bureau* of Investigation because it was immune from bureaucracy, and Schwartz was to some extent a prisoner of his own position. Jack's real beef wasn't with the FBI, anyway. It was with Duncan Fitz.

"He didn't have to involve the bureau in his pissant lawsuit," said Jack. "I know Hannah is your lawyer of record, but I'm not going to stand for this."

"What are you going to do?"

"I can think of a couple things," said Jack. A left hook to Fitz's jaw was high on the fantasy list.

"Please don't do anything while you're angry," she said.

Jack didn't answer.

"Jack, please. *Don't*."

"I promise on one condition. You need to go back to the office."

"Today?"

"Yes, now. You can't let this beat you. There's no reason for you to feel shame. I'll see you at home tonight. I love you."

The call ended.

"Everything okay?" asked Theo.

"Not really," said Jack. Andie had every right to feel

down, but it just wasn't like her to deal with adversity by leaving work early and going home.

Jack's focus turned to the root of the problem. "Drop me off right here," he told Theo.

Theo pulled up to the curb near the side-street entrance to Amir Khoury's office building. Jack's car was still in the parking garage. He got out and watched Theo drive away, but he didn't enter the garage. He walked to the corner and crossed Brickell Avenue—to the offices of Coolidge, Harding & Cash. Not even the pleasant greeting from the young woman at the reception desk could temper his resolve.

"I need to see Duncan Fitz," he told her. "Please tell him it's urgent."

She apparently remembered him from the prior visit. "Right away, Mr. Swyteck."

Jack stood by as she spoke into her headset. He couldn't hear the response, just the receptionist's stream of "Uh-huh, uh-huh, u-huh." Finally, she looked at Jack and relayed the message, straining with concentration to get it exactly right—oddly, the same face Righley made when spelling her name backward.

"Mr. Fitz thanks you very much for stopping by, and he asks that you please leave the check here with me."

"The what?" said Jack, and then his anger surged.

Treating him like the courier of the settlement check was beyond insulting. Jack knew the way to Fitz's office, and he started down the hallway.

"Mr. Swyteck!" the receptionist shouted, but Jack had too much of a head start to be chased down by a woman wearing high heels. The door to the senior partner's corner office was open. Jack went straight inside and closed the door behind him, startling Fitz, who was seated at his desk.

"You're lucky you and my father are old friends," said Jack. "Or I might punch you right in the nose."

"Trust me, Jack. There were times when the governor wanted to punch me in the nose, too. Sit, please."

"Don't downplay this. Filing the lawsuit was one thing. Lodging a complaint against my wife with the FBI's Office of Professional Responsibility is crossing the line."

"Easy, Jack. This is not personal. I believe it was Clausewitz who said war is the mere continuation of policy by other means. I think of litigation as the continuation of business by other means."

"This is beneath even you, Duncan."

Fitz rose, but it took longer than it should have. His hip seemed to be bothering him. "My arthritis is acting up," he said, grunting. "Getting old sucks."

It made Jack angry, but in a different way. His intention had been to shred the old man, and Fitz was making it feel like an attack on his own grandfather. Jack half expected him to offer a cherry Life Saver.

"I want you to know that this was not my idea," said Fitz.

"It's your case," said Jack. "If someone on your legal team has a Machiavellian mind, you're responsible."

"No, I meant the idea of lodging a disciplinary complaint did not originate from within this law firm. They asked me to do it."

"You mean your client? The school asked you to do it?"

"No," he said, grimacing as he massaged his hip. "I'm not making myself clear. Sorry. Damn this arthritis. I mean the feds."

Jack wasn't following. "Someone in the federal government asked you to report Andie to the FBI? That's what you're telling me?"

Fitz stood up straight, breathing out the pain. "That's exactly right."

"Who?"

Fitz shook his head. "I can't tell you that, Jack."

"Why did they ask you to do it?"

"I honestly don't know why. But as you know, this law firm has an all-star white-collar criminal defense team. We represent some of the biggest corporations in the world facing billions of dollars in fines for violation of the Foreign Corrupt Practices Act. When the feds ask for a favor, you do it. You never know when you might want to cash in your chips."

"Was it someone in the FBI who asked?"

"I can't say."

"You have to tell me."

He stepped closer and looked Jack in the eye. "All I can tell you is this: you're smack-dab in the middle of something much bigger than you can imagine."

Jack met his stare. "I think you're bullshitting me."

Fitz smiled a little, shaking his head as he returned to his desk. "Then I'll pray for you."

"I thank you for that."

"Oh, and Jack," Fitz said, before Jack reached the door. "Tell the receptionist to validate your parking ticket on the way out. What that garage charges is highway robbery."

"So I've heard."

Jack closed the door on his way out and went straight to the elevator. He wasn't sure what to make of Fitz's claim that someone in the federal government had solicited his complaint against Andie. But he knew one thing: it wasn't information he should keep to himself. The elevator doors opened to the main lobby. Jack speed-dialed Andie on her cell phone.

"Honey, are you at the office yet?"

"Almost. You don't have to check up on me, Jack. I'm going back to work."

"Sorry, I wasn't checking up. I just met with Duncan Fitz. There's something you need to know."

"What?"

Jack hesitated. Of all the federal agents he'd met over the years, no one was prouder of her work than Andie. She didn't warm easily to conspiracy theories, and neither did Jack.

"This came from Duncan Fitz, so consider the source."

"Jack, I'm walking into the building now. What is it?"

The lobby was more crowded than Jack would have liked, but he found a quieter spot behind a potted palm tree.

And then he gave her the painful news.

Chapter 35

Abe Beckham hurried back to his office, late for his meeting with Sylvia Gonzalez. It was his third trip of the day to and from the courthouse. A sentencing hearing before Judge Miller at nine a.m. Back to his office. A guilty plea before Judge Salvador at eleven. Back to his office. Another hearing at two. Back to his office. Thankfully, it was a short walk from the justice center to the Graham Building and its appropriately shaped footprint.

The Boomerang Building.

"Sorry I'm late," he said, as he entered his office and hurried to his desk. Gonzalez was waiting for him.

"Not a problem," she said. "Hopefully you've had time to reconsider our phone conversation."

Gonzalez had called him after her meeting with

Swyteck and explained how finding Xavier's accomplice was a "Justice Department priority." To that end, the State Attorney's Office needed to be "flexible" on the death penalty. Beckham had told her no. She'd asked him to think about it, which he'd promised to do. In no way had he encouraged her to fly all the way down from Washington to hear his final answer.

"I'm sorry you made the trip," said Beckham. "If you were under the impression that a face-to-face meeting might make me more amenable to dropping the death penalty, you were mistaken. The state attorney's position is unchanged."

"I'm sorry to hear that. I thought I'd made the DOJ's priorities clear."

"Honestly, I'm not convinced there *was* an accomplice. Maybe someone—his mother, probably—ditched the vest, the ski mask, the goggles, and the rest of his gear as an accessory after the fact. But an accomplice on the front end? No. I see Xavier Khoury the same way history records ninety-nine percent of mass shooters. A lone wolf."

"What if you're wrong about that?"

"Prove me wrong. Show me some evidence."

It was clear from her body language that Gonzalez was reluctant to do so. "I'm not asking you to drop your case, Abe. I shouldn't have to compromise a federal investigation to convince you that it's in the interests of national security to offer Xavier Khoury life without parole in exchange for the name of his accomplice."

"Threatening a man with death unless he names an accomplice is a dangerous game," said Beckham. "Even if you get a name, the accomplice will argue that Khoury just made it up to avoid the death penalty. And you know what? The man may have a point. Everything I see tells me no accomplice."

"Then where did Khoury get the extended magazines?" she asked.

"Really? That's your evidence of an accomplice? It's not illegal to own an extended magazine. Anybody can buy one at a flea market, online, or at countless other places. Unlike a handgun, you don't even have to register them under state or federal law. The important thing is we know exactly where he got the murder weapon."

"The gun with the unidentified fingerprint on it," she said.

"The gun with *Xavier Khoury's* fingerprint on it."

"Aren't you at all concerned that the extraneous print will raise a reasonable doubt in the minds of the jurors?"

"Not in the context of the totality of the evidence.

That print could belong to the guy who washes Amir Khoury's car."

"And Swyteck will argue that it could have been *that* guy who shot up Riverside Day School."

"Which the jury will find laughable. It was Xavier Khoury. And I can prove it. He murdered thirteen innocent children, fourteen now with the Abrams girl, and a science teacher—a hero—who died trying to save his students. Khoury deserves to die for what he did."

Gonzalez rose, seeming to realize that Beckham was not about to budge. "I'm very disappointed, Abe."

"Don't be," he said, walking her to the door. "Charge Mr. Khoury under federal terrorism laws as you see fit. But I answer to the people of this community, and fourteen of the youngest and most promising members of that community were murdered in cold blood. The Office of the State Attorney is seeking the death penalty. Period."

Jack was determined to leave his office before five o'clock.

One of the great things about Riverside Day School was its after-care program. Jack and Andie had used it to the fullest extent. With the change of schools, Abuela was filling in at the house from three till seven on school days. But 7 p.m. was practically bedtime—Abuela's, not Righley's. She was in her eighties and too proud to admit that she was slowing down. Max was getting on in years, too, the upside being that he no longer posed a danger of jumping up and knocking Abuela over. But Jack didn't like to push his luck or his grandmother. At a few minutes before five, he headed for the door.

"I have to show you this, Jack," said Hannah.

Two more steps and it would have been a clean getaway. "Can it wait till tomorrow?"

"Five minutes. That's all I need."

She was too excited for Jack to say no. "Two minutes," he said.

She led him to the kitchen, where her laptop was open on the table. On-screen was a frozen frame from what Jack immediately recognized as the surveillance video at Riverside on the morning of the shooting.

"Exactly what am I looking at?" said Jack.

"Xavier Khoury," said Hannah.

Jack looked more closely. The shooter was not in the frame. He saw only high-school-age students running in a hallway.

"I don't see him," said Jack.

Hannah pointed. Jack looked even more closely. It was a boy. Dark hair. About Xavier's build and skin tone. He was wearing the same uniform that all high school students at Riverside wore.

"I don't see it."

Hannah increased the zoom. The resulting pixelation only made the image worse. "Now I really don't see it," said Jack.

"You don't have to. I found a face recognition expert who will say *she* sees it. In her opinion, that is Xavier Khoury running from the gunman, like the rest of the students."

Jack was more than skeptical. To his eye, the zoomed image on the screen was little more than a scattering of magnified dots. "Hannah, there are so many problems with this, not the least of which is how are we going to afford a face recognition expert. How much does she charge?"

"Two thousand dollars."

In the world of expert witnesses, that wasn't much. "That's all? Total?"

"No. Two thousand *an hour.*"

Shades of the parking garage: *For the first fifteen minutes.*

"I don't like this," said Jack. "The jury will see how grainy this image is. Beckham will destroy this expert as a hired gun: 'Pay her enough and she'll say that's Christopher Columbus running down the hallway.'"

"She's highly respected in her field," said Hannah. "She uses an accepted video-pixelation-enhancement technique."

"Let's get real. Do you truly believe that's Xavier caught on video?"

"I believe my expert is qualified to render an opinion that it's him."

Given the day Andie was having, Jack was in no mood to debate the limits of a lawyer's ethical duty to be a "zealous advocate." He wanted to be home when Andie got there.

"We'll talk tomorrow." He said good night to Bonnie on his way out and headed to his car in the driveway. A couple of blue jays had dropped direct hits on his windshield. Jack loved the sprawling limbs of century-old oaks that canopied the front yard, but he wished the birds would find another bathroom. It was such a common occurrence that he kept a spray bottle in the trunk. He was rummaging around for a clean rag behind the spare tire when he heard a footfall in the pea gravel behind him and a voice that was vaguely familiar.

"How is Xavier?"

Jack turned around slowly. He knew he hadn't been seeing things in the courtroom, and one look at her face confirmed it. "Nice to see you, Maritza."

"Is Xavier going to be okay?" she asked.

"I was told you were deported."

"And the best thing is to let everyone keep on thinking it."

She had a black gym bag slung over her shoulder. "What's in the bag?"

"That's not important. A friend from the coffee shop told me you're looking for me. I want you to stop. I'm of no value to you. The alibi was a lie. I was not with Xavier during the shooting."

"I figured that out on my own. I want to know why you lied."

"Because I love him. And because he didn't do it."

Jack was much more interested in the second part of her answer. "How do you know he didn't do it?"

"Xavier got mixed up with some bad people. *I* got him mixed up with bad people."

"The imam told me you're a prostitute."

She paused, and it was apparent to Jack that the word wounded her. "Of course he would say that," she said. "But this is not about me. Xavier is not a murderer. He didn't do this. He's the fall guy."

"Then why doesn't he just deny it?"

"The same reason I want the world to think I've been deported to El Salvador. He's afraid."

"He could get the death penalty if he doesn't deny it."

"He's not afraid for himself. When I say these are bad people, I mean *bad*. They will kill his sister, his brother, his mother. He can't deny it."

"Who are these people?"

"Ask Xavier. I can't tell you."

"I need your help. He won't talk to me. Maybe he'll talk to you. Come visit him with me."

"I can't go anywhere near him! It's risky enough for me to come here and see you."

"Tell me how to break through to him."

"I've told you enough. You don't need me to figure this out. It's all there. Find it. And leave me alone."

"The name you used at the coffee shop was Maritza Cruz. I've run every background check I can legally run. There's nothing to connect 'Maritza Cruz' to anyone who even vaguely resembles you. That's not your real name, is it?"

"What do you think?"

"How do I get in touch with you?"

"You don't. Ever."

"I could tell the FBI we talked. Maybe they know who you are."

Her eyes narrowed. "That would be a very big mistake."

She walked away, and only then did Jack notice the taxi waiting across the street. The driver started the engine. Jack followed her to the end of the driveway, and then, suddenly, she whirled around to face him.

"*Don't* follow me."

Jack froze. Her hand was inside the gym bag, and he couldn't tell if the protrusion from inside was her finger or a gun.

"Please," he said. "Let's talk again."

She backed away slowly, then hurried to the taxi and climbed in the back seat. The door slammed, and as the driver sped away, Jack raised his cell phone, snapped a quick photograph, and enlarged the image on the screen.

"Got it," he said, looking at a clear string of six characters on the rear license plate.

Chapter 36

"Maritza" caught her breath as the cab pulled away.

"Where to?" asked the driver.

She gave him the address and settled back in the seat.

It had been a bold move, confronting Jack Swyteck. She'd gone back and forth on it, having chickened out at the courthouse, deciding at the last minute not to go through with it. That blunder had left her no choice. He'd obviously recognized her, or thought he had. Why else would he have followed her out of the courtroom, only to have lost her in the crowd? The real danger was not the encounter. The risk was that Swyteck would tell the FBI about it. She was somewhat confident that she'd discouraged him from doing so. Hopefully, he understood that the bulge in the gym bag was no bluff.

"Belt, *por favor*," said the driver.

"Excuse me?"

He apologized for his English, then reverted to his native tongue to ask that she fasten her seat belt. She knew the accent well. Her father, an engineer in the petroleum industry, had moved the family to oil-rich western Venezuela when she was six years old, and they'd lived in Maracaibo almost four years.

"You are from Venezuela, no?" she asked in Spanish.

"*Sí. Caracas. Y usted? De dónde es usted?*" And you? Where are you from?

She smiled back at him but chose not to answer. The driver let the conversation drop. He probably figured that she'd exhausted her knowledge of the Spanish language with one simple sentence that she'd practiced for a visit to Miami. He surely would have been surprised to know that Spanish was only one of four languages she spoke fluently.

It was getting dark outside, and her shadowy reflection appeared in the side window. The cabdriver's question returned to her, but only in her thoughts:

Where are you from?

She didn't answer, and she didn't even want to think about it. But riding in the back seat of a taxi, staring at her ghostly reflection in the window, brought the memories flooding back. She was fourteen years old. The man sitting beside her was probably forty. His name was Abdul. They'd met ten minutes before they'd climbed into the back seat of a taxi near the market in central Baghdad, a place called Kadhimiya, one of Shiite Islam's most important pilgrimage sites. The man driving the taxi said he was a cleric. His title, sayyid, meant that he claimed descent from the prophet Muhammad. Maritza—Rusul—had her doubts.

"What is your name, girl?" asked the cleric.

He made eye contact with her in the rearview mirror, as the cab pulled away from the busy market and into early evening traffic.

"Rusul."

She was wearing a black chador, a full-body cloak with a hood that covered all but her face, and beneath it a niqab, a scarf that covered her face below the eyes. The men didn't seem to notice how she was trembling beneath the garments.

"Your uncle tells me you are a virgin," said the cleric.

Rusul had been living with her uncle in Baghdad for almost a year, driven from her home in Mosul by ISIS militants, lucky to have survived the eighty-seven-hour trek on foot. Her father, an American expat, was shot in the face after bribing the wrong man to smuggle his family to Kurd-controlled Ebril in northern Iraq. He'd left Rusul with perfect English and Spanish, but not much hope. Last she'd heard, her mother was trapped in west Mosul with thousands of other civilians—the human shields ISIS used to conquer the city.

"Yes, I am a virgin."

Out of the corner of her eye she saw a smile crease Abdul's lips. She looked out the window at the passing cars, clenching her fists into tight, tense balls.

The driver continued, steering with one hand and smoking a cigarette with the other. "Rusul, be assured that I am licensed to perform the ceremony of marriage by the Iraqi Ministry of Justice. What we are about to do is permitted under religious sharia law. Mut'ah is an ancient custom that allows a man to help a woman in need. By doing so, Abdul is getting closer to God." He took a long drag from his cigarette, then exhaled. "Do you understand?"

"Yes."

"You must never tell anyone about this. Iraqi law is in conflict with religious law. We do not want trouble with the militia, do we, Rusul?"

"No."

Another long drag on his cigarette. The smoke was so thick that Rusul was beginning to feel nauseated. It poured from the cleric's lips as he spoke.

"Rusul, do you agree to the marriage?"

"Yes," she answered in a timid voice.

"A temporary marriage, right?"

"Yes."

"Open your hands and pray with me."

Her fingers ached as she opened her fists, she'd been clenching so tightly.

"Do you, Rusul, give me your consent to do this marriage? Abdul will pay a dowry of one hundred fifty thousand dinars for one day. If you agree, say, 'Yes, I give my consent.'"

She blinked, eyelashes fluttering nervously as she recited the words her uncle had practiced with her. "Yes, Saddir, I give you my consent to marry me."

"Abdul, do you agree to marry Rusul for one day and that you will pay her one hundred fifty thousand dinars? If you agree, say yes."

"Yes."

"Now you are both married and it is halal to be together."

Halal. Holy.

The cab stopped. They were outside an inexpensive hotel. Abdul reached across and opened Rusul's door. She climbed out first and waited on the sidewalk. The driver had final words for Abdul as they settled up the bill, and Rusul was standing close enough to overhear.

"The girl is a virgin, Abdul. You must not penetrate her from the front."

"What about the back?"

"The back is fine."

"What if something happens and she loses her virginity?"

"Then her uncle can come after you and force you to marry her. Then she is your responsibility, not his."

"There is no way to get rid of her?"

"Does her uncle know where you live?"

"No."

The cleric crushed out his cigarette in the ashtray, breathing out one last cloud of smoke. "Then no problem at all."

"Señorita, estamos aquí," said the driver. We're here.

The way he'd said it, as if repeating himself, she must not have heard him the first time. "Sorry."

She paid in cash, which made him more than happy. She had yet to meet a Miami cabdriver who didn't get pissed off by customers with a credit card. Fine by her. Cash was a way of life. No paper trail.

She gathered her bag, climbed out, and stepped onto the sidewalk. The cab pulled away. Rusul slung the strap over her shoulder and started walking along the street. Home.

Chapter 37

J ack got in his car but didn't back out of the driveway until the taxi was out of sight. Tailing Maritza home was not his plan. He was no James Bond. Surely she would have noticed and led him to a random place. The only way to find her actual destination was to let her go there and follow up with the driver. He dialed the cab company and gave the dispatcher the license plate number. She put him on hold for several minutes before coming back on the line.

"Sorry, that's not one of our drivers."

Jack had never really paid attention, but apparently the Yellow Cab Company did not have a monopoly over yellow taxis in Miami. Not until the fourth call did he get a match on the license plate, but the dispatcher would not give up the driver's cell-phone number.

"All I can do is ask him to call you," she said. "What's this about?"

Good question. "Tell him it's about his reward. A hundred dollars. I would like to hand it to him personally."

She promised to deliver the message, but Jack suddenly realized that Maritza might still be in the cab and overhear the conversation. "Wait. Tell him not to call me. Only text."

"Our drivers are not allowed to text and drive."

Right. And college students aren't allowed to drink at parties. "Tell him to text me as soon as he can," said Jack, and he gave her his number.

Two minutes later, Jack's cell phone chimed with an incoming text. It was in Spanish. There were times when that C minus in Spanish from Abuela was kind of funny. This was not one of them. Fortunately, this translation was relatively simple:

You say you have money for me?

Jack tried texting back, but he was losing precious time fighting with the autocorrect function on his phone, which kept "correcting" his Spanish with nonsensical English. He finally typed the English words into Google Translate, and then copied and pasted the entire Spanish block into the text bubble.

334 · JAMES GRIPPANDO

My friend got in your cab on 9th Court. Tell me where you dropped her and I will Venmo you $100.

He texted back with his Venmo address and a demand: Money first.

Jack wired him fifty dollars from the Venmo app with this message: The other 50 after I get the address.

The address popped up on Jack's screen, along with a little blackmail: Send 200 or I tell her you asked.

Nice guy. For all that driver knew, he was giving up a battered wife or girlfriend, which made Jack worry for the next woman. He sent no more money but texted back: Shame on you if you didn't tell her already.

Jack made a quick call to Theo, who agreed to check out the address. Jack had other plans. Attorney-client visits at the Miami-Dade Detention Center were allowed twenty-four hours a day, seven days a week. Jack called ahead to let them know he was coming, as he drove along the river toward the justice center.

Einstein is credited with defining "insanity" as "doing the same thing over and over again and expecting a different result." Perhaps Jack was insane to think that things would be different this time and Xavier would talk to him. Or maybe he was a little like Max, his ever-optimistic golden retriever, who woke up every morning convinced that "This is it, today is the day Jack is going to make me pancakes for breakfast!" Either way, instinct told him to take Maritza at her word: *"You don't need me to figure this out. I've told you enough. It's all there. Find it."*

Jack parked in the visitor lot, which had plenty of empty spaces. Dusk had turned to darkness. Traffic on the nearby expressway, which Jack never really noticed during daylight, was like the sound of running water at night. Another car pulled up beneath a glowing streetlamp. A car door slammed shut. Then another. Behind Jack, quick footfalls on the pavement became louder and even quicker as two men followed him toward the building. Either they were in a hurry or they were trying to catch up. Jack stopped outside the entrance door and turned to face them.

"I need five minutes of your time, Mr. Swyteck."

The bigger of the two men was doing the talking. Jack didn't recognize the voice or either face. "Who are you?"

He flashed a badge. "Agent Carter. Joint Terrorism Task Force."

Jack looked at it carefully. "Nice shield. How do I know you fellas are for real?"

"We saw you talking with Maritza Cruz in the driveway outside your office," said Carter.

"Did you follow me here?"

"Didn't have to. A corrections officer calls us every

336 • JAMES GRIPPANDO

time you come here to meet with your client. Go inside and ask her, if you don't believe us."

That didn't seem necessary, and it was more than enough to convince Jack that Carter was the real deal. "What's on your mind?"

"Here's the way it is," said Carter. "Save the 'my client is innocent' bullshit. Your client did it. Somebody helped him. We don't know who it was, but we need to know."

"You're not telling me anything I haven't heard from Sylvia Gonzalez at DOJ."

"This you haven't heard: if we don't get a name, there's going to be another shooting. And another. And another. Riverside Day School was the first of more to come."

It was sobering news. "How do you know that?" asked Jack.

"It's our job to know it."

Jack took a moment to wrap his head around this one. "Let's see if I understand the problem. Here's one situation. If I was sure my client was guilty, and if I knew ten schoolchildren were going to die tomorrow if Xavier didn't give me the name of his accomplice, I'd go upstairs, lock the door to the attorney-client conference room, and beat the living shit out of him until he told me."

"We're not asking you to get disbarred."

"That's good. Because I'm not a hundred percent sure he's guilty."

"We are," said Carter. "But let's get real. Your client is in jail. If we wanted to beat this information out of him, we'd have an operative in there right now shoving his face into a prison toilet until he talks. If our intelligence tells us that the next shooting is imminent, it may come to that—which I will deny having said if you ever repeat it. Just like this meeting never happened."

It was suddenly clear to Jack why this discussion was taking place with two agents in the dark, outside the detention center, rather than in a roomful of higher-ups in Washington, DC. *This meeting never happened.*

"If I hear you correctly, your intelligence isn't telling you that the next shooting is right around the corner."

"On the color code, I'd say we're somewhere between orange and red. But that could change quickly. This is no time to screw around."

"Then exactly what are you asking me to do?"

"We want the name of everyone involved in the Riverside shooting, we want your client to be the star witness against them at their trial, and we want his testimony to be clean enough to get the death penalty for every single one of those bastards. Do all you can, but do it by the book."

"I get it. But I wasn't blowing smoke when I told Sylvia Gonzalez that he doesn't talk to me."

"That's why you need to focus one hundred percent of your energy on your client. Stay away from Maritza. She can't help you make Xavier talk. *You* can make Xavier talk. We got Maritza covered."

Jack wasn't exactly eager to come face-to-face again with a woman who'd just threatened him with a concealed weapon, but any meeting with the government was an exercise in horse trading. "I'm happy to let you cover Maritza, if you're willing to give me your 302s on her."

The Form 302 was the federal agent's written record of a witness interview.

"That's impossible," said Carter.

"It's required, if you're serious about my doing this 'by the book.'"

"That decision is way above my pay grade. I will make sure your request lands on the appropriate desk."

"Thank you."

"One more thing," said Carter. "Tell no one we talked."

"Again, if you're serious about my doing this 'by the book,' I have to tell my client."

"Fine. No one else. Not even your wife."

Not telling Andie about a break in one of his active

cases was consistent with the way they'd always done things, but coming from one of her fellow federal agents, it didn't sit well with Jack. "Why not Andie?"

Carter only repeated the directive. "No one."

Jack made no promise. He opened the door and went inside to see his client.

Chapter 38

Molly was alone at her kitchen table. Amir didn't seem to notice her or the stack of mail in front of her as he entered from the hallway.

"Then we need a different lender," he said sharply.

His voice startled Molly, but he was holding his smartphone and she noticed the cordless earbuds in each ear. He continued on about the need to get this deal done, speaking not to her but to whoever was on the line, as he grabbed a can of diet soda from the refrigerator. Molly waited for the words that signaled the end of a call from Amir to his subordinates at the office.

"Get it done," he said.

Molly seized the opening. "Can we talk?"

The question snagged him from somewhere deep in his thoughts. "Now?"

"Yes. It's important."

Amir checked his messages on his phone, not even looking at her. "Sure."

"Amir!"

He looked up from his phone and seemed poised to say something about her yelling at him, but the worried expression on her face must have put him in check.

"Who died?" he asked.

"Nobody *died*. I opened the mail today."

"Oh, for God's sake, Molly. I told you not to do that. It's filled with hate."

"I have to open it."

"Why?"

"For Talitha."

"What are you talking about?"

Riverside had not officially expelled Xavier's siblings, but Molly knew they weren't welcome. She'd been homeschooling Talitha and her older brother since the shooting. Talitha missed her friends.

"Most of the parents have cut us off," said Molly. "But Rachel's mother lets her write to Talitha."

"Who's Rachel?"

Rachel had been Talitha's best friend since they were toddlers. "Forget it, all right? This isn't about a letter from Rachel." She pushed an oversized envelope toward the edge of the table. It was opened on one end. "It's about this."

"What?"

"Just look inside. But don't take it out."

Amir stepped toward the table, took the envelope, and squeezed the side seams to enlarge the opening. "What is it?"

"It's a footie."

"A what?"

"You wear it over your shoes so you don't leave footprints. Cleaning people use them. So did the shooter at Riverside."

Molly locked eyes with him, watching as his confusion turned to anger.

"This is how you choose to tell me?" he asked.

"Tell you what?"

"Oh, come on, Molly. The footie worn by the shooter just landed in our mailbox? Is that it?"

"I didn't say it was the actual footie. But it could be."

"Yes! It definitely could be, Molly! Because Xavier still had it with him when you picked him up after the shooting!"

"That's crazy!"

"It's what the police have been saying all along. *Somebody* helped him ditch his stuff after the shooting. Who else but his mother would do it?"

"It wasn't me."

He clutched the envelope. "Then where did you get this?"

"It came in the mail."

"Stop lying!" he shouted, slapping the envelope down on the table. "What did you do with all the other stuff? Burn it? Dump it in the Everglades?"

"I didn't do anything with it!"

"You got rid of all of it, or at least tried to. But like everything else you do, you fucked up. Somehow the footie got separated from all the other stuff. Where'd you find it, Molly? Under the seat in your car? The laundry room? The bottom of your four-thousand-dollar handbag?"

"Why are you saying this?"

"Because it's classic *you*. Brilliant Molly finds the footie and says, 'Hmmm, I'll mail this to myself from some random post office, and then I'll go to the police and say, "See, Detective, I told you my son was innocent. The real killer mailed me his footie!"'"

"Stop it, Amir."

"No, you stop! Your son did this. Do you hear me? He *did it*. This idiotic scheme of yours is just going to get you arrested as an accomplice after the fact and bring me down even further."

"Bring *you* down? Why is this about *you*, Amir?"

"Because I'm the only Muslim in this marriage!"

He grabbed the envelope and stormed out of the kitchen. Molly followed.

"What are you doing?"

Amir continued to the living room and went to the fireplace.

"Amir?"

He opened the flue, grabbed some kindling from the tinderbox, and lit it with the starter.

"You can't burn it!" shouted Molly. "That could be evidence."

The kindling burned quickly. Amir tossed the envelope with the footie into the fire. The flames shot up another foot, consuming the package and its contents.

"Not anymore," he said.

Chapter 39

Jack's meeting with Xavier entered its second hour of silence.

The opening monologue had taken about twenty minutes. Jack had laid out everything he'd learned about Maritza from their encounter in the driveway and from Agent Carter outside the detention center. Xavier had shown no reaction, except to make momentary eye contact with Jack each time he mentioned the name Maritza. Jack's last question was still pending. He broke an hour of silence by repeating it.

"Do you love Maritza?"

Xavier was slouching in his chair with his shackled wrists crossed in his lap. He cut a glance in Jack's direction, the mention of Maritza's name triggering another reaction. Then he lowered his eyes and retreated into his cocoon.

Jack rose and reached for the ceiling, giving his back muscles a good stretch. "She doesn't want you to die. She risked her own life to come and tell me that tonight."

Xavier didn't reply. Jack returned to his chair.

"I can wait all night for an answer, if I have to," said Jack. "Do you love her?"

It wasn't the most important question on Jack's list, but he was betting that it was the one Xavier was most likely to answer. All Jack needed was a trigger to get him talking. Another minute passed. Then—and Jack almost missed it—Xavier nodded. Just once, and ever so slightly. Jack smiled on the inside.

"Now we're getting somewhere," said Jack. "She clearly loves you."

Xavier made eye contact again. Jack moved to the end of his seat, getting a little closer. "She says you're afraid to deny the shooting."

Xavier looked away. Jack had switched gears to the shooting too quickly. He was losing him again. He tacked back in the other direction.

"Relationships are funny things, aren't they, Xavier?"

His client didn't look at him, but he seemed to re-engage.

"Sometimes, when you're in a relationship, you feel like you have no choice. In some cases, that's true. Hell, look at us. I don't have a choice. I can't quit being your lawyer. The judge won't allow it. I'm not complaining. That's just the way it is. But do you understand what that means?"

No answer.

"It means you can tell me anything. You don't have to be afraid when you're with me. Don't be afraid to deny it. Don't be afraid to tell me you did it. Don't be afraid to name the person who helped you do it. I can't tell anyone what you tell me, unless you allow it."

Xavier didn't look at him, but he appeared to be thinking about it.

"It's like a marriage," said Jack, "but it's a weird marriage. You can fire me, but I can't fire you. A marriage where only one person has all the power."

Jack waited, studying his client's reaction. Xavier's lips parted, and he seemed on the verge of saying something. And then he spoke.

"Like Rusul."

Jack could hardly believe that his client had finally spoken. But he didn't understand it. "Like whom?" asked Jack.

No answer.

"Like Russell, did you say? Who's Russell?"

Jack waited and watched. The body language went negative again. No eye contact, no sign of any willingness to speak further. Perhaps Jack should have let the silence linger another hour, if necessary, but he was losing patience.

"Does Russell have something to do with the shooting?"

Xavier sat up in his chair. For an instant, Jack thought he might say something, but he was only getting up to leave.

"Sit your ass down," Jack said harshly.

Xavier seemed taken aback by the tone, and the shackles rattled as he settled back into his chair.

"Like I said, you can fire me. You can walk out of this room right now. But here's what will happen if you do. Tomorrow, maybe the next day, you'll be in the shower. Two guys will grab you, hold you up by your ankles, and shove your head in the toilet until you drown unless you name your accomplice."

Xavier sat motionless.

"I'm not threatening you. I'm not suggesting that I will have anything to do with that. I'm telling you that I can't *stop* it from happening. So here's the choice I'm giving you. Tell me the name of your accomplice. Or sit for a polygraph examination and answer this question: 'Were you the shooter?'"

Jack gave his client a minute to consider it. But only a minute.

"Tell me what it's going to be, Xavier. Before you walk out that door, I want your answer."

Xavier glanced at the door, then back at Jack.

"I'll take the polygraph," he said.

Jack didn't respond immediately. He hadn't expected an answer, and he certainly hadn't expected that one.

"All right, then. I'll line up an examiner."

Chapter 40

It was long after dark when Maritza pulled her Toyota Prius into the lot behind the Mount Olive Baptist Church of Fort Lauderdale. Several RVs, a handful of SUVs, and about a dozen other cars had arrived ahead of her. Another Prius was parked in the usual place. Maritza wasn't the type to get to know her neighbors, but the guy in the Prius seemed to think that all Prius owners were members of the same club, so he'd introduced himself one morning. He was a grad student with about four hundred thousand dollars in student debt. The church didn't chase people away at night and had even installed a security light, a bathroom, and a shower for its homeless guests. For Cousin Prius, living in his car was the only affordable option.

Maritza hadn't told him her story.

She parked in her usual spot, not so close to the security lamp behind the church to keep her awake all night, but enough light to hopefully keep away the rapists. She got her blanket and pillow from the trunk and made up her bed in the back seat. Her "neighbor," the grad student, liked to fold down his back seat and sleep with his feet in the trunk, but Maritza wasn't interested in buying a mattress and turning the "Prius Motel" into a way of life. She plugged her phone into the USB charger in the console. An extra-long cord left the phone in reach in an emergency. She put her gym bag on the floor, also within quick reach. The pistol was inside and loaded, just in case. She would never have shot Jack Swyteck in his driveway, her threat notwithstanding. But that didn't mean she was afraid to use it, if necessary.

Maritza had figured that Swyteck might follow her, so the address she'd given to the cabdriver was a good three blocks away from where she'd parked on the street. When she was sure no one was on her tail, she'd walked to her car, hopped on the expressway, and headed north. The parking lot behind the church was her go-to bridge from one apartment to the next. She moved twice a month. It was a way of life for her—had been, for some time.

Damn, it's hot in here.

It was only her third autumn in South Florida, and like many natives, Maritza had come to hate October in the subtropics. When the rest of the country was enjoying crisp nights, sunny days, and blazing fall foliage, Florida was still stuck in the last vestiges of summer heat, humidity, and even hurricanes. The weather would make a glorious turn any day, bringing millions of snowbirds, some of whom would vie for a spot in the parking lot behind the church. Until then, there was at least one more night of misery on the calendar. She cracked the window open an inch for some air. It didn't help.

She checked the time on her cell phone. 11:28 p.m. The hour was late and she was dead tired, but she could tell that it was going to be another restless night. It had nothing to do with the heat or the fact that the car wasn't wide enough for her to stretch out the full length of her body. Her mind was too active.

The imam said you were a prostitute.

Swyteck's words had been weighing on her all evening, playing over and over again in her head. In hindsight, falling for Xavier had been a mistake—for obvious reasons. But the bigger mistake had been accepting his invitation to go with him to the mosque. Hoping for acceptance and forgiveness had been borderline delusional on her part. She'd trusted the imam for some reason.

What she'd told him in private was something she'd told no one since coming to this country.

"Have you been married before?" he'd asked her.

"Yes."

"What was his name?"

"Abdul."

"Abdul what?"

"I don't know. Just Abdul."

It had gone downhill from there. She was a grown woman, but the imam had made her feel like that fourteen-year-old girl in Baghdad who had gone back to the fraud who'd called himself a cleric to tell him that Abdul had taken her virginity and left without paying her the dowry.

"Now that you have chosen this path, you have no choice," the so-called cleric had said to her. "You are a pleasure wife. You will do many pleasure marriages. You will bring many men closer to God."

The tap on the car window made her start. She snapped quickly from her memories and grabbed her gun. The man outside the car took a step back, and she recognized his face in the glow of the security lamp. She put the gun away and lowered the window. He came closer to the car.

"Hello, Rusul," he said in Arabic.

"Hello, Abdul."

Chapter 41

Jack got home after midnight. Andie was asleep in their bed. He was too tired to eat, but he went to the kitchen anyway. He checked the trash. No empty wine bottles, which was a relief.

Jack had never known Andie to have a drinking problem, but he'd never known her to drink alone either, until he'd found her nearly passed out on their couch the other night. He knew virtually nothing about Andie's biological mother, except that she was an alcoholic incapable of raising her own child. A doctor had once told Jack that alcoholism was hereditary, but Jack still wasn't sure if it was genetic or "like parent, like child." It bothered him that the fallout from the shooting even had him thinking such things about Andie.

"You hungry?" asked Andie. She'd entered the kitchen so quietly that Jack hadn't even noticed.

"I'm sorry. Did I wake you?"

"It's fine. I was in and out of sleep."

She took a seat at the kitchen table. Jack joined her. Less than twelve hours had passed since she'd called to tell him that she was under disciplinary review. It seemed so much longer.

"I'm glad you went back to work," he said. "I really wanted to be here when you got home, but—"

"There's no need to explain."

"I want to."

"You weren't here, Jack. That's all there is to it."

"Trust me, there's a little more to it."

He didn't go into his meeting with his client, but he told her everything about the meeting with Agent Carter outside the detention center.

"Be careful, Jack," she said.

"Meaning what?"

"Carter looks like a nice guy—kind of like Theo when he's behind his bar at Cy's Place. But if you think Theo has another side, his is nothing compared to Carter's. He's a former Green Beret. His father was from Detroit, but his mother was Libyan. He's fluent in Arabic, so he was at the top of the food chain when

US Special Forces started training the Iraqi Special Operations Forces Brigade in counterterrorism."

"Sounds like he should be working in the Pentagon. Why did he leave the military?"

"I only have hearsay," said Andie.

"This isn't a courtroom," said Jack.

"Around two thousand and nine, US advisers were getting ready to transfer counterterrorism efforts to the Iraqis. It was literally called the Iraqi Counter Terrorism Service—CTS. Our exit from Iraq didn't go so smoothly. Troops were leaving, but Carter was one of the US advisers still on the ground conducting side-by-side operations with CTS. That's when things got ugly."

"Ugly for Carter?"

"For CTS. You stopped hearing success stories and started hearing about CTS conducting mass arrests, abusing women, using collective punishment, intimidating entire villages to apprehend a single suspect, and on and on. There was talk of a secret prison and torture."

"Was Carter part of that?"

"I don't know. You asked why he left the army. From what I've heard, it was entirely his decision."

"How'd he get into the FBI?"

"We're talking about the war against terrorism.

People as talented as Carter get a second chance. Sometimes a third or a fourth."

"All of what you say fits with the way he handled our meeting. Lots of implied threats. He told me not to tell anyone we even talked."

"Except me?"

"No. Including you."

Andie's expression turned to concern. "Then you shouldn't have told me."

"What?"

"Jack, I'm under disciplinary review. If they ask whether we've talked about the case, I'll have to say that you broke your agreement with the FBI and told me about Agent Carter."

"I didn't break any agreement. I never agreed."

"They won't see it that way."

"I don't care how they see it."

"Well, I do! The FBI is my career, Jack!"

"I didn't mean I don't care—not in that way."

Andie breathed out so hard that it was almost a groan. "I'm so tired of walking this line, Jack. Everything has a footnote."

"What does that mean, 'a footnote'?"

"All you lawyers love your footprints in fine print," she said, and then switched to her "Jack voice," which was about as flattering as any wife's imitation of her husband. "'Andie, I know you don't want me to defend a school shooter—*footnote*—but don't worry about it, because you and I won't talk about the case.'"

"That's not fair. I agreed to take on Xavier only to see if I could convince Abe Beckham to drop the death penalty for life without parole."

Her Jack voice continued. "'I never agreed to take Xavier's case to trial—*footnote*—but now I'm stuck because the judge won't let me out of the case.'"

"It's not a footnote, Andie. It's the law."

"If that's the law, then you should never have said yes to Xavier Khoury."

"I said yes to Nate Abrams, who doesn't want to spend the next ten years of his life attending court hearings, obsessed with whether Xavier Khoury lives or dies."

Andie rested her elbows on the table and massaged between her eyes, as if staving off a massive headache. Slowly, she rose and cinched up her robe.

"Nate Abrams is a good man, and I feel so sorry for him and his wife. But thirteen other families lost a loved one, too. Maybe for those others the death penalty isn't just an obsession, Jack. Maybe it's justice."

Jack watched as she walked away, leaving him alone in their kitchen.

Chapter 42

On Monday morning Sylvia Gonzalez left her apartment in Maryland at the usual time, caught the eight a.m. train, and rode the Red Line all the way into the district. Judiciary Square Station was flooded with the morning rush hour when she arrived, thousands of commuters climbing out of a big hole in the ground, robotic slaves to smartphones and electronic devices. On her way to the escalator she noticed a plaque that marked this station as the birthplace of the entire Washington Metro line. No one else seemed to pay it much mind. Sylvia did, but only because her father had operated a rapid transit train for forty-one years. She missed her dad and thought of him often, the proud man who'd put his daughter through Georgetown Law by going back and forth, traveling the same mile, thousands and thousands of times over four decades.

It was actually chillier as she stepped into the city than when she'd left her apartment. A fast-moving cold front was injecting a taste of winter into the middle of autumn. She buttoned her coat and forged ahead three blocks, fighting the wind all the way to her meeting at the J. Edgar Hoover Building. Ned Griffin, chief of Operations Branch I in the Counterterrorism Division of the FBI's National Security Branch, was waiting for her in a secured and windowless conference room in the building's basement.

"Nice hair," he said as she entered.

The cold wind had taken a toll, and the situation was pretty much hopeless.

"Nice gut," she said, referencing the extra ten pounds hanging over his belt.

As one of the top prosecutors in the DOJ's National Security Division, Sylvia had a close enough relationship with Griffin to allow for good-natured kidding. A little humor was good for the soul in this line of work. Operations Branch I was devoted entirely to al-Qaeda, and Griffin was a walking encyclopedia on the organization.

Griffin adjusted the audio on the LCD screen on the wall. Agent Carter was joining them by videoconference from the Miami field office. Carter had an image of sunny South Beach displayed on the green screen behind him. Agents who transferred from Washington to Miami or Los Angeles always seemed to do that for videoconferences, bragging about their balmy new location, until they caught on to the fact that no one at headquarters really gave a shit that they were living in the midst of palm trees and crime.

"What you got for us, Carter?" asked Sylvia.

"Pure gold," he said, the on-screen movement of his lips not quite in sync with his words.

Sylvia had drafted the court filing and coordinated with the US attorney in Miami to get the federal judge to approve electronic surveillance of the Khoury residence. Carter was responsible for monitoring and pulling out the gold nuggets of conversation between husband and wife. There was only audio, so Sylvia closed her eyes and imagined the scene as the entire exchange unfolded, from the argument in the kitchen over the footie that had arrived in the mail, to the shouting match in the living room:

"Because I'm the only Muslim in this marriage!"

Molly Khoury's voice was next, a series of pleas:

"What are you doing?"

"Amir?"

"You can't burn it! That could be evidence."

And finally, Amir: *"Not anymore."*

The audio recording ended. Sylvia opened her eyes.

"Well, what do think?" asked Carter.

"It's complicated," said Sylvia.

"How is this complicated?" asked Carter, incredulous. "It's just like Amir said. The mother managed to ditch everything but the footie on the day of the shooting. It turned up somewhere, and she got a crazy idea about the real shooter sending it to her in the mail. She was probably ready to call Jack Swyteck any second. We've got her, and now we've got her husband for destroying evidence."

"The point is not to build a case for accessory after the fact," said Sylvia. "We want the accomplice on the front end."

"I understand," said Carter. "We bring in mom and dad for questioning. We play the audio, and then I squeeze the shit out of them until they tell us who their son's accomplice was."

"Assuming they know the name of the accomplice," said Sylvia.

Carter scoffed. "Is there anyone on this videoconference who doesn't think *one* of them knows? Get real, Gonzalez. Amir Khoury has to know."

"No, he doesn't *have* to," she said. "You've been

eavesdropping since the search team executed the warrant and planted the devices. Almost a month."

"Twenty-six days," said Carter.

"And not a word has been spoken in that house to suggest that either one of them knew anything about the shooting before it happened. This audio doesn't change that. If anything, it makes it sound even more like the parents didn't know."

Griffin seemed eager to get to a decision. "What are you recommending, Sylvia?"

"We can do one of two things," she said. "We can pull the trigger now, like Carter recommends, and bring them down for questioning. Or we can let this play out and see if we hear what we really want to hear."

"I vote we haul them in now," said Carter. "If they know who helped their son, I'll get it out of them."

"Carter's interrogation skills are second to none," said Griffin.

Sylvia was well aware. Although his multiple tours in Iraq as a US Special Forces adviser to Iraq's Counter Terrorism Service had come to an abrupt end, the bureau had given him a second chance as a legal attaché in the US embassy in Baghdad. The official duty of a "legat" was to serve as a liaison between the FBI and the law enforcement agencies of other nations, but some—as Carter had—functioned as intelligence agents and more.

"I'm not denying his talents," said Sylvia.

"No, you're just chickenshit, and if we blow this opportunity, the next shooting is on you."

Rumor had it that Carter was once in line for Griffin's job as section chief, but his propensity for berating and even sacrificing his colleagues to achieve his objectives—which Sylvia was experiencing firsthand—was the untold story behind his obvious demotion from legat in Baghdad to a mere squad member in the Miami field office.

She kept things professional. "Bringing in the Khourys for questioning now is a risky proposition. At the end of the day, we could be left with nothing but a mother who made a really bad decision *after* the shooting, and a father who burned the evidence of her crime because he's tired of being the Muslim scapegoat."

Griffin glanced at the LCD screen, as if to see if Carter had changed his view.

"You know what I want," Carter said to him.

Griffin looked at the lawyer. "What do you think we should do?"

Sylvia appreciated his respect for her opinion, but the decision was not clear-cut. "What are you hearing on the ground about a possible second shooting?"

"I told Swyteck there's no time to waste," said Carter.

"It's good that he thinks that," said Griffin. "But we have some room to maneuver here."

"*Some*," said Carter. "Not a lot."

Sylvia's gaze settled on the phony palm trees on the green screen behind Carter. "Let's give the Khourys a little more rope. Smarter people have hanged themselves."

Griffin mulled it over for a moment, then came to his decision.

"All right. We wait."

Chapter 43

Jack was in the room for the polygraph examination, but he stood in the corner, behind his client and out of view. Xavier was seated in an old wooden chair with an inflatable rubber bladder beneath him and another tucked behind his back. A blood pressure cuff squeezed his right arm. Two fingers on his left hand were wired with electrodes. Pneumographs wrapped his chest and abdomen to measure depth and rate of respiration.

Seated across the table was Ike Sommers, a former FBI agent who, in the estimation of many, was one of the finest private polygraph examiners in the business. He was watching his cardio-amplifier and galvanic skin monitor atop the table. The paper scroll was rolling as the needle inked out a warbling line.

"All set," said Ike. "Are you ready, Xavier?"

He didn't answer. Jack wasn't sure his client was going to keep his promise and go through with the examination. He'd reverted to the silent treatment right after uttering the words *I'll take the polygraph.*

Ike tried again. "Xavier? Are you ready?"

He nodded.

"Good. Let's get started."

Jack had explained the basic process to his client in advance. The examiner's first task was to put him at ease. He started with questions that would make him feel comfortable with him as an interrogator. Do you like chocolate? Did you ever have a dog? Is your hair purple? They seemed innocuous, but with each spoken answer the examiner was monitoring Xavier's physiological response to establish the lower parameters of his blood pressure, respiration, and perspiration. It was almost a game of cat and mouse. The examiner needed to quiet him down, then catch him in a small lie that would serve as a baseline reading for a falsehood. The standard technique was to ask something even a truthful person might lie about.

"Have you ever thought about sex at your mosque?"

Xavier shifted uneasily. "No."

Jack didn't need a polygraph to know he was lying about that one.

The room was silent as the examiner focused on his readings. He appeared satisfied. The trap had worked, and now the examiner knew what it looked like on the polygraph when Xavier lied. It was clear sailing to test his truth telling on the questions that really mattered.

"Is your name Xavier?"

"Yes."

"Do you like ice cream?"

"Yes."

"Are you a medical doctor?"

"No."

"Do you own a gun?"

"No, my dad—"

"Just answer yes or no," said the examiner.

Jack couldn't overlook the irony: his client finally started to talk, and the examiner immediately shut him down.

"Is today Sunday?"

"No?"

"Have you ever climbed Mount Everest?"

"No."

"Did you kill Lindsey Abrams?"

Xavier hesitated. Maybe it was because he didn't know who Lindsey Abrams was. Maybe there was another reason.

"No."

The examiner continued. "Are you sitting down now?"

"Yes."

"Are you a woman?"

"No."

"Are you the Riverside School shooter?"

"No," he said, a little louder than his previous answers.

"Are you deaf?"

"What?"

"Yes or no, please."

"No."

"Are you fluent in Chinese?"

"No."

"Do you know who the Riverside shooter is?"

"No."

"Are you glad this test is over?"

Jack suspected that the last question was Ike's standing joke, a little levity intended to elicit a cathartic smile from the subject. He got nothing from Xavier. He turned off the machine and looked at Jack.

"You want to talk outside?" he asked.

Jack called for the guard, who unlocked the door from the outside, and the two men stepped into the hallway.

"Any initial impressions?" asked Jack.

"I'm a polygraph examiner, not a mind reader," said Ike. "I need to study the data."

"How soon can I have the results?"

Ike checked his watch. "Give me a couple hours."

"Sounds good," said Jack. "Call my cell."

Andie left Abe Beckham's office in the Graham Building with her suspicions confirmed.

Her visit had not been on Jack's behalf. She'd gone on her own account, as an FBI agent facing disciplinary review for her behavior during the Riverside school shooting. She had only one question for the prosecutor.

"Is the state of Florida on board with no death penalty if Xavier Khoury gives up his accomplice to the FBI?"

Beckham's response had come as no surprise. "Absolutely not. And I told Sylvia Gonzalez exactly that."

Ever since Jack had called and told her about his meeting with Duncan Fitz, Andie had been wrestling with the question it had raised: Who in the federal government would ask Fitz to lodge a disciplinary complaint against her? At first, she'd dismissed Fitz's claim as more hot air from a pompous old lawyer who was skilled in the ways of casting confusion to his adversaries. Her meeting with Beckham, however, had vaulted one suspect to the top of the list.

Andie drove straight to the field office, brought her ASAC fully up to speed, and laid her theory on the table.

"I think it was Carter," said Andie.

It nearly knocked Schwartz out of his desk chair. "Whoa."

"I know it's a serious accusation, but it adds up."

"How?"

"Jack and I don't discuss much about his cases, but he told me about his meeting with Carter outside the detention center. Clearly the pressure is being put on Jack to get his client to name his accomplice."

"As it should be."

"Yes, but not at my expense."

"You lost me there," said Schwartz. "How is this at your expense?"

"The original deal was that if Jack's client names his accomplice, he avoids the death penalty."

"Sounds good to me."

"Me, too. But it only works if the State Attorney's Office is on board. They're not. I just talked to Beckham this morning. The death penalty is nonnegotiable for him. Sylvia Gonzalez knows that—which means Carter knows it, too."

"I still don't see what that has to do with you, Andie."

She chose her words carefully, not wanting to sound

paranoid. But she was certain she was right. "There's no leverage on Jack if Beckham won't give up the death penalty. Carter and Gonzalez need a new pressure point to make Jack play ball."

Schwartz took a deep breath, seeming to sense where Andie was going with this. "You're saying Carter pushed Fitz to lodge the complaint against you."

"Yes. I think it's Carter's ace in the hole. He's of the badly mistaken view that Jack will give him whatever he wants—betray his own client, if need be—if Carter promises to make my troubles go away."

"Did Jack tell you that Carter put that quid pro quo on the table?"

"No."

"So this is just a theory of yours?"

"It's not *just* a theory," said Andie. "Carter has a history of throwing colleagues under the bus to get his way. That's why he's a squad member on the Miami Joint Task Force instead of the Special Agent in Charge of the Washington, DC, field office."

"How do you know that?"

"The man is grossly overqualified for his current position. Agents talk."

Schwartz leaned back in his chair, eyes cast toward the ceiling, thinking.

"I don't hear you saying I'm wrong," said Andie.

He lowered his gaze, looking straight at Andie. "His undoing was actually the Office of Security Cooperation–Iraq, part of the US embassy in Baghdad. The Iraqi government passed a law that said the Counter Terrorism Service couldn't hit a target without a legal warrant issued by a judge from the Central Criminal Court of Iraq who was independent from CTS. Carter didn't think that was such a good law."

Andie was surprised by the revelation—surprised that Schwartz had shared it, not that Carter had broken the law of a host country.

"But I do know this," said Schwartz. "Not everyone agreed with his demotion, and he still has friends in high places."

"He's using me," said Andie. "I'm an expendable pawn in his big plan to crack the big terrorist plot that will get him back in Washington."

Still no denial from Schwartz, but Andie felt an appeal to reason coming.

"Andie, this complaint against you from Duncan Fitz is bullshit. It won't amount to a hill of beans. Don't take on Agent Carter."

"Really? You want me to stand by and get steamrolled by a disciplinary review?"

"You won't get steamrolled. This complaint against you won't go anywhere. Let it play out, and the disciplinary review committee will see that there was absolutely nothing wrong with your response to the shooting. You don't have to pick a fight with Carter to clear your name."

"I should let it go? That's what you're saying?"

"Yes," he said, his expression very serious. "For your own good, let it go."

Andie rose. "Sorry, boss. Not in my DNA to let it go."

Chapter 44

Jack rode with Theo to Miami's Little Havana. It wasn't yet noon, but Theo had already scouted their lunch spot.

"Pinolandia! Let's do it. I could go for *fritanga*."

A *fritanga* was a restaurant that served a wide assortment and large quantities of home-style Nicaraguan foods, often sold by the pound. Little Havana was once known for everything Cuban, but a new wave of immigrants brought new culinary treasures. The carne asada at Pinolandia was so famous that reviewers wrote poems about it on the tables.

If you like dominatrix, go to Pain-o-landia.

If you like crap jokes, go to Pun-o-landia.

If you love Nic BBQ, go to Pinolandia!

"Work first," said Jack. "Then lunch."

Miami Senior High School's official address was on First Street, but its grand entrance, hailed upon its opening in 1928 as "befitting of a Gothic Cathedral," was on Flagler Street, Miami's east-west equivalent of "Main Street." The main structure had suffered from years of neglect, but a major twenty-first-century renovation had restored much of the Mediterranean-style architectural glory. The first graduates were the children of Miami's pioneers, all white. By 1984, the student-run newspaper had declared "Spanglish" the official school language. And in another three decades, the student body of nearly three thousand was 93 percent Hispanic, mostly Cuban, Honduran, Guatemalan, and Salvadoran.

"Did you know this is where my dad went to high school?" asked Jack, as they pulled into the parking lot.

Former governor Harry Swyteck was one of many famous alumni, including *I Love Lucy* actor Desi Arnaz, an all-star lineup of professional athletes, and the CEO of Apple Computer, Gil Amelio, who was replaced by Steve Jobs after an anonymous party—who turned out to be Jobs—sent the company into free fall by selling off 1.5 million shares of Apple stock in a single day.

"The more important question is, did Maritza Cruz go here," said Theo.

At Jack's first meeting with Maritza at San Lazaro's

Café, Maritza had told him that she was a graduate not of Fancy-Pants Day School, as she'd called it, but of Miami Senior High. Over the years, Theo had coached a number of boys from Miami High on his travel basketball team, and he knew the school's principal. She'd agreed to a meeting for eleven a.m. Elena Cantos took them back to her office, and after a few minutes of banter about the top ballers in the school, they got around to the purpose of the meeting.

"I remember Maritza," said Cantos. "Such a sweet girl."

With all the lies he'd gotten from Maritza, Jack tried not to show too much surprise. "You do remember her?"

"Yes." Cantos swiveled in her chair and ran her index finger across the spines of "MiaHi" yearbooks on the bookshelf behind her before pulling one that was five or six years old, guessing from its position on the shelf. She cracked it open and flipped through the pages, a nostalgic smile creasing her lips as she came to the right class portrait.

"This is her," said Cantos, and she handed Jack the open yearbook.

The student body was so large that headshots were about the size of a postage stamp. Jack examined this one closely. It looked a little like the Maritza he knew, but he wasn't sure.

"How old is she in this photograph?"

"Fourteen or fifteen. She was a freshman."

"Do you have any pictures of her as an upperclass-man?"

The question seemed to strike her as strange. "Well, no. Of course not."

Jack didn't understand. "Sorry, am I missing something?"

"Maritza was with us only one year. She was killed by a drunk driver the summer before her sophomore year."

Jack caught his breath. "I wasn't aware. So sorry to hear that. Are her parents still in Miami?"

"No. Her father never left El Salvador. Her mother was devastated after the accident. Last I heard, she moved back. I could look up the names of her teachers, if that would help."

Jack was about to accept the offer, then reconsidered. The phony Maritza Cruz was using the name of a deceased teenager who vaguely resembled her. Talking to the real Maritza's teachers, parents, or friends five years after her death seemed pointless.

"That won't be necessary," said Jack. "Thank you for your time."

Cantos walked them across the administrative suite to the exit. Theo reminded her that there was still room on his travel team and asked that she put in a good word with Jose Ramos, a six-foot-eight power forward on the Stingarees' varsity basketball team.

"He's another Udonis Haslem," said Theo. "Just sayin'."

Haslem played his entire NBA career with the Miami Heat, the local kid made good who'd grown up eating as many fish sticks as he could finagle for lunch at Miami Senior High and maybe a red box of raisins for dinner at home. Jack listened and enjoyed it as Theo recounted a half dozen Haslem highlights on the walk back to the car.

Jack's cell phone rang as he climbed into the front seat and got behind the wheel. The results of Xavier's polygraph examination were in. Jack put Ike Sommers on speaker as he backed his car out of the space.

"How'd he do?" asked Jack.

"I'm afraid I don't have great news," said Ike.

Jack stopped the car. "He failed?"

"No. But he didn't pass, either. The results are inconclusive."

"Does that mean he was lying or being truthful?" asked Jack.

"Neither. It means the results are useless."

Jack put the car in gear and continued out of the lot toward Flagler Street. Ike went on for another minute or so explaining the possible reasons for the inconclusive results. Maybe the questions weren't quite right. Maybe Jack's presence in the room, albeit out of sight, had made his client nervous.

"I can do a second test, if you like," said Ike.

Another thousand bucks. "I'll get back to you on that," said Jack, and the call ended.

"Sounds like that was a waste," said Theo.

"Not really," said Jack. "I don't believe in polygraphs. I've seen too many liars pass and too many truth tellers fail."

"White man's logic. Not even gonna try to understand that one."

"It's actually pretty basic. I believe someone's willingness to take the test is more reliable than the results of the test itself."

"Okay, I get it. So the fact that Xavier was willing to take a lie detector tells you he was telling the truth?"

"Not conclusively. But it says more than the test results. On the other hand, back when I first met her, I asked Maritza to sit for a polygraph examination. She freaked out and started screaming at me because I wouldn't take her at her word."

"What does that tell you?"

Jack stopped at the traffic light. "It tells me we shouldn't be surprised to hear that the real Maritza Cruz is dead."

Chapter 45

Maritza moved into a furnished efficiency apartment on Tuesday. She'd snagged a bargain on a daily rental in Hollywood through the end of the month. She was by far the youngest tenant in the complex, probably the only one born after Nixon was president, which was a good thing, as people would leave her alone. The rent would triple on November 1, the official transition from hurricane season to snowbird season, but she never stayed anywhere more than two weeks. Her job application was in the manager's hands at five different coffee shops, and surely one of them would bite. She just hoped they didn't call until the afternoon. That morning she would be away from her phone. Abdul had given her strict orders: no electronics on this trip. She left her cell phone on the kitchen counter and headed out.

She was driving to Palm Beach County but nowhere near the millionaires and mansions on the famous island off the coast. Abdul's directions took her west to the farmlands near Lake Okeechobee. Belle Glade was a city of fewer than twenty thousand residents that somehow managed to land near the top of so many lists. Highest rate of HIV infection in the twentieth century. One of the highest crime rates of the twenty-first century. Highest number, per capita, of high school football players to break out and play in the NFL. Maritza had read all those things on the Internet, none of which had anything to do with her visit. This was about open space. Vacant land. A place to target shoot.

She turned at the gravel road, exactly 1.1 miles east of the yellow building on Main Street, the one that still had the "temporary" blue tarp on the roof after a hurricane that had cut across the peninsula four years earlier, and a big sign out front that said WE BUY GOLD. She followed the road all the way to the barbed-wire fence at the end, another 1.3 miles. She stopped the car, turned off the engine—Abdul's instructions had been that detailed—and got out. The cloud of dust rising up from the road behind her evaporated. Empty fields stretched before her in every direction. It felt like the middle of nowhere, and she might have thought she was in the wrong place, but for one thing. Just as Abdul had promised, an array of paper targets was set up and standing in the north field. They were set at various distances, some just a few feet beyond the barbed-wire fence, others a good thirty yards farther away. Each a human silhouette.

Maritza opened the trunk. Inside was the long, rectangular plastic carry case Abdul had brought to her in the church parking lot. She opened the case, and for the first time—"Don't open it till you get there," he'd told her—she saw the weapon of choice.

It was the AK-47. She recognized it immediately, though she'd not actually seen one since leaving Baghdad. Not since her last meeting with Abdul in Iraq. He'd had one just like it when he took Rusul back to see the cleric.

"Another Mut'ah," said Abdul.

He was speaking to the cleric, who was seated behind his cluttered desk in an office that was barely big enough for the three of them. They were in Kadhimiya, central Baghdad, and Rusul could hear the typical noises of the shopping arcade just outside the office door. Millions visited the holy shrine, and couples often came to get married there. The certificate from the Iraqi Ministry of Justice that authorized the cleric to perform marriage ceremonies was framed and hanging on the wall behind him.

"For you?" asked the cleric.

"No. A friend."

"Another lonely colleague at CTS?"

Rusul was dressed as before, cloaked in a black chador, but she wondered if the dark blue niqab that covered her face below the eyes had hidden her surprise. She'd heard of the American-trained Iraqi Counter Terrorism Service, but this was the first she'd heard that Abdul was part of it.

"No," said Abdul, smiling. "Not from CTS. At least not directly."

Rusul sat in silence as the two men negotiated the "dowry" that Abdul's friend would pay to her, less the cleric's fee for performing the ceremony and the commission to Abdul as a finder's fee.

"The dowry from your friend is not enough."

"One hundred twenty thousand dinars is more than enough," said Abdul. "She's not fresh."

"She is still young. A beautiful girl. Your friend must pay more."

"He is a good friend. I treat him fair. The dowry is right."

The cleric lit up a cigarette. He and Abdul were

locked in the stare down of seasoned negotiators. The cleric inhaled deeply, then spoke.

"For this dowry, one hour."

"It's better for the whole day. A man gets tired."

"Two hours," said the cleric. "Final offer."

"Fine. Two hours."

Abdul opened his wallet, deducted his cut of the dowry, and handed the rest of the cash to the cleric. He counted it, then removed enough bills to cover his fee and locked them in the metal strongbox in his desk. He promised to deliver the rest to Rusul's uncle after the two-hour-long pleasure marriage to Abdul's friend ended. He could not pay the money directly to Rusul. She was, after all, "just a girl."

"Where is your friend?" asked the cleric.

"He is waiting by your taxi," said Abdul.

The first time, for her marriage to Abdul, it had struck Rusul as strange that the cleric performed the ceremony in a taxi. But she had since come to understand. No matter what the cleric told girls about the Mut'ah as an ancient religious custom, it was illegal under Iraqi law. If caught, a cleric risked detention by one of Iraq's feared Shia militias. Better to be in a moving vehicle than trapped in an office in the shopping arcade with no escape.

"Come with me," the cleric said.

The men parted ways outside the office. Rusul went with the cleric, remaining several steps behind him as they wended their way through the crowded arcade, along the cobblestone pedestrian-only walkway. A few minutes later they reached the taxi stand on the busy boulevard. The cleric's cab looked like any other in Baghdad, but she remembered it as "the one" from that ride she'd taken with Abdul as a fourteen-year-old girl. Even the smallest details continued to haunt her. The missing hubcap. The scratch on the right fender. The nauseating smell of tobacco that poured from the back seat as the door opened.

"Get in," said the cleric.

Rusul obeyed. She watched through the windshield as a man approached the cleric on the sidewalk. Abdul hadn't mentioned that his friend was black, and from the bits of conversation Rusul was able to gather through her open window, the cleric apparently had a problem with interracial "marriage," even if for plea-sure. The man opened his wallet, handed over more cash, and the matter was resolved. The cleric walked around to the driver's side. The man opened the rear door on the passenger's side. Rusul's heart pounded.

Just then, a black sedan pulled alongside the taxi on the driver's side. The man she was about to "marry" reached across, opened her door, and pushed her out of the taxi. He went with her, and in one fluid motion, the passenger's-side door to the sedan opened, the man pushed Rusul into the back seat, and he got in the sedan with her. The door slammed, and the sedan sped away.

Rusul was certain that she was going to die.

"Don't be afraid," the man said in English.

She could barely speak, overwhelmed by fear and confusion.

"Rest easy," said Carter. "You're safe with me. I'm getting you out of this hellhole."

Rusul caught her breath and forced out the words. "Who are you? How did you know I speak English?"

"I knew your father."

"From the oil company?"

He smiled sadly. "No, Rusul. Your daddy was one of the bravest men I've ever known. He didn't work for no oil company."

Maritza slammed the trunk closed, slung the rifle over her shoulder, and walked to the barbed-wire fence.

A trail of dust rose from the dirt road behind her. She watched as the approaching vehicle and the man behind the wheel came into focus. The car stopped right behind hers. The driver's door opened. Abdul got out. He walked toward her and stopped.

"This will be your only chance to practice," he said in Arabic.

"Do we have a date?"

"Soon. I will tell you the exact date when I know it. Now, let me see how much work we have to do."

Rusul inserted a plug in each ear, raised her rifle, and took aim at the nearest target. One squeeze of the trigger sent a bullet straight to the bull's-eye of target one, followed a second later by another squeeze and another hit, another squeeze, another hit, and another, and another. In less than twenty seconds it was over. Fifteen hits. She removed her earplugs.

"Not bad," said Abdul. "Not bad at all."

Chapter 46

Tuesday night was enlightening.

Jack had heard Andie complain about the bureau before, but it had always been the way anyone complained about a job. The boss is an idiot. So-and-so is a brownnoser. Tuesday night was unlike anything Jack had ever heard from his wife.

"Carter is using me," she said. "I'm a pawn."

They were sitting outside on their patio. The overdue turn in the weather had finally arrived, and Andie was covered with a cable-knit blanket. Jack was wearing the UF Gator fleece that he hadn't donned since March. Andie spared no details in laying out a theory that, not too far in the distant past, might have sounded like paranoia. He wondered if Carter would be the one to broach the quid pro quo, or if he was waiting for

Jack to be the one to come and say, "I'll give the FBI the name of Xavier's accomplice; just back away from my wife."

Jack was still steaming about it when he left the house on Wednesday morning. Sylvia Gonzalez was in Miami. It was the four-week anniversary of the Riverside shooting, and maybe that explained her visit, knowing how terrorists seemed to love anniversaries. Whatever the reason, Jack seized the opportunity and set up a meeting with her and Agent Carter at the US Attorney's Office in downtown Miami. They listened, along with the US attorney, as Jack explained all that Andie had pieced together. Then he added his own twist.

"This is more than just Agent Carter encouraging Mr. Fitz to lodge a complaint against my wife, though he certainly has a reputation for stepping on anyone and everyone if it helps him achieve his objective. I believe others are in on it," said Jack, and he was looking at Gonzalez as he spoke. "Including you."

Sylvia was too cool to be defensive. She said nothing and showed no reaction at all to the accusation. Jack continued.

"It goes back at least to the DOJ's opposition of my motion to withdraw as counsel for Xavier Khoury. All this BS you fed the court: 'Mr. Swyteck's a known quantity, we can trust him, he has a security clearance going back to his defense of Gitmo detainees.' Very smooth on your part. But let's get real. You wanted to keep me in the case because I'm married to an FBI agent. If push came to shove, you had a pressure point on me like no other defense lawyer."

Jack let the accusation linger. Sylvia and Agent Carter were looking straight at him. The US attorney, per usual, was checking messages on his phone.

"You done?" asked Sylvia.

"No. Not until I get an answer."

"We agreed to this meeting because we thought you were going to give us the name of your client's accomplice. Not to hear this nonsense."

Jack had implied as much when he'd called to arrange the meeting, so he gave her what he had. "Who is Russell?"

"Russell?"

"It's a name my client mentioned."

"Rusul," said the US attorney, looking up from his smartphone.

At once, the FBI agent and the lawyer from Washington shot him a double-barreled look that Jack read as *You're out of the club.*

"Interesting that my work at Gitmo comes back to bite you," said Jack. "Rusul. That's a woman's name. Quite common in Iraq."

Jack got no answer, but the wheels were turning in his head, and one thing after another fell into place.

"Maritza is Rusul, isn't she? She's Iraqi, not Salvadoran. And she's using the name of a dead girl, as I'm certain you're aware."

The US attorney took a shot at damage control. "Hispanics are actually the fastest-growing segment of converts to Islam. At least in South Florida."

Gonzalez shot him another look, this one translating roughly to *Shut the hell up.*

It was almost fun to watch, this living and breathing reminder that the position of US attorney was a political appointment, a highly powerful post that was not always filled with the sharpest tool in the shed. But Jack hadn't forgotten the reason for his visit—or his anger. He started with Carter.

"The FBI literally stood by and did nothing when Maritza ambushed me right outside my office and threatened me with a gun inside her bag. She could have shot me, for all you cared.

"And you," he said, bringing Gonzalez within his crosshairs. "You're standing by, if not helping him screw over my wife. So let me tell you something.

I've had enough. Tell me who Rusul is, or I'm going public."

"No!" said Carter.

"Yes. I will."

There was silence in the room.

"Would you excuse us for a minute, Jack?" asked Gonzalez.

"A minute," said Jack. He stepped into the hallway and waited outside the closed office door. A minute later, perhaps a little more, Gonzalez invited him back inside. He returned to the chair, facing them.

"I'm authorized to tell you that Rusul is a trained intelligence gatherer," said Gonzalez.

"Come again?" asked Jack.

"I met her when I was legal attaché at the US embassy in Baghdad," said Carter. "We used every asset at our disposal to fight terrorism in Iraq. Even teenage girls."

Jack wondered if that was "Carter's law" or US policy. "She worked for the American forces?" he asked. "Or for Iraq?"

"She was trained by us. But she worked for the Iraqi Counter Terrorism Service."

"What is she doing in Miami?"

"She's been here quite a while," said Carter.

"Why?"

"That's none of your business, Mr. Swyteck."

"She's working for the FBI?" asked Jack.

Carter was silent. Gonzalez answered: "Technically, yes."

"Technicalities worry me," said Jack.

"That makes two of us," said Gonzalez. "Honestly, we don't know which side she's on anymore. So the sooner your client coughs up the name . . . the sooner we can all feel safe."

Chapter 47

Jack went straight from the epicenter of federal prosecutorial power in South Florida to the Miami-Dade Pretrial Detention Center.

Xavier's communication skills had shown no improvement. Every attorney-client communication since Monday's polygraph examination had been a rerun of the Jack Swyteck monologues. Wednesday would be different, Jack resolved. He had leverage.

"Tell me about Rusul. Your Iraqi girlfriend."

Xavier's jaw nearly dropped. Jack had him. Maritza—Rusul—was the one topic his client could not keep quiet about.

"How'd you know where she's from?"

"It was certainly no thanks to you," said Jack. "But I'm not as dumb as I look."

The young man seemed concerned, or at least skeptical. "Did she tell you?"

"No. I heard it from the FBI."

Xavier was now fully engaged, no longer slouched in his chair. He leaned forward, his chest bumping right up against the table between him and Jack.

"Are they watching her because of me?"

"You might say that. She works for them. Or at least she used to."

"That's a lie."

"Did she never tell you she worked for the government?"

"She worked for the coffee shop. San Lazaro's."

Jack flashed the smile of the older and wiser. "Let me tell you something, Xavier. I'm married to a woman who has actually done undercover work for the FBI. She's had a lot of jobs. She may have even been a barista somewhere along the line."

"Undercover? What are you talking about? Rusul loved me. I loved her. I know why she called herself Maritza and pretended to be from someplace she wasn't. She was forced to marry the same man over and over again, every time he wanted pleasure."

Jack assumed the word *marry* was a euphemism. "So, when the imam told me she was a—"

"No! She was not a prostitute!"

"I understand. She was a victim of sex trafficking."

Xavier rose, his wrist shackles rattling as he pushed away angrily from the table. It wasn't news to him, but hearing Jack say it was clearly upsetting. He went to the other side of the room and leaned against the wall. Jack gave him a moment, then continued.

"What was the name of the man she was forced to marry?"

His client didn't answer.

"Xavier? Do you know the man's name?"

"Abdul," he said, muttering.

A man named Abdul from Iraq wasn't much to go on. "What more can you tell me about him?"

"I think he's here."

"Here in Miami?"

Xavier nodded.

Jack couldn't hide his frustration. "Xavier, why has it taken you this long to tell me this?"

No answer.

Jack tried a more understanding tone. "Xavier, I understand you love this girl. But you're looking at the death penalty. If you're trying to protect—"

"I need to talk to her," Xavier said, cutting him off.

"You're free to call anyone you want. But as your lawyer I need to remind you that every call from here is monitored. The police will hear everything."

"Then you need to talk to her for me."

"You want me to call her?"

"No. You can't trust phones. We never trusted phones. No texts, no emails, nothing like that."

No electronic trail was consistent with the evidence in the case so far. "How did you communicate?"

"In person. We had meeting places."

"So you had standing meetings, like every Tuesday at six o'clock in the park?"

"No. In my house it was impossible for the kids to have standing meetings. My mom micromanages everyone's schedule. I had to meet Rusul when an opening popped up."

"How did you arrange meetings if you didn't text or email?"

Jack detected the hint of a smile, the first he'd seen from his client. Xavier seemed proud of his own cleverness.

"Do you know Lincoln Road Mall?"

Interesting, thought Jack, the way teenagers assumed that anyone over the age of forty had never heard of the places young people liked to go on Miami Beach, even though young people had been going to those same places since the 1930s. It was more promenade than mall, a ten-block, pedestrian-only stretch of Lincoln Road running east-west in the heart of Miami

Beach. Thousands came every day for the cafés, bars, shops, and galleries in a treasure trove of art deco–style buildings that never seemed dated. The only vehicles were at the cross streets.

"Yes, I know Lincoln Road Mall."

"Something you probably don't know is that at the Pennsylvania Avenue intersection there's a live webcam twenty-four hours a day, seven days a week. It never moves. It's the same camera angle, forever. If you download the EarthCam app, you can see everything as it happens in real time."

"You're right," said Jack. "I had no idea."

"It's cool, right? I never got the app, cuz my parents were always checking my phone. But Maritza opened it every day at four p.m. If I wanted to get together, I would go to the intersection right before four o'clock, and that's how we knew where to meet."

"You met at the intersection where you were on camera?"

"No. In the middle of the intersection there's an oval-shaped island of grass. The island has two palm trees and two lampposts. I would bring a yellow ribbon with me. If I tied it around the nearest tree, we met at the coffee shop across from the candy store on Lincoln Road. The far tree meant our spot on Ocean Drive— the bench by the showers for the beaches. The near lamppost meant the mall at Brickell City Center. The far lamppost, midtown."

On the cuteness scale it was somewhere between teenage crush and puppy love, but Jack couldn't deny its effectiveness.

"What makes you think she still checks the web-cam?"

"She's smart. She knows that's the only way I can get a message to her."

Jack was starting to feel a bit like Cyrano de Bergerac. Or Tony Orlando and his hit song about the old oak tree. "So you want me to go to the intersection and tie a yellow ribbon around a palm tree?"

"Yes. Choose the palm tree closest to the camera. In thirty minutes she'll meet you at the coffee shop a block away."

"I know what I want to ask her," said Jack. "What do you want me to ask her?"

Xavier shrugged, and his answer told Jack pretty much all he needed to know about the two of them. "Ask her to stay safe."

Chapter 48

At four p.m. Maritza opened the webcam app on her cell phone.

For the first week after Xavier's arrest, she'd checked the Lincoln Road webcam every day at four o'clock without fail. She knew he couldn't call her from police-monitored pay phones in the detention center, and she obviously couldn't visit him. Her only hope of any word from him—even something as simple as "I'm okay"—would have to come through his lawyer at one of their old meeting spots. By the second week, she was checking maybe every other day. That Wednesday, however, she was sure to check. Something told her that if Xavier was going to reach out to her, it would be on the four-week anniversary of the shooting.

"Oh, my God," she said aloud, staring at her phone. The yellow ribbon was on the nearest palm tree.

She gave a minute of thought as to whether it was a trick or trap of some sort. She'd been waiting too long for this signal, and she couldn't ignore it. But she couldn't ignore the risk, either. She packed her gym bag accordingly. The traditional black chador wouldn't conceal her identity, but it would certainly conceal the 9 mm Glock she would carry beneath it. She grabbed her keys, got in her car, and drove to South Beach, speeding down the expressway like Danica Patrick.

The chador was something she hadn't worn since her first and last visit to Xavier's mosque. Agent Carter had given it to her and told her to wear it. Carter had choreographed her every meeting with Xavier, except the ones they'd arranged on their own through the webcam. It had taken him months to get clearance for her to work the assignment, and if her father hadn't been a CIA agent killed in Iraq in service to his country, she never would have been approved. But Carter had pull, not only with the bureau, but with her. She owed him. Carter had reminded her of that when he'd called in the favor from Rusul.

"I need you," said Carter.

They were at San Lazaro's Café. Rusul had been

working there almost a year as Maritza Cruz. Staying in Iraq as Rusul had not been an option. Not after word got out that it had been Rusul who had helped the American not only put that fraud who called himself a cleric out of business, but put him away for the next fifteen years in an Iraqi prison.

"Just ask," said Maritza.

"There's a family in Coral Gables. Well-to-do. Khoury is the name. They have a seventeen-year-old son named Xavier. We got our eye on him. I'd like you to get to know him."

He showed her a photograph.

"Handsome boy," she said. "But seventeen is a little young for me."

"Not for the role you're going to play it isn't."

"What role is that?"

He hesitated, clearly reluctant. Finally, he said it. "I need you to play a prostitute."

"Damn it," said Maritza, still in her car. It was 4:35 p.m. She'd made it to South Beach in record time, but she was wasting precious minutes hunting for a parking space, which was a form of extreme sport on Miami Beach, something that could quickly turn as violent as your average African safari. The trick was to target an unsuspecting gazelle walking along the sidewalk with her car keys in hand, stalk her at a steady and patient 3 mph all the way to her parked car, and then pounce on the opening as she pulled away.

Maritza found her mark and zipped into the opening. Getting dressed in her car was something she'd done on a regular basis when parking overnight behind the church, so slipping on the chador while still in the front seat was a piece of cake. She grabbed her Glock, concealing it beneath the chador, and then jumped out the car, walking as fast as possible to the coffee shop on Lincoln Road Mall.

Chapter 49

Jack and Theo waited at a café table beneath the palm trees outside the coffee shop. They were at the geographic heart of Lincoln Road Mall, across the street from Dylan's Candy Bar. The promenade was loaded with places like Dylan's, celebrity-owned shops with lines of tourists out the door, most of whom would buy nothing unless in need of a prop to hold in their storefront selfie.

"You and Andie doin' okay?" asked Theo.

Jack had brought Theo along because the last meeting with Maritza had ended with a gun. Jack didn't think of himself as a risk taker, but this one was worth taking if it meant stopping another school shooting.

"It's getting better," said Jack. "Things were pretty tense for a while."

"What'd you expect, defending a school shooter? You're lucky she didn't up and kick your ass."

"I suppose."

"Because she could, you know. Kick your ass."

"Yes, I'm aware."

"I mean literally. If Jack Swyteck versus Andie Henning was on pay-per-view, Andie would absolutely kick—"

"Theo, I get it."

Jack drank from his tall paper cup. It was decaf at this hour, but the Sumatra bean flavor was still there.

"That has to be her," said Theo, pointing across the street with a nod of his head.

Jack instantly knew whom he meant. He hadn't expected her to show up dressed as if she were still in Baghdad. Nothing was covering her face, however, so if the idea was to conceal her identity, it was beyond ineffective; it seemed counterproductive, more likely to draw attention than deflect it amid a crowd of tourists dressed in shorts.

Then Theo said what Jack was thinking. "I bet money there's a gun under that getup."

"I'm betting you're right," said Jack.

"You scared?"

"No. You?"

"Nope. If she's gonna shoot someone, it'll be you."

Maritza crossed the street and came straight to their small café table. Jack and Theo rose, and then they all took their seats.

"Brought your bodyguard, I see," said Maritza.

"Brought your gun, I'm sure," said Jack.

"Good to know we understand each other," she said.

Jack asked if she wanted coffee. Theo went inside to order it for her, leaving them alone to talk. Jack had not told Theo about his meeting with Agent Carter and Gonzalez in the US Attorney's Office. He told Maritza, right down to the final point.

"Sylvia Gonzalez says she doesn't know which side you're on anymore."

"Makes sense that she would say that. She wants to keep you afraid of meeting with me."

"Should I be afraid?"

"Only if you're afraid of the truth."

"What is the truth?"

She thought for a second. "The truth is I love Xavier."

"I'm guessing that falling in love was not part of your original assignment."

She laughed a little. "No. Not at all."

"What was the original assignment?"

The smile drained away. "Have you heard the myth of the seventy-two virgins?"

Jack had. It was the promise of dark-eyed virgins in

paradise that recruiters distorted to induce young men into suicide bombings and other acts of terrorism. Jack first read of it after the attacks of 9/11.

"Yes. I've heard of it."

"Agent Carter didn't think an American boy raised in the Western world of immediate gratification would be quick to act on the promise of what might come in the afterlife. I was to play his real-life virgin. Xavier's reward."

"Reward for what?"

"Martyrdom."

"You mean the shooting," said Jack.

"I didn't know it was a shooting. All I knew from Agent Carter was that Xavier was being groomed for a suicide mission."

"Groomed by whom?"

"Someone with connections with al-Qaeda. The whole point of the assignment was to figure out exactly who that person was."

"Could that be Abdul?"

The very mention of his name seemed to make her cringe. "Did Xavier tell you about Abdul?"

"I'm sorry," said Jack. "I shouldn't have just dropped his name on you like that."

"It's okay. There's a side of Abdul that Xavier doesn't know. Abdul has worked with Carter going back years in Iraq. Way back. They first met when Carter was a Green Beret and an adviser with US Special Forces. Later on, when Carter was the FBI's legal attaché in the embassy, he brought Abdul into the Iraqi Counter Terrorism Service."

"Was it Carter who brought him to Miami?"

"Yes. It's temporary. It was Abdul's job to find the connection between Xavier and al-Qaeda. Offering me up to al-Qaeda as the virgin for Xavier's sacrifice was part of his cover."

"So in this instance, Abdul is actually one of the good guys."

"He's not a good guy," she said firmly. "He's incapable of being good. I told Carter that."

"Told Carter what, exactly?"

"Abdul has gone rogue. He's training *me* for the next shooting."

"Why would he think you are trainable for such a heinous act?"

"He doesn't actually believe I'll go through with it, if you ask me. He's training me because he needs someone to pin it on after it happens."

"He's setting you up?"

"I believe he is," she said.

"The same way he set up Xavier?"

"You said it. Not me."

Jack was skeptical. "It's one thing to think a seventeen-year-old boy can be manipulated. You're savvier than that."

"Not in Abdul's eyes. He thinks I'm still the fourteen-year-old girl under his control—the pleasure bride who will do anything he says, even if she's crying in pain or gagging in disgust."

Jack had researched pleasure marriages and sex trafficking after his talk with Xavier. "You mean the Mut'ah?"

"I don't want to talk about that."

It was clearly a painful subject. "I understand. But help me understand. Why are you going along with this, letting Abdul train you for a shooting?"

"I allow him to *think* he can train me, because I want Carter to see him for who he really is."

"Why doesn't Carter see it?"

"Abdul is a very clever man. Devious with his explanations."

"What's his explanation for training you to be a shooter?"

"He told Carter he's being watched by al-Qaeda, so he's role playing with me, acting like he's really on the al-Qaeda team and planning the next shooting."

"Carter bought that?"

"Apparently. I wouldn't say Carter is naive enough

to totally trust Abdul, but Abdul has a proven track record of results for him going back to the Bush Two presidency. Carter's heart is in the right place, but his biggest flaw is that he's willing to cut a deal with the devil if it gives him a clear path to his objective. I guess Carter figures that if he gives Abdul enough latitude, they'll flush out the real al-Qaeda connection."

Jack took a minute to absorb all of it, then framed a question. "Do you know for a fact that Abdul trained Xavier?"

"I don't know for a fact. He probably did."

"Why do you say 'probably'?"

"Why else would Xavier go silent and say nothing in his own defense? He must think Abdul will kill me if he names the shooter."

"Are you saying Abdul was the shooter?"

"I don't know that. You asked me if I thought Abdul trained Xavier, and I gave you my best guess."

Jack didn't respond right away. He gave her words a moment to swirl around her, and he watched her demeanor. It wasn't exactly a lie detector test, but he noted that she didn't feel the need to fill the silence with nervous jabber the way most liars did.

"Let me ask you this, and I want an answer that is based on actual facts known to you and in your head. Was Xavier the shooter?"

"He was targeted and recruited to do it. No question."

"But did he do it?"

Her dark eyes met his, burning with intensity. "No."

"How do you know?"

She looked away, then back at Jack. "Because I wouldn't love him if he did."

Theo returned with Maritza's coffee.

"Theo, can you give us another minute?" asked Jack.

"That's all right," said Maritza, rising. "I have to go. I've said everything I came to say."

Jack believed that much. "We should talk again."

"If Xavier wants," she said. "He knows how to reach me."

Theo gave her the coffee to go, and she thanked him. "See you around, Jack."

"Hope so."

She turned and left, and Jack watched as the only hijab on the promenade disappeared into the early evening crowd of tourists.

Chapter 50

Jack and Theo were in no rush to leave their café table. Theo had scheduled himself for bartending duty starting at eight p.m., so he ordered a second espresso to help him power through till closing. Jack was still thinking of his conversation with Maritza. Theo was people watching.

"Why do you think it is that Brazilian women are so freakin' beautiful?" he asked in an almost philosophical voice.

Jack followed his friend's line of sight to the other side of the promenade, through a stand of potted palm trees, to four young women having dinner and cocktails outside a Brazilian steakhouse. They were smiling and cutting glances at the young men at the next table, and it was Jack's quick take that the ladies were trying to decide who among them had the best command of broken English to thank the Americanos for sending a round of drinks. Another case of girl from São Paulo meets boy from Saint Paul. Language was never a barrier on South Beach, but only if you were paying attention.

"I'm sorry. What'd you ask me?"

"Forget it. New question. You gonna spend the rest of your night inside your own head, or you gonna tell me what Maritza said?"

Jack had been too busy processing what he'd learned to waste time repeating it. But he took a minute to give Theo the gist.

"You want to know what I think?" asked Theo.

It had taken him all of thirty seconds to form an opinion. Theo was not the ruminator Jack was. "Okay, I'll bite. What do you think?"

"Your client either did it or knows who did it."

"You could be right," said Jack. "Or you could be wrong."

"If you think I'm wrong, then why'd you ask me what I think?"

"I didn't ask what you think," said Jack. "I think it was you who asked if I wanted to know what you think, and I thought I did—"

Suddenly, that old R.E.M. song that it had taken two days to get out of his head was back again: *I think I thought I saw you . . .*

"Can we drop this?" Jack asked, but there was no dropping it. "The thing is . . ."

"The thing is what?"

The question that had been nagging from somewhere in the back of his mind finally gelled. "Why would someone—Abdul, al-Qaeda, or whoever it was—target Xavier for recruitment and radicalization in the first place?"

Jack's cell phone rang. He checked the incoming number, then told Theo who it was.

"Mike Posten at the *Miami Tribune*."

Jack received at least five calls a day from reporters. He'd stated publicly that the trial of Xavier Khoury was going to take place in the courtroom, not in the media, and he'd meant it. He ignored ninety-nine percent of reporters' calls. Some numbers he'd even blocked. But Posten at the *Tribune* was an old friend, or at least as much of a friend as a criminal defense lawyer who was the son of a former governor could have in the media. Jack answered.

"How goes it, Mr. Posten?"

"I need a quote, Jack."

"Get in line."

"Come on. One sentence. That's all I need."

Jack was about to decline, but an idea struck. "Maybe we can help each other here."

"Wouldn't be the first time."

Posten was the reporter who'd broken the story that the weapon used in the Riverside school shooting was registered in the name of Xavier's father.

"I want to know the date of the first registration of the gun in the name of Amir Khoury," said Jack.

"You do realize that's not public information," said Posten.

"Yes. And even though your story didn't print the date of the *first* registration, I'm guessing you have that information."

"I probably do," the reporter said coyly. "But just so we're clear, you can't just go online or call the Department of Agriculture and get the name of registered gun owners. Florida law prohibits it. That information is exempt from public records laws."

"I understand."

"To put an even finer point on it," said Posten, "if I give you this information, there will be a very usable quote from you."

"Deal."

Jack could almost feel the journalist smiling through the line. "Hold on, Jack."

He waited with the phone pressed to his ear.

"What's this about?" asked Theo.

"I hadn't really thought this was important before. But talking to Maritza got me thinking that maybe I'm focused on the wrong lies and the wrong liars."

"How's that?"

"I keep asking myself the same questions. Did Xavier lie when he said 'I did it'? Was Molly lying when she said she had nothing to do with the disappearance of the clothes, the goggles, and all the other stuff the shooter was wearing? Is Maritza lying about her and Xavier? Then—boom—it hit me. What about Amir?"

"What about him?"

"Amir told me that he bought the gun after nine-eleven."

"So?"

Posten was back on the line. "Got it for you, Jack. The gun was first registered in the name of Amir Khoury on January seventeen, two thousand and one."

It was an easy computation—nine months before the terrorist attacks of September 11, 2001.

"Thanks, Mike."

"Hey, what about my quote?"

Jack said the first thing that popped into his head. "We intend to defend these charges vigorously."

"Bullshit, Swyteck. You're going to have to do a lot better than that."

"Give me twenty-four hours, Mike. This quote will be killer."

Chapter 51

Jack's drive from South Beach back to the mainland was against rush-hour traffic. Eastbound lanes on the Julia Tuttle Causeway were three long lines of monotony, but Jack was cruising toward downtown, making a blur of the evening glow from the waterfront homes of entertainment icons, Russian oligarchs, and pharmaceutical billionaires on Star Island. Theo took an Uber back to his bar in the Grove, so Jack had time alone in his car. A phone call was the last thing he wanted, and when his cell rang on Bluetooth, his first inclination was to answer only if it was Andie. He glanced at the number on the console. It was pretty unusual for Bonnie to call from the office after five o'clock. He answered.

"What are you still doing at work?"

"I had some filing to catch up on. Good thing. Molly Khoury came by. She needs to see you."

"Why?"

"She says it's important."

"Can you put her on?"

"She doesn't want to talk on the phone. She's in bad shape, Jack."

"You mean drunk?"

"I mean really bad shape. You need to come."

She was talking as if she couldn't say more. Perhaps Molly was standing nearby, and Bonnie didn't want to be overheard. Whatever the problem, a call like this from his trusted assistant of almost twenty years wasn't something Jack could ignore.

"Okay. I'll be there in twenty."

He called Andie and let her know he'd be home late, drove past his exit to Key Biscayne, and headed back to his office. He arrived sooner than promised, fifteen minutes later. Molly's Mercedes was in the driveway, but Bonnie's car was not. The door was locked, so he used his key. Molly was alone in the lobby, seated in the armchair.

"Where's Bonnie?"

"The freezer is broken on your refrigerator," said Molly. "She went to get some ice."

"Ice?"

"For what?" he was about to add, but then she turned her head, and Jack noticed her eye. The bruising was still fresh, but it was going to be one ugly shiner. Jack went to her, concerned.

"What happened to you?"

"Four-week anniversary of the shooting. A pretty awful day at the Khoury home, as you can imagine. Things got out of hand."

"Did Amir do this to you?"

She hesitated before answering. "I fell."

"You fell," he said in a tone that let her know he wasn't buying it. "Do you want to see a doctor?"

"No. I'm sure this looks a lot worse than it is."

"Has this happened before?"

Another hesitation. "People fall all the time, I guess."

"Molly, you have to be honest with me. You did the right thing by getting out of the house. You probably feel like there are not a lot of people you can turn to, with all that's happened in the last four weeks. But I'm glad you came here. I want to help, and you can trust me."

A tear from her good eye ran down her cheek. The drops pooled in her other eye, trapped by the swelling. Jack went into the kitchen and ran a paper towel under the faucet. Trying to get really cold water from a Florida tap was like the proverbial search for snowballs in hell, but something was better than nothing. He folded up the wet towel and gave it to Molly.

"This'll have to do until Bonnie brings the ice," he said.

Molly thanked him and gently applied it to the swelling.

"Where are you planning to stay tonight?" asked Jack.

"A hotel."

"Which one?"

"The usual."

"So this isn't the first time?"

"Xavier has always been a flash point in our marriage," she said.

"It might sound like a stupid question to ask why," said Jack, "but up until four weeks ago, I would have pegged him for the perfect son. Perfect grades. Accepted to MIT."

"Xavier was perfect. For a long time. Maybe he would have stayed that way if Amir had accepted him."

"Accepted him? In what way?"

She dabbed her eye, then looked at Jack. "Can I tell you a secret?"

"You can tell me anything."

"When Amir and I were engaged, he broke things off six weeks before the wedding."

"Why?"

"If you think he has a temper now, you should have known him then. The 'why' is not important. I was devastated and made a very dumb decision. I got really drunk and went to see my old boyfriend."

"We've all been there," said Jack.

"I suppose. Anyway, Amir and I obviously got back together. A month later, we were married. Eight months later, Xavier was born."

"Oh," was all Jack could say.

"Yeah. Oh."

"I'm guessing Xavier was not the product of make-up sex when you and Amir got back together."

"No. But my old boyfriend looked a lot like Amir. I've never been drawn to WASPy-looking guys. So it was never an issue outside our marriage."

"But inside?"

She lowered her gaze. "Relentless," she said in a soft but sad voice.

"Is that what tonight was about?"

She nodded. "The anniversary of the shooting brought it all to a head. He said Xavier's sin was Allah's punishment for my sin."

"You know that's not true, right?"

Molly didn't answer. Jack didn't know whether to take the conversation in its logical direction, or to let logic wait for her to heal emotionally. But he was running out of time.

"There's something important I need to tell you, Molly."

She looked up. "What?"

"I'm not in a position to share many details, but I can tell you this much. I'm having serious doubts about Xavier's guilt."

A car pulled into the driveway, the sound of tires parting pea gravel alerting Jack.

"That must be Bonnie with the ice," said Molly.

Jack had a completely different thought, knowing how abusers operated, and he went quickly to the door. Through the glass he saw Amir coming up the steps. Before he could turn the deadbolt, Amir charged the entrance and pushed his way inside, the door hitting Jack in the chest as it flew open, knocking Jack backward to the floor. He'd seen Amir's temper before, but nothing like this.

"Molly!" he shouted, in a voice that made his wife shrink.

Chapter 52

"Tell me what you said to him!" Amir shouted. Molly didn't respond, perhaps because she was too afraid to speak, or perhaps because experience had taught her that there was never a right answer.

Jack quickly climbed to his feet and stood firmly between them. "Back off, Amir."

Amir's anger shifted to Jack. "What did she tell you?"

"If you're going to stay, I need you to sit down and shut up. Either way, I'm calling the cops."

"Don't!" Molly shouted, but it wasn't an order. She was begging him. "Please don't do that. If the media gets wind of this, I can't handle it," she said, her voice quaking. "Have you seen my new name on the Internet this week? Machine-Gun Molly, mother of the Riverside School shooter. I just can't handle one more thing, Jack. I just can't."

Jack put his cell phone back in his pocket, then looked at Amir.

"She fell," he said, his tone lacking any hint of believing it. "That's what she told me."

Amir seemed relieved, or at least satisfied enough to take his anger down a notch. He looked past Jack. "I told you not to drink so much," he said, and then he looked at Jack, adding nervous laughter in a lame attempt to wring the awkwardness out of the air. "These women at the country club. They start with a glass of wine at lunch, drink all afternoon, and then come home and fall flat on their face. Literally."

It was a cheap shot, but things were de-escalating, and Jack hoped Molly would let it go. She didn't.

"Jack was just about to tell me what he learned today. He thinks *our* son might be innocent."

She went right for the hot button, choosing not to call Xavier by his name and instead emphasizing *our* son.

"Go on, Jack," she said. "Amir might be curious to hear too."

Jack was in one of the most dangerous places on earth, alone in a room with an abuser and his victim and standing right between them. He wanted nothing more than to help Molly, but she wasn't facilitating it.

"Amir, I think it's best if you leave now," said Jack.

"No!" said Molly. "Amir, you stay. Tell him, Jack. Tell him what you know."

"Yes," said Amir. "Tell me what you know, Jack."

"Molly, it's time for Amir to leave."

She didn't take his lead, and Jack knew it wasn't because she was stupid. Either she felt safer with him standing there, or she'd simply had enough of Amir.

"Just curious," she said. "When did the questions begin in your mind, Jack? Was it the curious lack of evidence that Xavier was radicalized? No social media posts? No suspicious Internet searches? No radical cleric at the local mosque? No crazy uncle visiting from overseas?"

Jack was listening to the voice behind him, but he was watching Amir. Part of his brain told him to call the cops, but the expression on Amir's face told him that he had better not reach for that phone.

"That left only two possibilities," said Molly. "Xavier didn't do it because he was never radicalized. Or he did it because he was radicalized at home."

"This is a very dangerous game you're playing," said Amir.

"I agree," said Jack. "The door is right there, Amir."

The man didn't move.

"Did you know our house has been under surveillance?" asked Molly, her question apparently directed to Jack. "They have listening devices."

"That's not true," said Amir.

"It has to be," said Molly. "I didn't think about this until I was driving over here to see Jack. Apparently, when the FBI or whoever is watching us does surveillance, they have the decency to call the Coral Gables Police when they hear a husband hitting his wife. The cops were at our front door in three minutes. Lucky for you the police can't do anything if the wife doesn't speak up. But who called nine-one-one, Amir? The kids weren't home. It wasn't me."

"I'm leaving now," said Amir. "And you're coming with me."

"No, she's not," said Jack.

"Why would they be watching us?" asked Molly, staying with her own line of questioning. "Unless they thought one of us had something to do with the shooting."

"Maybe they wouldn't be watching us if you hadn't tried to get rid of Xavier's clothes after the shooting," Amir said. "Or if you hadn't mailed the footie to yourself to make it look like someone else was the shooter."

It was the first Jack had heard of the mailing, but he assumed it was a reference to the foot coverings worn by the shooter, which the police never recovered.

"I didn't do either of those things," said Molly. "And you know it."

"We need to go now, Molly."

"No, we need to be honest now!" she said, her voice rising. "Why did they mail you that stupid foot covering? Was that to keep you in line, Amir? Were they afraid you were going to break under the pressure, and they needed to remind you that you were already in too deep?"

"You need to stop right now," said Amir.

"How long has this been going on, Amir? Months? Years? Is this why you wouldn't let me divorce you? The pretty blond wife was your perfect cover?"

Amir charged toward her. Jack pushed him away, knocking him to the floor. Molly hurried to the reception desk and grabbed the telephone. Amir pulled a gun from under his sport coat and fired one shot, which shattered the base of the phone and sent the pieces flying off the reception desk. He then turned the gun on Jack.

"Nobody move!"

Jack froze. Molly was standing at the desk, the receiver still in her hand and the now-detached cord dangling. She didn't move. There was complete silence.

Then, from the driveway, came the sound of a car pulling up.

"Who's that?" asked Amir.

"Bonnie, my assistant. She went to get ice for your wife's eye."

He pointed the gun at Jack, then Molly, then back again, as if not sure who was the bigger problem. The car door shut outside the building.

"We can deal with this," said Jack. "Just put the gun away, Amir."

"Fuck you, Swyteck! Is there a back door to this place?"

"Through the kitchen."

"Let's go."

Jack made one more appeal to reason. "If we go out that door, you go from assault to kidnapping. Twenty-five years to life."

Amir raised his pistol. "If we're not out the back door in ten seconds, you *and* your assistant are looking at a bullet in the head. Now let's move."

They started slowly.

"Move!" said Amir, and they hurried to the kitchen and out the back door. Amir's car was just a few steps away. He had Molly by the collar and his gun aimed at Jack's back.

"You're driving, Swyteck. Molly in front."

At gunpoint, they complied, Jack behind the wheel and Molly in the passenger seat. Amir got in the back seat right behind Jack and pressed the barrel of his pistol up against the base of Jack's skull. The car started with Amir's press of the remote key.

"Drive. And do exactly as I tell you," he said, as he pressed the gun a little harder against the back of Jack's head, "or that is going to be one messy windshield."

Jack had no idea where Amir planned to take them, but for the moment all he could do was obey. The back of the old house faced an alley, and with one streetlamp on the entire block, Jack used his high beams to cut through the darkness. He was turning out of the alley and onto the street when he heard the wail of police sirens.

"Damn it!" said Amir. "I should have taken care of your assistant."

Amir thought Bonnie called the police, but if Molly had managed to punch out 911 before Amir shot the phone off the desk, they had already been dispatched. Jack had done enough criminal defense to know that if you wanted the police to come, dial 911 and talk to the operator; if you wanted the police to come *in a hurry*, dial 911 and hang up. They were trained to assume the worst.

"Go!" said Amir.

"This is not going to turn out well," said Jack.

The gun pulled away suddenly, but it returned with

a vengeance, the metal butt striking behind Jack's right ear. The blow stunned him. The car swerved, but Jack fought it off and quickly recovered. Amir jabbed his gun at the side of Jack's skull.

"Do as you're told."

Jack felt blood oozing down the side of his face. It was clear that Amir had no intention of surrendering, but it was even clearer that he had no plan. Just ahead, the traffic light changed from green to amber. Jack noticed a squad car at the cross street, waiting for a green light. On impulse, Jack hit the gas, knowing that he couldn't possibly make the light. The squad car was already in the intersection as Jack sailed past at nearly double the speed limit. Jack's light could not have been redder.

Blue flashing lights swirled behind them as the squad car screeched onto the boulevard and gave chase.

"You did that on purpose!" said Amir. "Outrun him!"

Jack didn't react fast enough.

Amir pushed the gun so hard against the back of Jack's head that his chin hit his chest.

"Floor it, or I'll kill you!"

Jack hit the accelerator, and the car lurched forward. The squad car was a half block behind them and in hot pursuit, siren blaring. The engine growled, and the speedometer rose beyond seventy miles per hour. The squad car was right behind them.

"Faster!"

The streets around Jack's office were short and narrow, harkening back to the days when the neighborhood was purely residential. But at this speed they were quickly out of the old neighborhood.

"Turn here!" said Amir.

They were coming up on LeJeune Road, a major north-south corridor with three lanes in both directions.

"Turn!"

Jack had too much speed. He hit the brake and jerked the steering wheel hard right, which put the car into a skid, forcing a corrective hard left, which put the car into one of those smooth sliding maneuvers that professional drivers do on television commercials. But Jack was no pro. The car was out of control.

Molly screamed, but Jack could barely hear her over the screeching tires, as the car cut across three lanes of oncoming traffic. Horns blasted, vehicles swerved out of the way, and the bright white beams from several pairs of headlamps shot in every direction. The front tires slammed into the curb, and for an instant the car was airborne before coming down hard on an asphalt parking lot, headed straight toward a motor lodge.

Jack's childhood flashed before his eyes, memories of those road trips and cheap motels that all looked the same, a string of rooms with outdoor entrances that faced the parking lot, the flimsy front wall consisting of a door, a picture window, and a climate-control unit all in one prefabricated piece. They scored a direct hit on Room 102. It was like driving into a one-car garage without bothering to open the garage door. Both airbags exploded. The car leveled everything in its path, like a high-speed bulldozer, shoving lamps and dressers and two double beds against the back wall of the hotel room. The mountain of debris had acted like a giant cushion, not exactly a soft landing, but better than crashing into a concrete pillar. Jack's door had flown wide open in the crash, but the seat belt and airbag had saved his life.

"Molly, are you okay?" he asked.

She didn't answer, but he heard her crying, so he knew she was alive.

"Molly?"

The room looked as if a bomb had detonated. It was almost completely dark, brightened only by the streetlights that shined through a gaping hole that was once the front of the motel room. The ceiling had partially collapsed into a cloud of dust. Electrical wiring, twisted water pipes, broken furniture, chunks of drywall, and other debris were strewn everywhere. Jack refocused just in time to hear the squad car squealing into the parking lot. The blaring siren drowned out all sounds—except for the gunshots.

Amir was shooting at the cops as he crawled out of the car through the shattered rear window. The officers in the parking lot scrambled for cover and returned the fire. Jack ducked down in the front seat and told Molly to do the same.

There was another exchange of gunfire, and the 9 mm slugs fired by the police made a popping sound as they hit the interior walls of the demolished hotel room. The wrecked automobile was suddenly bathed in white light. The police had switched on the spotlight that was fastened to the squad car. Another shot rang out, and the light was history. Amir had nailed it with one shot from a distance of at least a hundred feet. The police returned fire.

Molly was able to push open the passenger's-side door and seemed ready to make a run for it. Jack grabbed her before she put herself at risk of getting caught in the cross fire. Another crack of gunfire from somewhere in the demolished hotel room sent an officer falling to the pavement. The other went to his aid. Another shot echoed from somewhere within the mountain of debris, and the second cop went down equally hard. Jack couldn't see Amir, but wherever he was—whoever he really was—he was one crackerjack marksman.

Sirens blared in the distance, signaling that more law enforcement was on the way. Jack spotted a fast-moving shadow on the wall. It was Amir, and the instant Jack realized that, he felt the gun under his chin.

"Move, move!" shouted Amir.

He was pushing Jack over the console and into the passenger seat. It was like the old Chinese fire drills Jack had run with his friends as a teenager—in one door and out the other. Amir pushed until Jack and Molly were all the way out of the car, through the passenger's-side door. Right in front of them was a side door that, Jack surmised, led to an adjoining motel room. With a single shot, Amir destroyed the lock, forced open the door, and shoved his hostages inside. A quick look around confirmed that this room had suffered no damage from the crash. Amir pulled open the drapes on the front window facing the parking lot.

"Molly, stand in the window, hands up! Now!"

He was using his own wife as a human shield.

Molly complied, her arms shaking as she brought them up over her head.

Inside and outside the motel room, all was quiet, but for the sound of their own breathing.

Chapter 53

Andie was at home with Righley when the call came. Righley's kindergarten class was learning all about shapes in school, and Andie was in the middle of a dressing-down from a five-year-old for identifying the little window in their front door as a diamond and not a rhombus. She apologized profusely and stepped into the kitchen to take the call from her ASAC.

"I have some bad news," said Schwartz, in a tone that made the words even more ominous. "It's about Jack."

He told her what he knew, but details were sketchy. He gave her the address. "Hostage negotiation team is on its way."

"So am I," said Andie.

It was a great help having Abuela with them on

school nights, but Andie didn't tell her where she was going. "Just don't turn on the news in front of Righley," she said on her way out the door.

Three minutes later she was speeding across the causeway toward a hostage crisis on the mainland. She felt guilty not telling Abuela what was going on, but she couldn't have handled her falling to pieces on the spot. Abuela was the best grandmother anyone could ask for, but she was a Cuban grandmother, which meant that she wailed when Jack caught a cold. Andie couldn't possibly have told her that she had no idea when she and Jack might come home. If Jack came home. The thought was enough to make her crazy. Or cry.

Her phone rang again. It was a number she didn't recognize, but this was not the time to let anything go to voice mail. She answered, and the voice on the line only confused her.

"Please don't hang up."

"Who is this?"

"My name is Maritza Cruz. I know what's going on with your husband. Probably more than you do. Agent Carter told me."

Mention of Agent Carter lent this call instant legitimacy, not to mention the fact that the media had not yet gotten wind of the hostage taking. But she sounded too young to be an agent.

"Are you FBI?"

"I've been helping Agent Carter infiltrate the Khoury family."

Infiltrate? That was news to Andie. "What do you mean by 'infiltrate'?"

"That's a very long story."

"I'm listening."

"The problem is that you're not in the need-to-know universe."

Andie knew what she meant in the strict FBI sense, but she begged to differ. "My husband is a hostage. If there's something you can tell me to help, I *need to know.*"

"Just understand: if I tell you, I have to go dark."

She seemed to mean "go dark" in its military parlance, as in breaking off communication from her contact—in this case, Carter.

"If you can live with it, I can live with it."

A few seconds of silence followed. And then Maritza started talking.

Chapter 54

"More, more, more!" said Amir, barking out orders to Jack.

At gunpoint, Jack was turning the motel room into a makeshift fortress. Anyone trying to rescue the hostages by barging through the front door that faced the parking lot, or through the side door to the adjoining room that was now a pile of rubble, would have to get past a mountain of furniture and a hail of bullets. The dressers, the mattresses, the bed frames, the nightstands—the entire room had been cleaned out, except for the television. There was a crack of light at the edge of the wall and along the top of the window. The drapes were so old and worn that, in spots, the lining had lost its blackout quality. The room brightened every few seconds as the intermittent swirl of police lights seeped in from the parking lot.

"Get a blanket over those drapes!"

Jack grabbed the extras from the closet. The room was the typical old-style motel with the climate-control unit below the big picture window. Jack stood on the unit to hang the blankets from the curtain rod. It made the room even darker, but Jack's eyes had adjusted. Amir tried the light switch again. Nothing. They were obviously without electricity. That didn't stop him from pushing the on-off button on the TV every few minutes, determined to get a picture.

"Can't you see that the power's out?" said Molly.

"Shut up!"

The constant blare of sirens over the past twenty minutes told Jack that an army of police had taken up positions outside the motel. He'd heard helicopters as well, though he had no way of knowing if they were part of a tactical team or the media. His guess was that the police were regrouping and tending to the fallen officers. Jack prayed they were alive.

"Too damn quiet out there," Amir said, muttering to himself.

"Gunfight is over," said Jack. "Time to negotiate."

Amir shot him an angry look. Jack hoped this hostage taker would stay calm enough to appreciate that police didn't deal for dead hostages. Amir went to the corner and peeled back the edge of the drapes for a peek at the parking lot.

"What are you going to do?" asked Molly. "Shoot your way out of here?"

"I'll shoot *you* if you don't shut up. I only need one hostage. Remember that. Both of you."

That kind of talk to his own wife spoke volumes, but Jack still had to believe that the lawyer was the more expendable of the two.

Amir looked at the ceiling. "What was that?"

Jack had heard it, too.

"Someone's on the roof," said Amir.

Jack didn't correct him, but it wasn't that kind of sound. Perhaps they were snaking some kind of listening device through the attic. Or, Jack wondered, did law enforcement have the technology to listen through walls remotely and wirelessly these days? Jack wasn't sure. But the very fact that, one way or another, they *were* listening gave him an idea. It was tied to something Molly had said earlier, back at his office, right before Amir had gone apeshit.

"Molly really hit a nerve when she said she was the perfect cover," said Jack. "The perfect cover for what, Amir?"

Amir pointed his pistol at Jack. "Did you not hear what I said? I only need one hostage. And in case you're counting rounds," he said, pulling a second magazine from his coat pocket, "I have more than enough ammunition. Don't mess with me."

Jack had to say something for the benefit of whoever was listening.

"Did you grab that extra magazine from your car, or did you already have it in your pocket when you barged into my office?" asked Jack.

Amir ignored him, but Jack didn't care about the answer. It was all about conveying information to the hostage rescue team. Jack knew they were out there. Somewhere. And it wasn't just about saving Molly and himself. Agent Carter's warning about another school shooting was more pressing than ever.

"How long have you had that gun, Amir?" asked Jack.

"What's it to you?"

"Ah, forget it. You'd probably lie to me anyway. Like you did about the other one. The one used at Riverside."

"I told you why I bought that gun. Do you know what it was like to be a Muslim living in this country on September twelfth, two thousand and one?"

"People were scared, and they made a lot of mistakes. I hear you on that. Problem is, you bought the gun before nine-eleven."

Molly went ashen, as if unable to handle the exposure of one more lie about her husband.

"Is that true, Amir?" she asked.

"So what?" he snapped back. "It's an old gun. Who gives a shit when I bought it?"

"You're right," said Jack. "Why would anyone care? Which raises a better question."

The two men locked eyes, staring at each other in the dark room.

"Why would you lie about it?" asked Jack.

Chapter 55

Andie slammed the brakes, and the front bumper nearly kissed the pavement as her car came to an abrupt halt at the police barricade.

LeJeune Road was completely shut down, both north and south, for as far as Andie could see. Eerie was the mood on a normally busy street that was suddenly deserted, particularly at night, with the swirl of police lights coloring the neighborhood. Andie rolled down her window as the Miami-Dade police officer came toward her.

"Agent Henning, FBI," she said, flashing her badge.

Schwartz had made good on his promise to alert perimeter control that she was on her way. She parked at the curb, where another traffic control cop was dealing with media vans with satellite dishes jockeying for position. Andie counted at least three helicopters whirring overhead, their bright white search lamps cutting through the clear night sky to improve the images on television.

Schwartz came out to the barricade to get her.

"Jack's alive and sounds unhurt," were his first words to her. "We snaked a microphone through the attic and heard his voice."

Andie was so happy she could barely speak. "What about Molly?"

"Heard her voice, too. Also got a visual. Amir put her right in the window to make sure we knew he had a hostage. Or to keep us from shooting."

Amir was clearly in contention for worst husband ever.

Schwartz led her down the block toward a fast-food restaurant. Law enforcement was setting up a command post in the parking lot. Its location was strategic—close, but not too close, to the motel—and a ready source of burgers, fries, and coffee didn't hurt. The FBI SWAT van was parked in the drive-through lane. The tactical teams stood idle outside, drinking coffee—decaf, Andie presumed, so as not to get too stimulated. Behind the van was an ambulance at the ready, just in case. Andie hoped Jack wouldn't be the one to need it.

"Well, look who's here," said Schwartz.

A large motor van bearing the blue, green, and black logo of the Miami-Dade Police Department rolled into the parking lot and stopped. The antennae protruding from the roof signified that it was equipped with all the necessary technical gadgets to survey the situation and make contact with the hostage taker. The rear doors to the SWAT vans flew open, and the tactical teams filed out. They were armed with M16 rifles and dressed in black SWAT regalia, including helmets, night-vision goggles, and flak jackets.

"Wait here a sec," said the ASAC, and he started toward the MDPD van.

Almost immediately, Schwartz and the MDPD team leader were in a heated discussion, as if the face-to-face confrontation were a mere continuation of an argument they'd been conducting by telephone or radio. Andie was too far away to overhear, but she knew a turf war when she saw one. A helicopter whirred overhead—low enough for Andie to read the *Action News* logo on the side.

"Too close!" shouted Schwartz, this time speaking in a voice that Andie and everyone else could hear. "Get them to back off—now!"

An officer grabbed a loudspeaker from his patrol car and told the intruding chopper to mind the restricted airspace. It seemed to have no effect.

Schwartz and the MDPD officer continued to haggle for control of the situation. A pair of tactical teams at the ready awaited instructions, doing exactly what many believed to be the true meaning of the SWAT acronym: sit, wait, and talk. Andie's patience was at an end. The FBI's hostage negotiation team had already set up shop in the mobile command center across the street. Andie went alone. Agent Carter stepped out as she arrived.

"You're on the negotiating team?" asked Andie.

"I'm lead negotiator. I did hostage negotiation in Iraq. I speak Arabic. I know how al-Qaeda thinks."

"You're saying Amir is al-Qaeda?"

He didn't answer her question. "I'm sorry, but you can't come inside."

Andie knew that a hostage negotiation mobile command center left little room for visitors. But there was always a secondary negotiator, if only to take notes.

"I can be secondary," said Andie.

"Got one," said Carter. "It's Jones."

This was not the negotiation she'd come for. "I'm going in, Carter. And no one's going to stop me."

"Look, I'm not being petty or sexist or whatever you think I'm being. Last thing I need as lead negotiator is a demand from Amir Khoury to talk to Jack Swyteck's wife."

"Amir doesn't have to know I'm in the van."

Carter looked away, then back, for no apparent reason except that she was annoying him. "It's just not a good idea for you to be at the nerve center of this operation. Aren't you still under disciplinary review?"

It was a shitty thing to say, even from a guy with Carter's reputation for crushing out anyone like a spent cigarette if he or she didn't fit his personal vision of the mission. Andie decided to fight friendly fire with friendly fire.

"Awful lot of media out here," said Andie. "You don't want me talking to them. Not after the earful I just got on the phone from Maritza Cruz."

That got his attention. His gaze drifted toward the mobile command center.

"Sounds like you're in, Agent Henning."

"Good call. But first I have some questions for you. About the fingerprint on Amir's gun."

"Which gun?"

"Don't play stupid. The one used in the school shooting."

"Oh," he said. "That fingerprint."

"Are you going to enlighten me?"

"Here's the only thing I have to say to you, Henning. And this doesn't go beyond you and me."

She didn't commit herself to any of his conditions.

Carter took a half step closer and looked her in the eye. "I've been working this case for almost a year, and I've been watching the Khoury family almost that long. If I have to lose the Riverside School shooter's mother and his lawyer to stop the next school shooting . . ."

He let her draw her own conclusion. It didn't require much brainpower on Andie's part.

"Now, you're welcome to come inside," he said. "But it is what it is."

He turned and disappeared into the van. Andie glanced down the street toward the motel, where Jack was at the mercy of whoever this Amir really was.

Chapter 56

Jack's feet were killing him. He and Molly had been walking for so long that, had they not been trapped in a motel room, they probably could have made it all the way to Key Biscayne and back.

"Can we *please* sit down?" asked Molly.

The furniture was piled to block the door and most of the front window, but motel furniture didn't stack up with the precision of a jigsaw puzzle, so there were openings here and there—where the trash can butted up against the desk, the chair against the valet stand, and so on. The double layer of drapes and blankets should have alleviated Amir's concerns about sniper fire through the window, but he was taking no chances. On his order, Jack and Molly had started on opposite sides of the room and were on a loop: walk toward the other wall, pass each other in the middle, continue to the other wall, turn around, and repeat.

"Keep walking," said Amir.

He had the desk chair, the only place to sit in the room, other than the floor. And the floor was looking pretty good to Jack.

"I believe this is a violation of the Geneva Convention," Jack said with sarcasm.

"Shut up, smart-ass. Since when does this country follow the Geneva Convention?"

It wasn't the response Jack had anticipated, but it offered insight as to what he was really up against. Alleged violations of the Geneva Convention had sparked numerous challenges to the treatment of al-Qaeda detainees by US interrogators.

Amir's cell phone rang. He checked the number. It kept ringing.

"Aren't you going to answer it?" asked Molly.

"Just keep walking," he said.

The ringing stopped. The call had probably gone to voice mail. Amir's phone rang again. Jack couldn't be certain, but a call from a hostage negotiator would have made sense.

"They probably want to talk," said Jack, still walking.

Amir silenced the ringer on his phone. "When I want to talk, I'll call them."

Jack was no expert in hostage negotiation, but a hostage taker who didn't want to talk was not a good thing.

A ringtone pierced the silence. Amir had all three cell phones, and Jack knew that Madonna's "Material Girl" was definitely not his ringtone.

Amir jumped up from his chair, clearly agitated. He silenced Molly's phone, and then silenced Jack's.

"Please talk to them," said Molly, pleading.

"Shut up!"

Jack and Molly exchanged looks of concern as they passed each other on their endless loop. Without talk, there was no negotiation. Without negotiation, there was only one ending to this crisis. Jack had to do something. He was betting that the FBI was eavesdropping through some kind of listening device. He had to get Amir talking, if not directly to the FBI, then indirectly—through Jack.

"If you're hungry, you could negotiate for food," said Jack.

Amir didn't say anything. The fact that the suggestion didn't draw the usual vitriol told Jack that maybe he was on to something.

"Just a thought," said Jack. "No telling how long this might last."

Molly picked up Jack's lead. "I'm kind of hungry."

"You can stand to lose a few pounds," said Amir.

The hostages crossed paths on their walk. Jack made eye contact, and they reached a silent agreement to let him do the talking. The mere sound of Molly's voice was enough to set off her husband.

"There's a great little Cuban restaurant not far from here," said Jack. "You could tell the FBI to leave the food outside the door. Arroz con pollo. Plantains. Maybe a little tres leches for dessert. Whatever you want."

Amir didn't answer. He removed the magazine from his pistol and checked the remaining rounds. He was definitely more concerned about ammunition than food.

"You think they'll bring me more bullets?" he asked, clearly facetious.

That was the one thing Jack was certain was off the negotiating table.

Amir shoved the magazine back into the butt of his pistol. Jack hadn't noticed before, but it was a 9 mm semiautomatic, the same type of pistol that had been used in the Riverside shooting, though probably a newer model.

"You like the Glock?" asked Jack. "My wife swears by the Sig Sauer."

Amir studied his weapon, as if actually considering Jack's question.

"Easy to clean, she tells me. I've actually seen her

take the whole thing apart and put it back together again in less than a minute."

Jack wasn't just making small talk. Over the past four weeks, he'd spent many hours thinking about the old Glock used in the Riverside shooting. Many of those hours had been spent wracking his brain over the unidentified fingerprint—the lone print that didn't belong to Amir or his son.

"How easy was it to clean that old Glock you owned?" asked Jack.

"What does that have to do with anything?"

"Just curious," said Jack. "You must not have cleaned it very often. Or maybe you didn't do it right."

"Are you some sort of expert marksman?"

"No. But my wife is. I've watched her clean a pistol. You wouldn't find any stray fingerprints on her Sig Sauer. So, when the forensics team examined the murder weapon and found a fingerprint that didn't belong to you or Xavier, my first thought was, didn't they ever clean that thing?"

Jack and Molly passed each other again. She was dragging but pushed on. Jack kept talking.

"Then I saw where the forensics team found the print. It was actually inside the gun, under the slide, a place that would come in contact with a person's fingers only when the gun was completely disassembled."

Jack stopped at the wall, turned, and started back toward the other wall.

"So I asked myself, why would someone disassemble a gun? To clean it, obviously. Or a gun could also be easier to conceal if it's in pieces. Anyway, my conclusion was that the unidentified print belonged to the last person to completely disassemble the gun, whatever the reason. It was on the inside, so it was never smudged or wiped away in normal handling or external cleaning."

"And whose fingerprint do you think it is?"

"I don't know. But I know this, Amir. If that fingerprint belongs to the real shooter, there's a way out of this for you. I've defended clients in much deeper shit than you're in right now. You don't have to go down in a gunfight. Talk to them. Answer the phone and just talk."

A minute passed. Jack had him thinking.

The phone rang. The FBI was definitely listening.

Jack kept walking. The phone kept ringing. Jack tried the most reasoned voice he could muster.

"Pick up, Amir. You have the power in this negotiation. Only you can tell them whose fingerprint is on that gun."

Chapter 57

Maritza parked her car on a side street and walked toward LeJeune Road. In the neighborhoods just outside the police perimeter, MDPD officers were going house to house asking residents to stay inside for their own safety. But this was excitement, Miami-style, and onlookers were lined up three deep on the civilian side of the police barricades. Maritza wormed her way to the front and looked all the way down the street, her gaze landing on the old, half-lit sign outside the motel that proclaimed there was ACANCY.

She probably shouldn't have come, but after the phone call to Agent Henning, she found it impossible to stay away. Maritza had done most of the talking, but in each response and follow-up question, Henning's fears and worries for her husband had come through on the phone, no matter how hard she tried sticking to the role of staid FBI agent. There was probably nothing Maritza could do to help resolve a hostage standoff, but she was curious in a way that no other onlooker was curious.

She wondered if Abdul would show up.

If he was there, somewhere in the crowd, Maritza was the only person who knew he alone was rooting for the hostage taker. Carter seemed blind to it. *Indispensable* was the word he'd used to describe Abdul in their Baghdad operations.

Carter had been right about her. Fighting bad guys was in her blood, this daughter of an American CIA agent. Carter had been a Green Beret when he'd met Rusul's father, and though he'd moved on to the FBI and was no longer army when he'd rescued Rusul from that fraud who called himself a cleric, Carter had even more pull at the US embassy in Baghdad as a legal attaché. He put her to work for the Iraqi Counter Terrorism Service, where she was an invaluable set of eyes and ears in the mosques, in the schools, in the markets—anywhere people gathered and talked. He trusted her with the intelligence she brought him from her sources, and she trusted him to keep her out of any mission that might bring her face-to-face with Abdul.

It was Carter who'd handpicked Abdul, trained him, and brought him to CTS. He had too much invested in Abdul to get rid of him, even if the man was a pig who married one fourteen-year-old virgin after another. Carter had saved her life, but if Abdul was indispensable in Carter's eyes, she simply had to swallow that pill, no matter how bitter.

But this was Miami, not Baghdad. They were no longer in a war zone, even if they were still "at war" against al-Qaeda. It was mind-boggling to Maritza the way Carter refused to see Abdul for the man he really was three thousand miles from the world in which he'd made himself "indispensable."

Agreeing to be part of Carter's Operation Khoury without first getting the name of her handler had been Rusul's mistake. Naming Abdul as her handler had been Carter's betrayal.

"I'm not asking you to do *me* a favor," said Abdul. "This is Carter's decision."

They were in the parking lot at San Lazaro's Café in Little Havana. She was five weeks into the Khoury operation, working under the name Maritza Cruz. Carter had placed her there because it was Xavier's regular coffee shop.

"I've done everything Carter asked," she said. "I

talk with Xavier almost every morning. Every time he comes in."

"We need to take this to the next level."

"What does that mean?"

"What do you think it means?"

She couldn't find the words to respond. "I need to hear that from Carter himself."

"You know he can't speak to you directly," said Abdul. "He's breaking the FBI's rules by using you. He tried playing it by the book, but the bureau gave him three agents to choose from. The youngest was twenty-five, and not one of them could have pulled off playing a teenager. We're playing this by Carter's rules, and my directions to you are coming straight from Agent Carter. You owe him, wouldn't you agree?"

Rusul had no doubt in her mind that she would have been dead long before her nineteenth birthday had she stayed in Iraq. Still, the irony of Abdul speaking of her rescue—from men like *him*—was more than she could stomach.

"What would he have me do?"

"Carter wants his net to snare as many operatives in this country as possible. That means we have to let Amir and his son play this out to the very last step. Obviously, it's critical that we not push this too far. We need to know when the attack is in motion so we can stop it. We can't be left with egg on our faces and dead victims on the ground."

"How do I help with that?"

"Casual chitchat with a customer at the coffee shop isn't going to get us the information we need."

"You want me to ask him out? Like on a date?"

His expression turned very serious. "We need you to do whatever is necessary."

The words repulsed her, especially coming from him. "I don't believe Carter would ask me to do what I think you're asking."

"You're right. He wouldn't. But that's because he's under the impression that you hated doing what you did for the cleric in Baghdad. I know differently."

"You don't know anything about me, Abdul."

"Do you want this operation to succeed, or don't you?"

"Yes, of course. But—"

"No buts. You're in a position to be our best set of ears in this operation. Xavier's an easy mark. He's being taught to understand that a reward of seventy-two virgins awaits him in the afterlife. Whet his appetite. Be his virgin in this world."

"That's not who I am, Abdul. I am not a prostitute."

"And you're definitely no virgin," he said. "But I play the cards I'm dealt."

A flash of light assaulted her eyes, as a sudden glow from the parking lot outside the motel lit up the night.

LeJeune Road was already alight with permanent streetlamps, but law enforcement had brought in portable trees of vapor lights to bring virtual daylight to the immediate area around the motel. Maritza was in the darkness, but the people on the other side of the street, closer to the motel, were within the outer reaches of the portable glow, bathed in white light.

Rusul's memories burned hotter than vapor lights. Five months into the operation, Carter had finally spoken to her directly to ask what the hell was going on between her and Xavier. She'd confessed that one thing had led to another, and that she'd "developed feelings for Xavier." Carter had gone ballistic and said she was out of line, and when she'd told him that it was Abdul who'd ordered her to cross the line in the first place, her accusation rang hollow.

Across the street, MDPD officers were moving the crowd back, beyond the reach of the vapor lights. Rusul watched, and then she froze, her gaze locking onto the man with the dark beard wearing a baseball cap. It was him.

It was Abdul.

She backed away from the barricade. She had to get to the other side of the street. This would be the night—the night she made it clear to Carter that it was a mistake to trust Abdul more than her.

Chapter 58

Andie waited for the phone to stop ringing, hoping to hear Amir's voice on the line.

She was inside the mobile command center, just a few feet from Carter. It was tight quarters. Carter, as lead negotiator, was seated behind a small table. On it was his coffee mug, a bone mic to communicate with his team leaders in the field, and a telephone within easy reach to speak to the hostage taker. Nearest to him was the secondary negotiator, and next to him, a staff psychologist to evaluate the subject's responses and recommend negotiating strategies. Schwartz was seated next to Andie, facing the team.

"Hello, this is Amir, I'm sorry I can't take your call . . ."

Carter hung up.

"Try Molly's phone," said Andie. "Amir probably has all of them."

Carter didn't seem to appreciate the advice. "Tried that already, as you might have guessed. Let's give him a few minutes."

He put down his headset and breathed in and out.

Andie needed to know more about his approach. His earlier expressed willingness to sacrifice hostages if it would stop the next terrorist attack was weighing on her mind.

"Are you planning to ask Amir about the fingerprint on the gun?" she asked.

"That's not your territory, Henning."

"That's my husband in there. I'm not interfering, but I think I have a right to know if the priority is to gather information or to save the hostages." She was speaking more to her ASAC than to Carter.

"The priority is always to save the hostages," said Carter.

"I told you I spoke with Maritza," said Andie. "She said the fingerprint belongs to a known and confirmed member of al-Qaeda."

Carter was stone-faced.

"That's true, isn't it?" asked Andie, again speaking more to Schwartz.

Carter didn't answer, but she'd apparently gotten through to her ASAC.

"Tell her," said Schwartz.

Carter grumbled, but Schwartz called the shots in this group. "We ran the fingerprint through the dead terrorist data bank. It came up."

"Who?"

"The name wouldn't mean anything to you," said Carter. "He's dead. Been dead for years."

"You're saying that fingerprint does not belong to the Riverside shooter?"

"Only if he rose from the dead," said Carter.

"I'm still not okay with this," she said.

"Not okay with what?"

"You have physical evidence that confirmed a connection between Amir and a known, albeit dead, member of al-Qaeda. And yet you used my husband. You pressured him to get his client to name his accomplice, but you never told him how dangerous this family really was."

"I'm not hearing a problem," said Carter.

"You should have told Jack."

"How do you know I didn't?"

Schwartz leaned forward in his chair, as if to draw the line. "Let's not lie to her, Carter. We didn't tell Jack."

Andie tried to control her anger. "And look where we are now."

"It was your husband who chose to defend Xavier Khoury," said Carter. "Not me."

The phone rang. Carter quickly put on his headset and gave everyone the *quiet* signal. Then he answered.

"So good of you to call back, Amir."

"I want to speak to Swyteck's wife."

Andie was silent. Carter did not so much as glance in her direction.

"I'm afraid that's not possible, Amir. She's not here."

"I don't believe you."

"Let's you and I talk, all right?"

"No, not all right. I think she's sitting right there with you, but she's afraid to talk."

Carter did what a good negotiator was supposed to do, keeping it friendly, no argument.

"Ah, come on, Amir. I'm not lying to you. I promise you, I won't lie to you as long as we keep talking."

"You are so full of shit. I know she's afraid. I read the newspaper article about the lawsuit against her. She ran like a coward. A trained FBI agent ran away from a boy with a pistol, when all she had to do was listen and wait for him to reload—and then overpower him. Her daughter is home safe. The children who followed her the wrong way down the hall, thinking she was leading them to safety, are all dead."

The command center was silent. Not even Carter had a response.

"Nice work, Agent Henning. Now pick up the phone and call me." Amir hung up.

Andie was staring at the floor, stunned.

Schwartz spoke first. "Ignore him, Andie."

Andie took a breath, then looked her ASAC in the eye. "No. I can't ignore him. I want to make the call."

"Not gonna happen," said Carter.

Andie's gaze remained fixed on her ASAC. "I'm asking you, Guy. I want to call him."

Jack wanted to hit him.

He had no idea why Amir wanted to talk to Andie, but he hoped she wouldn't take the bait. He applied the same rule to himself, not taking the bait. The last thing he wanted to discuss with a terrorist was his own family. He turned the conversation back to Amir's.

"Still pinning this on Xavier, are you?"

Jack was doing the loop at the front of the room by himself, walking from one wall to the other, running sniper interference for Amir. Molly was in the bathroom.

"What are you talking about?"

"You said Andie 'ran away from a boy with a pistol.' I assume you meant *your* boy."

"Her boy," said Amir, pointing with a jerk of his head toward the bathroom. And then a look of concern came over him. Molly had been in there an awfully long time.

"Molly, time to get out!" said Amir.

She didn't answer. The thought crossed Jack's mind that she might hurt herself.

Amir went to the door and pounded twice. "Molly!"

"Just a minute, all right?"

Jack was relieved to hear her voice.

The toilet flushed. The bathroom door opened. Molly stepped out tentatively, started across the room, and then stopped.

"I can't walk anymore," she said.

"Didn't you see *American Sniper*?" said Amir. "These guys will shoot through a pinhole if they think there's an opening. Keep walking."

She dragged herself back to the path she and Jack had cut in the carpet. To the far wall, turn. Back to the other wall, turn. Molly was over it.

"I have to sit down, Amir."

"You just spent ten minutes in the bathroom."

"I have cramps, okay?"

"Fine. Take turns. Sit with your back to the wall."

She walked very slowly, her feet shuffling as she passed Jack. Then she whispered to him, "You can hear everything in the bathroom."

Jack kept walking. Molly continued toward the wall and sat with her back to it. Amir apparently hadn't heard what she'd said, and Jack didn't fully understand the point. He continued to the far wall, turned, and started back toward Molly. She cut her eyes, telling him to go. It was his deduction that she had something to say to Amir. Or no—she wanted him to say something to her, and her strategy was that he wasn't likely to say it with Jack in the room.

"I need to use the bathroom," said Jack.

"You got cramps, too?"

"It's been a few hours."

"Go."

Jack walked to the bathroom at the back of the room and closed the door behind him.

"Molly, you have to walk while Swyteck's in there."

Jack heard Amir's voice loud and clear. Molly was right. The walls were like paper. The FBI didn't even need electronic listening devices.

"I'll walk," she said. "But there's something I have to say to you."

"I don't want to hear it."

"Oh, you're going to hear it. Twenty years, Amir. I've had this inside me almost twenty years. You're going to hear it. Whether you want to or not."

Chapter 59

Amir took a seat in the armchair, the only stick of furniture that wasn't piled up against the front door and window. He needed a negotiating strategy. He could release one of the hostages. In return for what?

Money? How much?

A plane? To where? Havana was just ninety miles south of Miami. Fidel Castro was dead, but Cuban airspace was still hostile to American interests. US fighter jets couldn't follow him there, unless they wanted to take on Russian-made MiGs. The motel was just a few minutes away from Miami International Airport. This plan could work. But there was an alternative.

A plea. Ratting out . . . who?

He rose and crossed the room to the front barricade. He'd left an opening at the peephole. A sniper's bullet could pierce the door, so there was some risk, but he needed to see what was going on outside. He leaned forward and got a quick fish-eye view of the parking lot. It was brighter than before, thanks to whatever portable lighting the cops had brought in. Obviously, they thought more light was to law enforcement's benefit, but Amir liked it, too. Hard to pull off a sneak attack in virtual daylight. LeJeune Road was quiet. Plenty of flat-roofed buildings across the street for snipers to position themselves on. He counted the cars in the parking lot. Seven. No change since the start of the standoff.

"Are you going to tell them about Ziad?" asked Molly. She was on sniper-fire-intercept duty, walking.

Amir backed away from the door. "Don't say that name."

"Why? Are you afraid the FBI might be listening?"

The thought had crossed his mind. "Just don't say that name."

She stopped. "Ziad Jarrah, Ziad Jarrah, Ziad Jarrah."

He grabbed her by the collar, raised his hand to slap her, and then stopped. What if the cops *were* listening? Beating a hostage and her screaming for help might bring SWAT crashing through the door and charging into the room. At the very least, it might encourage Swyteck to play hero.

"Don't ever say that name again," he said, glaring. He released his grip on her collar.

Molly resumed walking. "The FBI must know by now," she said. "How you two met in Hamburg. How you two reconnected when he came to Florida for his flight training."

"Molly, that's enough."

"It can't possibly take them as long as it took me to figure all this out. Nineteen years. I probably still wouldn't know, if it weren't for Maritza."

Amir froze. From the get-go, he'd suspected that girl was trouble.

"When did you realize you were cooked, Amir?"

She was talking way too much, and Amir was on to her. She was betting that the FBI was listening, and this was her negotiation: let me go, or I bury you. She was overlooking the fact that there was another option.

He opened a music app on his cell phone and played it at full volume. Then he grabbed Molly by the throat, shoved the gun under her chin, and whispered into her ear. "I could strangle you to death, and they wouldn't hear it over the music, even if they are listening. I'm giving you a choice. Fly to Cuba with me. Or go out that door feetfirst on a gurney, and I can fly there with

Swyteck. Like I said, I only need one hostage. It's up to you. Keep your mouth shut, or pay the price."

Her eyes bulged. Her fingers pried at his grip. He released her. She gasped for air. He gave her a moment to recover and then killed the music.

"Keep walking."

She caught her breath, and then put one foot in front of the other.

Amir returned to the armchair, thinking. Molly was right. The FBI must have pieced it all together by now. He'd managed to put Hamburg, Ziad, and al-Qaeda behind him for twenty years and lead a respectable life. Then all of it had come back to haunt him, jeopardizing everything he'd built for himself. He'd thought he could pull it back together, even after the shooting. But Molly had asked the right question. "When did you know you were cooked?" For Amir, that realization had come through a deposition transcript, the moment he'd read the printed colloquy of Swyteck's examination of the fingerprint expert. When the chief of the MDPD Forensic Bureau's Latent Unit had testified that fingerprints could remain on a gun for ten, twenty, or even forty years. Right about then, the FBI could have stuck a fork in him.

It all went back to his final meeting with Ziad, almost twenty years earlier.

"Nice gun," said Ziad, speaking in Arabic.

They were at the kitchen table in Ziad's apartment in Lauderdale-by-the-Sea, just a few blocks away from the South Florida fitness center where Ziad was taking close-quarter-combat training from a master. Amir watched as Ziad disassembled Amir's brand-new Glock 9 mm pistol and laid the pieces on the table. It took him even less time to put it all back together.

"Is that how we get the guns on the plane?" asked Amir, also speaking in Arabic. "Take them apart and then put them back together once on board?"

"That was the idea. But that's changed. No guns."

"How do you hijack a plane without a gun?"

"We use these." Ziad opened the kitchen drawer and showed him.

"That's not much of a knife," said Amir.

"It's a box cutter. We can get through airport security with these."

"We need guns. What if the shit hits the fan when the plane lands?"

"The plane isn't going to land."

"What do mean it's not going to land?"

Ziad's expression turned very serious. "I'm flying it into the White House."

"Whoa. *What?* I didn't sign up for a suicide mission."

"We need five, Amir. I don't have time to find another replacement. Mohammed al-Qahtani never made it out of the Orlando airport. You agreed to step in when Immigration sent him back to Saudi Arabia."

"I didn't agree to a suicide mission. I'm no martyr."

"Come on, Amir. There are seventy-two virgins waiting for you."

It was an odd attempt at humor under the circumstances. He knew Ziad wasn't in it for that. He had a girlfriend back in Germany whom he called or emailed almost every day. He was close to his family in Lebanon. He would even go out for a beer every now and then. Amir detected a hint of apprehension in his friend's voice, but he respected his choice.

"Looks like you're in line for a hundred and forty-four virgins, Ziad. I'm out."

Amir's cell phone rang. He answered it immediately. "This better be Agent Henning."

He had a strategy. If anyone inside the FBI would push for his plane to Cuba, it would be Swyteck's wife. But the friendly voice on the line was Carter's.

"Good news, Amir. She's on her way. Ten minutes. Fifteen, tops."

The bathroom door opened and Swyteck stepped

into the room. Amir raised his pistol shoulder high and stopped him in his tracks, aiming straight at his chest. Then he spoke into the phone.

"You're on the clock. If she doesn't call me in ten minutes, tell her she's lost the chance to say good-bye."

Chapter 60

The mobile command center was silent. Amir's warning had given the FBI plenty to ponder, but Andie was more focused on the separate audio feed from the motel room, which had captured the entire conversation between Amir and his wife, less the part drowned out by music.

"Ziad Jarrah," she said, looking straight at Carter.

It wasn't a question. There wasn't an FBI agent over the age of thirty who didn't know the name of the 9/11 hijacker who took over as pilot of United Flight 93. The fact that no one in the command center was talking about it told her that she was the only one outside the loop.

"You heard right," said Carter. "It took us twenty years. But we finally made the connection."

"How?"

Carter glanced at the ASAC, as if asking for permission not to tell. Permission was denied.

"Tell her," said Schwartz.

"When United Airlines Flight Ninety-Three crashed into an open field in Pennsylvania, there wasn't the complete incineration that occurred with the direct hits on the Twin Towers or the Pentagon. In fact, the passports of two of the Flight Ninety-Three hijackers were recovered in the debris."

Andie wasn't aware of that. "When you say recovered, you mean in good condition?"

"Good enough," said Carter. "The FBI was able to obtain fingerprints of those two hijackers. Those are the only fingerprints the US government has for any of the nine-eleven hijackers. Before nine-eleven, fingerprinting wasn't part of routine visa applications under US Immigration laws."

With the mention of fingerprints, it all clicked for Andie. "Are you saying the unidentified fingerprint on Amir Khoury's gun belongs to . . ."

"That's exactly what I'm saying," said Carter. "It belongs to the Lebanese-born pilot of Flight Ninety-Three."

"How did it get there?"

"We don't know. But there's no question about the

match. It appears they first met in Germany. Jarrah was a student at Hamburg University of Applied Sciences when he joined al-Qaeda's Hamburg cell. Amir did a semester abroad in Germany while he was at Wharton. We assume they reconnected when Jarrah came to Florida to take flying lessons."

She was angry at Carter but directed her response to the ASAC. It was one of incredulity.

"You approved this operation, using my husband, without telling me or him about a direct link between Amir and one of the nine-eleven hijackers?"

"Andie," said Schwartz, fumbling for words. "Would it have made a difference if I had told you?"

She took his point. "You're right. Jack would have done it. But maybe he would have finally listened to me and kept a gun in his office to protect himself. I've always told him he's a sitting duck. Maybe this time he would have been in a position to protect himself instead of ending up a hostage."

"Now is not the time for finger-pointing," said Schwartz. "You heard Amir. We're on the clock."

"I can talk to him," said Andie.

"I can't imagine why you would want to do that," said Carter.

It wasn't a question of "want." It had started with the way he'd tormented her with his accusations of cowardice, and it had continued on through the threat against her husband. "I *need* to talk to him," said Andie.

"This could go very badly," said Carter.

"Carter's right," said Schwartz.

The quick decision against her came as a surprise. "You heard Amir," said Andie. "He threatened to kill a hostage—my husband—if I'm not on the line in ten minutes."

"That's one interpretation," said Schwartz.

"You have another one?"

He looked at the tech agent. "Play back that last sentence."

The techie tapped away on the computer, then brought up the audio recording and played it for all to hear.

"If she doesn't call me in ten minutes, tell her she's lost the chance to say good-bye."

The recording ended. Having heard it a second time, Andie understood Schwartz's concern, and she voiced it for both of them.

"He's going to kill him either way," she said.

Schwartz elaborated. "If you don't call, you lose your chance to say good-bye. Either way, you lose Jack."

Carter put a finer point on it. "And the idea that he's gracious enough to let you say good-bye is bullshit. He's a fucking terrorist. He's probably going to blow Jack's brains out while you're on the line, so you can hear it."

"I get the picture," said Andie, meaning that it was hardly necessary for Carter to have painted it so graphically.

"Then we all understand what we have to do?" asked Schwartz.

Andie nodded.

"All right," said Schwartz. "I'm giving SWAT the yellow light. In T minus five it's green."

Chapter 61

Jack was pacing more than walking, his mind working furiously to drill down on what exactly Amir had meant by that last warning: *tell her she's lost the chance to say good-bye.*

As a lawyer, Jack argued constantly as to whether words were ambiguous. If the language in a statute or agreement was susceptible of more than one meaning, lawyers were allowed to drone on endlessly about what was really meant. But if the language was plain on its face, that ended the matter. Judges would shut down any arguments about the true intent behind the words or any discussion of what the speaker had really tried to say. The plain language spoke for itself.

Amir's words were not ambiguous: whether Andie

got on the phone or not, Jack was a dead man. He figured he might as well take Amir down with him.

"Ever see that movie?" Jack asked. "*Flight 93*?"

Jack had. The true story of how the passengers of United Airlines Flight 93 were able to overcome the hijackers and prevent them from achieving their terrorist mission was well known. But he probably wouldn't have recognized the name "Ziad Jarrah" as that of the pilot if he hadn't seen the film.

"Most of the nine-eleven hijackers were Saudi. Jarrah was Lebanese, as I recall. Aren't you of Lebanese descent?"

"I'm American," said Amir. "Born in this country. Fucked by this country."

Jack was glad Molly didn't fan the flames with another chip-on-the-shoulder comment. He wanted to keep this focused. He talked while he walked, his tone somewhere between the peripatetic delivery of a college professor and the cross-examining technique of a trial lawyer.

"Jarrah was part of the notorious Hamburg cell. You ever spend any time in Germany, Amir?"

"He was a college student there," said Molly.

Jack moved on quickly, not wanting to make this a three-way conversation.

"I remember for sure that Mohammed Atta, the

pilot of the first plane to crash into the World Trade Center, took his flight training in Florida. I don't recall specifically about Jarrah. I'm guessing he trained in Florida, too. For every disaster, there's always a Florida connection."

Amir checked the time on his cell phone. "They got seven minutes. Talk all you want, Swyteck. I'm not extending the deadline."

"I remember—not just from the movie, but from everything I've read—all of the planes hijacked on nine-eleven had five hijackers except for one: United Flight Ninety-Three. There were only four on that flight, including Ziad Jarrah."

"So?"

"I've never talked to anyone who thinks that having only four hijackers on Flight Ninety-Three was part of the plan. Either somebody backed out or didn't get through immigration. There was some kind of problem with the fifth guy."

"Old news," said Amir. "What's it matter?"

"It matters because, until now, I've never heard anything about al-Qaeda trying to replace the missing guy."

"Guess he was just lucky. The others are all dead now."

"Yeah," said Jack. "Fifteen on the three planes that

hit their target. Four on the one that didn't get there. All dead. All *nineteen* of them."

Jack stopped walking. He locked eyes with Amir, who stared right back at him.

"Were you twenty?"

Chapter 62

Andie took a sip of water. Her mouth was desert dry. Her stomach was in knots.

Schwartz had made the call. An FBI tactical team armed with M16 rifles and outfitted in black SWAT regalia—helmets, night-vision goggles, and flak jackets—was ready, eager, in fact, to go on a moment's notice. Andie felt anything but ready. Definitely not eager. Negotiation was by far the preferred way to end a hostage crisis. If something went wrong, she'd never forgive herself for standing down and letting her ASAC pull the trigger, so to speak, on the tactical team option.

And the very last thing she needed was to be caught in the middle of a disagreement between Carter and Schwartz.

"I need you to tell SWAT to stand down," said Carter.

"The team is already moving into position," said Schwartz. "We can't change the plan every two minutes."

"I've seen SWAT called back later in the game than this—as late as the breacher's boot in the air, ready to kick the door down."

"With good reason, I presume."

"There's good reason here," said Carter.

"Look, Carter—"

"I want to hear it," said Andie. "If there's good reason to think this is not the best way to get the hostages out alive, I want to know."

"Losing your nerve is not a reason," said Schwartz, a little too harshly, but they were all under stress. He adjusted his tone. "To revisit a decision like this, something in the calculation has to have changed."

"It has," said Carter. "We all just heard it on the audio feed."

"You mean Jack and Amir talking?" asked Andie.

"Yes."

"Mostly what I heard was Jack talking," said Schwartz. "And Amir listening."

"Exactly," said Carter. "Jack essentially accused him of being linked to the worst terrorist attack in history, and Amir didn't shut him down. I think he's ready to talk."

"What I heard," said Andie, "is that the clock is still running no matter how much Jack talks."

Carter directed his response to the ASAC. "We need to keep this dialogue going. Everything we've learned so far tells us that Riverside was job one—the North Tower, if you will. If Amir knows something that could stop the next attack, we lose that the minute SWAT sets foot in the room."

Andie took a deep breath, recalling Carter's warning to her outside the command center: *If I have to lose the Riverside School shooter's mother and his lawyer to stop the next school shooting . . .*

"This is the moment I've been working toward for nearly a year," Carter added.

"You actually had me," said Andie. "Until you made it about you."

Schwartz was of like mind. "What you just said goes double for me, Andie. But Carter's first point still has merit."

Andie couldn't disagree. "We can't just let the deadline pass. We need an extension."

"I can get it," said Carter.

"Or maybe I could," said Andie.

"No," said Carter. "So far, talking to you has been

his only demand. Once we put you on the line, there's no leverage to string this out."

For an instant, all Andie could think of was Jack in that motel room, the clock ticking on the five-minute deadline. "What if he shoots him?"

They seemed to understand that it wasn't really a question. Just her fears, out loud.

"You know something?" said Schwartz. "Most people in Jack's position right now would probably be begging for their life. I don't know Jack well, but well enough. He wouldn't have started this dialogue and gone down this road if he wasn't on board with what Carter is proposing."

Those were kind words, and Andie knew her ASAC wasn't just blowing smoke.

"Okay," said Andie, and then Schwartz gave the order.

"Do it, Henning. Get us more time."

Andie did a double take, but it was Carter who put her thoughts into words.

"You said Henning," he pointed out. "You meant me."

"No," said Schwartz. "I definitely meant Andie."

Chapter 63

Jack had one eye on the bed frame.

There were two of them in the pile of furniture that was their makeshift barricade, but the one that had caught Jack's attention was broken. It had been broken before Amir had given the order to turn the beds on their sides and shove them up against the front window with the couch, the dresser, and all the other stuff that, throw in a few "angry men," reminded Jack of the battle scene out of *Les Misérables*. The one in good condition had a crossbeam bolted to the frame that kept the full-size mattress from sagging in the middle. The other had lost its crossbeam, probably to children jumping on the bed, or perhaps something more X-rated. The replacement beam was a flat strip of metal; it looked as though the motel's handyman had cut it to order and just shoved it into place, no bolts. *Cut* was the operative word, as it appeared that maintenance had used metal-cutting shears instead of a hacksaw, leaving a jagged end to a six-foot length of metal that was sharp enough to draw blood if applied with enough force. With enough courage. At the right opportunity.

"Why'd you back out, Amir?"

Jack was still walking as he spoke. Molly was seated cross-legged on the floor, her back against the wall. Amir was on the other side of the room. He checked the time on his cell phone, offering no response.

Jack was slowly shifting into cross-examination mode, which was comfortable territory for him, or at least as comfortable as he could be under the circumstances.

"I've heard it said that not all the nine-eleven hi-jackers knew they were on a suicide mission. Is that true, Amir?"

Amir rose from the armchair. He seemed agitated, but Jack's read was that it was something other than his questions that had the hostage taker so wound up. Time was running out, and maybe Amir didn't know what to do when the deadline inevitably arrived. Or maybe he knew exactly what needed to be done, and he was coming to terms with it. Jack kept talking.

"Some people think the reason Ziad Jarrah failed is that he had only three muscle hijackers to keep the passengers out of the cockpit. If there had been a fourth, who knows what might have happened?"

Amir checked his phone again. Time was ticking.

Jack had exhausted his knowledge of facts and theories about Flight 93. But if he followed his cross-examination instincts and climbed farther out on this limb—if he could tie Amir to Ziad Jarrah's failed mission in a way that would cause Amir to let his guard down for just a moment—maybe Jack's opportunity to draw blood, literally, would present itself.

"The argument could be made that the missing hijacker is what caused the mission to fail," said Jack. "And just imagine if, after all the years of planning and training, someone who'd promised to be the fifth hijacker backed out at the last minute. Wow. *That* would have to piss people off."

Amir returned to the armchair, took a seat, and breathed in and out. He looked mentally exhausted, and not just from the stress of a hostage standoff. Maybe Jack's initial read had been wrong. Maybe his questions were getting to Amir. *Tormented* was the word that came to Jack's mind. Tormented by Jack's words. And the past.

"I didn't go looking for this," said Amir.

Molly bristled. Jack kept walking. He didn't prompt Amir with another question. He just let the man say

494 · JAMES GRIPPANDO

what he apparently wanted or needed to say. He was looking at his wife.

"Sometimes the past comes back to bite you," said Amir. "Out of nowhere, someone steps into the life you've worked so hard to build for yourself and your family and says, 'You owe us. Pay up. Make this right. Or we ruin you.'"

Molly looked right back at him. "You could have gone to the police."

"Yeah, sure. Like they'd cut a deal with—" He stopped short of saying the twentieth hijacker. "With me."

It wasn't clear what reaction Amir was trying to draw from his wife, but whatever it was—pity, understanding—Jack wasn't feeling it. He did what any trial lawyer would do when cracks appeared in the target. He moved in for the kill.

"You owed them," said Jack, again following his intuition. "So you gave up the one thing that would forever make you and al-Qaeda square. Radicalize your own son."

Amir was still looking at his wife, but slowly his expression changed, as there was not an ounce of pity or understanding coming his way from Molly's direction, either.

"*Her* son."

Jack seized on it. "And Xavier failed, didn't he?

The shooter's tactical gear didn't disappear because his mother burned it. It disappeared because the real shooter got away."

Amir checked his ammunition one more time, then shoved the magazine back into place. The stress drained away from his face, as if he were satisfied that he had both the bullets and the nerve to get the job done. "Crazy thing is, if he hadn't met Maritza, they might have actually talked him into doing it."

"Who's they?" asked Jack.

He glanced at Molly. "The same people who put the footie in our mailbox when they thought the Khoury family might step out of line. A not-so-subtle reminder that they had us by the short hairs."

"Who's *they*?" Jack asked again.

Amir smiled, but only slightly. "Well, if I told you that, then I'd have nothing to negotiate with. That's my ticket to Cuba."

His cell phone rang. He rose, pointed his gun at Jack, and said, "This better be your wife."

Jack hoped it wasn't. Not yet.

Amir starting pacing. "That you, Henning?" he said into the phone.

Jack couldn't hear, but he knew from Amir's reaction that it was indeed Andie on the line.

"Let me put you on speaker," said Amir, a hint of

sarcasm in his tone. "This is America. We'll do this democratically. Say it again, Carter."

The agent's voice filled the room. "I'm willing to negotiate. But first I need to talk to Jack."

"I vote no," said Amir. "Swyteck, how do you vote?"

Jack stopped walking. "I vote yes."

"Molly?" said Amir. "It's up to you."

The look of distress on her face was something on the order of what Jack had seen back in his office when the beating from her husband had chased her out of their home. She didn't answer.

"See?" Amir said into the phone. "It doesn't work. This democracy you presume to force on every culture in the entire world—it doesn't even work."

"Come on, Amir," said Andie, her voice carrying over the speaker. "You put in a tall order when you asked the FBI to put me on the line. We gave it to you. All I'm asking in return is to hear Jack's voice on the phone. And then Molly's."

Jack was certain that the FBI had already heard their voices through listening devices. Clearly Andie was just getting the hostage taker in a bargaining frame of mind.

"Sounds like you think my demands are negotiable," said Amir.

"We haven't heard your demands," she said. "What

if I get you some food? Or maybe I can get the power turned back on. Is it getting hot in there?"

Jack watched, and Amir seemed to be getting comfortable again, more confident.

"Food and electricity aren't going to cut it."

"Then put something else on the table," said Andie.

Amir stopped pacing and gripped the phone a little tighter. "I want a car with a driver to the airport. I want a plane with a pilot to Havana. And I want room on the plane for me and one hostage. Just one. You can keep the other."

"That's going to be very difficult," said Andie.

"I'm giving you five minutes."

"I need you to work with me on this. It's a big ask. I can't do it in five minutes."

"I'll give you ten. But the next time my phone rings, it better be you calling to tell me the car is here and the plane is on the runway."

"Okay," said Andie.

Amir seemed surprised. "Okay then."

"We're going to get this right," said Andie. "I understand what you want, and we're going to get it right the first time. There are no do-overs."

"You're damn right." Amir hung up and tucked the phone into his pocket.

Jack didn't move. He'd totally understood the message from Andie. That was his favorite expression with Righley as peewee soccer coach: no do-overs. Jack read it to mean, *Take whatever shot you get, Jack. There's not going to be a plane to Cuba.*

He was three feet away from the crossbeam in the broken bed.

"Walk," said Amir.

Jack didn't even glance in the direction of what was the weapon of last resort, if not of choice. He turned and started walking, counting down from ten minutes in his head.

Chapter 64

Maritza started the walk back to her car.

She'd lost sight of Abdul shortly after crossing to the other side of the street. Had she been allowed to walk straight from point A to point Abdul, all would have been fine. But the MDPD on perimeter patrol had forced her to take the long way, outside the barricades. Before she could reach the spot, Abdul was gone. Maybe it hadn't been him after all. It was petty of her anyway, this urge to spit in his eye and tell him to his face that all his lies were about to catch up with him.

Another thought came to her. Maybe he'd seen her coming. She checked over her shoulder as she crossed back toward her side of the street.

"Keep walking, folks," said the officer at the barricade. "Nothing to see."

The police were doing their best, but with media vans at every barricaded cross street and the *Action News* helicopter whirring overhead, the crowd wasn't buying the "nothing to see" baloney.

"Are they filming a movie?" Maritza overheard someone say.

"Quick, selfie!"

"Move along," said the officer.

An MDPD squad car was parked at the curb, beacons flashing. The driver's-side door was open. A handful of officers were standing near it, talking. From the looks of things, it wasn't just idle chitchat. Something was up. With the door open, the console-mounted computer workstation was in plain view. Maritza glanced at the glaring rectangular screen as she passed, and she did a double take. There were a pair of images on the screen, both the face of the same man. Abdul with facial hair. Abdul clean shaven. She was too far away to read the on-screen message, but she could see the large bold letters directly above the photographs: BOLO. Even the occasional watcher of police dramas knew what that meant.

Be on the lookout—which explained Abdul's sudden disappearance.

Maritza kept walking, exhilarated, wishing Xavier were with her to slap a high five. She couldn't be certain that Xavier had broken his silence. But maybe he'd heard about the hostage standoff on the news and realized that, no matter how many threats Abdul made against his mother, brother, and sister, taking the fall for a crime he didn't commit was no way to protect his family. It was time to hold the real terrorists accountable.

"Don't scream," said Abdul, and suddenly he was walking alongside her, his arm around her shoulder, and his gun pushing up below her rib cage.

They were still a block away from where she'd parked her car, but they were well away from the crowd and commotion on LeJeune Road.

"Just keep walking normally," he said. "We're taking your car."

"There's a BOLO issued for you."

"Yes. It looks like Amir cracked."

Maritza hadn't considered that possibility. Maybe Xavier hadn't broken his silence. "You won't get away."

"I will if I have you with me. They have to give me something for giving up the next school shooter."

"Just like you pinned the first one on Xavier. Except I don't have a family you can threaten to make me take the fall."

"I have ways to make you cooperate."

Maritza was all too aware, and she couldn't deny it,

but the voice from behind them made a response un-
necessary.

"Police! Stop right there!"

They stopped on command. Abdul whispered in her
ear, poking her ribs with the muzzle of his pistol. "Tell
him your father is deaf."

She hesitated.

"Do it!" he whispered.

"My father is deaf," she said.

"Then why did he stop when I told him to?" the cop
asked.

"Because I stopped," Abdul whispered.

Maritza repeated his answer.

"Okay. Well. Then . . ."

Maritza estimated that the cop was about fifteen
feet behind them, and even though she and Abdul were
looking down the street in the opposite direction, she
could tell the officer was flummoxed.

"Do what you need to do to get your father to put
his hands in the air," the cop said.

"I have to sign," Abdul whispered.

Maritza hesitated. She knew Abdul was trying to
create a distraction, but he was pressing the gun so
hard into her abdomen that her eyes teared.

"I have to sign," she said.

The cop took a moment. "I just want you to raise

your hands in the air, and raise his with yours. Nice and slow."

Maritza started to comply, raising both her hands and taking Abdul's left hand with hers. The gun in Abdul's other hand was still poking her in the side as the officer's radio crackled.

"This is Officer Michaels," he said. "Just got off duty and was walking over to the sub shop, and I spotted—"

"He has a gun!" Maritza shouted, but before the cop could say another word, Abdul whirled around and fired two quick shots. Maritza screamed and saw the officer drop to the sidewalk, as she dove between two parked cars on the street for cover.

Abdul fired one shot in her direction, shattering the taillight just above her head. Then he ran. Maritza hurried to the fallen officer. At least one of Abdul's rounds had hit its mark, and it was an obvious kill shot—a through and through wound, with point of entry to the left of his nose and a deadly exit through the back of his skull. He was probably dead before he'd hit the sidewalk.

"Oh, my God," said Maritza.

She grabbed the radio and told them where they were, what had happened, and who was on the run.

"Stay right there," the dispatcher told her.

She saw no point. The officer was dead. She couldn't help him. Abdul was getting away.

She laid the radio on the sidewalk and made a promise to the dead officer. "I got this," she said. She ran to her car, popped the trunk, and grabbed the AK-47 that Abdul had trained her to use.

Then she ran after him.

Chapter 65

Andie watched the cursor on the computer screen. The hand-sketched plan as mapped out by the tactical team leader told most of the story. It looked like a play drawn up by a football coach on the blackboard. But this team was already in position, and its SWAT leader had gone silent. So Schwartz filled in the details for the negotiators inside the mobile command center, referencing the on-screen diagram as needed.

"It will be a simultaneous breach from two points of entry," he said.

The cursor moved to the common wall that separated the hostages from the adjacent room. It had been virtually demolished by the crash entry of Amir's car, but SWAT had descended like ghosts to assess the damage and its potential impact on a breach.

"Cameras and on-site inspection confirm that the south wall is seriously compromised," said Schwartz. "There's a section about midpoint that can withstand a blast of explosives needed to create an entry point."

"Explosives?" asked Andie.

"The doors are barricaded," said Schwartz. "We could blast through it, but it could send debris flying and injure the hostages. And we can't have SWAT tripping all over stuff on the way in."

The cursor moved across the screen to the back wall.

"In all these old roadside motels, there's a service corridor that runs right behind the rooms from one end of the building to the other. This motel is so old it's not even close to being up to building-code requirements. SWAT tells me there's only one sheet of drywall on this back wall. The working side, facing the corridor, is exposed studs. And they're thirty inches apart, not the usual sixteen or twenty-four inches. Easy point of breach with enhanced percussion."

Easy. Andie found the word choice interesting. There was nothing easy about breaching the den of a hostage taker.

"Questions?" asked Schwartz.

His cell rang. He checked the number and didn't hesitate to answer, even at such a crucial point. "Keep us apprised," he said into the phone, and the expression on his face made Andie fear the worst.

"Officer down just outside the perimeter. We think it was Abdul."

The words seemed to leave everyone numb. Then Carter spoke. "I guess you were right, Henning. I should have listened to Maritza."

It was probably the first time in his life Carter had eaten crow, but the Pyrrhic victory of an "I told you so" was not what Andie wanted.

Schwartz laid a hand on her shoulder. "You did your job, Henning. I'm confident that Amir is expecting at least one more phone call from us before we breach. SWAT has the element of surprise. And we've done all the talking we can do."

Andie was silent. And then she nodded.

The ASAC put on his headset, adjusted the microphone, and spoke directly to the team in position.

"Green on your ready," he said.

Chapter 66

Maritza was running at full speed. Even with a rifle in her hand, she was faster than Abdul. She'd closed the distance between them to about twenty yards, when he stopped, turned, and looked back. Maritza stopped and raised her rifle. She wasn't close enough to hear him or even see his lips move, but everything about his reaction to her weapon screamed *Holy shit!*

He fired a shot in her direction, which missed, and then ran into the alley.

The chase had taken them away from the residential area. Abdul was heading toward the airport. They were in the warehouse district, where every building looked the same and everything shut down after dark. Warehouses were built to zero lot lines, each long and rectangular building separated from the next by a narrow alley. Maritza dialed 911 on her cell phone, still running. She told the dispatcher she was chasing the man in the police BOLO but didn't have an exact address.

"Five blocks east of LeJeune Road," she said, breathing into the phone, "by the hostage standoff."

"Stay on the line, please."

"I can't."

Maritza stopped at the front corner of the warehouse, at the entrance to the alley into which Abdul had disappeared. She put away her phone and caught her breath. With her back against the wall, a rifle in her hand, and the enemy somewhere in the dark alley, it was all eerily reminiscent of another time and her darkest days in Iraq. She poked her head around the corner and peered cautiously down the black alley. The warehouses were much deeper than wide, nearly the length of a football field from front to back. The alley had no streetlamp, or at least not a working one. The moonlight did little more than create confusing shadows in what seemed like an endless black tunnel. She knew he was still in the alley. The run had left her winded, and Abdul had to be in even worse shape. Surely he needed rest.

Maritza could have stayed right there and waited for the police. She chose not to, repeating to herself the words she'd shared with Abdul's latest victim: "I got this."

She entered the alley, keeping close to the wall, her rifle at the ready. Ten feet into the darkness, she stopped, listened, and reassessed. Roll-down steel shutters covered the windows and doors that faced the alley, blocking off escape routes. Corrugated boxes, flattened and stacked one on top of another for disposal, rose in cardboard towers along the wall near the Dumpster. She took another step forward, then stopped. There was a noise. Something—or someone—was behind the Dumpster. She took cover behind a thick stack of flattened boxes and waited. Her heart pounded. The chorus of sirens in the distance grew louder. Police were on the way. It gave her comfort, and yet it heightened the sense of urgency.

Two quick shots rang out, followed by pops in the stacked cardboard that was her cover. Maritza returned fire, squeezing off ten quick shots.

Abdul cried out in the darkness, and then she heard something hit the pavement. It was not at all like the sound of the fallen police officer hitting the sidewalk. It was something inanimate, metallic, like a gun.

Slowly, sliding her back against the wall, Maritza moved deeper into the alley closer to the Dumpster.

She heard Abdul groaning on the other side of it. He was definitely wounded. She maneuvered around the Dumpster, leading with her rifle, and saw him. He was down on one knee and clutching his bloody hand. She'd shot the pistol right out of his grip. There was no telling where it had landed, but Abdul was disarmed.

"Don't move," she said.

"You shot me, bitch!"

"Move a muscle and I'll shoot you again." She dug her cell phone out of her pocket to dial 911 again.

No service.

Abdul chuckled through the pain. "Better service in Baghdad, no?"

She put her phone away. "Nothing is better in Baghdad."

"Wrong," he said, grimacing. "Prostitutes are better."

"Shut up."

"You think I wanted the life of pleasure marriages, Rusul?"

The use of her real name was clearly intentional.

"I don't care what you wanted. You're a monster."

Another mirthless chuckle, and then he looked up at her, his expression deadly serious. "Agent Carter used me. His country used me. I gave him everything I had for eight years to fight al-Qaeda. It cost me my wife, my sister, my mother. Everything."

"How could you join a terrorist organization that murdered your family?"

"It wasn't al-Qaeda. They were murdered by ISIS. The Americans left us at their mercy by pulling out before the job was done. Does Carter care? No."

"That wasn't Carter's fault."

"For nine years, I risked my life fighting terrorists for the Americans. Carter owed me more than 'Goodbye and good luck.' Do you know what ISIS did to men like me who helped 'the invaders'?"

She did. She'd witnessed it with her own eyes.

"My wife, my mother, my sister were not enough," said Abdul. "They took my son, my daughter, and all their classmates. They gunned them down like animals."

"At school," she said, purely a reaction.

"Yes. At their school."

"So Riverside was *your idea*. When Carter asked you to help root out Amir Khoury's connection to al-Qaeda, it was you who put the idea of a school shooting in his head."

"Justice. Put down the gun, Rusul. Carter used me. He used you, too."

"No," she said, her voice quaking. "Carter saved me."

"Saved you?" he said, scoffing. "He needed young women to gather intelligence in Iraq."

"And then he brought me to this country, where I would be safe."

"And he paired you with *me* to infiltrate the Khoury family. Saved you," he said, almost spitting out the words. "It's all about the mission, Rusul. He *used* you. The Americans use everyone."

"You're the user, Abdul. You used Xavier. And when he wouldn't do as you asked, you took Amir's pistol and did it yourself. And Amir went along with it. What kind of sick father allows a man like you to pin a school shooting on his own son?"

"Better than letting him fall in love with a whore."

"Shut up, Abdul!"

"Did you kid yourself into thinking you could actually have a boyfriend, Rusul?"

She wanted to pull the trigger.

"Did you think you could undo the thoughts I put into that boy's head? The hatred Amir put into his heart? Did you think the two of you would live happily ever after, Rusul?"

She wanted to pull it so badly.

"Do you honestly believe you can ever be more in this life than a tight virgin for lonely men?"

His words alone might have been enough to push her

over the edge, but as he dove to his right, Maritza saw the gun, and she had no choice. She squeezed the trigger, again and again, faster and faster, releasing round after round until the flurry of bullets took Abdul down to the pavement.

The sound of blaring sirens grew louder. The police were near.

Maritza dropped her gun, fell against the Dumpster, and wept until they arrived.

Chapter 67

On edge. Stressed out. At the breaking point. From Jack's vantage point, all of the above applied to Amir. The deterioration of his emotional state over the past seven or eight minutes had been precipitous. The darkness was getting to him. Streaks of light seeped through the cracks in the draperies, and his cell phone added a little more. But it wasn't enough.

"Too dark in here," he said for the fifth time in the last five minutes.

"Use my cell phone," said Molly.

"No. I need to save batteries."

"I could peel back a corner of the drapes," said Jack.

"No!"

Amir's worries about a sniper shot had steadily grown to paranoia. Even with the drapes pulled shut, he had both hostages walking from one side of the room to the other as human shields.

"Faster," said Amir. "Both of you. Walk faster."

"A sniper can't see through the drapes," said Molly.

"They have infrared sensors. They can pick up body heat."

Jack had heard of such devices from Andie. They were different from night-vision goggles and actually allowed law enforcement to "see" through solid walls. Maybe Amir wasn't just paranoid.

"I want to sit down," said Molly.

"You can sit when they start taking me serious."

"Serious*ly*," said Molly. "When they start taking you serious*ly*."

He aimed his pistol. "Keep it up, Molly, and you'll be the one who gets the bullet when this deadline passes."

"Nobody needs to die," said Jack, which drew the pistol in his direction.

"Do I hear another volunteer?"

"What I meant is that you're going to get your plane to Cuba," said Jack.

"You'd better hope so. Because either way, the FBI gets one hostage. In ninety seconds we'll know if they want him dead or alive."

Jack glanced at the crossbeam on the bed frame. By his guesstimate, walking at this pace, he'd pass it five or six more times in the next ninety seconds. He was down to his final handful of opportunities.

No do-overs.

"Mix it up a little," said Amir. "Confusion to the enemy. Don't go all the way across the room from wall to wall. Meet in the middle and then turn back."

Molly was on the side Jack wanted. His final handful of opportunities had just slipped through his fingers.

"Andie will get you what you want," said Jack. "Just give her the time she needs."

"I've given them more than enough time."

"What do you think is going to happen when they hear a gun go off in this room? Shooting a hostage is like shooting yourself."

"Not if the other one is still alive."

"My God, Amir," said Molly. "Who *are you?* You talk about killing human beings like we're insects."

"Zip it, Molly."

"How could you—"

"I said, zip it!"

"How could you have anything to do with a school shooting?"

"I didn't know, all right! They gave me a year— one year to figure out how to make amends for backing out of Flight Ninety-Three, how to make my own mark on the twentieth anniversary of nine-eleven. They never said school shooting! I never said it! Not until Xavier pussied out on blowing himself up in the mall did Abdul—"

Amir stopped. Jack watched as Molly stepped toward her husband, as if confronting the devil himself. "I'm not sure I even believe in hell, but if there is one, you're going there."

"Not today, I'm not."

"Say hello to your friend Ziad Jarrah when you get there."

"Shut up!"

"I'll bet that whole virgin thing didn't work out so well for him."

Amir shoved her the way he'd surely shoved her many times before, knocking her into the barricade. She hit with so much force that the desk stacked on top of the dresser came tumbling down, taking the bed frame with it. The unbolted crossbeam shook loose and landed on the floor. Jack grabbed it and swung it like a baseball bat, hitting Amir squarely on the side of the head. As he staggered into the wall, a gunshot rang out—and then it was suddenly like the Fourth of July, with two quick and even louder explosions to follow the first.

Jack hit the floor. He heard Molly scream, but it was

the least of the noises that suddenly filled the room—
walls crashing, boots stomping, and men shouting.

"FBI! FBI! FBI!"

Sharp beams of light cut like lasers through smoke
and dust. In the confusion, Jack saw Amir on his back,
raising his pistol in answer to SWAT's knocking. Jack
had an answer of his own, swinging the crossbeam like
an axe and bringing it down with all his strength.

It was impossible to discern what he heard next,
whether it was the cracking of Amir's skull or the bar-
rage of gunfire from SWAT rifles. It didn't matter.

"Are you hurt?" the SWAT leader asked him.

Jack was looking up at him from the floor. Amir was
three feet away, flat on his back, lifeless.

"Sir! Are you hurt?"

Jack could breathe again. "I need to see my wife."

Epilogue

The autopsy was inconclusive as to the exact cause of Amir's death, whether it was the blunt trauma to the head or multiple gunshots. That bit of uncertainty didn't change the headlines:

DEATH PENALTY LAWYER EXECUTES TWENTIETH HIJACKER.

Jack was actually okay with it. Andie was more than okay.

"I'm proud of you," she said.

It was mutual. The FBI's Office of Professional Responsibility dismissed Duncan Fitz's disciplinary complaint against Andie. Under subpoena, Fitz testified that Agent Carter had pressured him to lodge the complaint against Andie so that Carter could use it as a quid pro quo, if needed, in his dealings with Jack: "Pressure your client to give me the information I want, and I'll get Fitz to withdraw his complaint against your wife." It wasn't the most outrageous thing Carter had done in his controversial career, but it was enough to get him reassigned to background checks on low-level government hires for the foreseeable future. The very next day, Fitz filed a voluntary dismissal of the school's lawsuit. Andie's good name was restored.

Jack's meeting with the state and federal prosecutors was more of a mixed bag. He paid one last visit to the detention center to give Xavier the bottom line.

"The good news is that the state attorney dropped all charges against you, including homicide."

Xavier didn't jump for joy. His reaction was that of a guy whose head had been held under water for five weeks, and he'd finally been let up for air.

"The other good news is that the US attorney has agreed to bring no charges related to the school shooting."

"*Yesss,*" Xavier said, like a tennis player who'd just served an ace. But Jack didn't smile back, which sent the appropriate message.

"The rest of the news is not so good," said Jack.

Xavier's smile faded. "Okay. What's the bad news?"

"There's a catch to the Justice Department's offer. You have to plead guilty to conspiracy in violation of federal antiterrorism laws."

His mouth fell open, but it took a moment for words to follow. "I don't understand. I wasn't the Riverside shooter."

"We know."

"Abdul did it. He used my father's gun to make it look like me."

"I know."

"He said he'd kill Mom, Talitha, and Jamal if I didn't say it was me."

"I get all of that," said Jack.

"Then why do I have to plead guilty?"

Jack had given much thought to what he might say in this meeting, but there was no point in sugarcoating it.

"The FBI was listening to everything that was said in the motel room. They heard Amir say you backed out of a plan to blow yourself up in a shopping mall."

"That's a lie! He is such a liar! We never talked about anything like that. I would never hurt anyone!"

"I'm sure Maritza would completely back you up on that."

"Yes! She knows me! She knows that's not true!"

Jack believed him, if only because it was consistent

with Amir's twisted logic to say the school shooting was Xavier's fault because he—*Molly's* son—didn't have the courage to be a suicide bomber.

"There's still a problem," said Jack.

"I didn't *do* anything."

"That's the point, Xavier. You did nothing."

"What was I supposed to do?"

"I can tell you how the Department of Justice sees it. All this could have been avoided if you had done just one simple thing. If you had just told someone."

"Told them *what*?"

"You're not a stupid kid, Xavier. You knew Amir was up to no good. You knew he was putting thoughts in your head, grooming you for something, even if at the end of the day you wanted no part of it."

He didn't deny it. "But I'm eighteen years old."

"There are a lot of eighteen-year-olds in Arlington National Cemetery. Different people make different choices in the war against terrorism."

The frustration was all over Xavier's face, which then turned to worry. "What's going to happen to me?"

"The government's offer is two years, with credit for the time spent in here. Your sentence would be served at a minimum security federal correctional facility, which is a heck of a lot better than Florida State Prison. I recommend you take it."

Xavier was looking at the floor. Jack waited.

"What does my mom think?"

"Why don't you ask her," said Jack. "She'd love to hear from you."

And then there was Maritza.

Everything she'd told Carter about Abdul—and then some—had proven true. It was unusual for a member of the Iraqi Counter Terrorism Service to turn against the US adviser who'd trained him. When Carter asked Abdul to help root out the Khoury family's suspected connection to al-Qaeda, the FBI had no idea how much Abdul had come to hate America.

Five days after Maritza riddled Abdul's body with the bullets he deserved, Jack and Andie visited her at the coffee shop. She still worked there, but no longer under an alias. The story of Abdul, phony clerics, and the abuses of Mut'ah had gone viral. Whether she liked it or not, social media had turned "Rusul" into a household name.

"Get you something?" she asked, as she arrived at their booth.

"Can you sit for a second?" asked Jack.

She shrugged, then slid into the booth beside Andie. "What the heck. So what if they fire me. Today's my last day."

"Where you going?"

"Not sure yet. Far away from here. Maybe the West Coast."

"Of Florida?"

"No. I mean *far away*."

"Seattle's a cool city," said Andie. "And plenty far. That's where I'm from."

"Really? Where did you guys meet?"

"Florida," said Jack.

"Ginnie Springs," Andie added. "Underwater. In a cave."

It was only slightly inaccurate.

"That's a very long story," said Jack.

Andie turned the conversation back to Rusul. "Wherever you land, we wish you well. But I was wondering. Have you thought about law enforcement?"

"You mean as a career?"

"Yes. You speak Arabic. Your father was CIA. I see you more as FBI. It's a long road, but you're still so young."

Rusul smiled, but then shook her head. "I don't think so."

"Why not?"

"I dunno," she said, looking at Jack. "I was thinking maybe I'd be a lawyer."

"Oh, dear God," said Andie.

Jack laughed. "There's hope for the profession."

The manager came by. "You on a break, Maritza?"

"Yes. Permanently." She removed the cap that was part of her uniform and laid it on the table. "And my name is Rusul."

Acknowledgments

A huge thank-you to my editor, Sarah Stein, and her team at HarperCollins. Richard Pine is the best literary agent in the business, and I am so grateful for all these years together. Janis Koch is so much more than a beta reader. With her wit, love of words, and incredible knowledge of the rules of words, Janis makes me actually look forward to the marked-up galley pages bleeding with good ol' fashioned fountain pen ink.

This book also seems to be the appropriate place to acknowledge the kindness of strangers my wife and I encountered during our 9/11 experience. I was on a book tour of Australia. Tiffany and I mingled with fellow authors at the Melbourne Book Festival, took in *Faust* at the Sydney Opera House, climbed the Sydney Harbour Bridge, snorkeled in the Great Barrier Reef, and simply fell in love with Australia. But after seventeen days, we were more than ready to get back to our children for our son's third birthday—on September 11, 2001. Before leaving the hotel, we got a call from Qantas Airways and turned on the television in time to see the South Tower collapse. All flights were canceled indefinitely.

For days, we and thousands like us followed the same routine: go to airport, get bad news, return to hotel. One morning the line was so long at Sydney Airport that we almost decided to turn around and go back to the hotel without waiting to speak to a ticket agent. We could hear others in line ahead of us getting the same answer: no flights to America. When it was our turn, the ticket agent suddenly did a double take at the screen in front of her and said, "Oh, my God, we're flying." The bad news was that the flight was full and we were last on the waiting list. Then she did the most extraordinary thing. This Australian from Australia's leading airline grabbed the microphone, announced that a flight to Los Angeles was leaving in ninety minutes, and asked if there were any Australians with confirmed reservations who would be willing to give up their seats in favor of Americans who were trying to get home. In a snap, she had a couple of volunteers. Moments later, she had two more. They kept coming.

I don't know how many Australians stepped forward to help stranded Americans get home that day. But even twenty years later, their kindness toward total strangers still brings a lump to my throat. And from the bottom of my heart, I wish to say, "Thanks, mates."

—JG

About the Author

JAMES GRIPPANDO is a *New York Times* best-selling author of suspense and the winner of the Harper Lee Prize for Legal Fiction. *Twenty* is his twenty-ninth novel. He lives in South Florida, where he is a trial lawyer and teaches Law and Literature at the University of Miami School of Law.